THE DEADLINESS OF LIGHT

THE DEADLINESS OF LIGHT

DARK GATE ANGELS™ BOOK FOUR

RAMY VANCE

MICHAEL ANDERLE

THE DEADLINESS OF LIGHT TEAM

Thanks to our Beta Team:
Larry Omans, Rachel Beckford

Thanks to the JIT Readers

Veronica Stephan-Miller
Deb Mader
Diane L. Smith

If we've missed anyone, please let us know!

Editor
The Skyhunter Editing Team

LMBPN Publishing
PMB 196, 2540 South Maryland Pkwy
Las Vegas, NV 89109

First US Edition, October 2020
ISBN (ebook) 978-1-64971-198-4
ISBN (print) 978-1-64971-199-1

DEDICATION

To Baby Orla – my own Dark Gate Angel.

—Ramy Vance

*To Family, Friends and
Those Who Love
to Read.
May We All Enjoy Grace
to Live the Life We Are
Called.*

— Michael

PART I

CHAPTER ONE

New York had always been a city in flux. There was something magical about the way it had shifted throughout the decades. The city never remained the same, always growing in one way or another.

This was the first time it had ever been literally magical, though.

The streets and buses were as crowded as usual, but the character of them had changed. Humans, elves, gnomes, and dwarves walked side by side, many of them on their way to work, the rest making the rounds as tourists.

Abby had only been in the city for a night, and she was amazed at what she'd seen. Most of it had been from her hotel window because Anabelle wanted to continue with mission prep until Sarah arrived.

Still, there was much to see through the window—so many sights to behold.

The universe had changed since the Dark Gate Angels defeated the Dark One, and this world was nothing like it had been before.

She looked down at her hand and slightly flexed her fingers. Nanobots came out of her pores and covered her hand with metallic black armor. Her finger stretched to a fine point, which she used to scratch her head.

Anabelle burst into the hotel room. She was full of energy, and her makeup was fiercely done. You would have assumed she was about to walk the runway; if it wasn't for her sharply pointed ears, anyone would assume she was a human supermodel.

When Abby had first met Anabelle, the elf had worn her hair so it covered her ears. Now, Anabelle kept the sharp tips of her ears as visible as possible.

Terra was behind the elf, carrying a few bags in her lean, muscular arms. The warrior wore a bright, toothy smile and sported a cleanly shaven head, even though the war was over. She said she liked not having to fuss over it in the morning.

Looking at the two side by side, Abby never would have guessed these two women would have become her best friends. Nor would she have thought that after defeating an interdimensional being a year ago, they'd have spent the last few months hunting down black market tech left over from the war.

Life was full of surprises.

Terra spilled the contents of the bags on the desk in the room. "Dude, you would *not* believe the crap you can find down in the dining hall! All-you-can-eat buffet with gnome, goblin, and orc foods."

She pulled out a leg of orcish mutton and handed it to Abby. "If Cire got his hands on this, he would freak. They even have Three-Tiered Wood-Elf Cake."

Anabelle jumped onto the bed as she flipped on the television. "Nah, tried it. More like Three-Tiered Crap than cake." Anabelle contorted her face in disgust.

"Give them some slack, they're probably all human cooks. Most of us don't have your distinguished four-hundred-year-old palate."

Anabelle glared at Terra, who was smirking behind her mutton. "I am not four hundred years old," the elf fired back.

"Whatever, sis. I only know you're ancient and picky."

Abby closed the window's blinds and came over to the bed to look at the spoils from Anabelle's and Terra's kitchen raid. "Did they have any *ubjul?*"

When Abby had first started working with the DGA in the technology department, her coworker, a fastidious goblin, had introduced her to his race's breakfast foods. They had left a lasting impression on Abby, and she found herself craving them nearly as much as her mother's cooking.

Terra rifled around in the plastic bag and pulled out a container filled with a slushy green meat stew. "This stuff, right?"

Abby snatched the container and popped it open, and the room filled with a musky aroma. "Yes! Thank you!"

A serious silence fell as the three of them tore into the bounty, trading containers and hunks of meats and vegetables with unpronounceable names.

Unpronounceable for a human, at least.

Finally, Abby, who was thoroughly stuffed, laid back on the bed and belched. "Wait, we should have saved some for Sarah."

Anabelle picked up a second bag. "Don't worry, I made sure to get one Terra didn't know about."

Terra, who was busy sucking down a tentacled dish, snorted loudly. "Psh, I would have found it eventually." She pointed at her nose. "This thing is all-powerful."

The door opened, and a human with deep-red hair poked her head in. Sarah. She was the only one of the four who wore the DGA uniform, hers being altered to be sleeker and black with an insignia that disappeared on command.

Abby wasn't as close to Sarah as she was to Terra and Anabelle, but that was purely circumstantial. Sarah rarely had the time to go on missions with the rest of the DGA.

Today was supposed to be a treat.

"What the hell are you guys doing eating?" Sarah asked, "I specifically said for you not to. That was the only criteria I gave in the mission brief. Don't eat. This is a mission best done on an empty stomach."

Terra belched again as she rolled over on the bed. "I don't do anything on an empty stomach." She tossed Sarah a gnomish cookie.

Sarah bit into the cookie, which crackled and shot out little sparks of electricity as she chewed. "Whatever. We better get a move on. Anyone have any questions?"

Terra sat up as she rubbed her stomach. "No. This mission sounds like it'll be as boring as the last one."

Abby stood up, went over to her luggage, and started rummaging around. "Not everything can be as exciting as breaking into the Netherverse and waging an all-out war with the Dark One. We have to at least *try* to adjust to the new normal. Or did you want to go back to what you used to do?"

Terra scrunched her face in thought. "Hm, that's a really good question. What did I used to do?"

Abby pulled out what she was looking for: three brand-new HUDS. "We made these for you guys. Figured shiny new toys might make things a little more fun this time. These bad boys have a few upgrades."

Terra leaped off the bed as the scientist threw her one of the HUDs. Before she slipped it on, she eyed Abby suspiciously. "You didn't fill this with nanobots or any of the other weird crap you're into, did you? Not that I don't trust you, but I wouldn't put it past you to try and add us to your growing army of mindless robot drones."

Abby laughed as she handed HUDs to Sarah and Anabelle. "No, we aren't trying to assimilate you. Now, Martin and the AI consciousness?" Abby shrugged.

Terra's HUD turned on and projected an image of Martin, Abby's AI, who took his preferred shape of a paper clip with huge eyes. "Nope, humans. When I start my empire, it's going to be robots from the ground up. That's where everyone always screws up. The Borg? Too many human bodies. The Daleks? Now, those guys know how to kill all humans, isn't that right, my sweet AI consciousness?"

Then he popped out, no doubt laughing with the other AI consciousness that also existed in the recesses of Abby's being.

Martin and the consciousness had started to do something like dating. Abby tried not to think about it too much. It was strange enough that she talked in the second person plural. Obsessing about a technological tryst in her head was a little too weird.

Sarah slipped on her wrist HUD and looked it over. "Anything we should know about it?"

Abby stared out the window, watching the people beneath her go about their business. "Nope. They should work better."

"Well, if that's it. Wait, Anabelle, you like doing that whole thing, right?"

Anabelle blushed as she smiled. "Not really. It's just a thing. You can go ahead and do it."

"No, no, I insist. Go for it."

"Fine." Anabelle stood, clenching her fist. "All right, Angels. Let's go fuck someone up!"

The four of them arrived at Little Tito's in formal attire.

Terra had made a huge deal about not having enough time to pick out a decent dress, but Anabelle had vetoed her appeal to go shopping and put the mission off for another day.

"You don't even like shopping," the elf had argued.

"I do like New York, and I'd like to see some of it," Terra had retorted.

In the end, they'd come to a compromise. After the mission, they would take a couple of days off to have a real vacation and see what New York had to offer.

Until then, there was a mission to take care of.

The maître d' at the restaurant quickly seated the DGA. Terra instantly grabbed her menu and started looking through it. "You guys, you know we're going to look very suspicious unless you at least pretend you're at a restaurant."

Abby groaned, still stuffed from the hotel. Still, Terra was right. They were on a mission and needed to blend in. She picked up her menu, which offered the general run of Italian fare alongside a modest list of elvish dishes. It had only been a few months since the Realm Integration guidelines had passed, but New York had wasted no time adapting.

The restaurant was full of different species from the Nine Realms. Elves, dwarves, and gnomes were seated with humans, talking and joking. There was even a table of orcs dressed in tuxedos eating with forks and knives, which was very different from the typical orc table manners of gorging and fighting.

Abby reflected that it had only been a few months ago when humanity didn't believe magic was real.

Anabelle put down her menu. "I still find it hard to believe this place has a decent bottle of Ehue Spirits, but hey, it's on the menu, so I might as well give it a try." She called the server over and pointed at the bottle.

Sarah, who was peering over her shoulder, turned back around. "For all the illusion of smoothness, you'd be amazed at how much work is going into this."

Terra nodded in agreement. "That's putting it mildly. Things are a fucking mess on the orc world with all this red tape. Can you believe they had me and Cire do forty extra pages of immigration paperwork that the elvish ambassadors didn't have to?"

Another server came by to see if they were ready to order, which they weren't, so he left. "Well, people are afraid of orcs."

"Yeah, I know, and it's—"

"Fucked up. But you and Cire are putting in the work to change that. You can't expect humans to suddenly be comfortable with their whole world changing."

The first server returned and poured them each a glass of wine. "I wish we could handle it like we do back home. One ring. Two axes. "

Anabelle stared blankly at Terra. "You have to acknowledge the irony of what you just said."

Abby was happy to be sitting with the DGA. She never got tired of hearing Anabelle and Terra bicker. It reminded her of being back home, when her siblings would get into it.

Anabelle and Terra behaved like any normal family would.

Sarah stood up abruptly. "Okay, my contact says it's go time."

Anabelle stared down at her glass as she swirled her wine gently. "Really? Our drinks just got here."

Abby dragged Anabelle along as she followed Sarah, who was weaving her way through tables and customers toward the back of the restaurant. "Just down it. That's what I did."

Anabelle's eyes widened. "You're still under—"

"The nanobots process everything. We don't get even a little bit buzzed, but it does taste pretty good."

Sarah beckoned for them to follow as she held open the door to the eerily abandoned kitchen. They walked in, and Terra snatched a sausage off a cutting board before stopping in front of what looked like a large walk-in freezer with a security keypad.

"A lot of security for something that keeps things cold," Terra said. "Don't tell me it's a portal to another dimension."

Sarah typed a code into the security pad and opened the door. "Nope. Just leads to a secret underground base."

Terra poked her head in and then smiled at Abby. "Okay, this might be fun."

CHAPTER TWO

Sarah shut the freezer door tightly behind them as she turned on her flashlight, illuminating a long staircase that led into darkness.

Abby was curious about what they were going to find. Over the last few months, the DGA had been working much more mundane cases.

As it turned out, all of the races had different systems set up for policing themselves.

Humans were the only ones who had to play catch-up, so for now, there were a lot of odd jobs.

Abby's eyes flashed bright white, converting to flashlights to light their path. "Who or what are we expecting to see down here? The debriefing notes were a little confusing."

Anabelle scoffed. "That's because Blackwell is trying out a new encrypted messaging system. Makes everything a riddle. I hate it. Also, please don't do that with your eyes. You look like a monster from an elven horror movie."

Terra raised her arms, moaning as she shuffled forward. "It is I, the Flatwoods Monster, and I have come to...uh, does anyone know what that guy does?"

Abby's eyes flicked to night vision. "Never seen it."

"Monsters and movies aside, I think we'd best focus on the mission," Sarah interrupted. "And to answer your question, this is a mob takedown. We got a tip-off that this particular family has been buying magical weapons. They also might be building a bomb, so try not to blow anything up."

"Boring!" Terra complained.

The path straightened out and led to what looked like an empty warehouse. "Could be an illusion spell," Abby muttered as she cycled through the different types of vision her nanobots offered: night, heat, gamma, magic.

Anabelle flashed fire in her palm. "You know, we need to get someone who can do real magic on the team. That was a massive oversight. Or, maybe our resident genius could figure out how to detect—like this?"

Abby raised her hand as she continued to scan the area. "We aren't picking up any objects of interest, and we do have the ability to scan for magical illusions. We just can't do anything about them."

Terra, who had wandered a few steps ahead, suddenly stopped like she'd bumped into a wall and let out a quiet "Umpf" as she crumpled to the floor. "I'm okay! In case anyone cares."

"What the hell was that?" Anabelle shouted.

The lights suddenly cut on, illuminating a giant box. It was about the size of a single-story house and was made of metal. There were heavy grooves that looked similar to runes carved all over it.

As Abby and Anabelle helped Terra to her feet, the grooves of the metal box began to glow pale yellow. The light made the box look as if it were cracking open from the power as a sound like thousands of gears gurgled out of it.

Sarah's eyes narrowed. "Oh, I don't think this is good."

The box exploded, breaking into four different sections, two of which lodged into the ceiling, the other two striking the walls on either side of the room.

From the bottom two sections of the box came four humanoid robots that shone in the light.

One raised a mechanical arm. "Intruder alert. Intruder alert. Annihilate intruders."

Abby's armor flowed over her body, covering every inch of her in sleek black metal. She raised her hand as she charged a plasma blast in her palm. "Seriously? That's a little bit on the nose. Destroy humans, destroy humans. Cliché much?"

Terra cracked her knuckles. "I really don't give a shit as long as I can hit those fuckers." She sprinted toward two of the robots and tackled one of them to the ground. "Hey, this fucker didn't break." Terra's excitement was cut short as an energy blast from the other robot sent her flying.

It was preparing another attack on Terra when Anabelle, who had raced after Terra, slashed it across the neck with her hand.

The robot stumbled forward, somehow managing to stay on its feet. Its head whirled around, and it looked at Anabelle. "Hm. That usually does the job," the elf mused as she dodged the robot's plasma blast.

Across the room, two more robots emerged from the second hunk of box.

Sarah pulled out her plasma rifle and fired as she backed away, looking for cover.

Anabelle and Terra had natural defenses against most attacks. The elf was able to instinctively deflect most weak magical attacks, and Terra's body compensated by growing denser the deeper she went into a blood rage.

Sarah was the only person on the team who worried about getting shot.

Abby blasted her thrusters and skidded forward with her arm out in front of her as she fired at one of the robots. Then she shifted to the right and headed over to Sarah.

She slammed her hand into the floor in front of Sarah, causing a jagged piece of it to shoot up. "Good enough cover?" Abby asked.

Sarah pressed her back against the slab and pointed in the direction of Terra and Anabelle, who were fighting the two new robots.

"Could you cover my six? I don't want to get tapped in the back of the head."

Abby fired a sonic wave from her shoulder, sending a seismic shiver through the ground as another section of floor shot up, providing Sarah with cover.

"You want to take these two with me?" Sarah asked.

"Why don't you guys just go all Super Saiyan on everyone like you used to?" Abby asked.

Sarah reloaded her rifle and attached a scope to it. "Don't know what we're up against down here. Don't want to get too tired and find out we got four Groks on the other side. Strong's not the same as being smart."

Terra slammed into the side of cover Abby had created as a robot leaped on her chest and kneed her in the sternum. Terra laughed as she head-butted the robot.

The robot grabbed her head and slammed it into the stone slab.

Abby pressed her hand to the side of the robot's head and fired a concussive blast, shattering its skull.

Terra yelped, "Wait, what are you doing?"

Abby's mask peeled back so she could look Terra in the eyes. "Uh, we're helping?"

Terra sighed. "Dude, that's the first close-quarter fight I've had in like a month."

"It was winning."

"Nah. I was using some basic techniques for practice. You know, keep up with the basics."

Sarah looked over her shoulders. "Same here. Why do you think I put the scope on? I need the practice too." She fired, not even bothering to look over her shoulder, and nailed one of the robots in the head. "We haven't had a challenge for a while."

"Yeah," Terra said. "We aren't goofing off. Well, we *are* goofing off, but with a purpose."

Anabelle, who had a robot's throat gripped in her hand, turned around to partake in the conversation. "Seriously, what were you thinking, Abby? Terra literally caught a bomb last week."

Terra sheepishly looked at her feet. "Well, I mean, I didn't catch it so much as got caught in it."

Sarah fired again at the other robot, taking its head off. "Yeah, well, I can't get to the level of power output Terra and Anabelle can manage, but even I don't have to worry about simple human tech and shit."

Abby stood up as one of the robots fired at her. She absentmindedly raised her hand, blocking the attack and sending it back with a reflective plasma shield. "Is this what it's going to be like from now on? Did we peak already?"

Terra shrugged as the members of the DGA started to make their way through the room, walking under the pieces of the metallic box that had launched into the ceiling. "Don't know? You never see the in-between things from action movies. Like, what was John McClane doing between *Die Hard 1* and *2*? Did he take a vacation, or was he really bored, going through police reports and shit? Maybe *we* should be bored for a bit. We've done a lot. We deserve a bit of boredom, don't you think? Sarah, especially. She just got married."

The two metallic sections fell from the ceiling, extending metallic legs from their sides. Rocket launchers snapped onto what seemed to be a cockpit as two machine guns detached from their bottom sections.

The DGA split, Sarah rolling to take cover behind a piece of debris. "True, but that's got its own list of problems."

A rocket flew toward Terra, who grabbed it. She kept it from exploding and sent it back at the ceiling, where it blew up and tore open a huge hole. "Wait, is there trouble in paradise?"

The machine gun from one of the box hunks blasted Sarah's cover apart, forcing her to flip backward to avoid the bullets heading toward her. "Hardly. Everything with Kravis is great. But there's all this extra bureaucratic shit we have to do with work visas and other bullshit paperwork, and because Kravis can't get a work visa, he can't run his own missions. He's getting antsy."

Terra shuddered as she slammed her fist on the floor and levered up a person-sized piece of rubble. "Ugh. Paperwork. I'd rather be tortured."

Anabelle smirked. "That what you and Cire do in your free time?"

She tossed the debris, and Anabelle magically covered the rock with flames until it was molten slag. She kicked her lava-hot creation at the spider-like robot, tearing a simmering hole through it.

Sarah grabbed a grenade from her side and tossed it into the hole.

The spider-robot stumbled as Terra slid beneath its body, snatching one of its legs out from under it and driving it into its body. "I'll have you know we are the model of a perfectly normal couple. All of our bruises are consensual."

Abby pretended to shudder as she walked past the exploding bot. "Ew, gross. We didn't ask for details."

Terra walked past the scientist and clapped her on the back. "One of these days, someone is going to have to give you a talk about the birds and the bees. Or is it just birds? *Or* maybe just bees and stingers. I certainly shouldn't be the one giving that talk."

"We went to high school," Abby muttered. Terra dug her knuckles into Abby's scalp before the scientist vented kinetic energy from her suit, pushing her away.

Sarah pointed down the hallway. "God, two weeks without a world-saving mission, and you guys turn into the Golden Girls."

Anabelle shook her head. "We should all be honored to be compared with Betty White."

"I didn't know elves watched much human television."

"We don't. Terra showed me *Golden Girls*. It was life-changing, to say the least. I still find it hard to imagine how elves got so philosophically advanced without the great Betty White's influence."

Sarah and Abby burst out laughing while Terra tried to keep it in. "Didn't think you had such a savage sense of humor, Abby. Now come on, let's hurry up and finish this up. I think it's anime night. Right, kiddo?"

Abby smiled as she looked over her shoulder at the destruction she and her friends had left behind. "Yeah, and I haven't even read the manga for this one."

Terra shoved Abby lightly. "All you got to do is say anime around her and she's a completely different person."

"What? Anime is great, and I know you guys aren't watching it ironically anymore. Let's get this over with."

CHAPTER THREE

The Dark Gate Angels continued making their way through the dim underbelly of the restaurant, talking to pass the time. Since the release and nearly immediate destruction of the security robots, there was nothing to do other than walk.

After a considerable amount of pestering, Terra had finally got Abby to tell them what Persephone was working on.

Abby went into detail about her lover's new job as a cultural sensitivity trainer for the different races trying to integrate on Earth.

Terra pretended to snore loudly. "Yawn. This is what the great heroes of the war against the Dark One have been reduced too? Sensitivity trainers? And that's only if they can get a work visa? What about us? I haven't been decently stabbed in months."

The darkened halls were filled with far too much laughter for a serious mission.

Abby didn't care. Terra was right. There hadn't been a real challenge since the Dark One. Missions like this and the others they had gone on could have been completed by other agents.

But Myrddin wanted to keep them in the loop and in the field.

Eventually, the conversation turned to Anabelle. "So, how have things been going with you?" Terra asked. "You keep such a tight lid on everything, we would have assumed you're living in a cave someplace off the map."

Anabelle shrugged as she scanned the area. "No different than anyone else. Most I can say is, I've gotten in touch with a couple of cousins of mine. It would be nice if they weren't the most annoying people in all the Nine Realms. I'm supposed to take them to Santa Monica next week."

Sarah groaned. "Sounds tedious. Glad I don't have to entertain any family. I think I would kill myself."

The pathway they were following stopped abruptly at a large steel double door, much like the freezer door they had initially entered.

Terra pressed her ear to it and listened. "Do you think this place is sturdy enough to contain a bomb?"

Sarah reached into the bag hanging loosely at her side and pulled out a small detonator. "That's what we've been trying to figure out for the last few weeks. This might be an assembly plant, a place for pieces to come before they're shipped out to be put together somewhere else. Step back."

She placed the detonator on the door and secured it with a yellow gel.

Anabelle leaned against the steel and rested her hand on it. "Why don't you let me blow it?"

Sarah motioned for everyone to step away. "Because not everyone can just barrel through each situation in front of them. Maybe you guys should look into diversifying your own skill sets. Not every job needs to end with punching something in the face."

Terra raised her hands in the air. "Oh, can you cut the holier than thou act? You end up either punching or shooting someone in the face, regardless of what you're doing."

Sarah pulled out the switch for the detonator. "I'm just saying, sometimes warming up to face-punching can be the engaging part. Like foreplay. Cover your ears."

Terra, Anabelle, and Abby did as they were told, and Sarah blew the door open.

Thirty men stood in a steel room, some of them wearing exo-suits and others armed to the teeth with plasma rifles and pistols. Many of them were wearing black suits and sunglasses; it looked as if the room were filled with middle-aged pallbearers.

Even though they were all facing the Dark Gate Angels when the door blew open, they seemed to be surprised by the sudden intrusion. A handful of the men were still sitting at a table, playing poker.

A seated man who was wearing the largest exo-suit coughed uncomfortably. "Oh, blimey, didn't think you'd make it here."

Abby glanced at Anabelle. "Wasn't this an Italian restaurant? What's a Brit doing here?"

Anabelle nodded slowly, boredom evident on her face. "Yep, Italian and elvish."

The man spat on the floor and then stomped on the spittle. "Don't mean only Italians and elves work here. Don't mean they won't hire no British chaps, either."

Anabelle clenched her fist and flexed, shooting out sparks of mana. "Glad to hear your boss is inclusive in his hiring practices. Now, what the hell are you guys up to down here?"

The man looked from Anabelle to the squad behind him. "Yeah, we got all kinds of people here. And as for what we're doing, ain't it obvious? We're here to stop you."

Terra looked around the room. "I don't know how to say this politely, but you guys are going to get fucked up. We tore through your robots without even getting close to thinking about sweating. And you guys have, what…guns?"

One of the men at the table, who was wearing a fedora along with his exo-suit, stood up as he slammed his fist on the table. "Do you think we can't hold our own? Come on, give us a try!"

Sarah stepped between the rest of the DGA and the armed goons. "Hey, we can settle this without all of you leaving without your teeth. We're here to see where you're getting all this tech from. Tell us, and we can let you walk away. Or you can try to fight us, get the shit kicked out of you, go through a less than pleasant interrogation with me, and then tell us. What is it going to be?"

A man near the back pulled out a rocket launcher and fired.

Abby raised her hand and sent a signal to neutralize the rocket, causing it to hit Terra in the chest and fall dead on the floor at her feet.

"That means we get to kick their asses, right?" Terra asked.

Sarah nodded solemnly. "We gave them a chance. Do you want to—"

Terra leaped into the crowd of men, knocking over three of them as she belly-flopped onto them. She grabbed one by the hair, yanked him up, and headbutted him, breaking his nose while laughing loudly. Then she swung him around by his feet, knocking over a few more of the guards.

Anabelle closed her eyes and created flames around her body, forcing the guards back from the heat.

One fired his plasma rifle at the elf. She dodged to the side, ran up the wall, and flipped down onto him, breaking his clavicle.

Abby busied herself with scanning the enemy's tech. Their rifles hadn't come from Myrddin's forces or any of the caches left over from the Dark One, either. Someone else was supplying the mob with weapons. She transferred the data to the rest of the team.

Sarah glanced down at her wrist as she checked out one of the mob guys. "Wait, where the hell are they getting the guns then? This tech shouldn't be on the market."

Terra flipped over a goon and brought her arm down on the one behind him, breaking through his exo-suit. "You mean, not even on the black market?"

Sarah turned around and shot a guard in the chest. "You don't have to take that tone."

"I'm just saying. Obviously, wherever the mob is getting their guns is the most illegal of illegal places."

Anabelle broke the jaw of a guard, then dropped to one knee and sent a shockwave of electricity through a handful of guards. "Why don't we just ask someone?" She picked up one of the stunned guards. "Who are you working for?"

The guard trembled as he spoke, looking around at his fallen comrades, who were writhing in pain on the floor. "He's in the back. Jesus, please don't hurt me."

Sarah walked up to the guard Anabelle was holding and punched him in the face, knocking him out. "Ugh. Even the interrogations are boring." She pointed at a door in the back of the room. "Come on, he's probably in there."

Abby looked around the room. All the guards were lying on the floor, groaning as they clutched their broken limbs. "What do we do with all of these guys?"

Sarah pulled up her HUD. "I'll send in a team once we finish all of this. They're waiting upstairs. I wanted to make sure we didn't send anyone into anything dangerous. I doubt these guys will give the clean-up crew any trouble." She knelt and pinched the cheeks of one of the guards. "Isn't that right? Because the clean-up crew is ordered to shoot on sight."

Terra was already at the door leading to the mob boss. She threw it open theatrically and peeked in. When she turned to face the rest of the DGA, she looked worried. "Uh, this is kind of a weird door."

Abby and Anabelle walked over to Terra. "Looks like a pretty normal door to us," Abby said.

Terra pointed at the black emptiness behind it. "Most doors don't open up to nowhere. I mean, most non-magical human doors don't."

Sarah joined the rest of them and gestured at a fingerprint pad next to the door. "Gimme a minute." She walked over to one of the guards, who strained up and spat at her. "Okay, I was just going to ask you, but then you had to do that."

She grabbed the guard's hand and pulled out her knife. He screamed as he tried to pull his hand away, but Sarah was too fast. She severed his index finger and walked back to the fingerprint pad.

"Probably should have asked which finger they use," she muttered.

Terra shook her head. "Dude, you gotta stop the psycho stuff all the time. Abby's here. Try to be more child-friendly."

Abby glared at Terra, who smiled widely. "We are not—"

"I'm just fucking with you, kid."

"We're not sure anymore. You joke about it so much, we're starting to think this might be a not-so-subtle dig at us for embodying your lost youth."

Terra stared blankly at Abby for a few moments. "Damn, Abs. You didn't have to go savage on me. I might never recover from that."

"You'll recover. Martin already requisitioned some burn cream for you."

Abby raised both her arms as her mask peeled back so Terra could see her face. "Booyah!"

Terra feigned being struck in the heart, stumbling backward. "Two sick burns in a row? How can I go on?" She dropped to her knees, wringing her hands in mock pain.

Sarah pressed the guard's detached finger to the pad.

Lights shone in the room, and they saw that there was no floor.

"Huh. That was anticlimactic," Anabelle said as she peered in, eventually looking down when a draft blew up. "Guess we're going down there." She stepped into the darkness and plummeted downward.

Terra watched Anabelle disappear. "Is it just me, or does she always look really cool doing that?"

Sarah walked into the darkness and spun on one foot, smirking at Terra. "You only say that because you're always overthinking your own cool exits." She disappeared.

Abby floated past the door's threshold. "We think you have pretty cool drops."

Terra leaped over the threshold toward Abby, who caught her. "Trust me, this is going to look super cool. Let's go."

Abby descended slowly down the darkened shaft, shining a light below. She could see Anabelle and Sarah wading in what looked like water.

Once they got to the bottom of the shaft, Terra let go of Abby's arms.

Anabelle was shaking her head. "I'd give that two out of three. You looked like a giant baby."

Terra groaned as she ran her hands over her bald head. "Ugh. You are impossible to impress."

Abby landed next to Terra. The water came up to her shins.

The air smelled musky and dank. Crickets chirped, and in the dim light from overhead, could be seen leaping about.

Abby touched the water. "Was there anything in your intel about there being a swamp under this place?" She started scanning the fluid, hoping for a clue.

Sarah was walking down a hall that branched off from where they had landed. "Nope, but that means this could at least be a *little* interesting."

The four of them continued on their way, the water growing incrementally deeper until they were all waist-deep in it.

Anabelle suddenly shrieked and leaped out of the water into Terra's arms. "Something just bit me."

Terra laughed loudly. "Okay, who's the baby now?"

Anabelle scowled as she got back on her feet. "Shut up. It spooked me is all."

Sarah cried out as well. She spun, drew her pistol, and fired into the water.

The body of a dead grindylow floated up to the surface. The creature had a goblin's upper body up to the head, which was malformed and sharkish. Its torso was that of an octopus.

Sarah picked up the dead thing. "What the hell is a grindylow doing down here?"

Behind them, the water started to foam.

Anabelle looked over her shoulder to see dozens of grindylows poking up through the surface. They gnashed their teeth fiercely.

She waded in the opposite direction as fast as she could. "Move!"

More grindylows poked their heads out, cackling maniacally as the DGA agents headed away from them.

They had run into a large cavern that looked as if it had been ripped straight off the coast. The walls were sleek stone covered in barnacles and luminescent seaweed that glowed like it was filled with fireflies.

The water in the room started to get choppy, then erupted into a vortex that shot toward the ceiling.

A cecaelia sat atop the watery throne. He had the torso of a man, with fair skin and long white hair that matched his eyes. His bottom half was like an octopus, and he wore a drenched white shirt and a suit jacket on his upper humanoid half. "What the hell are you doing in my office?" he shouted.

Sarah swam to the surface, sputtering. "I saw the boss' name was Trident, but you are not what I was expecting."

Trident reached behind his back and pulled out a long, sharp steel trident. "Y'all got a lotta 'splaining to do."

Terra splashed around, trying to stay above the water. "Okay, now that is *too* close."

Trident spun his weapon, causing the water to swirl into a vortex. The DGA agents were sucked into it as grindylows flooded the room.

Abby let loose a blast of kinetic energy, breaking the grip of the water around her, allowing her to escape.

Anabelle leaped out of the vortex and landed on a rock near the wall. "Now this looks like a decent fight."

CHAPTER FOUR

The mob boss spun the trident around his head. He twisted the water around him into a funnel and sent it flying at the elf.

At the last second, the elven warrior raised her hands and let out a blast of fire, which evaporated the water and created a wall of steam between her and Trident.

While the mob boss was distracted, Sarah screamed as she used her abilities to enhance her strength. Once she had powered up, she leaped to the ceiling, wedging her feet into the rocks and holding tightly with her hands.

From there, she had a clear path to Trident.

Terra was trying to swim against the current Trident had created. She was about to pull herself out of the water when she felt something wrap around her leg. "Goddamn it," she muttered before being pulled underwater by a grindylow.

Abby saw Terra slip under the water. She slid into the water and sped through it like a torpedo.

Grindylows had surrounded Terra and wrapped their tentacles around her arms and legs, keeping her from getting back to the surface.

A few of the grindylows noticed Abby and jetted toward her.

There were at least thirty of them and possibly more. Abby couldn't see well under the water, but she could see Terra, and that was what was important for the moment.

Abby fired a plasma blast at the grindylows. The blast was hampered by the water, but it was enough to scare the grindylows off Terra and into the darker parts of the cavern.

Abby hit her thrusters and scooped Terra up, and the two of them burst out of the water together. She flew around in a quick circle, looking for a place to drop Terra off.

She saw Anabelle fighting back Trident's water onslaught and headed over to drop Terra by the elf. "We'll take care of the grindylows. We can move faster than you underwater."

Terra spat out water as she huddled behind Anabelle. "You don't have to tell me twice. I fucking hate swimming." She turned to the elf. "Any game plan? Can't say I have a whole lot of ideas for how to go about fighting in a giant fishbowl."

Anabelle nodded, her forehead furrowed in concentration. "Working on it. Doesn't seem like we're going to be able to blast our way through this. He's got a huge advantage over us."

Above Trident, Sarah prepared to attack. She let go of the ceiling and fell toward him.

One of Trident's tentacles lashed out and grabbed Sarah by the ankle. He effortlessly tossed her away.

Sarah hit the wall hard. The wind was knocked out of her, and she gasped as she fell into the water. Before she had a chance to get out, Trident's tentacle slammed into her chest, forcing her down.

Sarah pulled out her katana to hack through the tentacle, but before she got a chance, several grindylows raced toward her.

Abby swooped into the water, getting between the grindylows and Sarah. "Martin, can you do anything about our visibility?"

Martin's voice rang in Abby's ear. "Working on it. The water keeps shifting. Trident must be affecting it magically, and I might not be able to work through that."

Abby slammed her hands together, sending a sonic shockwave

through the water that dispersed the grindylows. That gave Sarah enough time to get to the surface.

She pulled out a grappling hook and launched it into the ceiling, using it to pull herself up.

Across the room, Trident was making his move on Anabelle and Terra, who were stuck behind the wall of steam and water.

Terra poked her head out to get a better look. "Uh, you got anything? He's getting closer."

Anabelle smiled smugly. "Don't worry about it. This is like a game of rock, paper, scissors, except with water. Guess what always beats water?"

"Yeah, got it." Terra returned the smile, but it fell. "Wait, are our suits insulated?"

Anabelle shrugged. "You might want to make sure you don't get any more soaked than you are. You know, just to be safe."

Trident burst through the wall of water and brought down his weapon on Anabelle. She leaned back and knocked the trident to the side as she charged her arm with electricity, then punched Trident in the chest with a thunderous boom.

The cecaelia smiled grimly. "Little elf, ya think ya can hurt a creature born of the storm?"

Trident slammed his trident into the rock, sending thousands of volts of electricity into the stone as his tentacles wrapped around Anabelle.

Electricity flowed through her body, shocking her and wracking her body with pain.

Trident lifted her into the air and slammed her back into the rock. He raised her once more.

Terra uppercut Trident, knocking him back.

As he stumbled back, he whipped around, commanding the water into a giant fist that rammed into Terra, smashing her into the wall.

Terra tried to fight with the watery hand, but every time she punched it, her fist went straight through the liquid.

As Terra fought, Trident began to wave his weapon around his head, pulling some of the water in the room toward him and covering himself in watery armor.

From the ceiling, Sarah fired her pulse rifle.

The pulse hit Trident's armor, stopping instantly.

Abby shot out of the water, covered in grindylows, and charged Trident, trying to break through his armor. The grindylows' tentacles grabbed her arms and legs until she was covered with odd appendages.

Trident slammed his weapon into Abby, knocking her back into the water.

Anabelle was back on her feet. As she leaped, her foot grew denser until it was as solid as a diamond. It connected with Trident's water armor but didn't pass through.

Realizing her attack had done nothing, Anabelle flipped backward, using her mana to skid across the surface of the water without sinking.

Sarah leaped onto the water as well, using her chakra energy to keep from going under.

Terra, who had made her way over to a piece of stone, gasped in awe. "Wait, how are you guys doing that?"

Anabelle glanced at Terra and smiled. "Years of practicing mana manipulation. Probably the same as Sarah."

Terra frowned as she crossed her arms. "Fucking showoffs."

Anabelle returned her attention to Trident. "Haven't even started showing off yet." Her eyes flashed brightly as she shot mana sparks, then the elf transitioned into the Path of the Lost. "*Now* this is over."

She surged forward, her fist crackling with energy, and slammed it into Trident's water armor.

It exploded outward.

As the steam passed, Trident still stood.

"You're kidding me." Anabelle groaned. "There's no way you're stronger than Grok."

Trident laughed defiantly. "Don't know who you're talking 'bout, but I'm gonna let you in on a little secret. Ain't nothing stronger than water."

He waved his free hand, and a fist of water slammed into Anabelle.

Sarah opened all of her inner gates, and her power increased until she was on the same level as Anabelle. Her skin vibrated as she launched at Trident, who threw up a water wall. Sarah spat a ball of fire that turned some of the water to steam, then tried to punch through it to no avail.

Trident spun his weapon again, and the water formed two humanoid figures nearly seven feet tall. The figures went after Anabelle and Sarah, forcing them both to stop paying attention to Trident. The mob boss dove into the water, then sprang back up in front of Terra. His tentacles gripped the rock she stood on and crushed it to dust.

Still, he was distracted long enough for Abby to fire a precise laser blast that cut through the creature's stomach.

Water rather than blood poured from Trident's wound. It was the first he'd received since the fight started, and he let out a roar as the water level in the room decreased significantly.

Terra leaped, her eyes wide and mad with fury and an insane smile on her face as she brought her fists down on Trident's armored head.

The force of Terra's attack didn't break through the armor, but it forced Trident to buckle under the pressure. Before he could stand again, Abby charged into him, knocking the creature off-balance.

Terra climbed onto his chest. "I don't need all those fancy tricks, homeboy. I punch really hard."

Terra drove her fist into Trident's armor, sending waves of water flying off him. The shockwave from her punch and Trident's writhing caused Terra to fall, but luckily, Abby was close enough to swoop down and grab her.

Trident dissolved the two water warriors fighting Anabelle and Sarah and drew even more water from the room. He bolstered his defenses so much that the DGA were only up to their knees in water.

The remaining grindylows looked around the room at the corpses Abby had left after being underwater. She had killed most of their kin. They took off, leaving Trident alone.

Terra leaped back onto him, seeking to use sheer strength to rip through Trident's water armor.

The mob boss looked afraid. "You can't break through," he muttered.

There was a flash in Terra's eyes as she smiled wider. "Oh, I can't? How much do you want to bet?"

Terra crouched on Trident's chest and then sprang into the air. She landed on the water armor, which bent under her weight, then she cupped her hands together and brought them down.

The force behind Terra's fists broke the armor, and waves flooded the room.

Once the water was out of Trident's control, Anabelle slipped out of the Path of the Lost. She used her other elemental skills to scoop the water into the air so it hung like a curtain, where she flash-froze it.

Trident scrambled across the ground, his octopus tentacles trying to get traction so he could make a quick escape. Unfortunately, his suction cups stuck to the stone.

Terra made her way to Trident, her eyes dark as she cracked her knuckles. "My honor hath been offended for the last time, squid-man." She punched him in the face, cracking his jaw and sending him flying across the room. By the time Abby reached the mob boss, he was unconscious.

Anabelle walked over to Terra, whose eyes were returning to their normal color. "Damn, that was more annoying than I thought it was going to be."

Terra dabbed her forehead. "Oh, shit! Do you see that? Sweat! I worked up a sweat."

"Did you even go into the Path of the Lost?"

"Nope. Just got a rush, you know?"

Anabelle crossed her arms as she stared at Terra. "Fucking showoff."

Sarah, who was crouched next to Abby as she cuffed Trident, shouted at Terra and Anabelle, "If you two are done comparing dicks, we got a perp to question."

Terra clapped her hands together. "Oh, this is my favorite part. It's my turn, right?"

Anabelle shook her head as they joined Abby and Sarah. "Nope. It's Abby's turn."

The scientist sighed as she stood up. "No, we pass. Terra can have it."

Anabelle looked at her sternly. "You know you're going to have to start doing it eventually. I know you don't want to be the bad guy, but you have to learn how to get information out of assholes like this."

"Fine, fine. We'll do it. We've been practicing."

Abby slapped Trident across the face. "Where are the bomb parts?"

Trident's eyes were still trying to focus. "I ain't tellin' you broads nothin'."

Abby's hand converted to a long funnel. She pointed it away from Trident's face, and a jet of fire shot out from it. "Once more, where are the bomb parts?"

"Okay, okay, I'm sorry. They're in the back room. Swear to the gods. You're not gonna torch me, right?"

Sarah pulled out a taser. "Nope, but you're going back to sleep. Without your water shield, this should do the trick." She jammed the taser into Trident's side, shocking him and knocking him out.

Abby grumbled as they walked toward the back door in the office. "We could have figured this out on our own."

Anabelle draped her arm around Abby's shoulder. "True, but now we know for sure. Besides, it's fun to watch you be all scary."

Terra kicked the door down.

It was a small room, but it was crowded with weapons and magical artifacts. In the middle of the room was a partially-built bomb.

Abby scanned the bomb while the rest of the team scoured the room. "Looks like this was made with technological and magical parts. Whoever built this knew what they were doing. This is pretty advanced stuff."

Terra, who was playing with a crystal orb, looked at Sarah. "You think they were doing this themselves or working for someone else?"

Sarah shook her head as she looked at the bomb. "These guys are just muscle. Security. But it's a lead."

"Eh. I guess detective work can be fun."

Martin popped up on their wrist comms. "Hey, I got bad news. Something popped up on Abby's scan. You're not going to believe it."

Abby projected a hologram of the bomb's internal workings. A vial separated from the rest of the bomb. Within the vial was a black liquid, moving around and attacking the walls of the vial.

Anabelle stared at it. "No way. Is that Dark Melody?"

Abby nodded grimly. "Yep. That's exactly what it is."

CHAPTER FIVE

Anabelle was in her room, meditating, thinking over the events of the day. Since their battle with the Dark One several months ago, she had been having an easier time settling into meditation.

The brush with death had put a lot of things into perspective, and the process had made her less of a mystery to herself. Many of her memories were still lost, as was the way with elves, but more often than not, if she needed to recall something, she could.

The fight with Trident had bothered her. Even though Terra, Sarah, and she had all uncovered the Path of the Lost, albeit all in different ways—some of which Anabelle was tempted to think were inferior—they still had struggled with Trident. How could they have defeated the Dark One and not been able to wipe the floor with the mob boss?

Anabelle continued to pore over the question as she concentrated on her breathing. The Path of the Lost offered strength, a wild abandonment of power drawn from losing yourself in battle, but it hadn't been useful against an effective defense.

Defeating Grok had required brute force. The Dark One had required the combined energy of more than the DGA, and Rasputina had never truly been subdued.

Maybe the Path of the Lost wasn't enough, simply another tool in a list—one she should not rely on.

Anabelle remembered the strength Terra had shown without accessing that power. She made a promise to herself not to depend too heavily on the Path. There were other tactics to be learned and practiced. Even Sarah still played with her guns, knowing full well she could eviscerate anyone in front of her with her hands.

But that was not what was really on Anabelle's mind. It was a pleasant distraction from what was gnawing at her.

The Dark Melody was a substance created from the decaying bodies of the old gods who existed in the Netherverse. The Dark One had harnessed the Dark Melody for his own infernal uses. Luckily, he had been caught at the beginning stages of that particular tactic in his evil plans, and the Dark Gate Angels had managed to destroy what little of it had made it out of the Netherverse.

The Netherverse Gates had been destroyed. How the hell had anyone smuggled more of the Dark Melody out of a place that couldn't be accessed throughout any of the Nine Realms?

There was a simple answer; it was obviously old. The Dark One had used multiple backend channels to move the Dark Melody throughout the Nine Realms. It had initially been discovered on the gnome world. It wasn't too big a stretch to believe it could have been smuggled onto Earth.

Anabelle didn't pretend to understand the complex criminal network that Sarah had made it her mission to root out. Human crime was already difficult for Anabelle to understand. Coupled with a handful of opportunists looking to take advantage of the sudden influx of magic coming to Earth, she could imagine a magical group trying to make a profit off selling humans something they didn't understand.

The mob boss hadn't even been human, and the bomb had been created by someone with an understanding of magic and technology that could be used in tandem with it. That was more than most humans knew anything about, let alone mobsters without an extremely well-funded science department.

Anabelle almost felt bad for humanity. Earth had to go through so many changes. They'd managed to deal with all the superficial ones, adding simple gestures to welcome their new interdimensional guests and providing guidance on the cultures of the other races. All good stuff, but the humans weren't ready for the complications that would come with these new visitors.

And Anabelle knew humans.

They had a capacity for violence that made orcs look like pacifists. The biggest problem was that they lacked the nobility of orcs, something humans didn't grasp yet.

Anabelle couldn't help but laugh. She would never have thought she'd be worrying about humans.

But she was.

One in particular occupied her mind: Roy.

She hadn't seen him in days. They'd both been wrapped up in work. He was now the head of Interdimensional Policing, a position Anabelle had turned down. Seeing how much time he spent buried under paperwork, she was more than happy with her decision.

There was a knock on Anabelle's door. She opened her eyes, letting them adjust to the light. "Come in."

Her door slid open, and Terra stepped in. "Okay, so what the hell was that all about?"

Anabelle stood and went to her fridge, poured herself a cup of water, and grabbed a beer for Terra. "What are you talking about?"

"Crab Boy gave us a huge run for our money, which makes absolutely no sense since we fucked the shit out of the Dark One. Yet here we are, having troubles with middlemen mob bosses? The Hand of the Orcs spent twenty minutes tap-dancing with Crab Legs."

"You know he had tentacles, right? Not crab legs."

Terra cracked her beer and sat on Anabelle's bed. "His nautical parts weren't worth remembering. Seriously, Anna, what the fuck? I thought we were badasses?"

"You can't chop down a tree with a hammer."

Terra took a sip of her beer and pointed it at Anabelle accusingly.

"You know I hate it when you get all Bruce Lee on me. What are you trying to say?"

Anabelle leaned against her desk. "A tool that works for one purpose doesn't mean it works for all. Maybe we needed a Path to take care of Grok and the Dark One. We shouldn't rely on one skill to deal with everything we come across."

"That's easy for you and Sarah to say. You have the Path of a Traveler, and Sarah's a trained assassin who can kill anyone in six different ways. All I can do is scrap. It's not the same."

A hologram of Abby and Martin projected from Terra's and Anabelle's wrist HUDs.

Terra screamed in surprise and rolled off of the bed. "Jesus, Abby, you're supposed to send us an email or something when you're going to do something invasive like that."

Abby shook her head, and Martin did the same. "Nope. Ruins the fun. We need you two to come down to the Tech and Magic department. Martin and us, I guess. That's probably the only time that's sounded awkward. Anyways, we need you to come here. There's something you should see."

Anabelle drained her water and placed the cup on her desk. She was always happy to see Abby in her element. Taking charge was a good look on the kid. "We'll be there in a second."

Abby disappeared, leaving Terra and Anabelle alone. "We'll finish our heart-to-heart later," Anabelle said. "But remember what I said. Think about it."

Terra waved away her words as she walked toward the door. "Yeah, yeah, I got it. Don't try to water a garden with a plant."

"Yeah, you definitely got it."

In the Tech & Magic workroom, Abby and Creon had their own section, separate from the rest of the department. It was here the two of them worked on their experiments, many of them off the record. The faint of heart were advised never to visit. The area was known for a variety of explosions.

Tea and cookies were ready for the two agents when they arrived.

Terra looked suspiciously at the food and drink. "When did you two go all Victorian?"

Abby, who was munching on a cookie, leaned over to see if Creon was down the hall. "He's been trying to get into human culture more, and unfortunately, he's on a Jane Austen kick. Don't get us wrong, she's great, but we can only deal with so much bland food."

Terra took a seat and sipped a cup of tea. "Some people would say the British have very nuanced palates."

Anabelle broke her cookie in half and watched it crumble. "Eh, I'd say they might want to look up the definition of nuanced."

Abby took a bite of her cookie and washed it down with tea. "Regardless, don't be a dick about it to him. It's the only human thing he's taken an interest in."

Creon walked into the room as Terra was about to say something. Anabelle thought she looked like she had a mouth full of food as she tried to swallow her retort. "Good to see you all here," Creon said as he settled at his desk. "You don't stop by as much since you don't need a world-saving solution as often."

Anabelle sighed as she checked her makeup. "Creon, we went out to dinner last week."

"True, perhaps, but I still enjoy a visit to the office. But Abby and I didn't ask that you come here to go over the amount of time you are expected to visit your friends."

Abby, Anabelle, and Terra exchanged knowing glances. "Well, what are we here for?" Terra asked.

Abby brought up a hologram of the vial they had retrieved from Trident's bomb. "We ran a series of tests on the Dark Melody we found. It isn't old. This is brand new."

Terra shook her head as she continued to poke at a cookie, only stopping when Anabelle hissed at her. "That's impossible. The Netherverse Gates are closed. There's no in or out. Myrddin said so himself."

"True, that was what Myrddin said, but my research shows it can't be true. This has been carbon-dated and studied alongside every bit of the Dark Melody we have. It was mined within the last two weeks."

Anabelle crossed her legs and leaned back in her chair. "Do we have reports of it showing up anywhere else?"

"We went through all of the reports for the last year. This is the first case of Dark Melody since we shut down the gates."

Anabelle didn't like the news, but it seemed straightforward enough. Someone had found a way into the Netherverse, and whoever it was intended to weaponize the Dark Melody. "Well, what's the big problem? We neutralize it with your nanobots like we did before, then we find whoever is responsible for this and lock 'em up. They can't be too high-level if they're working with humans. No offense."

Terra slammed her fist on the table. "I take offense on principle but also agree. Humans haven't had time to get a grip on any of this. If someone is working with humans, they're obviously willing to risk dealing with a huge learning curve."

Abby shook her head. "No, we think differently. It's probably someone banking on the fact that we're going to think this is too mid-level for us. It could be someone trying to make a name for themselves, or it could be something much worse."

Silence enveloped the room. Anabelle knew what everyone was thinking—the same thing that was running through her head. She shuddered. What if the new peace was a lie? If her fears were true, it meant everything they'd put themselves through had been for nothing.

Terra broke the silence. "He can't be back. We killed him."

Anabelle shook her head. "No, you remember what Myrddin said at Sarah's wedding."

Terra waved away the elf's words. "Oh, Myrddin always expects the worst. He's been fighting this war for the last thousand years. He's probably not ready to give it up."

"You doubt the person who knows the enemy the best?"

Terra's eyes dropped, avoiding Anabelle's. "It's supposed to be over. We finished it."

"What if we didn't?"

Abby, Anabelle, and Terra avoided looking at each other. Creon, on the other hand, stared at them all. "Haven't you been bored anyway? Isn't this the challenge you've been waiting for?"

Terra summed up everything Anabelle felt. "We gave it everything we had, and it still wasn't enough to stop him. What if we can't?"

No one could answer.

CHAPTER SIX

Terra waited for Anabelle and Abby in the transportation hangar. She was pacing, not because she was nervous but because there was nothing else to do. For some reason, she'd woken up earlier than she'd planned.

She'd spent the morning in the cafeteria, responding to the backlog of messages and requests she'd received since she took on the mission in New York.

Imagining the amount of paperwork she would have had if she still had the position of chieftain to all the orcs blew her mind. She hardly had anything to answer as the Hand to the Council. Most of the busywork she had to fill out was for Myrddin, and it looked like it would take the rest of the week and the weekend as well.

Guess I'm not taking any leave this week.

If she were honest, the paperwork was a pleasant distraction. It gave her something to look at other than the news.

There weren't many people with whom Terra had remained in contact since she joined the DGA. Not that she didn't have friends before. It was just that her life had so suddenly and drastically changed since she had been abducted by the orcs and dragged to the arena to fight for her life.

The few she still talked to were constantly bombarding her with questions about the other races. Even though Terra wasn't involved with the human race like she had been, she was able to pick up on the anxiety the planet was feeling.

It was an odd sensation. That was one of the reasons Terra was avoiding the news. Still, you'd have to live in a cave to miss it all, and she'd caught wind of a few stories.

There was unrest.

Lots.

She didn't know the extent of it, but she had a fairly good idea.

Terra had been the public face for the Myrddin Initiative—the public's given name, not Myrddin's—since her fights had been broadcast from the arena. She'd enjoyed her time away from the public eye, but that time had come to an end. Now the entire DGA would be in front of the camera.

Surprisingly, Terra wasn't worried about Anabelle. The elf had come a long way since Terra met her. Whatever Anabelle had witnessed in New York, maybe even before then, had changed her opinion of humans.

Abby was Terra's main concern. An all-American girl drafted into a war across the Nine Realms who'd sacrificed part of her humanity for a cause humans didn't quite understand could easily be flipped and given a negative spin.

Terra was mulling all this over when Abby and Anabelle walked into the hangar, followed by Myrddin. The wizard was lecturing them on talking points, not that Anabelle seemed to care. She was obviously not listening. Abby, on the other hand, was hanging on his every word.

Terra had to laugh. She had no idea why she was worried about any of this. Both of them were going to do great. If anything, Terra should have been worried about herself. She was the one with the big mouth.

Once Terra and the rest of the DGA got to the studio, it was business as usual, but the particulars were a complete surprise to Abby.

Makeup artists gushed over the girl's natural beauty. They lavished compliment after compliment on her as they played with her hair and did her makeup and ran back and forth to pick out outfits they thought she'd look good in.

Initially, Abby wasn't receptive to any of it, particularly about having her hair touched. Eventually, she came around. Terra assumed the compliments had worn her down.

The former gladiator watched the madness in the green room as she munched on a cheese and meat plate left for them. Once the makeup artists left, Abby whirled around in her chair, giggling loudly before stopping and looking at herself in the mirror. "Can you believe this? We've never had anyone do our makeup before. This is how they pampered you, Terra? You were making it sound like you were being martyred."

Anabelle took a seat next to Terra and popped a piece of cheese into her mouth expertly, careful not to smear her lipstick. "Don't get too comfortable. This is mostly a ploy to get you to lower your guard. The real shit show is when they start asking questions."

Abby was hardly listening. "Why would they put this much work into making us look this good if they were going to be jerks to us?"

Anabelle and Terra smiled at each other. "Oh, if that's the case, you can take the first round of questions," the elf offered.

Abby wheeled her chair over to the table of treats. "We're not falling for that. You two can do all the talking. We'll just keep our feet out of our mouth."

Terra couldn't help being proud as she watched the girl. She'd once asked herself if she would have been able to accomplish what Abby had at her age. The answer was fairly obvious. Terra could see that Abby was a special kind of person. She hadn't needed years to mature into her position. Instead, she'd let the position mature her, stepping up whenever she was needed and sacrificing what she thought she had to. Her parents would have been proud of her. Terra sure as hell was.

It was a panel show where three different opinions were being debated.

Another panelist was a dwarf named Nigel, a stuffy male with a tightly groomed beard and gray eyes. His co-panelist was Meredith, an elf who was nearly as striking as Anabelle. They were strictly anti-integration.

The final opinion was provided by the human host, Derek Withers, an elderly nebbish with a flat nose and large glasses. He was supposed to take a moderate, centered view of things.

Derek introduced the guests to the audience. It was polite enough, but the introduction was the last bit of civility in the whole affair. As soon as they sat down, the barrage began.

"So, tonight, our esteemed guests from the Myrddin Initiative are meeting with—"

Withers was interrupted by Meredith, who politely cleared her throat, murder in her eyes. "I think the fact that the initiative is named after one man sums up the very issue with it: an individual pushing an agenda and mindless drones following it."

Anabelle and Abby were taken aback by Meredith's claim, and neither of them answered. Terra shook her head, already irritated with the direction the interview was taking.

Terra leaned forward and spoke into the microphone. "Okay, first off, we didn't choose the name of the initiative. It was given to us by Earth's diplomats. Second, we aren't serving in an official capacity, merely facilitating the directives that have been given to us."

Nigel sniffed loudly. "And we are to believe that? What it looks like to most of the other races is an aggressive campaign by humans to begin infiltrating the Nine Realms and staking their claim."

Withers tapped his mic to redirect the attention of the debaters. "Why are you claiming that? Humanity has its own issues, given the onslaught of other races that have poured into our country and our world. Many are saying that orcs are taking jobs that many humans could be working instead, and elves are—"

Meredith sneered. "What jobs would humans have that elves would want?"

"Well, what do you have to say about the recent rise in crime since orcs started to travel to the human realm?"

Abby and Anabelle both looked helplessly at Terra, who folded her hands in the most aggressive fashion as possible. "That statement is pure anti-orc rhetoric. The orc diplomats have records of each orc traveling legally or illegally to this realm, and there have been no reports of aggression toward humans by any human authorities. Read the papers, not the tabloids or the bloated press conferences of the President."

This shut everybody up for a moment.

Withers cleared his throat. "Are you saying our president is an idiot?"

Meredith fidgeted in her seat, growing more agitated. "Obviously, he's an idiot. Human politics are so backward. For instance, our reports have shown that the reports of the Dark One being destroyed is total nonsense. It is a narrative being pushed by Myrddin, his cronies, and human diplomats to gain access to our world to appropriate the resources they've stripped from their own planet. Humans are dangerous. Your viciousness is known across your own planet, and now you're spreading it to ours like a cancer."

At this, Anabelle's eyes lit up. "You want to talk about violence? Have you forgotten the Three Hundred Year war the elves waged against the drow? Our own kin? Or perhaps you've neglected to remember that the first blow against the orcs was struck by elves."

At this, Meredith's face closed up, giving the impression of a clam. "That is not human business. Those are—"

"The secrets of elves? And therein lies the problem. The time for secrets is over. The time for division is finished. Look, I understand; getting used to this is difficult, but can you imagine how the humans must be feeling? They only found out about all of us less than two years ago. Now their entire civilization is being restructured. They need to give *us* a chance, not the other way around."

Nigel raised a pen. "Yes, those are all good in words, but what do you have to say about the Dark One? Is it true he still lives? How about we start with some honesty?"

Before Terra could say anything, Abby answered, "Yes and no. The answer is more complicated than that. We know beyond a shadow of a doubt that the Dark One was removed from our realms, all nine of them. We *don't* know if he's been destroyed, and we are working tirelessly to find out."

Meredith's hawk eyes zeroed in on Abby. "You see? They've been lying to us. How can we trust Myrddin's Initiative when they've already spun the truth so much?"

"God, would you shut up for a minute?"

Meredith's jaw dropped as she glared at Abby. "How dare you speak to me like that? A child has no right—"

"A child who has given everything she has for the Nine Realms. Who has lost..."

Abby's voice trailed off, and she looked down at her hands. She wiped the tears from her eyes as she continued, "My father died in the first wave of the Dark One's attacks, killed by orcs under the Dark One's mind control. I joined Myrddin to kill orcs. To get revenge. What I found was a much more complicated world than I had thought. I sacrificed my humanity to free the orcs. The least humanity and the rest of the races can do is try to work with each other because it's happening whether you like it or not. We all know about each other. It doesn't matter if Myrddin works with the human diplomats to make this easier for everyone involved. It's happening regardless."

Meredith and Nigel looked at each other before the dwarf meekly said, "How do you propose to accomplish that?"

Abby smiled and relaxed. "Well, here are a couple of strategies we've prepared to be reviewed by all of the races of the Nine Realms. *All* of them."

***

Terra, Abby, and Anabelle sat in the green room, watching the recording of the debate.

"I think you three did a remarkable job," a voice said.

They turned around to see a magical projection of Myrddin. "I don't think I could have said any of it better myself."

Anabelle grabbed Abby and squeezed her tightly. "That's because we had a junior debate leader on our team. Abby killed it."

Terra nodded, glad to know Abby and Anabelle could hold their own in the public eye. Particularly Anabelle. This was loads better than her first television appearance.

Myrddin smiled softly. "You all did fantastically. If only Sarah could get through an interview without threatening to murder someone."

Anabelle shrugged. "Everyone has their own style."

"Understood. I trust you will all be returning shortly?"

The members of the DGA nodded in unison. "Of course," Abby replied.

"Wonderful. I will see you soon."

Myrddin fizzled out of sight. As soon as he was gone, Anabelle pulled a set of keys out of her pocket. "Guess who snagged the chauffeur's keys?"

Abby gasped before breaking into laughter. "Sarah should have never shown you how to pickpocket."

"Who's ready to finally see New York?"

CHAPTER SEVEN

Abby didn't get back to her room until long after midnight. If her body had been anything like a regular human's, she would have been exhausted. Luckily, she was able to control her body to such a degree that she never got tired. Instead, her nanobots could do any and all micro-repairs on her body and internal systems that created the need to sleep.

But there was only so far that could go, and she was close to her limit.

It had been worth it, though. Anabelle had taken her and Terra all over the city, showing them her favorite spots from her modeling days. But that wasn't all. It had felt wrong for them to be in New York without visiting the site of the lich's return.

They had stood where Rasputina had erupted from the earth and visited the city blocks she'd used for a mass ritual to summon a Jotuun. It was a good way to end the day.

None of them wanted to forget what they were fighting for.

If they hadn't seen the wreckage before, they would not have known this part of the city had been reduced to rubble.

The only sign of destruction was a monument erected to the victims of Rasputina the Lich's attack.

A lot had happened since then, even though it didn't feel like it because there was always something to take care of. Abby could see it in herself. She hadn't felt like a child when she originally signed up with Myrddin, and she didn't feel like an adult now that she was eighteen. It was more complicated than that.

Abby looked at herself in the mirror, watching the light reflect off the nanobots that formed a collar up to her chin.

That was part of what made her feel different. She'd never been insecure about the changes to her humanity. They had been judgment calls and sacrifices for the team and the war. But it was still hard for Abby to get her mother's worried face out of her mind.

The week after they defeated the Dark One, Abby had returned to the farm. Her mother had looked at her like—

Abby didn't want to think about it. She decided to go to the shooting range.

As she was preparing to leave, her comm pinged with a message from Creon to the team. He'd found a lead on the Dark Melody.

Terra messaged back first. We just got home. Can it wait until tomorrow?

Anabelle was next. Yeah, we had a long day.

Then Creon. That's your call. If you want to take the chance that we might lose the one lead we have to find the contact who is supplying criminals with a possible world-destroying material, well, that's up to you guys. I'm a simple scientist. Who am I to question the great Dark Gate Angels?

Terra sent a string of expletives, followed by a set of aggressive emojis, then, **Fine, I'll see y'all at the Collider.**

As Abby made her way to the Collider, she stopped by Persephone's room and knocked. She stood there for a few minutes, but there was no answer. That was what she'd expected.

Persephone had hardly been home over the last three months. She was traveling between the realms, leading classes on cultural sensitivity, opening training workshops, and in some cases, mediating the more confusing social issues that arose.

Persephone had been surprised when Myrddin offered her the job, but Abby hadn't. The recommendation had originated from her, after all. Abby knew her drow girlfriend and how big Persephone's heart was. Her compassion was coupled with the practicality needed in such times.

If there was anyone who could help this transition along, it was Persephone.

But the job came with sacrifices, and right now, one of those was their relationship. The two of them still hadn't been able to make time for a date in over a month.

Abby sighed. She missed Persephone, the sound of her voice, her soft skin pressed against her own. Hopefully, things would slow down a little bit, and they would be able to spend some time together.

It was amazing that they had seen more of each other when the universe was on the edge of collapse.

The complications of peace, Abby thought. When you're on the edge of death, you make time for those who matter. When you're not, well, life seems to get in the way.

Terra and Anabelle were already at the Collider by the time Abby arrived. Roy was there as well, talking quietly with Anabelle a few steps from Terra.

Abby tilted her head in Anabelle's and Roy's direction. "What's up with those two?"

Terra shrugged as she fiddled with her wrist comm. "I think they were supposed to have a date tonight or something. Don't ask me how. If Cire suddenly showed up, I'd give that orc a kiss on the cheek and pass out. I'm fucking exhausted."

Roy walked over to Abby and Terra, his face frazzled. During his tenure heading the operations of the DGA, gray had salted his perfectly black beard and hair.

Still, he looked a lot healthier than he had before. He'd finally put the weight he had lost back on. "Good to see you two. It's been a while."

Terra hugged Roy tightly, lifting him off the ground. "Hell, yeah. You can say that again. How you been living, my dude?"

"Same ol' shit, different day. Blackwell's finally getting used to the new job, so that's making my life a lot easier."

"Sorry we're taking Anabelle away from you tonight. Creon didn't think it was a good idea to put this off."

Roy waved away Terra's concerns. "Don't worry about it. I'm heading out too. There's been an altercation on the orcish world with a few humans."

Terra's smile fell, replaced by a tense frown. "What the hell is happening? I didn't hear anything."

"That's because it's not a problem with the orcs. It's the humans who are being shitheads. A bunch of rowdy humans on a work program went off on an orc, and it got messy. As a result, it fell into my jurisdiction, but don't worry. We already solved it. I have to go pick up the pieces. Guess they weren't prepared for what happens when you're a racist against someone who is willing to kick your ass. They're lucky the orc didn't tear their heads off."

Terra shrugged as she started to brood. "Where's the fun in that? I can't believe that shit is still happening."

Roy watched the Hadron Collider turn on. "We're doing our best to cut down on it. Weed out the crazies. Every so often, we get an anti-orc nut. The more we can keep that kind of news off-planet, the better. The orcs have been making a good show of faith by opening up to us, largely because of you. I'd really hate for humanity to fuck it up."

Abby stepped aside to give some workers a way to get past. "Have there been any incidents on Earth? Like on the orc world?"

Roy shook his head. "No, but honestly, we're expecting one. People blew each other up for this shit for years. Now the same hate groups are looking for someone else to terrorize." He forced a tired smile. "But again, don't worry. We're on the lookout."

Anabelle came over and kissed Roy on the cheek. "Later, babe. We gotta go."

The former mech rider nodded solemnly. "I'll leave you guys to it. Be safe."

Terra saluted Roy as she walked by. "Always do." Then she turned to Abby. "Hey, how come you don't just teleport us there?"

Abby raised two fingers. "One, teleporting uses a lot of our energy, especially if it's going to be you two in addition to ourselves. Secondly, Tesla."

Anabelle gave Abby a confused look. "I thought you left him locked in an in-between realm or something?"

Abby shrugged. "People say they know how all that works. We're not sure. Rather play it safe. Sometimes we have nightmares he's going to find us. What we did was torture, but it was the only way. It scares us to think about what he would do if he ever got out."

"Don't think about it. You're wasting your time and energy. We do what we have to do. That's our job. Now let's go."

Anabelle stepped through the Hadron Collider. Terra and Abby followed right after.

Abby and Terra stepped out of the Collider. Anabelle was tossed out and landed flat on her ass. "Goddess damn it!" she grumbled as Abby helped her to her feet.

Terra looked around. "You gotta get better with your landings, Anna. You'd think you didn't grow up with magic, the way you always bomb that."

Anabelle brushed off her uniform. "The Collider is not magic. And shut up. I haven't fallen out in a while."

While Anabelle and Terra argued, Abby scanned the area they had arrived in. The mission briefing had said this was an island off of Greece. The Dark Melody had been traced to a cave on the island.

The island was covered by a heavy thicket of greenery that started not far from the beach, which was where the portal had dropped them. The crashing waves gave Abby the creeps as she wondered what could be hiding in the island's dark interior. "Come on, let's get this over with so we can go home."

Terra followed after Abby. "I'm not gonna argue with that."

Abby led them into the thicket, illuminating the path she was trying to make. "Martin, can you scan for odd life forms?"

Martin popped up in Abby's peripheral vision. "All forms of organic life are odd to me."

"Stop being a smartass."

"Might as well tell me to stop breathing. Oh, wait, never mind. All right, this is what we got. Tons of plants, like a shit-ton, but nothing weird for this region. Little scurrying things here or there, and a lot of decomposing animals. I think that's a good place to check out."

Abby converted her arm into a long blade and slashed through the branches in front of her. "Thanks. Will do." She looked over her shoulder. "Martin says there's something suspicious up ahead. A bunch of dead animals."

One of the vines Abby moved out of the way snapped back and hit Terra in the face. "What's so special about dead animals? Isn't that the law of the jungle or something?"

"Depends."

They continued walking and finally came to the dead animals Martin had spoken of.

Carcasses were piled high. There were at least twenty of them, stripped of nearly all their flesh. Their polished bones reflected the somber moonlight.

Anabelle knelt to get a closer look. "Looks like we've stumbled onto a predator's trash bin." She picked up one of the bones. "It's been picked clean. See the claw marks?"

She tossed the bone to Terra, who looked it over, then handed it to Abby, who scanned it. "Those are teeth and claw marks. Whatever did this ate nearly everything," Abby said. "There wasn't a whole lot left over to decompose."

Abby looked around the island for a moment before bringing up her map. "The island is too small to have a predator this large living here. What the hell would it even be?"

Anabelle scratched the back of her head before pulling her hair up in a bun. "Could be something from one of the Nine Realms, someone dropping off animals for illegal transporting. There's that huge big cat thing in the States. How many of those people would be willing to drop a fortune for something from another realm?"

Terra shook her head. "That would make sense if we were someplace near the States. There's no market like that near Greece. And there's only one? Why would they only bring one?"

"Well, what are the other options?"

Abby pointed her scanner at the ground, highlighting footprints in the dirt. The footprints were nearly three times the size of her feet. "How about we follow these and find out?"

They followed the trail through the trees until they came to a cave in the side of a ridge. There were fresh footprints outside the cave, along with the remains of a fire. The ashes were still smoldering in the firepit.

Abby checked out the fire. "Looks like we got us a real live person. Guess smuggled animals are off the list."

Terra kicked a rock. "Damn it. I was really hoping for something weird to wrestle."

Their conversation was interrupted by the sound of trees cracking to their right.

Pushing over all the trees in his way, a cyclops came toward them, wearing a tattered blue robe with a hood pulled down to his eye. The staff he gripped in his right hand was about a foot taller than Abby.

"What about something to kill you?" the cyclops bellowed.

Terra laughed as she jerked her thumb toward him. "This is the guy who's selling the Dark Melody? Give me a break."

The cyclops raised his staff and slammed it on the ground. The ground beneath Terra tumbled into a hole, which she promptly dropped into, narrowly escaping by grasping the edge. Anabelle dove forward and helped her up.

"Ugh. Magic," Terra grumbled.

CHAPTER EIGHT

The three DGA agents squared off against the cyclops.

He walked right past the DGA to the entrance of his cave, where there was a large stone, and sat down. "Before we get into this, I want to know who the hell you are and what the hell you are doing here."

Abby and Terra exchanged glances while Anabelle laughed. "We're the ones who are here to ask questions. Like, for one, how the hell did you get your hands on the Dark Melody?"

The cyclops reached behind the stone and pulled out the body of a half-eaten lamb. "Oh, you must be Myrddin's girls."

Anabelle bristled at the term, the hair on her neck standing up. "Before we go any further, I'm going to tell you not to say that again, or we will make this much more painful for you than it needs to be."

The cyclops bit into the lower body of the lamb, easily tearing it apart and swallowing the entrails. He didn't bother to stop chewing as he spoke. "Why? You are his lapdogs, aren't you? He says run, and you ask how far."

"Whose lapdog are you?"

"Don't matter to you. You'll be dead in a couple of minutes. Hmm. You'd probably go well in a stew. I haven't had elf in a while."

The cyclops stood and removed his robe, revealing a body with tightly corded muscles and a misleading beer belly.

Anabelle had fought cyclops before. They weren't much different from giants, maybe a bit easier because of the lack of depth perception. "Fine, your funeral."

Faster than the eye could register, Anabelle ran forward. Her fist went up as she leaped, ready to crack the cyclops on the head.

He waved his staff, vanishing for a moment and reappearing behind Anabelle. He swung his staff at her and she ducked as she landed, swiping at his legs with a spinning kick.

The cyclops jumped out of the way, flipping backward, moving remarkably gracefully for someone so large. Anabelle figured he must be using magic to augment his movements. That didn't matter. As long as she put him down fast, he wasn't going to be a problem.

Abby and Terra watched from the sidelines as Anabelle and the cyclops circled each other.

The elf surged forward and burst into a cloud of smoke, then reappeared behind the cyclops. He leaned back and blocked her attack with his staff, then kicked at Anabelle, forcing her to move back. He slammed his staff into the ground, causing jagged chunks of rock to shoot in her direction.

It only took a small effort to deflect the attacks. "Are you two going to stand there, or are you going to help me?" Anabelle shouted.

Terra and Abby pointed at each other. "Oh, you mean us?" Terra asked. "You walked out there like you had all of this taken care of. We thought you were—"

"Get your asses over here."

Abby's armor flowed over her body, and she lunged at the cyclops as Terra stomped her foot, breaking up the ground, and pulling a reasonably sized rock out of it. She hurled it at the cyclops as Abby flew above him and fired.

The cyclops melted into the sand, re-forming next to the trees that encroached on the open space they fought in. He tapped the tree with his staff, knocking down a few coconuts that floated around him. The coconuts caught fire, and he tossed them in front of Terra.

The coconuts exploded in front of Terra, sending her flying through the air, screaming.

She hit the ground and rolled as she desperately tried to put out the fire. Small cyclopes walked out of the cracked coconuts. They ran after Terra and threw a rope around her, rushing to pin her to the ground. "What the ever-loving fuck is this?" she shouted.

The cyclops was laughing. In the brief time Anabelle and Abby had taken their eyes off of him, he had gathered more coconuts. "I'm just nuts for these things!"

Abby groaned as Terra screamed for help. "Ugh. Is he one of *those* kinds of bad guys?"

Coconuts sailed through the air. Abby wasn't going to risk any more surprises. She auto-targeted the coconuts and fired, blowing apart all ten of them.

As the coconuts split, drakes the size of small cats flew from the wreckage. They went straight for Abby, who tossed up an energy shield to block the fire spewing from their mouths.

One of the drakes didn't bother turning away from the shield, instead crashing into it and exploding into flower petals. Then the flower petals vaporized into green gas.

Abby stumbled back, holding her breath and waving her hand in front of her to scan the cloud of gas. "Don't inhale it! It's poisonous."

Using the distraction to its advantage, a drake managed to get behind Abby. It grew larger, contorting and shifting into the cyclops. Once he was fully formed, he cracked Abby across the head with his staff.

Anabelle let out a roar, slamming her hands together and launching a jet of fire at the cyclops. He whirled his staff in front of him like the blades of a helicopter, repelling her fire.

"Ah, magic, the ever-versatile tool." The cyclops laughed. "Looks like that might be where you draw all of your strength. Did you think we hadn't been watching your techniques? A one-trick-pony, I'm afraid, using magic to make you strong. The human is just strong, and the little girl likes fancy toys that go boom. Too easy."

The cyclops slammed his staff on the ground, causing a hole to open beneath Anabelle. She flipped out of the way and took cover in the trees.

Terra was still struggling with the small cyclopes, which had split into doubles of each other. Some were walking on top of her, shocking her with their staffs as others hurried to finish pinning Terra down.

Abby was flying ahead, trying to shoot the drakes speeding after her.

Anabelle watched, assessing what she could use to her advantage. She hadn't fought a wizard one-on-one before. Anytime the team had come across one, they'd had a magical heavy hitter with them.

The war elf's magical understanding wasn't very detailed. She could manipulate the energy and elements around her, but that was about it.

Still, that said, all she needed was one good punch, and he'd go down.

"Everyone has a plan until they're punched in the face," Anabelle muttered to herself. *And only a stupid warrior relied on one technique.* She concentrated on the shadows of the ropes holding down Terra.

The ropes had to be magical if they were strong enough to hold down the gladiator, but even magical ropes still had a tangible existence.

Anabelle hit her comm. "Abby, I'm going for Terra. Can you cover me?"

"Got it!" Abby answered, turning in midair and releasing an electric shockwave that gave her some room to breathe before heading back down toward the cyclops.

Anabelle leaped out of the trees, looking as if she were going to attack the cyclops. Even though she had no intention of following through, she watched him closely and noticed he looked much more frightened by her approach than before. She couldn't worry about that now. She needed to focus.

Her body turned into mist and passed straight through the cyclops, who yelped loudly. She floated over to Terra, converted to water, and fell to the ground in a mini-tidal wave that swept away the small cyclopes.

With the little bastards gone, Anabelle re-formed and reached for the magical ropes binding the gladiator, then she snapped the ropes shadows. With the magical tether gone, the ropes disappeared.

Terra leaped to her feet. "I'm going to kill that fucker."

She ran at the cyclops, pulling her axe from her back. She swung at him, but he managed to step back at the perfect time, dodging her attack.

There was no way the attack wouldn't have landed. Anabelle had seen it. Terra's blade had barely missed him. The cyclops could not have managed to move back so slightly and avoid being hit by a fraction.

Terra attacked again, undeterred. The cyclops dodged that attack as well. Terra continued to swing her axe, stepping closer to the cyclops, who smiled smugly, effortlessly dodging Terra's blade.

That can't be right, Anabelle thought.

The cyclops leaped back and pressed his hand to his ears. "Do you hear that?"

There was a loud oinking coming from the forest. "My children have returned."

A herd of wild boar came running out and encircled the cyclops, whose staff was held high. "Kill, my piggish children, kill!"

The boars reared back on their hind legs, grunting loudly, their eyes full of blood lust and foam coming from their mouths. Three of them rushed Anabelle, who was so caught off-guard that she slashed in front of her, creating a wall of fire to give herself a few moments to figure out what the hell was going on.

There wasn't a whole lot of time to think. Coconuts were flying through the air.

A boar stepped through the flames. As it approached Anabelle, it grew larger and more human-like. Some of the tiny cyclopes were climbing up the boar man's dense fur, holding staffs and creating magical fireballs.

More of the boar men were stepping across the flames, undeterred by the fire.

Anabelle saw Abby trying to outrun a few of the boar men who had sprouted obscene fleshy wings.

She turned to Terra, who was behind her, and asked, "Do you think you can take care of these guys? I'm going to try to get that staff out of that asshole's hands."

Terra pulled another axe from her back and spun both in her hands. "We're eating pig tonight, baby!" she shouted as she ran into the throng of boar men, slashing in a hurricane of blades and cutting through whatever she could. Abby flew above, raining down small plasma mines that exploded anytime one of the boar men got close to her.

Anabelle leaped over the wall of fire. The cyclops gave her an infuriatingly smug smile.

"I'm going to beat that smile off of your face." She ran at the cyclops and slid under him. Before the cyclops could turn around, Anabelle kicked his wrist, sending the magic staff into the air.

He backed away, eyes wide, as Anabelle caught the staff. "And I'm going to use this."

Anabelle swung at the cyclops' head, throwing everything into the attack. She was going to take his head clear off.

Somehow, the cyclops was able to move out of the way. Anabelle screamed in rage as she set fire to the staff. She swung it at his head again, narrowly missing, then at his legs, which he nimbly sidestepped. Anabelle slashed and lunged at the cyclops repeatedly, yet he stayed narrowly out of reach, smiling as he did.

It made no sense. She had managed to kick the cyclops' staff from his hand effortlessly, yet here he was, dodging her attacks. She was fast, but the cyclops was faster. She'd never faced anyone as fast as him. He was faster than Grok.

"Make way!" Terra shouted.

Anabelle turned just in time to move out of the way as Terra flew back, propelled by one of the boar men.

She crashed into the cyclops and the two of them tumbled together, scrambling to get away from each other.

"Wait!" Anabelle shouted. "Abby, get over here."

Abby, who had finished dealing with the boars that had been chasing her, hovered a few feet away. "Yeah?"

"Shoot him in the foot."

"What?"

"Go for it."

Abby took aim and fired, and a plasma bolt blasted through the cyclops' foot.

He yowled in pain.

Terra scratched her head. "I don't get it. How come we couldn't hit him before?"

Anabelle ran up to the cyclops, stopping a few inches from him, and punched him in the shoulder. "Magic." She grabbed the cyclops by his neck and lifted him into the air. "Care to explain to my friends before I make a carefully curated selection of which bones to break?"

The cyclops threw up his hands. "Okay, okay, I surrender. I didn't think you would figure it out. It's a spell, a precog that lets me see how I'm going to die."

"Pretty ingenious. In a field where everyone's trying to kill you, it would pretty much nullify any real threats. And that's how we beat you. We stopped trying to kill you, and with that threat gone, your little precog spell was useless." Anabelle headbutted the cyclops, knocking him out.

She knelt and handcuffed him. "Let's get out of here. We have some information to get."

Terra pointed over her shoulder at the boar men. "Shouldn't we take care of those?"

Anabelle glanced at them and flexed, sending a blast of mana from her body. "All right, but let's make it quick."

CHAPTER NINE

The cyclops was escorted beneath HQ, where a labyrinth of dungeons held captured warlords, double agents, and high-level military.

As Terra prepped to go down to the lower level to interrogate the captured cyclops, she received a message from Cire. It simply read: **I'm coming. Can we speak?**

One thing Terra had needed to get used to over the last year was the personality change that had come over Cire since he had taken over the role of shaman. Part of the ritual had been absorbing all of the memories of past shamans, as well as having his soul stored in Terra's body.

The result was a surprisingly serious demeanor. Granted, Cire had always been fairly serious, but he had also been a shy, lovable goofball. That was gone now.

Yeah, Terra responded. **I have to interrogate some loser, but I'm free after that.**

There was a loud knock on Terra's door. She sighed as she walked over to open it.

When Terra flung the door open, she gasped loudly.

Cire was standing in the threshold, holding a bouquet of flowers wrapped around a battle-axe. "Are you surprised?"

Terra jumped onto him, knocking him to the ground, and covered his face in kisses before rolling off and admiring the axe. She pulled the flowers off and put them in a vase that held the flowers Cire sent on a regular basis.

The axe had a good balance to it, better than either of the two Terra was using at the moment. "Where did you get it?"

Cire reached for the axe, turning it over in his hand until the inscription on its pommel was visible. "This was crafted by the dwarven lords of Mototh. They haven't smelted an axe for an orc in hundreds of years. It was sent as a sign of goodwill between our people. I thought you would have more use for it than I do."

Terra took the axe back and sliced the air with it. "I love it. You're getting your soul fucked out of you tonight." She attached the axe to her back. "How did you manage to get away?"

Cire walked farther into the room, admiring Terra's orcish decorations. "The council is ancient. They must remember that. They must remember they have wisdom. They must then remember to rely on that wisdom. My departure will, hopefully, help those memories surface."

Terra leaned over Cire and kissed his forehead. She had missed him, and it felt good to have him so close and be able to feel his body beneath hers. "It's about time you came to visit me. I don't know the next time I'll be able to make it back to sleep here. Do you have royal beds?"

Cire shook his head as he smiled. "No, the shaman has only a cot in a poorly insulated hut. It is to remind us of our fragility and strength. But the Hand, well, he has an entire wing dedicated to him."

"We're going to have to take advantage of that sometime soon, but for now, I have work to take care of."

"Do you mind if I join you? It has been too long since I've seen Anabelle and Abby."

Terra was already heading toward the door. "Of course, come on."

As they walked down the halls, Cire talked about what had been happening on the orc world in her absence. Their homeworld was still being flooded by emissaries from other realms. At times, it was difficult to tell who was coming to the council with genuine interest and who was planning on exploiting the orcish people.

Cire was blunt about the issue with humans. Generally speaking, most of the other races were trying to mend the ties that had been broken with orcs. Even the elves were putting forth effort, though they weren't ready to issue a formal apology. The humans who had come to the planet were problematic, however. Recently, as anti-orc sentiment had increased on Earth, there had been an alarming number of terrorist attacks.

Terra was embarrassed. Even though she had nothing to do with the attacks, she felt somewhat responsible.

As if he could read Terra's mind, Cire said, "You needn't worry. You have not lost the support or love of the orcish people because of the humans. None question your loyalty. You and Abby will never be forgotten for what you've done for the orcs."

"What about Anabelle?"

"Old grudges die hard. Perhaps that will change with the decisions of the elves."

As the two of them stood in the elevator descending into the prison, Terra and Cire switched roles. She told Cire about the recent change to human crime. Too many people had gotten their hands on the leftovers of the Dark One's tech, and there were enough people smart enough to figure out how to use it. That didn't even touch on the sudden introduction of magical items.

"For the most part, you know, people don't see it," Terra said. "They see the gnomes and elves walking around and all the small, cool stuff. But wrong people are getting their hands on this shit. Governments and armies are buying it up, and there's nothing we can do about it. Myrddin's taken a pretty strong stance on not interfering in global politics. We're handling the integration aspect and trying to help things move along smoothly. We also put down anything that gets out of hand."

Cire nodded solemnly. "So, humans are doing what everyone was afraid they would?"

"Who knows if that's what's going to happen? We have our fingers crossed. I would have thought this would unite everyone, but we'll see."

"It is the cruel fate of mortals to consume each other."

Terra pointed a finger at Cire. "Hey, what did we talk about? No ominous lich-like phrases."

Cire smiled as he relaxed, reminding Terra that he was nothing like Rasputina. "Sorry. Existence is a complete and utter pleasure."

They turned the corner and spotted Abby and Anabelle waiting outside the cyclops' cell. Terra smiled back as she turned to face Cire. "That's what I'm talking about. Pure, unreasonable positivity."

Abby jerked her thumb at the door. "It's your turn to get answers."

Terra groaned loudly as she banged her head against the cell door. "Ugh, really? I hate doing this. I'm not good at being mean."

"Terra, you head-butt and decapitate people all the time."

"That's not mean, that's war! It's not like I walk around cutting people's heads off."

Anabelle, who was looking through the glass portal on the door, turned to face Terra. "Okay, we have a job. This is part of it."

Terra whined as she leaned against the wall. "Are you sure you don't want to do it? You love being stern and mean to people."

Anabelle crossed her arms and glared at her, the same look Terra remembered receiving from teachers. "I do not enjoy being stern or mean, and you are going to get in there and beat that cyclops to a bloody pulp if you need to."

Terra stood up, muttering under her breath, "Fine, but I'm only going to enjoy it a little bit." Secretly, she hoped the cyclops gave up the information quickly. She hated interrogations. If Sarah had been there, Terra would have pawned it off on her.

She opened the cell door and stepped inside.

The cyclops was sitting on his bed. The cell was comfortable-looking. There was a desk with a few flowers and one of Myrddin's conjuration pads for food or other things.

Terra sat in one of the extra chairs as the cyclops looked up at her. "So, we can do this the easy way, which is the one both of us would probably prefer. Or we can do this the hard way, which I know for a fact you won't like. It involves my fists."

The cyclops sighed, his face drooping and heavy. He didn't look like he was willing to put up a fight. "What do you want to know?"

"Uh, really? Just like that?"

The cyclops leaned farther into the light, showing his black eye. "I haven't been punched in the face for a long time. Can't say I'm a fan. Why do you think I stick with the magic? The way I figure it, you guys won, and as long as I cooperate, no one is going to hurt me in here. Maybe I can work out a plea deal or something. Heard you guys ain't that bad. Especially you."

Terra tried not to show that she was flattered. "Oh? Where have you heard these rumors?"

"Working with a couple of orcs, pulling jobs. Apparently, you're a sweeping win on their planet."

Terra tried not to betray any emotion, but internally, she was leaping for joy. "Okay, let's start off with the basic shit. What was going on with the mob?"

The cyclops leaned back, crossing his legs. "Real simple shit. Humans are looking to make a buck off of the Dark One's leftover tech and shit, but they can't get to it on account of the lack of magic. Those of us with connections find us some leftovers and bring 'em back. Like I said, real simple."

"Who are you working for?"

"Me? I ain't working for anyone but myself. Just trying to make a buck before all that shit gets shut down."

Terra was surprised by the answer. She'd thought this went deeper than a couple of petty thugs. "You're not working with the Dark One?"

"Uh-uh. Ain't ever met the guy."

"Then how did you get the Dark Melody?"

The cyclops looked at Terra, squinting as if trying to understand what was being said. "What the hell is that?"

"You know, the black goop you were selling."

The cyclops laughed. "Oh, that shit. You know—"

The cyclops stopped talking. He blinked rapidly, then looked at Terra blankly. "What were we talking about?"

"The Dark Melody. The black goop."

"Oh, yeah, you know—"

He broke off again, this time staring straight ahead as if his mind had been turned off.

Terra stood and waved her hand in front of the cyclops' face. He didn't seem to register it. "That's not good," she mumbled as she got up and left the room, closing the door and locking it behind her. "Did you guys see that?"

Anabelle nodded. "Looks like his memories have been tampered with. He thinks he's not working for anyone, but that might not be true. And whoever messed with his head knows the Dark Melody is important."

"Do you think it could be the Dark One?"

Abby was staring at a holoscreen and she peeked out from behind it. "Let's look at what we know. We only removed the Dark One from the Nine Realms. The Netherverse could connect into other dimensions as well. We ran across some very weird stuff when we were using Tesla's teleportation device."

"Okay, Abby, I don't have a degree in nerd physics. What are you trying to say?"

Abby scowled at Terra. "The Dark One could still be in the Netherverse, manipulating things in his favor until he gets stronger. What better time to invade a reality than when it's in the middle of a species-wide war?"

Terra groaned as she threw her arms in the air. "Well, how are we going to get into his brain? None of us knows magic. Whoa, never mind." She turned to wrap her arms around Cire. "Hey, babe, could you break into that guy's brain for us?"

Cire closed his cloak as he shrugged. "Sure, I'm not doing anything."

The two of them walked back into the cell, and the cyclops looked up. Before he could say anything, Cire raised his hand, and the cyclops flew back and hit the wall.

Terra yelped, "Hey, you don't need to hurt him."

Cire's hand was already pressed against the cyclops' face. "Look into my eyes."

The cyclops stared into Cire's eyes and his body went limp, his large eye rolling back. The air in the room went cold and suddenly warmed back up.

Cire turned, and the cyclops gently floated down to his bed. "He will be fine in a few minutes."

Once they were outside, Anabelle asked, "What did you learn?"

Cire frowned, the lines in his forehead growing more pronounced. "It would seem there is another route into the Netherverse. We must speak to Myrddin immediately."

CHAPTER TEN

Anabelle, Terra, Abby, and Cire met in Myrddin's office. The elf hadn't seen much of the wizard since Sarah's wedding. Even Roy had hardly heard from the man. Anabelle had been surprised to hear Cire mention meeting with Myrddin so casually.

They'd been sitting in the wizard's office for nearly half an hour so far. The space was drastically different from the last time Anabelle had met with Myrddin. The bookcases filled with arcane scrolls and books were gone. There was no longer a desk, and many of the artifacts found over the course of thousands of years had been removed. The only remaining relic of the past was Myrddin's conjuring pad, which they had used to make chairs to sit on.

A single Persian rug was placed near a window that overlooked a garden with vividly green grass and a healthy cherry tree.

Terra walked around the room as the rest of the team sat awkwardly in their chairs. "Looks like someone has been spring-cleaning."

Abby nodded as she looked at the bare room. "Yeah. Looks like when our dad decided he needed to update his life. There was a long period of trying out new cars and motorcycles."

Terra glanced at Abby. "Can you have a mid-life crisis when you're over a thousand years old?"

Terra and Abby looked at Anabelle. "What are you asking me for?" the elf asked. "I'm not *that* old."

Terra shrugged as she continued pacing, trying to find something to catch her attention. "I don't know. I never thought I'd make it to forty. I can't imagine what being that old feels like, especially after being in the Netherverse. Like, fuck, why not experience the afterlife? How do you come back and live a regular life?"

"You don't," said a voice from the doorway.

Myrddin walked into the room. He was thinner than he'd been at the wedding, and his skin had taken on a glossy sheen as if it weren't composed of skin cells but had been molded from light.

Anabelle had seen this in some of the older elves. It was as if their bodies grew tired of continuing, and the only thing keeping them going was the magic flowing through their veins.

The wizard glided past the DGA and sat on the rug near the back of the room. "Unfortunately, the body remembers the trials you put it through. But we don't need to bore ourselves with conversations about me. How are you all getting along?"

Before anyone could speak, Cire stepped forward. "There has been a breach into hell. A serious one."

Anabelle thought she'd heard the wrong thing. Hell wasn't a real place. There was the Netherverse, the place where souls went. They existed in the perpetual dreams of the Old Ones, each soul experiencing an afterlife built from their living expectations.

Myrddin's brow furrowed, but he did not answer immediately. Apparently, he knew what Cire was speaking about.

"How?" Myrddin finally asked.

Before the shaman could reply, Abby interrupted, expressing what Anabelle had been thinking.

Myrddin's eyes looked tired. They were shining lights beneath a dead sea. "There is another part of the Netherverse which we have not talked about. An anomaly, you could say. Few people know about it.

Think of it as a backdoor, a very specific one. It should not be accessible to mortals, or at least, it hasn't been for some time."

Anabelle leaned forward. "Wait, what? Why is this way in any more special than the Netherverse Gates?"

"Because it is only shared by three realms. It is difficult to explain without an extensive understanding of arcane metaphysics."

Abby, who seemed the most interested in the conversation, sat up straighter, her eyes zeroing on Myrddin. "How about you try us?"

Myrddin's eyes flitted from Cire to Abby. "Fine. The Netherverse realm is between the rest of the Nine Realms. Each of them connects to the Netherverse through a nexus, but since the Netherverse is not composed of matter but of psychic energy made tangible, it is capable of morphing into different levels of existence within itself."

Terra leaned her head against her chair back as she reached out to the conjuring pad and got herself a beer.

Myrddin continued, "There are only three realms with a concept of hell. It would be more accurate to say these three realms have a concrete understanding of a place that exists in the Netherverse: orcs, humans, and gnomes. At some point in history, someone from those three races explored hell, albeit for different reasons. Crude at first, the propagation of the story has created a place that has a tangible existence in the Netherverse and is extremely difficult to get to through conventional means."

Anabelle didn't understand what Myrddin was saying. "So, this place didn't exist, now it does exist, and it only exists because people think it exists?"

Myrddin waved his hand, and the door to the office opened. A book flew through it and into the wizard's hand. "Dante Alighieri. Beautiful poetry. One of the lesser-known agents seeding the artistic world with tales of the reality we live in. There are gnomish and orcish versions of the same tale, more or less."

Cire nodded. "The orcish version is quite similar. It does not take as much artistic license as the gnomish text."

Abby narrowed her eyes. "So, there's really a hell? How do you get there? I'm assuming it has nothing to do with the typical religious dogma."

Myrddin stood and waved his hand once more, pulling down a holoscreen in the middle of the room.

The holoscreen showed an ancient depiction of Dante's Inferno: the nine circles of hell and their *malebolge*. "Hell is other people, as Sartre said. The vast majority of souls go to the Netherverse, but those who believe they deserve hell end up in this place. It's mostly a playground for demons. Some of them are so lost they believe they are the souls of humans. Others are merely playing. And others— what's the expression? It is better to rule in hell than serve in heaven? Some of the more enterprising demons have formed kingdoms, amassing their own armies for conquest. We've been keeping tabs on it for some time. Typically, there is enough infighting to take care of anything large.

"We rarely have anyone breaking into hell. Usually, demons are trying to get out. But if it is the most viable way into the Netherverse, then it would make sense that it has garnered more attention."

Anabelle thought back to the stories she'd been told as a child, those meant to scare her into good behavior. They were drastically different than those told by humans, but she couldn't help wondering if there was any truth to them. If hell was real, what else was?

Myrddin held his hand to his mouth and coughed. A table appeared at his side, complete with a teapot and mugs. He poured each of his guests a cup. "If there is a backdoor into the Netherverse, we must shut it down, and we need to investigate whether the Dark One is involved with this recent surge in arcane weaponry."

Terra put her hand up palm out to let Myrddin know she was sticking with her beer. "I thought we already took care of him? You said we'd removed him from the Nine Realms. If he's in someone else's universe, that should be their problem, unless we're going to have a universe-hopping adventure. I'm down for either option."

Myrddin blew the steam off his tea. "We were able to remove him from the Nine Realms, but there is still a high possibility that he is in the Netherverse. He's substantially weakened and perhaps trying to gather forces to do his bidding while he gathers strength. We could kill two birds with one stone."

Anabelle was glad to see Myrddin's time away from his body hadn't dulled his pragmatism. "How do we get into hell?"

His eyes dropped to his cup for a few moments before he answered. "Cire will have to help you. Hell is sealed by a variety of magical defenses. One of the reasons I suspect the Dark One is active is due to the difficulty of coming and going from hell. It requires a wizard of extreme talent and power. The last person to break into hell was a lich. That is how difficult the process is."

Anabelle nodded. "Which brings up a good point. Could this be Rasputina's doing?"

Myrddin shook his head. "I doubt it. She conquered Death, so her purpose was fulfilled. Turning her attention to the Nine Realms by sowing discontent and supplying criminals with weapons is not something I believe she would do. Still, it is worth bearing in mind that there may be other players besides the Dark One."

Cire placed his tea back on the table. "I can take a short leave from my council duties to work on this. I'm assuming you have the relevant texts."

Myrddin nodded, tossing Cire a ring. "Yes. You can find them in the archives. There is an entire section dedicated to them in the restricted area. You'll need that ring to disarm the area's defenses."

Cire bowed slightly in Myrddin's direction. "I'll begin immediately. The faster we deal with this, the better." He kissed Terra on the forehead and left the room.

Myrddin waved away the tea set, leaving only the cups in the DGA's hands. "I would suggest you prepare for this journey. Hell is not a place to be taken lightly."

"What can we expect?" Abby asked.

"Torture, mostly of the psychological sort."

Terra groaned as she leaned back in her chair, nearly tipping it over. "Ugh. How the hell are we supposed to prepare for that? And don't you say therapy because I'm already up to my ass in sessions."

"How you choose to prepare is something only you can figure out,"

Myrddin replied. "If there's nothing else you need, there are other concerns I must attend to."

Anabelle watched Myrddin closely. "We're talking about possibly going up against the Dark One again. What could be more important than that?"

Myrddin, who was already at the door, his body looking more ghostlike than earlier, smiled faintly. His age showed plainly on his face, with thousands of years of worry ingrained into his forehead. "Unfortunately, the Dark One is only one of many problems. Good luck, Angels." And With that, Myrddin left the room.

Abby, Anabelle, and Terra exchanged glances, mystified by Myrddin's cryptic words. "What the hell does that mean?" Terra asked.

Anabelle stood and stretched, thinking that Myrddin could stand to conjure more comfortable chairs in his study. "We'll probably end up roped into whatever the hell Myrddin is talking about. For now, let's take care of the problem in front of us. I guess we should take some time to prepare, however we do that."

The three of them stood watching each other, Anabelle thinking about what she had said, and trying to figure out what the other two would believe was adequate preparation for the journey ahead.

Abby and Terra exchanged glances. "Uh, do you want to hang out before we get started with all of this?" Abby asked.

Terra shook her head, looking down the hall at Cire. "No, I think I know what I need to do to prepare."

Anabelle watched Abby, realizing the kid was trying to figure something out. Abby was going to have to do that for herself. She knew what *she* had to do to prepare. She lightly punched Abby in the arm and said, "Good luck. Call me if you need anything, but that 'anything' has to be pretty damn important, all right?"

Abby nodded, and Anabelle left it at that. She messaged Roy as she walked away.

There was no way she wasn't going to see him before their next big mission.

Roy's legs were draped over Anabelle's. His head was resting on her chest, and she could feel his warm breath on her skin. He had promised he wasn't going to fall asleep, but she'd known that was going to happen anyway. The rings around his eyes had given him away.

She was left with her worries about what they were going to come across in hell. It wasn't just worrying, though. She felt a strange excitement too.

She was finally going to be challenged.

Thankfully, Myrddin hadn't prefaced what they were up against with a load of bullshit. He'd been straightforward and to the point. Hopefully, the Dark One wasn't still alive, but now was the perfect chance to find out.

Anabelle rolled over and threw her arm over Roy, breathing him in as they lay there together. There couldn't be a better way to spend this night.

Then her comm pinged.

Anabelle groaned as she reached out and picked it up. It was a message from Abby.

"By the goddesses." Anabelle sighed as she opened the message.

It was brief. **Please come over. Now. Please.**

Anabelle looked at Roy's sleeping body. It was covered in scars, muscular, and lean, and it breathed with perfect contentedness.

He would understand.

Anabelle arrived at Abby's room as Terra walked around the corner. "She call you too?"

Terra yawned loudly. She was wearing an animal-skin coat made from a beast Anabelle had never seen. Terra had probably killed it with her own hands on the orcish world. "Yeah. I figured Cire's got a lot of work to do anyway. Might as well see what's going on."

Anabelle raised her hand to knock on the door when Martin

projected himself from her and Terra's wrist comms. "Oh, thank God you two are here. I've been waiting for you forever."

Anabelle raised an eyebrow. "Is everything okay?"

Martin looked over his shoulder at Abby's room. "Uh, I don't know. I think it's a human thing. I tried to talk to her, but I don't understand what's wrong. The AI consciousness tried too but didn't get anywhere either. Abby didn't message you, I did. I can't figure out what's going on, but I think she needs something I can't regulate."

"Open the door."

The door whizzed open, and Anabelle and Terra stepped through.

Abby was pacing, holding herself tightly before suddenly sitting on the bed, her right leg bouncing up and down as she looked at Anabelle and Terra. "Oh, hi…" She didn't finish her sentence. Her voice cracked as she started shivering and crying, covering her face one second and trying to wipe away her tears the next.

Anabelle froze, uncertain of what to do.

Luckily, Terra was there. She ran over to Abby and tossed her arms around the young woman. Abby burst into heart-wrenching sobs, as if she were trying to cry out her entire soul.

Terra was whispering something into Abby's ear that Anabelle couldn't make out. Suddenly, Abby leaned forward, her head between her legs as she ran her hands through her hair. She started breathing heavily, gasping as if there were no air in the room.

Anabelle understood that. She'd seen and had her fair share of panic attacks. She rushed over to Abby and knelt in front of her. "Abby, you need to breathe. Just breathe in slowly. Breathe slowly."

Abby tried to speak through broken gasps. "We can't get in touch with her. What if something's happened? What if she isn't safe? She could be hurt! We can't get in touch. *I* can't get in touch."

"Abby, it's going to be okay. Trust me."

Abby looked up at Anabelle. Her eyes were wild and bloodshot from crying, and her lips trembled as her face collapsed in on itself. "How do you know that?" she screamed. "How do you know she's not going to die like he did?"

Anabelle and Terra looked at each other. "Like whom?"

Abby's eyes fell to the ground. "Like Papa. We…I never said goodbye to him. Everything was normal like every other day, and then he was gone, and I don't know where he is. The Netherverse? Hell? Could my Papa be in hell?"

Anabelle understood. Abby had processed her father's death as something final and forever. Now they were going where souls went, somewhere terrible. "There is no way your father is in hell."

"How do you know?"

"Because of this." Anabelle touched Abby's tears. "You loved him deeply, and no one who was loved that much could be so lost that he'd be in hell. It couldn't happen."

This seemed to calm Abby, who nodded. "I miss him. So much. I wish I could speak to Persephone. I miss her, too." Abby crumpled against Anabelle, sobbing harshly. "What if she never comes back, and this is forever?"

Anabelle didn't have an answer, nor did she think there was one. She didn't speak, just held Abby as the tears and the stuttered, nonsensical words came and went. She and Terra wrapped their arms around Abby as she cried until there were no more tears. Then she sat there in silence, breathing quietly.

They all continued to sit together in the silence of their company.

CHAPTER ELEVEN

Abby woke up in a cold sweat in the middle of the night, her heart pounding through her ribs. She looked around, trying to figure out where she was. She didn't remember getting into bed, but here she was, nicely tucked in as if she were a child.

As her mind adjusted to being awake, Abby saw Terra, who was curled up on the floor like a cat, and Anabelle, who was leaned up against the wall, a blanket lying over her.

It all rushed back in. She felt a pang of guilt in her stomach, strong enough to make her feel like she had to leave the room. There was no way she would be able to get back to sleep with that on her mind.

She woke Terra by nudging her.

Terra's eyes opened slowly and she stared at Abby, sleepily trying to make sense of what was going on. "Tehrek al-Jorak," she muttered before her head dropped back down to the floor as if it were weighed down by rocks.

When Abby stepped over to Anabelle to wake her, a pulse of mana shot out of the elf's body, warping the air around her. Her defenses were up even when she was sleeping.

Abby didn't want to sit around in her room. The walls felt like they were too tight. She decided a walk was a good alternative, even if she felt shitty because Anabelle and Terra were sleeping on her floor.

She left her room and let her feet take care of business, her mind drifting between anxieties and worries with no clear distinction. She knew the fear she felt for Persephone was tangled in her repressed feelings concerning her father, but that didn't make it any easier to deal with.

The tears came without warning, and she leaned against the wall. She didn't bother fighting them. She did try to fight the thoughts, though. The pain of Persephone never coming back was nearly unbearable. It had happened once before. There was no way she could handle that kind of loss again.

"Are those tears meant to be shared, or may others join your sorrow?" a voice asked.

Abby straightened, wiping her face to see who was talking to her.

Cire stood in the shadowed hallway. His eyes seemed to beam out from the darkness, two stars in an infinite galaxy.

Abby shook her head, pushing down her sniffles. She hated feeling this exposed. She didn't know anything about Cire, and she almost felt naked in front of him. "No, it's nothing. We're okay."

"You cannot sleep. That's obvious. Would you prefer to sit with your thoughts or have something to distract you from them?"

Abby was surprised by Cire's straightforwardness. "A distraction would be good."

"Then follow me, little warrior."

Cire turned and walked down the hallway as Abby jogged to catch up with him. That was the most the orc had ever spoken to her. All the words that had been exchanged between them before had concerned war.

They continued down the halls to a section of HQ Abby had never been in, the library. There were rows upon rows of books. The ceiling was a painting of the sky and the sun, but when Abby looked closer, she saw that the sun was slowly making its rotation as clouds ambled across the vast blueness. The air was heavy with the smell of ancient tomes. "This place is beautiful," she muttered.

Cire nodded as he walked past a couple of dwarfs squatting over books. "Yes, it is. I take it you don't come here often?"

"Never a need. Martin provides any information we need. Never occurred to us to come down here."

Cire continued walking through the library, weaving between the rows of books. He looked like he belonged in this place. Since he'd become the shaman of the orcs, he'd begun looking older. Not as if he had rapidly aged, but rather that his eyes were from a place long lost to the memory of those still living.

As he walked, books floated off of the shelves toward him, trailing behind him like a regal cape. Finally, he stopped in front of a humble wooden door. He pressed his hand to the door and it popped open, revealing a circular room filled with candles, the floor covered in a pentagram with a steel rod at each point of the sigil.

Creon was in the room as well, bustling about, grabbing bizarre ancient artifacts and juggling a handful of books. He beamed when he saw Abby, a smile that looked extremely out of place in the satanic room. "Abby! I wasn't expecting to see you here. I didn't think you had any interest in magic."

Abby crossed into the room, trying to ignore how uncomfortable the pentagram made her. "Didn't think you did either."

Creon pushed up his glasses. "All goblins have at least a cursory interest in magic. It isn't my strong suit, but I know a few tricks here and there. Enough to help out if I need to. Thinking about broadening your horizons?"

Abby swallowed her anxiety and took a good look at the arcane symbols on the floor. "You know, never really thought of it. Guess we weren't curious after finding out that humans need familiars to use magic. What we have seemed to work well enough."

Creon shook his head disapprovingly. "You should never let your ability to do something determine your level of curiosity. Look at me! Still useful at something I'm not great at. Besides, knowledge is knowledge, magical or technological. For all intents and purposes, technology isn't anything other than magic. Both are ways for us to manipulate our physical and—if you're lucky—metaphysical realities. The only difference is the means."

Cire, who was crouched in the center of the pentagram, his face covered in shifting shadows, looked up. "And it is a misconception that humans cannot use magic, one Myrddin does his best to circulate. Humans cannot use magic the way that the rest of the races can without a familiar, but there are many other ways for humans to access magic. Take Dante, for instance."

Cire raised his hand, and a book floated over to him. He motioned for Abby to come closer. He opened the book, showing a complex map of nine circles, arcane symbols scrolled all throughout the geometric patterns.

The orc traced his hands in the air, making one of the signs from the book. As his finger trailed, it burned the sign into the air, causing smoke to float up to the ceiling. "Sigils are one of the foundations of magic and one of the most ancient arts. Mere writing, yet capable of so much. They require no mana, no connection, merely knowledge and understanding."

Abby watched the sigil burn out and fade away. She'd never thought of herself as being jealous of magic, but at that moment, whatever was inside her crystalized. "How do we learn?"

Cire's toothy grin was as far from intimidating as it could be. "I was hoping you would ask. Creon didn't think you would be interested."

Creon, who was now busying himself painting sigils on the wall, turned and shrugged. "It's hard to read humans when it comes to magic. It's so unbelievable that you never know if they're going to take a chance until it's thrust upon them."

Cire motioned for Abby to join him in the circle. He opened another book and passed it to her.

Abby stared down at the book of symbols. To her, they were nothing but nonsensical squiggles on paper, but that was all calculus had been at some point. And binary, and everything else she'd pushed herself to learn over the last two years.

For the first time in a while, Abby was excited to learn something.

Terra woke up punching the air, a habit she'd gotten into because of Cire. It was a part of orcish childhood games: first thing in the morning, punch your sibling in the jaw and then wrestle your way out of bed to see who makes it to breakfast first. Terra and Cire played a similar game, but it was not breakfast they were trying to get to.

As Terra stretched, Anabelle also stirred. The elf's hair was a mess. It looked like a beehive had come unraveled. Her makeup was smeared, so it looked like half of her face was dirty in the most beautiful way. "Where's Abby?"

Terra looked around the room, searching for the young woman. "How does she keep her room so clean?"

Anabelle stood and stretched, then touched her toes easily and twisted her body into an odd posture that implied she did not have bones. "She's got a computer program in her head. The least it could do is make sure that she's not living in a pigsty like you do."

Martin popped up on Anabelle's and Terra's wrist comms. "Abby is down in the library with Cire in the restricted tomes section. She's been up all night, working with Creon and Cire. Your presence is required. Furthermore, it is suggested that you suit up, as Abby put it."

Anabelle scratched her head, still trying to get over the last bit of sleepiness. "Guess we're going to hell," she said as she gathered her gear. "What is Abby doing down there before us anyway?"

"You're going to be as surprised as I was."

Anabelle shrugged and headed toward the door as Terra followed her. "I swear, that kid is up to no good."

Terra took one last look at the pristine room, then she grabbed a pillow from the bed and tossed it on the floor. "There we go. That looks better. Now you can tell someone lives here."

Anabelle chuckled as she waited for Terra to walk out of the room. "Cire doesn't dabble in technology, does he?"

Terra shook her head. "He's not a Luddite, but orcs have never used much of it. Recently they've started to pick it up. We have a whole goblin research team starting up a school, and there are HQ initiatives. Makes sense that after the Dark One's bullshit, they would go into it."

Anabelle could see why the orcs were working so hard to get up to par with the rest of the Nine Realms in the technological arena. The Dark One had used advanced technology from another universe to enslave nearly all of the orcs. It only made sense that they didn't want that to happen again.

"You know that the council is making a statue of Abby?" Terra asked.

Anabelle stopped and turned to face her. "Are you serious?"

Terra raised her hands to defend herself. "Hey, don't look at me, I don't make those kinds of decisions. And don't even start getting jealous. I'm not getting a statue either, and I'm the fucking Hand."

Anabelle waved away Terra's criticism as she shook her head. "I don't care if I don't get a statue. It just surprised me. I've never known orcs to be big on monuments of any kind."

The two of them reached the library. Terra opened the door for Anabelle. "They aren't. They have maybe three of them on the entire world. One of them is the first shaman. The others honor the greatest warlords. I'm hoping to get up there someday, but they're definitely erecting one for her. I mean, she did kind of save the entire orc race."

Anabelle had nearly forgotten about that. Last year had been one crisis and then the next. They'd been fighting the war at a breakneck speed. But among all of that, Abby had found a way to reverse the Dark One's techno-grip on the orcs. She'd liberated them and nearly lost her life doing it, and she'd altered her humanity beyond repair.

The two of them stood in front of the library's restricted area. "Hope it's a good one," Anabelle said. "She deserves it."

Terra scratched her armpit. "Had to convince them not to give her four arms."

"Why four arms?"

"No idea. It's an orcish tradition. They give all their heroes an extra set of arms. I'll have to ask Cire about it some time. The only problem is, I'm sure his answer will be long and full of detailed battles from centuries ago. I'll probably have to block off an entire weekend for the answer. Don't worry. I'll send you the CliffsNotes."

Anabelle and Terra stepped into the room. It was dark, lit only by candles, but there were hundreds of them on the floor and in sconces on the walls. Some were even floating in the air.

The floor and walls were covered in sigils, none of which Anabelle recognized. She doubted if Terra knew any of them either.

Creon was in the corner, running some kind of scanner over the sigils on one of the walls.

Cire was standing on a ladder, painting sigils on the ceiling as if he were afraid too much pressure would break the plaster. Abby was floating by his side, carving sigils into the wall with a laser in one hand and a dusty tome in the other. She looked at Anabelle and Terra when they walked into the room. "Hey, guys!" She drifted down to them as Cire made his way down the ladder, smiling.

Abby landed and looked away bashfully. "We're sorry about last night. About the whole freak-out. We were—"

Terra put her hand on Abby's head and shoved her away. "Don't even trip about it. Glad you were able to find something to do. As if you aren't always doing something."

The girl's smile returned, youthful and excited. "Cire's been teaching us how to write sigils. That way, we can do bits of magic. Not a lot, but it's still pretty fun. We've been doing the protection sigils on the hell-mouth portal so nothing comes through."

Cire nodded as he clapped his hand on Abby's shoulder. "She's a natural."

Abby beamed. "It's not that much different than coding."

Anabelle looked at the sigils. She didn't know much about how they worked, but she knew enough to tell when they were done well. Abby's not only looked as aesthetically beautiful as Cire's but were also just as functional. Anabelle could feel power humming from them. "Okay, well, let's get this portal open and get going."

Cire walked to the center of the room and motioned for Abby to join him. "Would you like to do the honors?"

Abby squealed and clapped her hands together as she ran over to join the shaman. She took a piece of chalk from his left hand and scrolled a sigil on both of her palms before pressing them to the center of the pentagram.

Light burst around the edges of the pentagram as a portal opened in front of her. She poked her head around the portal. "Why the *hell* not? See what I did there?"

Terra lumbered over to the portal and looked around it. "You going to start doing standup next?"

Anabelle walked over to Cire. "Anything we need to know about this place before we go in?"

Cire nodded grimly. "Don't trust demons. Other than that, you should be set. Abby seems to have a good idea of what human hell is supposed to be like. Terra probably does as well. Once you've finished your mission, Abby will be able to open a portal to get you out."

Anabelle turned her attention to the portal. "All right, Angels. Let's get the *hell* out of here."

Terra groaned loudly. "I swear, if you two are going to be doing this the whole time, I'm quitting. Two weeks' notice is going in as soon as I get back."

Abby poked her hand through the portal. "Whoa. It is *warm* on the other side." She stepped through, and Anabelle and Terra followed her.

The portal closed behind them.

CHAPTER TWELVE

T he three Dark Gate Angels stepped out of the portal.

There was no visible sun or moon. It was difficult to see where the light was coming from, but it seemed more like grayness than blackness. Even in the gray darkness, a path could be seen, dirt stamped into dust.

Terra knelt and touched her hand to the path. "Looks like we got a direction to head in. I would have expected hell to be hotter than this. You know, fire and brimstone and shit. At least it doesn't smell bad. God, could you imagine if there were shit demons in here? Like from *Dogma*?"

Abby and Anabelle gave Terra confused looks.

Terra put her hands on her hips and clicked her tongue at her partners. "Are you telling me you guys found out you were going to hell and didn't put on the greatest movie about demons ever? Greatest comedy, at least. Peasants, the both of you."

They began walking down the path, the grayness all around them. A howl pierced the eerie stillness.

"That's ominous," Anabelle muttered under her breath. "At least hell isn't lacking in absurd thematic consistency."

They continued on, their feet dully hitting the dusty road beneath them as the air grew thicker and wetter. A foul humidity settled over them until their uniforms felt as if they'd been drenched.

Terra continuously pulled at her suit. She was glad she hadn't brought the fur armor she'd made of the pelts Cire had given her. The humidity made her feel like she was drowning. "Either of you two religious?"

Anabelle pointed up ahead where the sky was a little bit less dark.

The tree line of a great forest could be seen in the shadows. Another howl screeched like an angry wind.

Abby picked up a stone and rolled it in her palm as they walked. "No. Ma and Pa didn't take us to church. We grew up around Mormons, but we never talked religion much. All this is new to us, except for what we've seen in video games or read about. I read Dante in high school. That's about it."

Anabelle was staring at the forest. "All elves are spiritual. Wouldn't say religious, though. Most of us don't bother with the whole organization thing, except for the drow. The high and wood elves have a lot of gods. Some of the older high elves still keep the old ways alive, but they've been fading for a long time."

To the right, in front of the tree line, there was a large hill. Atop it was a she-wolf who stood nearly as high as the tree line. Her red eyes glowed in the darkness, and saliva dripped from her steaming, growling mouth.

The three Angels stopped to watch the creature as she peered at them.

Abby raised her hand, trying to scan the wolf from afar. "Do you think everything in here is going to try to kill us?"

Anabelle shook her head. "I doubt it. Myrddin sent us a dossier earlier this morning. Doubt either of you had a chance to read it." She paused to look at the other two Angels, who both shook their heads. "Good thing I did, huh? Apparently, the kingdoms in hell are pretty concerned with themselves. All of them are still infighting, trying to take down the ruler, archdemon, or whoever is in charge around here. We just have to play nice by hell's rules, and we'll be okay. So—and this should go without saying—don't open fire unless you're provoked."

Terra, who had her axe in hand, sighed and put it away. "Fine."

The wolf watched the DGA walk into the forest.

The trees around them managed to obscure the little light that was starting to break through the fog. The branches were worn and old, stretching out like fingers forever unable to reach one another. They looked sad, and Terra noticed the sense of dread they inspired.

The trees grew thicker, making it harder for the DGA to make their way through the forest. They resorted to crawling, climbing, and cutting their way through since the path had all but disappeared. Finally, Terra threw her hands up and shouted, "How the hell are we going to get out of here if we get lost?"

Abby snapped her fingers and pulled out a compass. "Cire said we have to go west. The sun rises in the east, but in hell, it rises in the west, and all paths follow the sun."

Anabelle's arm flashed bright with fire as she cut through a tree. Then she held her arm up, casting light all around them. "Thanks for the little lesson."

Abby raised her hand, palm toward the sky, and a book materialized in it. "Cire said if we can't figure out what's going on, we can check this. He said it might be a little hard to understand. It's all poetry."

Terra, who was once more tangled up with the creeping branches of the tree, groaned with irritation. "You just leave the poetry to me. I had a long goth poetry phase."

"But you never read *Dante's Inferno*?"

Terra slashed through more branches and caught up with the other Angels. "I was much more of a *Paradise Lost* kind of goth. Satan was pretty sexy."

"Figures you'd end up dating a semi-lich."

As those words left Abby's lips, a leopard stepped out in front of them. It was as large as the she-wolf, its black- and yellow-spotted coat shimmering in the sudden moonlight. The cat bared its fangs.

Abby and Terra looked at Anabelle. "This one looks like it wants to eat us," Terra said. "Beyond the shadow of a doubt."

Anabelle shook her head as she folded her arms. "Just because it's big, it doesn't mean—"

The leopard charged, covering an obscene amount of distance in the blink of an eye, and plowed into Anabelle. The elf wrapped her hand around the leopard's neck, trying to gain leverage, but she couldn't get a grip on the creature.

She fell to the ground, hitting it hard enough to knock the wind out of her. Before she could get back on the defensive, the leopard was above her, slashing at her with its claws.

Terra was already on the move. She rammed into the leopard's side, knocking it back as it hissed and spat.

The cat sank into the shadows to regroup and take advantage of the darkness.

Abby flew to the other two agents, spinning as she shone her eye lights into the dark forest. They seemed to have no effect. "It's a magical forest, isn't it?" she muttered to herself.

The leopard struck from the shadows again.

Terra barely had enough time to raise her battle-axe to catch the giant cat's jaws. The leopard pivoted, standing its ground as it shook its head and flung Terra into the air. It then leaped and slamming down on Terra, treating the human as no more dangerous than a large rat.

Abby fired a plasma blast at the giant cat, singeing its fur and causing it to back away from Terra. The Hand picked up her axe and swung it at the beast, cutting its leg.

The leopard hissed and stumbled back before opening its mouth and unleashing a barrage of thorns.

Anabelle ran forward and slid between Abby and Terra, throwing up a mana shield to take the bulk of the impact from the leopard's attack. "Oh, come on, leopards can't do that."

The cat didn't seem to care. It darted forward as Abby lined up her aim.

She fired as the leopard dodged to the side, skidding in front of the

DGA. The leopard swiped at them and connected with the scientist, sending her flying into a tree, which cracked.

The girl threw the broken trunk at the leopard.

The tree hit the cat in the face, knocking out one of its fags. The cat stared at its broken tooth on the ground and hissed as it clawed at the earth, its claws stretching and growing. The hair on its back stood up, catching fire as the cat's claws burst into flames.

Terra swung her axe over her head and leaped at the leopard. "Hell, yeah, this is more like it!"

The cat swiped Terra out of the air. Anabelle ran past them, pulling earth up in front of Terra and then transmuting it to powdery ice for Terra to fall into.

Then the elf slammed her hands together as she stomped on the ground, sending boulders into the air. The boulders exploded into icicle shards that flew at the leopard.

The shards hit the cat in the chest, piercing its skin.

As the cat stumbled back, Abby flew after it, her body filled with kinetic energy. She hit the monster hard, forcing it to stumble. Terra came up behind the cat and wrapped her arms around it as it shot fire into the air, then lifted with all of her might and threw the leopard on its head.

The cat scrambled to its feet, bleeding from the mouth, and hissed loudly before running into the forest.

The DGA watched the creature go.

Terra sheathed her axe. "Well, that was weird as fuck, but if all we have to deal with is big-ass cats, I think we'll be cool. That *was* a large cat, though."

Abby looked at her compass until she found west. "Come on. We should keep moving."

They went through the forest until it began to thin out. Ahead, Terra could see a river but could not hear running water.

There was a dock on the river and a frail old man with blue skin and a bald head, draped in a black cloak, stood near a boat. His eyes bulged from their sockets, and the skin around his mouth was tight, showing the jawbone beneath.

He smiled grimly when he saw the DGA agents approaching. "Ah, a new fare. Allow me to introduce myself. I am Charon, ferryman of the dead. And you are?" Charon's smile dropped. "Still among the living. How do so many of you mortals make it into this place?"

Anabelle stepped forward. "Us? Have more mortals come through here?"

Charon yawned lazily. "Of course. Mortals are always trying to sneak in here before their time. Don't know why. Everyone else is dying to get here."

No one laughed.

Charon shrugged. "That one doesn't usually go over well with the living."

Terra raised an eyebrow. "Does it fare better with the dead?"

"Most people who find themselves in hell after they die are ready to laugh at anything."

Anabelle waved her hands in front of her face. "Okay, okay. When was the last time a mortal came through here?"

Charon scratched his leathery blue skin. "Last time...hm, probably three hundred years ago? A loud-mouthed kid named José. Tore another hole in the damned place."

Anabelle sighed and shook her head. "One mortal in three hundred years is hardly 'all the time.'"

Charon stuck his oar in the water and swirled it around. "Listen, I've spent an eternity on this river. Let's say dates aren't my strong suit. Well, what do you want?"

"That's a good question."

Anabelle turned to Terra and Abby. "Any idea what we want?"

Abby took out her book and scrolled through it, then turned to Charon. "We want passage to the first circle of hell."

Charon's face drooped a little bit. "You don't want the river tour? It's to *die* for. Honestly, it's beautiful. There's a wonderful waterfall of blood a little north of here."

"No. Just straight to the circle."

"Wouldn't be a problem if you three weren't so full of life. Only charter is for the dead."

Abby frowned as she crossed her arms. "You helped Dante and José get across."

Charon looked back down to his oar. "I only let Dante across because he was with Virgil. And José because he had special permission from on high."

"How high?" Terra asked.

"Very. All the way to the top. Permission you three don't have." Charon paused as he considered his next words. "But there are ways around the rules. I'm not allowed to say. The bosses get pissy, and they got tempers."

Terra groaned as she leaned her head back. "Ugh, didn't we have something to deal with this before? Like, a temporary solution to being dead?"

Anabelle was cracking her knuckles in frustration. "Honestly, we've picked up so much crap I can't remember. We probably never used it. I don't remember ever being dead."

Abby was still flipping through her copy of *Dante's Inferno*. She let out a squeal of joy. "Oh! Does anyone have any coins?"

Terra and Anabelle looked at Abby like she was crazy. Charon, on the other hand, looked delighted. When no one answered, Charon cleared his throat and tilted his head to the boat, where a large pile of shining coins sat in a pile. "Oh, look! I found something very interesting in the water," Charon said as he stared down.

Abby walked over to the pile of coins and took six, two for each of the DGA agents. "Put these on your eyes."

Anabelle accepted her coins, leaned her head back, and placed them on her eyelids. Terra did the same, and then Abby. "Okay, Charon, how about now?" Abby asked.

Charon smiled widely, his yellow teeth shining. "Ah, looks like the dead have arrived with the proper toll. Come this way, my suffering souls. Let's get you to your torturous afterlife."

Terra reached out to find her way until she felt a cold, damp hand wrap around her wrist. She jumped, nearly knocking her coins off of her eyelids.

"Uh-uh," Charon said. "Try to keep those on. Just follow me."

Terra tried to relax as Charon guided her to the boat, which had tripled in size.

Charon helped Terra step in. "Go ahead and lie down."

Terra held the coins to her eyes and laid back. The bottom of the boat was oddly comfortable.

The boat started to move, and Terra could feel it rocking in the waves. What she heard next surprised her.

A beautiful baritone voice rose around her, singing in Latin. It continued as the boat rowed down the river Styx, only stopping when the boat hit the bank.

Charon plucked the coins from the DGA's eyes and pocketed them. "Thanks for that. Not often I get a living audience. I'm assuming you have some business to take care of. If you see the Big Guy, could you kindly not mention this? Oh, and try to stay sane."

The ferryman smiled as he pushed off, and his boat continued down the river.

Abby watched Charon float away. "Can't say we were expecting such a pleasant ride."

Terra nodded as she walked over to Anabelle, who was interested in the large stone wall ahead of them. "I guess hell's full of surprises."

CHAPTER THIRTEEN

Abby, Terra, and Anabelle stared at the vast wall separating the vestibule from the first circle of hell.

It was cracked and looked ready to come apart. Some of the cracks were filled with a sealing compound that looked like blood.

Abby scanned one of those spots to satisfy her curiosity. "Ugh." She looked up at the top. "We can fly up there right quick. See if there's anything we need to be prepared for."

Terra picked up a rock and sent it sailing toward the top of the wall. She whistled as she watched it go over. "Not a bad idea. If that hit anyone, would you apologize for me?"

Abby flew up the side of the wall, coming over its rim in a few seconds.

Thick fog stretched out over what looked like nothing. She couldn't make out if there was any ground, or if there were any enemies.

She headed back down and reported what she had seen. "Kinda weird that the first circle wouldn't have anything in it." She pulled out her book and cracked it open.

Anabelle grabbed her hand. "Do you want to suck the fun out of this?"

Abby laughed as she looked at Terra, who seemed to share Anabelle's opinion. "You guys are having fun?"

The elf shrugged as she headed toward the wall. "Brand new realm? No idea what's ahead of us? Feels like an adventure for the first time in a long time. Definitely beats beating up mobsters."

Terra followed Anabelle to the wall and kicked it, breaking through the stone. Then she punched another hole higher up in the stone, anchored her hand, and lifted herself. "Hopefully, this circle has something cooler than a giant leopard. Ugh. If this is a realm of giant creatures, I'm giving hell a zero out of ten."

Anabelle's feet and hands glowed light blue as she touched the wall, and she effortlessly pulled herself up. "Meet you up there, Abby?"

The girl nodded. "Sure thing," then took off toward the top. She sat on the edge, her feet hanging over, staring at the heavy fog.

Martin popped up in Abby's HUD. "Is this place a big deal for humans?"

Abby kicked her feet as she nodded. "For a lot of people, yeah. You could say we humans are obsessed with the idea of heaven and hell."

Terra pulled herself over the top of the wall. "Heaven, hell, another dimension…whatever this place is, you'd think someone would have installed an elevator or something."

Anabelle jumped up onto the wall beside Abby. "Why? Can you think of anything more torturous than dying and then having to climb a wall to get into hell?"

Terra smirked as she nodded. "Yeah, I guess that makes sense. So, who wants to take the plunge?" She leaned forward and spat over the edge.

"How about on the count of three?"

Terra jerked her hand at Abby. "That's not fair. She can just float down."

Anabelle stepped off, her mana suspending her in the air. "So what? I can too."

Terra crossed her arms as she glared at the elf. "I'm really tired of all the cool powers everyone has. Path of the Lost, my ass. I still can't even fly."

Abby stared down at the drop. "We'll rig you up something when we get back. You'll be like Power Woman, minus the cleavage."

Terra stood up as she peered down into the fog. "What if I want the cleavage? I happened to be a fan of that look. All right, catch you guys at the bottom."

Terra leaped off of the wall, screaming wildly as she dropped.

Abby took a deep breath. "Guess it's only fair." She cut her thrusters and plummeted into the fog.

The rush of wind brought tears to her eyes, but she didn't pull her armor up. This was the first time she'd free-fallen in over a year. It was pretty exciting.

Below, she heard Terra's impact.

Abby covered her waist and legs with armor, shock absorbers replacing her thrusters. She hit the ground hard, making a crater under her feet.

Terra was waiting for Abby, axe drawn. "Where's the princess?"

Anabelle hit the ground with a heavy thud, sending a shockwave of mana out. She stood as the fog dispersed around her. "Is that what you call me when I'm not around?"

"First time, but I like the sound of it. Would you prefer 'Your Majesty?'"

Anabelle breezed past Terra and followed Abby, who was heading west into the fog. "I don't mind it."

The girl went farther into the fog, ready to convert her arm to a plasma cannon whenever necessary. But the farther they walked, the less likely it seemed that there was anything there. "Hello?" Abby called. "Anyone here?"

Terra and Anabelle laughed. "I thought we'd be hearing more screams by now," Terra remarked.

"Hello? Is someone there?" a voice called.

The DGA agents exchanged glances. "Uh, yeah," Terra replied. "Are you being tortured?"

The fog directly in front of the DGA agents swirled and formed into an old man with a spindly beard and an oddly strong-looking constitution. He wore a toga and stroked his beard pensively as he beheld the DGA agents. Then he politely nodded his head. "Plato. Nice to make your acquaintance."

Abby's jaw dropped. "Wait, as in, *the* Plato?"

"The very one."

Abby extended her hand to the philosopher. Terra jerked her thumb at the two. "Figures there would be a circle in hell for nerds."

Plato shook his head. "There is nothing nerdy about preparing for one's death in the most virtuous way possible. How do *you* prefer to spend your time?"

Terra opened her mouth, but Abby stepped in front of her. "Be careful about answering his questions. It could be a trap."

Plato laughed jovially. "I see someone is familiar with the dialectic. I assure you, this is not a teaching moment. Besides, I have enough people to pester with the pursuit of wisdom. You three do not belong here. It doesn't take an undergrad degree to see that. I assume you are making your way through our humble limbo on some Herculean adventure of sorts?"

Anabelle, who was still eyeing the philosopher suspiciously, nodded. "Yeah. You wouldn't know the way through here, would you?"

Plato smiled and pointed at the ground. All of their shadows were facing the same direction. "I'll accompany you. The fog of limbo is much like philosophy. It is easy to get lost on your way, turned around. To walk in circles and eventually end up in the same spot." Plato clapped his hands together with glee. "Ahhh! It's been a while since I've been able to guide anyone."

Plato's joy was cut short by an electric feeling in the air when a familiar visage appeared out of the fog.

Tesla. His body was vibrating, fading in and out of existence.

Plato nodded solemnly. "We philosophers spend our time here because we could never make up our minds, but since philosophy is pointless, we've never harmed anyone. So, we have our own heaven here. Infinite conversations with peers. But this man...I believe you know him, correct?"

Abby nodded, remembering how she'd stranded Tesla in a pocket dimension to die.

"One leg in the land of the living, the other in the land of the dead," Plato continued. "He has yet to make up his mind."

Abby looked down at her shadow. "We should keep going."

"You needn't worry about him. He only sees what he wants to see, and it is not here."

Plato continued walking, the last of his shade companions vanishing as the fog dispersed.

Ahead was a faded green valley, and there was a glint of light in the distance.

Plato pointed at the glint. "Just touch the source of the light. Your shadows will disappear, and you'll see hell for what it truly is. Please be safe, and tell Arthur I said hello."

With that, Plato vanished.

Anabelle looked over her shoulder at the fog. "Hm. That was interesting. I thought he'd be more aggravating."

Abby didn't answer, nor did she hear what Terra said. She was too busy racing toward the light. She would never have guessed she'd be excited in hell.

The source of the light was the hilt of a sword buried in a stone as tall as Abby.

The girl walked around the stone and yelped when she came to the other side.

A man in gleaming silver armor sat on a stone bench. He had a thick red beard, and a golden crown was perched on his head. A red cape flowed from his back. He was easily ten feet tall.

"What are you yelping about?" Terra asked as she rounded the rock. She promptly yelped as well.

King Arthur got to his feet. "Hm, you have the blessings of my old friend. I wonder how he's doing? You wish to pass farther into hell, correct?" He smiled as he spoke, his face shining nearly as brightly as the light from the sword. "Allow me to help you."

He scooped the DGA agents up in his arms so they could each reach the hilt of the sword. "Please tell Myrddin that Arthur wishes him well."

Abby nodded, flabbergasted. "Plato says hello. Oh, and we'll tell Myrddin." She reached out for the sword, as did Terra and Anabelle.

They tumbled into darkness, and the circle of hell disappeared behind them.

CHAPTER FOURTEEN

Terra found herself shoved up and out of the earth, only to fall back down, flat on her ass. She rubbed her bruised coccyx as she got to her feet. "Glad to know I can still crack my tailbone."

Anabelle and Abby were vomited out of the hole in the ground next, landing in puffs of dust.

The ground closed up. There was no sign of a hole having ever existed.

The first thing Terra noticed was the wind. It was harsh, blowing as if they were in the middle of a hurricane. The gale was strong enough to make standing difficult. In addition, it was hot and dry. Terra felt the moisture being sucked out of her body.

A desert stretched out before the DGA, red sand dunes that reminded Terra of NASA footage of Mars.

Terra dusted her knees off. "There we go. Now, this looks a lot more hellish."

Abby, who was consulting her book, glanced up for a second. "Looks like the circles work differently than on the map. They're stacked on top of each other, hence the falling *up* we just did."

Anabelle walked over to look at Abby's compass. "So, what circle are we in for this time?"

Abby smiled mischievously. "Thought you guys were looking forward to the adventure?"

"You don't have to be a smartass. Just lead the way."

"It's the circle of lust. Promise, we didn't read anything else, so if you guys can, try to keep it PG."

Terra scratched her navel. "I'm always parent-approved."

The DGA headed west across the dunes that sloped down on either side of them. If it weren't for the compass, there was no way they would have been able to see through the storm.

Terra trailed a little behind Abby and Anabelle. She couldn't see as well as the other two. Anabelle had great vision because she was an elf, and Abby also had upgrades to her vision. Terra suddenly remembered something she always packed. She hit her wrist comm, and a pair of aviators appeared on her face. "Hey, how long do you think our comms are going to keep working?"

Abby looked back at Terra. "That's a really good question. Didn't even think about that. If we're going deeper or higher, there's a good chance we'll lose range if this is moving between the realms. We'll ask Creon."

Abby's wrist comm opened and projected a holographic image of Creon's lab. No one was there. "Guess he must have taken a break. We'll leave a message."

Anabelle pointed ahead. The dunes dipped down, opening up into a sinkhole. That was not what the elf was pointing at, though. A tornado a mile high stretched up to the sky, weaving in and out of the black clouds. "Looks like we found the main event of this circle."

Behind the DGA agents, the sand sank, and a bony spine shifted beneath it, rising for a moment before falling back.

Anabelle started to walk in the direction of the tornado. "We probably just have to jump into that, and it'll launch us into the air. This is easier than I thought it was going to be."

As they headed toward the tornado, a hoarse, rattling whisper blew through the desert.

Terra spun, her axe raised high. "Did you guys hear that?"

Anabelle nodded. "Yeah. It sounded like someone talking."

"Romeo..."

The voice was cracked and muffled, but Terra could tell which direction it came from. She turned around as the sand shifted behind her.

A long spine pushed its way out of the ground. Shoulders followed, jutting out against stretched skin rubbed raw by the sand. A hand shot onto the surface, its nails bitten badly enough that the fingertips were raw. Next came a head covered in faded makeup that masked the contours of youth, with a mat of stringy hair atop a scab-covered scalp. The eyes of the giant were sunken, and the eyelids had been cut off. "Romeo," the giant rasped, "wherefore art thou, Romeo?"

"Holy fucking shit!" Terra shouted as she stumbled backward.

The giant stretched out its flayed arm to grab the gladiator, who scrambled away from the slow-moving monster.

Abby and Anabelle helped Terra to her feet as they all watched the giant. It looked like a beached whale, its teeth chattering as its lidless eyes rolled back and forth, staring into the sand. Its mouth hung open, tongue lolling, and it kept rasping, "Romeo, wherefore art thou, Romeo?"

Frozen with horror, Terra stared at the thing. "Fuck, that's Juliet. From the Shakespeare play."

Another hand tore through the sand. And another. Then another. Hundreds of hands burst from the sand, grasping at nothing as the associated heads forced their way to the surface. They all belonged to the same pale-skinned boy, ligaments hanging from his face as his eyes hung from their sockets.

"Her vestal livery is but sick and green," the identical skulls wheezed. "And none but fools do wear it. Cast it off."

The hands grasped at Terra and the rest of the DGA as they tried to step out of range.

Abby fired her thrusters and rose into the air as Anabelle flipped away.

Terra crouched and then bounded over the garden of pale, rotten appendages.

The hands stretched toward the DGA, their bodies struggling to free themselves from the red earth.

"Guess that must be Romeo," Terra explained. "Dude can't keep his hands off the new girls. Definitely wasn't boyfriend material."

One of the Romeos popped up out of the ground, then another. In a few seconds, they were all above the ground.

The army of Romeos stared at the DGA and wheezed in unison, "Oh, she doth teach the torches to burn bright! It seems she hangs upon the cheek of night."

Each one of the Romeos' eyes turned to Abby. "Like a rich jewel in an Ethiope's ear..."

Abby glanced at Terra. "Uh, isn't he supposed to be in love with Juliet?"

Several of the Romeos pointed at Abby, all of them shrieking like banshees, "Beauty too rich for use, for earth too dear!"

The Romeos screeched again and stampeded toward the DGA agents.

Anabelle screamed, "Run!" and the three of them bolted toward the tornado.

Behind the wall, Juliet wrenched herself out of the ground, her words bellowing through the air as she chased the horde of Romeos, "If thou wilt not, be but sworn to love!"

Terra glanced over her shoulder and saw the teetering Juliet chasing them, bloodlust in her eyes.

"We're almost there!" Anabelle shouted.

Terra was focused on getting to the tornado. It was only a few feet away. She was preparing to jump when she noticed something. "It's made of fucking fire!"

She skidded toward the tornado and stopped right in front of it, the heat from the flames bringing her whole body to a dripping sweat.

Abby, who came up from behind, grabbed Terra's wrist. "We don't have a choice! This is the way!"

Abby leaped into the fiery tornado, and Anabelle jumped in beside her.

Terra turned around, saw the horde of Romeos closing in, and fell backward into the tornado.

The flames did not burn, and the wind caught Terra and pulled her off the ground.

The Romeos stared up at the DGA agents as they were swept away, wailing loudly. Juliet descended upon them and crushed their frail bodies between her hands as she wept.

Not that Terra cared. Right now, she was trying to figure out which way the tornado was taking her. She breathed a sigh of relief when it spat her out on solid ground.

Abby and Anabelle were already out. They were both staring straight ahead.

A mirror stood in front of each of them.

Terra walked toward hers. She couldn't see her reflection in it. She looked at Annabelle. "Do you have a reflection?"

Anabelle shook her head.

The mirror in front of Anabelle flashed brightly.

Terra covered her eyes to keep from being blinded. When the light faded, Anabelle was gone.

Abby ran over to where Anabelle had been. "Belle? Belle, where are you?"

Abby's mirror flashed and, even though she wasn't in front of it, she was gone.

Terra whirled, looking for something she could do, but there was no time. Her mirror was flashing.

Terra woke up in a lush bed, covered in the furs of exotic creatures she could not remember ever seeing but for some reason knew intimately.

The door to the room opened. Cire walked in, wearing nothing but his loincloth, holding a plate of raw meat. "Didn't think you were going to wake up after last night."

Terra scrunched her face and got ready to move, then she felt the soreness between her legs. "Oh. I guess that was good enough to deserve breakfast in bed."

Cire sat on the edge of the bed, passed Terra the plate, and poured her a glass of wine. "Not that you don't already deserve it, but yes. Did you get enough rest?"

Terra picked up a slice of meat and tossed it in her mouth. "Yeah. Feel like a hundred bucks. Just out of curiosity, what's going on?"

Cire chuckled as he stood up. He walked toward the window.

Terra couldn't keep her eyes off of his muscled back and ass. She faintly remembered why she was in the room. There had been a mirror. A few of them.

Cire threw back the curtains, letting in the light.

Terra covered her eyes, the sudden brightness blinding her. Cire motioned for her to come over to the window. "How did you already forget?"

The window was calling. Terra felt its pull. She got out of bed and went to stand next to the shaman. "Forget what?"

Outside the window, the orc horde stood, more mighty and vast than Terra had ever seen it.

Cire drew a battle-axe from his side and handed it to Terra. "They're waiting for you. We ride against the last humans today."

Terra looked at Cire, confused. "What do you mean, the last humans?"

"We're joining with your elf and goblin troops first, and we march on the humans. After today's victory, your empire will be complete. The troops are waiting for you to give them your words."

The window opened to a podium the whole horde could see.

Terra stepped out onto the podium, with Cire's encouragement. As she stood above the horde, he came up behind her and wrapped her in a flowing purple fur cape. Then he placed a helm on her head, its ancient horns curling down past her ears.

She looked out at the horde, and she felt something welling up in her that she hadn't felt in nearly a year. There was to be a battle. A real battle. *Her* battle.

The words came from her mouth before she realized it. "We are forever the horde. We grow each day. Orcs. Elves. Goblins. Gnomes. All together as one. The humans have tried to wage war with us long enough. Either they take our heads, or we will crush their skulls."

The horde cheered.

What happened next was hard for Terra to understand.

She was no longer on the podium.

She was on the battlefield, staring at one of Myrddin's dragon mechs.

She didn't have time to think. She merely acted, leaping into the air as she spun her axe, twisting and slamming it against the side of the mech's head, causing the beast to stumble.

Before the dragon mech could get its footing, Terra leaped onto it and tore open the cockpit.

Roy was looking up at her.

Terra dropped her axe. "No! I'm not going to..."

The face was different now, and Terra didn't recognize the rider.

Terra leaped off of the mech and backed away until she hit a wall.

Cire was facing her when she turned around. "Why didn't you finish him? He's the one leading the charge."

Terra shook her head. "No, Roy's my friend. I'm not going to kill him. I wouldn't even be fighting him."

Cire smirked. "What are you talking about? Roy and the others already joined you. They're your generals."

Abby, Roy, and Anabelle stepped out from behind Cire.

Cire handed Terra his sword. "We're all here for your war."

Terra took the sword and looked down at it. It was a beautiful piece of craftsmanship, perfectly weighted, with a golden hilt.

Not the sort of sword an orc would carry.

Terra spun, praying she was right, and lopped Cire's head off.

Fire spewed from his neck as hundreds of hands clawed out of the wound.

The whole world around Terra fizzled away until she was back at the bottom of the tornado.

Annabelle and Abby were standing there, the elf tapping her foot impatiently. "What took you so long?" Anabelle asked. "I didn't think you were that gullible."

Terra looked around, trying to get her bearings. "What the fuck was that?"

"A temptation or something. Obviously, you figured it out. And I thought *Abby* took forever."

Abby blushed and looked down at her feet while she muttered something unintelligible.

Terra folded her arms, trying to pass herself off as confident. "What did you see? And how did you know it wasn't real?"

Anabelle laughed. "It was Roy, and it was easy. He was so grabby. Roy's a fucking softy in bed. This thing just lumbered toward me, going on about how well he was going to fuck me." Anabelle rolled her eyes. "My Roy knows that isn't what I want him doing with his mouth —and don't you dare tell him I called him that."

Terra looked at Abby. "What about you?"

Abby spoke very quietly and quickly. "It was Persephone."

"How did you know?"

Abby muttered something as her eyes went back to her feet.

Anabelle was trying to keep from laughing. "What was that, Abby?"

Abby looked up, her dark cheeks rosy from blushing. "She didn't want to use her tentacles."

The elf couldn't hold it in any longer and burst out laughing.

Abby spun, pointing her finger at Anabelle. "Don't laugh! We didn't say anything about all the pet names you make Roy call you!"

Anabelle's laughter died. "That was said in secrecy, Abby. How dare you violate the sacred elvish oath?"

"There's no such thing! You're just saying that."

Anabelle laughed again and raised her hands. "Okay, okay, I promise I won't tease anymore. Not a word. How about you, Terra? What gave Cire away?"

Terra cleared her throat. "Oh, his sword. He never carries a sword."

Anabelle looked disappointed but didn't press it. Terra silently thanked God.

Abby looked around the eye of the tornado. "So, what now?"

The mirrors shattered, the glass flying into the air and swirling in the same direction as the tornado.

Anabelle's arms caught fire. "Guess we're about to find out."

CHAPTER FIFTEEN

The broken glass continued swirling, floating higher in the tornado until it finally crashed down and cut into the ground as if it were flesh. Blood bubbled up as the gash opened.

A demon with many heads stepped out of the hole.

One head was that of a man with pointed ears like an elf's. His eyes were as black as coal and he had a broad nose, and there was a lopsided crown on his brow. The head of an ox hung limply on one side of his neck and that of a goat was on the other, lashing back and forth, braying incessantly.

The demon floundered forward, his legs forming beneath him.

Anabelle shook her head. "Human demons are so uncouth. Ugh. Elves would have never dreamed up something so undignified."

The demon spouted drivel as his body continued to form well-defined, lean muscles on a human torso, even if his head was nightmarish. Leathery black wings stretched out as he stretched to his full ten-foot height. "Who dares break the profane mirrors of Asmodeus?" he bellowed.

Armor coated Abby's body. "Guess this is the prince or general of hell we have to beat."

Asmodeus laughed, his other heads making sounds as well, the ox only gurgling. "Some prince? Bitch of a human, I am the Prince of Lust and Revenge, one of the nine princes of hell. I will tear your bodies apart and torture your souls for eternity."

Abby scowled. "Ew. And you guys talk about our swearing?"

Anabelle closed her eyes, unshackling her mana. "Fuck off, *Ass-modeus!* You're gonna talk to the Dark Gate Angels with respect. Now, we want further passage into hell. Either you're going to let us through..."

Terra cracked her knuckles as her muscles tensed. "Or we're going through that ass."

Anabelle cast a glance at Terra. "Uh, that was a weird ending."

Terra frowned, still trying to look tough. "You have to give me a better setup than that. Next time Abby or I will go first."

Asmodeus roared with rage. "How dare you challenge me within my domain?"

Abby raised her hand and fired a bolt of plasma into the air. "Mocked you, too. Don't forget that one."

Asmodeus pulled a sword from his back and raised it high. Behind him, the tornado vomited out the butchered corpse of the giant Juliet and the hundreds of Romeos. The pieces of flesh started to reform, jamming into each other, bones splitting from skin, teeth forcing themselves out as the pounds of flesh rearranged themselves into something grotesque.

Juliet's body was mostly whole but was hunched over on all fours. The arms were pointed outward and her mouth hung open, her jaw slack, nearly touching the ground. A massive cock hung between her legs, dragging on the ground and leaving a thick, yellowing trail of mucus as dozens of Romeo's heads burst out of her heaving breasts like boils, all of them screaming and yammering. The side of her shoulder split open, leaving a gaping hole lined with the open mouths of the Romeos, their white teeth flashing alongside the hands that reached from the flesh, grabbing at any fold of skin or hole close by.

The DGA stared at the monstrosity for a moment as Asmodeus leaped onto its back, grabbed Juliet's hair, wrapped his palms in it, and snapped it like reins.

Abby curled her hands into fists, charging her body up. "That is disgusting. What, is that supposed to be, a metaphor for lust or something?"

Terra rolled her shoulders. "Don't want to fuck too much or you'll become horror porn, I guess."

Anabelle shrugged. "I don't know. Still kinda seems worth it."

Asmodeus and the Juliet monster charged, and the demon raised his gleaming sword. "Die, Angel Bitches!"

Abby and Anabelle broke to the right and left, while Terra stood her ground.

The demon brought his sword down on the Hand, who dropped her axe, raised her hands, and caught the blade.

Juliet swiped at Terra, sending her toward the tornado.

Abby shot toward her, caught her, and dropped her on her feet, then flew back around and fired on Juliet's and Asmodeus' backs, her plasma blasts tearing through the demon's and the monster's flesh.

Asmodeus bellowed and pulled Juliet's hair back, forcing her onto her hind legs as she spewed teeth and blood into the air.

Anabelle ran through the mist of blood and leaped, her hands crackling with lightning. She struck Asmodeus in the face.

The demon leaned back before slashing at Anabelle with his sword, catching her in the stomach and sending her flying into the tornado.

Anabelle screamed as her body caught fire and was torn apart.

Abby shouted, "Anabelle!" and went to fly to her when Terra grabbed her.

"No, we can't help her," Terra said. "We finish this."

Abby looked at where Anabelle had disappeared and then nodded. "You're right."

She blasted toward Asmodeus, slamming into him with a kinetic charge. As the demon reeled from the attack, the girl flew backward, connected her hands to form a large cannon, and fired.

The blast obliterated the ox head.

Abby retreated, needing time for her nanobots to cool down. As she backed away, Terra stepped forward to keep the pressure on.

Terra flung one of her axes at Juliet, slashing through the monster's arm.

Juliet fell forward and Terra moved in, trying to close the space between her and the demon.

Asmodeus slashed at Terra and she dodged, the blade narrowly missing her. She followed the move by rolling forward and scooping up her axe, then ran both of her axes down the middle of Juliet's torso, dragging her blades all the way down to her cock. "I've always wanted to do this!" Terra shouted as she brought both axes around and sliced through the engorged phallus.

Juliet screeched in pain and threw Asmodeus off as she thrashed about, her blood and entrails falling to the ground.

Asmodeus got to his feet, using his sword for support.

A plasma blast hit his goat head, severing it.

Terra rushed forward and threw one of her axes, which caught Asmodeus in the chest. She cut through the demon's leg with the other.

The demon fell forward, blubbering. Terra caught his jaw with an uppercut, knocking him off balance.

Her eyes flashed as she grabbed the demon's head and drove hers into it, following it up with a crushing punch to the face. She cracked her knuckles. "I'm going to enjoy this," she said as she slipped into the Path of the Lost.

"Not as much as they will," a voice called.

Terra looked over her shoulder.

Anabelle stepped out of the flaming tornado, bits of her skin flying back onto her. Behind her, thousands of naked humans were stepping out of the tornado.

"I think they want to have words with the Prince of Lust."

Terra and Abby moved out of the way, and the horde rushed at Asmodeus, punching, kicking, and gnashing their teeth. They tore the demon limb from limb as he threatened them, his words quickly turning to howls of pain. Then there was nothing more.

When the humans stepped aside, Terra saw that only a mound of flesh was left.

Over to the side, the malformed body of Juliet started to convulse. Light shone from her eyes and her wounds. Skin and appendages melted into a pile of smoldering flesh as a portal opened in front of Abby, Terra, and Anabelle.

The elven warrior clapped Terra on the back. "Good job staying focused. That must have been hard. I know you wanted to get in there and save my ass."

Terra shrugged. "Wasn't too hard. I figured the whole place was keyed to Asmodeus' power. If he was fucked up, he probably wouldn't be able to keep all this going. Also, we lived when we jumped into the tornado the first time."

Anabelle frowned. "That was a pretty big gamble."

"Same thing you would have done."

Abby cleared her throat. "We would have tried to save you first."

Terra tapped Abby's nose. "Which is why everyone likes you the most. Now come on. Let's see what else hell has to offer."

Romeo and Juliet walked over to the DGA agents. "Wait. Before you go, we wanted to thank you," Juliet said. "We've been like this for too long, and all we ever did was want to be together. Punished for hundreds of years for yearning for each other, for—"

Terra raised her hand. "Yeah, we get where you're going with that. No problem."

The rest of the humans wandered off as grass began to sprout across the sand.

Juliet and Romeo bowed slightly toward the DGA. "We should join the rest of them. We've all been apart for too long."

After the two of them joined the rest of the humans, Anabelle gave Terra a look. "We created the perfect realm for the horniest people in history."

Terra nodded approvingly at all of the buttocks walking away from her. "We're saints."

Abby was checking out the portal. "We give it a day until this is an orgy realm. Wait, and those weren't even souls. Romeo and Juliet weren't people. They're characters in a play. Hell doesn't make any sense."

Anabelle and Terra walked over to her. "You didn't see Cire, did you?" Anabelle whispered.

Terra groaned. "Will you drop it?"

"Nope. Abby guessed what it was. I'm sure she was right. She thought you were a warlord or something. I said you saw yourself."

Terra burst out laughing as she looked into the portal. "Okay, you got me. I *was* a warlord."

Anabelle shook her head. "Damn it."

Abby looked from the portal to Anabelle. "You owe us twenty bucks." Then she glanced at Terra. *"Belle* thought you were going to see yourself." She jumped into the portal.

Anabelle followed Abby.

Terra laughed to herself. "I guess I'll take both of those as compliments."

***

Persephone slid her fingers into the three dark holes and curled them together. She lifted her bowling ball and walked over to her lane.

Myrddin, Roy, Blackwell, and Naota had taken her out bowling. Naota had made it sound like it was his idea, but Persephone had her suspicions that this was as much for him and Blackwell as for her.

Life had been nothing but work for months. She hardly had time to see Abby. Their communication was purely online at the moment, and she traveled between the Nine Realms so much, she didn't even know where she was half the time.

Persephone didn't know anything about bowling (or any human sport, for that matter), but it was nice to be doing something other than work.

As the drow lined up her roll, looking down the lane at her pins, she felt a shiver run up her spine that set her teeth chattering and gave her goosebumps on her inner thighs. She was suddenly hot and flustered as she swayed to the side, barely catching herself before returning to the group's area and putting her ball down.

Naota looked over from the plate of buffalo wings in front of him. "You okay, Percy?"

Persephone raised her hand, signaling she was fine. "Yes. I just felt weird is all."

Roy, who was leaning back in his chair, sipping a beer, nodded as he met Persephone's eyes. "Yeah. Same here." He shook his head like he was trying to shake something away. "That was really freaky. I thought I smelled Anabelle's perfume for a second."

Persephone had definitely felt Abby's lips on the nape of her neck, but that was impossible. Abby was in hell right now.

Myrddin cleared his throat. He was wearing a polo shirt and a pair of slacks. Everything about him looked wrong for a bowling alley. "Whatever the reason, it is probably minor. Maybe the two of them are thinking about you particularly hard at the moment. Let's wish them luck and continue with the game."

The wizard waved his hands, and a drink appeared in front of each of them. "Cheers to some well-deserved time off. Now, who's playing Time Crisis with me?"

CHAPTER SIXTEEN

Cire stood behind Creon, watching the goblin work, before clearing his throat. "It's hard to concentrate when you're being watched by an orc."

Cire chuckled and stepped back. "My apologies. I didn't realize I was being intrusive. I'm merely curious. There are many things you and Abby are capable of that I do not understand."

Creon leaned back in his chair. "When it comes to Abby, we are equally baffled. She is a genius."

Cire nodded. "Still, you gnomes have got so far and seen so much. We orcs are playing catch-up with the rest of the Nine Realms, a task we are accomplishing quickly, thanks to you. I cannot extend enough thanks to you." He bowed deeply to the gnome.

Creon was taken back. Even with everything he'd seen and done, having an orc bow to him was something he'd never imagined possible. With a smile, the gnome extended his hand to Cire. "I'm glad we can get you up to date with the rest of the realms. The next thing is to work with the elves. A little too dependent on magic, in my opinion. Everyone needs to have options, especially in light of what the Dark One was capable of. Who knows what we might all have to face next?"

Cire's brow darkened, and he seemed hesitant to speak. "Do you think there could be another threat? One as serious as the Dark One?"

Creon shrugged as he turned back to the computer. "Never hurts to be prepared. That was what screwed us over last time. Myrddin had thousands of years to prepare, and it took nearly that long. Hopefully, the realms won't make that mistake again."

Cire pulled up a chair next to Creon. "What are you doing at the moment?"

Creon smiled, happy to explain his work. "I'm trying to reestablish comm links with the DGA. The farther they go into hell, the harder it is to keep track of them. Martin's still functioning, but it's only because he's located in Abby's body. As for the rest of their tech, well, it's slowly going out of range. I'm working with Martin to reinforce the signal before he disappears entirely."

"That is difficult, I gather?"

Creon shrugged. "Tedious is more like it. I can try to explain the ins and outs to you. It will be confusing, but then again, learning something new always is. Interested?"

Cire nodded. "If I am to lead the orcs to strength, it would be remiss of me not to take advantage of every chance I get to learn. To grow. And after seeing how easily Abby picked up the sigils, I have been inspired. Perhaps this old orc can learn new things, after all."

"I suspect this old orc will learn faster than most young ones." Creon turned to his computer, angling the monitor so Cire could better see. "Thanks to Martin, most of my duties are automated now anyway. I'm mostly monitoring, waiting for something complex that needs my attention. While I wait, it would be nice to have company and a new student. Abby caught up to me far too quickly."

Cire leaned forward, staring at the computer screen. "I shall not fail you where Abby did."

Creon looked at him curiously.

"I will not learn too quickly and make your role redundant."

Creon and Cire shared a laugh. Who would have thought a gnome and an orc would ever be friends?

There was a blip on the monitor, interrupting their laughter.

Creon snapped his fingers and leaned back in his chair, staring smugly at the holoscreen. "That would be our agents. Looks like they've made it to the fifth circle. Guess there was more lag than I thought."

———

Abby, Terra, and Anabelle were walking through what looked like a shattered version of New York. In truth, it could have been any city. There were skyscrapers, but none Abby could place. The streets seemed familiar, but only because they could have been any urban street.

As Terra walked, she rubbed her stomach, which was noticeably bloated. "Dude, you can send me back to Gluttony anytime. I have never had that much good grub."

Anabelle chewed on a toothpick. "You know if we sent you back, you wouldn't have passed, right? You would willingly be choosing to be in the ring of gluttony."

"Of all the rings we've been in so far, that's my favorite. There wasn't even a demon. Easy. Free food. Plus, the folks there were a riot. Except for the drunks. They were kinda weird."

Abby, who was still distracted by the uncanny nature of this ring, shrugged. "How would you feel if *you* were trying to get drunk, and it never happened?"

Terra scrunched her face as she thought. "Don't know. How do you feel? You can't get drunk, right?"

Abby shook her head, unable to take her eyes off of her surroundings. "No, we can't. But we aren't really trying to. Plus, we've never been drunk. There isn't anything to miss. Martin could probably simulate the experience if we asked."

Before Terra could say anything, Abby pointed at her and said, "Don't ask."

Anabelle was walking a little ahead of the rest of them. She held the compass. "I would have thought the ring for Greed would have been harder too. Like, I know I'm a greedy person. I love having shit, and all they tried to get me with was a couple of diamonds. Human demons probably only know about human vices, though."

Terra kicked a stone ahead of her, launching it through the air. "What do you mean? Elves have different vices than the rest of us?"

"Every race is unique in how they think of morality. Granted, we all think murder is wrong, but humans have a vastly different opinion on assisted suicide than elves do. We wouldn't even think of calling it murder. Stuff like that."

"So, what does elvish greed look like?"

"Jewels would have worked well on a dwarf. You know, mining and everything. It's a huge part of the culture. Elves? Oh, should have tempted me with land. Long stretches of open plains. That would have gotten me."

Abby and Terra stifled their laughter. Anabelle turned around, frowning. "What's so funny about that?"

"What are you, an early American settler?" Abby asked. "Land? You planning on homesteading?"

Anabelle crossed her arms and harrumphed at the two humans. "I'll have you know, I'm a descendant of wood and plains elves. We spent most of our time in the wild. It wasn't until we were absorbed by the high elves that we lost that. A lot of us still have dreams about it. It's a deep ancestral memory."

Neither Abby nor Terra looked swayed.

"What the fuck would have gotten you?" Anabelle spat, her voice taking on an edge Abby had never heard directed toward them before. "Abby? Another couple of personalities to help you be more neurotic about your dead dad?"

Abby was speechless. She couldn't believe what Anabelle had just said.

Terra stepped forward and put her hand on Abby's chest, pushing her back. "Fuck you, Anabelle! That's a horrible thing to say. Figures it only takes someone poking a little fun at you to remind us that you're a heartless, knife-eared bitch."

Abby was even more surprised by what had come out of Terra's mouth. She knew Anabelle could be short when she was stressed, but she'd never heard Terra speak like that before.

What came out of her own mouth was even more surprising.

"Don't fucking push me out of the way. We...*I* am not a fucking kid, and I'm sick of both of you acting like it. As if you're both so goddamn mature."

Abby could hear her voice. She was shouting. The blood was pumping, and her face was hot. And it felt good.

"If you two could get your heads out of your own asses, you wouldn't be at each other's throats."

Anabelle threw up her arms and pretended to curtsy. "Oh, meek little Abby finally decided to stand up for herself instead of letting someone else fight her battles. Or was it Martin? Is he speaking for you this time? Just like he fights all your battles? Admit it, you aren't anything without that AI running your brain for you. Underneath all the technology you've had to add, you're still just a weak, pathetic human."

Terra laughed. it was a cold, harsh sound. "Here we go again. Done pretending you don't hate humans, you racist piece of shit?"

Anabelle held her hand to her heart. "Me? Racist? I'm the only reason you backward-evolved monkeys even got a chance."

A plasma blast shot past Anabelle, gazing her chin.

Smoke floated from Abby's hand cannon. "Don't you ever call me a monkey," she said, pulling back her hair.

Mana pulsed around Anabelle. "Do you really want to do this, girl? Because I will rip you apart."

Abby's body vibrated with kinetic energy. "Try us."

"Having another one of your special moments?" Terra spat. "We already know you're in love with Anabelle. You don't have to broadcast it. Persephone might get pissed."

Abby whirled and hit Terra in the face with a plasma blast. The pulse sent Terra flying through the air with so much force she crashed through the building behind her.

Abby spun back, ready to fire at Anabelle.

The elf was already moving, energy crackling off her as she slipped down the Path of the Lost. Her eyes turned white and she screamed in rage as she punched Abby, her hand filled with energy.

The girl threw up an energy shield that took the bulk of the attack. She fired her thrusters, spun around Anabelle, converted her hand into a plasma blade, and went for the elf's throat.

Anabelle broke apart into mist and reappeared behind Abby, who shot into the air. The elf jumped after her, grabbed Abby by her wrist, and slammed her into the concrete.

Terra leaped and landed on top of Abby, driving her body into the ground. The girl spat blood. She stomped Abby's head for good measure, then pivoted and elbowed Anabelle in the face, the gladiator's eyes glowing red as her muscles bulged.

Terra was finding her own way into the Path of the Lost.

Before Anabelle could recover, Terra kicked Anabelle in the chest.

Abby shouted to Martin, "Increase my nanobots!"

Martin flittered into Abby's field of vision. "Abby, something is wrong. You're fighting—"

"Do what I fucking said!"

Abby's thrusters fired and she launched into the air, then spun and hit the ground. She fired her thrusters again and charged at Terra, who turned around just in time to pull out her axe.

Abby's arms hardened, deflecting the axe's blade, and she plowed into Terra. She opened her mouth and a plasma beam fired, engulfing her entire head.

Terra fell to her knees, her face smoking.

Abby leaped up and roundhoused Terra in the face before realizing Anabelle was floating above them both.

Abby fired two plasma bolts from her shoulders and slung more from her hands as she sped toward the elf.

The two collided, their fists moving faster than any mortal could have seen. Abby teleported behind Anabelle, and the elf burst into mist and recombined to avoid the attack, then launched her own.

Abby could hardly see in front of her. All she saw was the seething bright red rage of her desire to murder her friends. She wanted to wring the life out of Anabelle's neck and drive a knife through Terra's skull.

Out of nowhere, Terra exploded from below, grabbing both Abby's and Anabelle's heads, dragging them back down with her as she drove them both into the ground.

Terra lifted Abby by the throat, crushing her windpipe as Anabelle struggled to charge her hands with all of her mana.

As she gathered her magic, Anabelle darted for Terra, who threw Abby at her.

Abby teleported out of the way as the elf burst into mist, but she reformed too early, colliding with Terra's fist.

Terra grabbed Anabelle as she fell and drove her kneecap into her forehead.

Abby sped forward and caught Terra off-guard, slamming her hand into her nose and shattering it.

Terra stumbled backward as Abby fired two more plasma shots, hitting Terra in her kneecaps, shattering both of them.

Then Abby's hand shot a net that caught Anabelle as her other hand converted into a cannon. She diverted all power to the cannon and pressed it against Terra's head.

Terra spat in Abby's face, tears trickling down her cheeks. "Do it! I fucking hate you! Just do it!"

In the net, Anabelle tried to stand up. Abby mentally increased the pressure until she heard Anabelle choking.

Abby vented extra energy in her arm as her cannon started to sear the flesh on Terra's forehead. She could see Terra's skull exploding from the back, showering brain and blood and bone across the concrete.

Like what had happened to her father.

Abby recoiled and fell to her knees.

Terra surged forward, grabbing Abby by the throat and lifting her into the air. "You fucked up. This ends now."

"You're right."

Abby deactivated all of her systems.

Her armor disappeared, leaving her vulnerable.

Terra looked at Abby with a mixture of anger and confusion. "What the hell are you doing?"

Before Abby could answer, Terra punched her in the face.

"What are you doing?" Terra shouted as she kicked the girl in the ribs.

Abby rolled over, coughing blood as she struggled to her feet.

"Get up!" Terra shouted. "Fight me!"

Abby stood, but she didn't raise her fists. "Why would I do that? You're one of my best friends. I love you."

Terra drew her axe. "Fucking idiot." She swung it at Abby's throat.

Abby closed her eyes, waiting to feel the blade hit her throat.

It didn't happen. She slowly opened one eye.

The blade was a centimeter from her throat, trembling.

Terra was crying, one hand over her mouth. "Oh, my God, Abby, I'm so sorry."

She dropped her axe and ran to the scientist, and the two of them collapsed into each other's arms. "I'm so sorry, are you okay?"

Abby nodded, the motion sending pain shooting down her body. "We'll live." The nanobots were already starting their repairs.

"All those things I said, I didn't mean them. I don't know where they came from. It came out, but I don't know from where."

"Hey, guys!" Anabelle called. "Can you let me out? I'm not murderous anymore either. I want a hug too."

Abby released Anabelle, who looked extremely embarrassed as she hugged Abby and Terra. "The moment I stopped moving, everything slowed down," Anabelle explained. "And I could see what was happening. Resentment, that's what got us. Old anger. You know exactly where that came from."

Terra nodded. "I was hoping we could have a cute moment without talking about that."

Abby shook her head. "That's all we need to say. It was old. That's not how we feel now."

Anabelle nodded. "Yeah. Abby's right. I love you guys."

Terra hung her head, still crying a little. "I love you two. Both of you. You're my best friends. The best damn thing to ever happen to me." She turned over to Anabelle. "And you owe me twenty bucks."

"For what?" Anabelle gasped.

"Remember we bet that if we ever got in one of those anime fights, Abby would kick our asses? She definitely won."

Anabelle crossed her arms. "I was tied up. That does not count."

Abby stood up and looked at her compass. "We'll call it a draw. We should get going and find this demon before anything like that happens again."

Terra walked over to Abby and slung her arm around her shoulder as Anabelle walked by their side. "All jokes aside, that was probably the best fight of my life. Glad I could share it with you two. Let's never do that again."

CHAPTER SEVENTEEN

"Let's never do this again."

Sarah was sitting with Kravis in their tent on the outskirts of the gnomish city. They were both looking at a table covered with stacks of paper. "Never again," Sarah repeated.

Kravis climbed onto the table and kicked over one of the piles. "I'm more than happy with that. This was your idea to begin with."

Sarah glared at Kravis. "Don't act like you didn't want to get married."

Kravis hopped off of the table and sat in his chair. "Yeah, I definitely did, but you were the one who got the ball rolling. So, naturally, I'm going to take the chance to shift the blame to you."

Sarah grabbed a handful of papers and hung her head. "We can unseat the Dark One from the gnome planet, but we can't deal with tax forms?"

Kravis drew his knife and stabbed one of the piles of paper. "We can't kill our tax forms. We *could* just not do them. What do we have to pay taxes for? The whole world is going through a reformation. They're building entirely new infrastructures. How are they going to keep track of this if we don't do it?"

Sarah shook her head, then removed Kravis' knife from the paper pile. "It doesn't work like that. If we don't fill these out, we're not going to be eligible for any of the repopulation programs."

Kravis sheathed his knife and avoided Sarah's eyes. "We don't have to do that, you know. It's not our responsibility."

"Yeah, I know it isn't, but you need to tell me what you want. You can't wait for me to drag it out of you. That's not fair."

Kravis nodded as he looked at the paperwork. "If it requires all this, I'd say let the gnomes die out. If we're strong enough, we'll survive. Though, I'm not sure if anyone would survive this much busywork. Can't we just go back to killing things? And you're right. I'm sorry."

Sarah grabbed a pile of paper and rolled it up, then bopped Kravis on the head with it. "It's okay. Just don't forget we need to be talking, and even if we hate these forms, we have to take care of them. We're an example to everyone. So, no. We'll kill things when we're done."

Kravis picked up a pen. "You act like you wouldn't prefer to be killing the remainder of the Dark One's forces."

Sarah looked up from the worksheet she was filling out. "I'd prefer to be. But I know we won't be doing that until this is finished. Myrddin's not going to let us go out in the field."

"We could go rogue again..."

Sarah tossed her pen at Kravis. He dodged, and the pen hit the canvas of the tent. "Hurry up so we can get to bed. There's repopulation we need to take care of."

"I was trying to repopulate this morning."

"You did. You fell asleep right after. And we're not calling it that from now on, just so you know. Now come on, let's finish this up."

Kravis sighed but blew a kiss at Sarah. They hunched over their paperwork.

Terra, Abby, and Anabelle were still making their way through the circle of anger, looking for the demon who was in charge.

Even though they had ended their argument and fight, Terra could still feel the rage in the back of her head like a snake waiting to strike.

The three women were giving each other space, making sure not to speak much. Even after they'd stopped fighting, they'd still snapped at each other. They quickly decided Anabelle would continue guiding them with the compass, neither Terra nor Abby were going to ask any questions, and they would speak as little as possible.

So far, it was going pretty well.

The familiar part of the city had disappeared. The towers and skyscrapers had been replaced by sparse trees that towered as high as skyscrapers.

The trees had windows, and Terra saw eyes peering out from them at times. If she stopped paying attention and cast her eyes up toward them, she saw figures moving in their shadows as the windows shifted and changed shape.

They journeyed farther into the dead city as it became a forest. Above, screeching harpies flew about, paying no attention to those who journeyed below.

Suddenly Terra became aware of a horrid stench. It was like nothing she'd ever smelled, a sweetish scent, like incense muddled with decomposition. Terra wasn't certain how she could tell it was something dead.

They came to a hole in the concrete. It reminded Terra of the pit she'd seen the lich climb up through.

She leaned over to get a better look. "What do you think is down there?"

Anabelle took a deep breath, composing herself before she answered. "Probably whatever ugly son of a bitch we need to kill."

Abby, who was grinding her teeth, nodded. "We should do this as fast as possible." She leaped into the pit.

Terra almost said something about Abby's impetuousness but thought better of it. She bit her tongue and followed, and Anabelle leaped after her.

Terra's feet hit the ground, sinking into moist earth. The smell was even stronger down here. Whatever it was they were looking for, they were getting close to it.

The ground sloped down into the darkness as they journeyed into the heart of hell.

Abby raised her hand, silently stopping Tera and Anabelle. "Do you guys see that?"

Terra moved closer, her eyes adjusting to the darkness. Then she saw it.

A great winged creature lay at the bottom of the pit. The size of a submarine, the creature's wings were tightly folded around his body, with only his head exposed. His face was caked in blood and covered in maggots, but that wasn't the most disturbing thing about him. No, what was most disturbing was his expression of utter defeat, a face whose complete sadness somehow also carried with it no hope.

Abby gasped as they walked closer to the bloated corpse. "Is that an angel?"

Terra shrugged, taking her time to inch closer. She swatted at her face, killing a fly that had landed on her.

Millions of flies swarmed around the decomposing celestial body. "Fuck if I know."

The body started to twitch and convulse. The head split open, and an oozing trail of maggots poured out. One, larger than the others, forced its way out, and as its putrid, thin-skinned body flopped onto the ground, six insect wings sprouted from its back as hairy fly legs ruptured from its sides.

As if that wasn't weird enough, a crow's head tore out of the front of the maggot as its wings flapped, pulling the demon into the air. Another head, that of a possum, punched out of the middle of the maggot's body. Finally, a human head melted out of what Terra had assumed was its ass.

She thought the head bore a striking similarity to Christopher Columbus.

The skin of the maggot hardened, growing thick with coarse hairs as its legs twitched. The flies that had tended the angel's corpse swarmed around the demon. "How rare for the living to walk among the damned!" The demon cackled. "Count yourselves lucky, mortals. Not many gain audience with Beelzebub, Lord of Flies, Prince of Revenge, Second only to Lucifer himself, Scourge—"

Terra sneezed loudly, blowing snot out of her nose onto the ground. "Ew. Sorry. Didn't mean to interrupt you. Are you the demon for this circle?"

Beelzebub raised one of his insect arms as if saluting himself. "Demon of this circle? Human, I am the second prince of hell. I was known as Baal for hundreds of thousands of years, eater of children, devourer of—"

"Okay, cool. You sound pompous enough to kill."

Terra winked at Anabelle. "You see what I did there? The direct, quippy nature of my taunt? Abby, you want to finish this one off?"

The girl's arms converted to cannons. "You can call us the extermination squad."

Terra fist-pumped. "You see, Anabelle? That's how it's done."

Anabelle shrugged as her hands filled with fire. "Whatever."

Beelzebub let out a rage-filled roar and flew at the DGA, along with the swarm of flies surrounding him.

Abby fired her plasma cannon.

The swarm of flies flew in front of the demon, absorbing the blast. A pile of them fell dead to the floor, but it made no difference. There were still enough flies to obscure Beelzebub.

Suddenly the demon appeared behind the DGA, then opened his mouth and vomited forth a stream of flies and snakes.

Anabelle stepped forward. She slammed her hands on the ground, creating a flaming shield as Terra unsheathed her axe and flung herself at the possum head.

Terra held on tightly as she started to hack at the head. Flies swarmed around her, biting her skin. "I'm assuming no one brought bug spray!"

Abby flew through the swarm of flies, firing plasma bolts as she went. "Why don't you get angry? You practically tore our heads off before!"

Terra drove her axe through the possum's neck, severing the head from Beelzebub's body. "That was easy! You guys are easy to be pissed at. This guy is just gross. Reminds me of a couple of my old roommates!"

Beelzebub rolled over in the air, the swarm rolling with him as he spun, vomiting flies and bile. Terra was tossed off.

Anabelle slammed her fist on the ground, sending up a pillar of stone that drove into Beelzebub's soft stomach.

The stone spear ripped through his abdomen, which spewed rotting food and garbage.

Abby threw up a shield as the contents of Beelzebub's stomach showered her. "God, this is so gross."

Beelzebub fell to the ground and weakly crawled over to the corpse of the cherubim. Once he was above the corpse, he vomited a white substance on the decomposing angel and shoved his head into the sticky mess, gnawing on it while the wounds in his body started to heal.

Abby aimed her cannon at Beelzebub's backside. "He probably shouldn't be doing that, huh?"

Anabelle shook her head as a flaming aura surrounded her. "Nope. That's probably a bad thing."

Terra threw one of her axes at Beelzebub's exposed backside. It sank deep into the demon's body and he reeled back, screeching in pain.

The three DGA agents sprinted at him. Abby launched into the air and peppered his bulbous body with plasma bolts. Anabelle stopped a few feet away, slammed her hands together, and shot forth a jet of flame, while Terra ran along the side, slicing along the demon's ribs with her axe.

Beelzebub flailed as his entrails poured onto the ground.

Terra tried to step back, but the tidal wave of filth knocked her down. "Tell Cire I love him and I died in the entrails of my enemies!" she called as she was washed away.

Abby flew alongside Terra, then scooped her up and away from the sludge gushing from Beelzebub's writhing frame. She landed behind

Anabelle, who was pulling up dozens of earth spikes and impaling the demon.

Terra tried to wipe off the muck covering her. "Ugh. Why does this always happen to me?"

Anabelle's stone spires burst into flames, setting Beelzebub on fire. "Because you always get as close as possible."

"It's not my fault I don't have any long-range attacks! I'm not all magical and shit."

Terra and Anabelle glared at each other, then Anabelle laughed. "I don't know, you seem pretty magical to me."

Terra waved away the elf's compliment. "Aw, you're just saying that 'cause I'm cute."

Beelzebub was still gurgling, choking on his own blood.

Terra motioned toward the demon. "Uh, whose turn is it this time?"

Abby picked up Terra's axe and walked over to him. She stood before the main head and brought the axe down, slicing clean through the neck.

Beelzebub's flames flared and he disintegrated. A portal opened among the bones.

Abby tossed the axe back to Terra. "What is that, three more levels?"

Terra ran past Abby and jumped into the portal. "Who cares? I'm having a blast!"

Anabelle walked past the scientist. "It *has* been pretty fun."

Abby bowed theatrically. "After you."

"Hey. I'm sorry for all the—"

"Don't worry about it, Belle. I know that wasn't you."

Anabelle smiled and looked away. "Thanks. Catch you on the other side." She dropped into the portal, disappearing.

Abby cast one final glance at the half-eaten angel corpse, then followed her friends.

CHAPTER EIGHTEEN

They walked across concrete pavement flanked by decrepit dead buildings, rust, and rot covering them all. Flies filled the sky, and the stench of decay was in the air. Time seemed to lose all meaning since each building was the same, no distinction between them, stretching on for as far as Abby could see.

Finally, there was a break in the monotony. They saw a lake of ice in the middle of a parking lot the size of a football stadium.

As they got closer, Terra drew her axe. "Anybody down for ice-skating?"

Abby scanned the ice, hoping to learn something about it. "Hell isn't about subtlety. Might as well have a sign that says Bad Guy Here."

They crossed the rest of the concrete until they were at the lake of ice.

Anabelle tentatively stepped onto the frozen lake. "Seems stable enough."

Abby looked up from her scan. "Looks like there's something under the surface. It isn't moving, though. Must be frozen."

Terra sighed loudly. "I hope we aren't going to have to dig our way down to it. Personally, I don't think we should have to work to get to the demons we're going to kill."

Abby slid onto the ice, her feet converting to ice skates. "We usually don't have a say in things like that. Maybe we won't have to kill anything, it'll just give up. We've already torn through most of hell."

Anabelle skated by on a thin layer of mana. She waved her hand over Terra's feet, casting a similar mana field around the human's boots. "Yeah, you would have thought it applied to everyone we've had to fight. After we got through the first three circles, I would have called it quits if I was a demon."

Abby led the agents to where she was picking up the vital signs. It was in the middle of the lake. They stood over whatever was beneath the ice and stared down, trying to see something beneath the surface. "Can't really make anything out."

Terra heaved her axe up and brought the blade down on the ice. "Might as well get cracking."

She let her axe fall one more time when the ice shook violently.

Anabelle looked around for the source of the commotion and gasped.

Terra continued to hack at the ice. "What is it?"

"Us."

Abby and Terra turned around, facing where Anabelle was pointing.

A few feet away, in the surface of the ice, were the DGA agents' reflections.

Abby converted her hand to a plasma cannon. "That's a little unsettling."

The reflections shimmered and then pulsed. The ice beneath them cracked and water shot up, swirling and then forming doppelgangers of the DGA agents.

Anabelle's doppelganger took a step forward. "The reason nobody gave up is they all know you're wasting your time. You won't accomplish anything you're trying to do. You're a terrible leader."

Anabelle scrunched her face and pressed her hand to her chest. "Me? A terrible leader?"

Terra's doppelganger, which was hunched over like an ape, dragging her axe with one hand and grunted. "You hardly have the brains to get to the bottom of this. All you are is an idiot with a big axe."

She had turned back to the small hole she'd been working on and was busy deepening it. "Wait, huh?" she asked as she looked over her shoulder.

Abby's doppelganger floated into the air, her feet only a few inches from the ground. "At least it's better than me. I shouldn't even be here. Without these nanobots, I'm nothing. Just dead weight."

Abby tried to come up with a retort, but nothing came to mind. She tried not to think about what the doppelganger had said.

But she did think about it. Only a little bit, but still.

A fiery aura shot out and consumed Anabelle. She commented, "Could this be any more boring?" and dashed forward, covering the ground between her and the doppelganger in seconds. Her hand sliced through the surprised doppelganger's neck, severing its head.

Terra was still hacking. "Would you mind taking care of mine?"

Anabelle flipped over and brought her foot down on Terra's doppelganger, crushing its skull. "Done and done. How about you, Abby?"

Abby was caught off-guard by Anabelle's words. She wasn't certain when she'd stopped paying attention. "Uh, yeah, sure."

Anabelle sliced at Abby's doppelganger. Her hand passed through it, but the doppelganger continued to stand. It smiled and turned to Abby. "See? That big brain of yours is already failing to take care of this. What happens when you can't figure out the solution to your next problem?"

The girl didn't have an answer. It was something she was constantly worried about. Luckily, Martin was always there to help. But what if he wasn't?

Anabelle punched the doppelganger again, her hand once more passing through it. "Huh. Abby, I think you have to take care of this one."

The scientist raised her hand to convert it to a cannon.

Nothing happened.

She peered at it. Concentrated on bringing her nanobots out to cover her body with armor.

The nanobots didn't come.

Abby slammed her hands together as she tried to keep from panicking. "What's going on?"

Abby's doppelganger laughed wildly as her body dissolved into water and slipped back into the lake.

Anabelle walked over to her. "Hey, is everything all right?"

Abby shook her hand as fear began to settle in. "Something's wrong. I can't feel them in me anymore. Martin, the nanobots, they're gone! What's happening?"

The ice trembled.

A loud crack made everyone jump. The ice between Terra's foot split open. "Oh, shit, not again."

A column of water burst through the ice beneath Anabelle, and she tried to steady herself as a geyser blew up underneath her.

Terra cracked up. "It's about time that happened to someone else."

The ice continued to break apart.

A feathery white wing with an eagle's talons at the tip tore out of the ice, grasping at the slippery surface. More followed until there were six. The wings were covered in eyes, which were scanning the area, looking for prey.

A seraph flew into the air, its six wings swirling around a black nexus that seemed to be a fetus. An eerie screech came from the fallen angel.

Anabelle hit the ground, then got to her feet, rubbing her sore ass. "That's not something you see often. That's an excessive number of eyes."

A beam of celestial energy flew from the seraph. Anabelle and Terra leaped aside.

Abby tried once more to summon her nanobots, but nothing came. She threw herself out of the way of the beam at the last minute. "Something's wrong! I can't do anything!"

Terra made a beeline for the seraph. She leaped into the air, axe drawn, ready to bring down one of the wings.

The seraph's wings began to spin faster around its nexus, creating a forcefield.

Terra hit the wall of energy, which shocked her and knocked her back. She hit the ground with a thud, groaning as she tried to get up.

Anabelle ran toward the seraph. She slid underneath it and raised her hands, causing water to explode upward around her. She froze the water as it headed toward the seraph, the water forming sharp, jagged shards.

The ice melted as the seraph launched a wave of energy and converted the falling droplets of water into knives.

Anabelle dodged, sending a wave of fire at the knives for good measure.

Abby just watched, concentrating on her nanobots and screaming for Martin to help her. Behind her, the doppelganger reappeared. "What are you waiting for?" it whispered. "Aren't you going to help your friends?"

Abby turned around to face the doppelganger, who stared back at her with a lopsided smile. "What did you do?"

The doppelganger took a step back and spread her arms. "What did *I* do? This is all your doing, Abby. Your weakness will be the death of your friends."

Across the ice, Terra threw her axe at the seraph. Before it could connect, it was transformed into a swarm of wasps which promptly went after Terra.

Anabelle let out a roar of rage as her eyes flashed and she slipped into the Path of the Lost. She slammed her hands into the ice, ripped up a piece, and tossed it at the seraph.

The fallen angel vanished, instantly reappearing behind Anabelle. It hit her with a white energy blast.

Anabelle fell to her knees, smoking.

The doppelganger was behind Abby again, whispering into her ear. "You're going to watch them die because you can't help them. You are nothing. Everything you've ever accomplished has been because of someone else. The most you ever did was give yourself that AI—your crutch. You can't even think of yourself as separate from the AI consciousness. You're hardly even a person anymore. No personality. No skills. You're just meat, wishing it was something better than it is."

Abby spun and hit the doppelganger in the face. "Shut up!" Then she marched toward the seraph Anabelle and Terra were fighting.

Anabelle looked at Abby. "Thought you were never going to join us."

Abby gestured at Terra. "Give me one of those axes. I don't know how, but this asshole cut me off from Martin and my nanos."

Terra tossed Abby the axe. "And you need an axe to reestablish contact?"

"No, I need an axe to help you guys kill this thing."

Anabelle and Terra looked at each other. "You mean, without your powers?"

Abby was still staring at the seraph. "Yes. Without my powers."

Terra raised her axe. "Fuck, yeah! No-power Abby combat! I've been dying to see this."

The seraph floated toward the DGA agents, its wings spinning faster. Abby watched them. "Terra, could you attack that thing? I'm working on some math," she said.

Terra cracked her knuckles as her eyes burned white. "You know it." She slashed with her axe, tearing up the ice and sending a sheet of it at the seraph.

A blast of energy destroyed the ice as it approached the angel.

A telepathic voice blasted through Abby's head. "Humans, you are wasting your time. I fell from the heavens to hell, and even this place was not strong enough to reduce my powers. What do you think you will accomplish?"

Abby watched the spinning wings. "Belle, could you hit it with something too? I need a little more time."

Anabelle slammed her hands together and slowly pulled them apart, lightning crackling between her palms. She molded the lightning into a spear and let it fly.

The spinning wings connected with the lightning spear, shattering it and sending bolts in all directions.

Abby bit her lip as she thought. "Okay, that's it." She spread her legs for balance, taking a knife-throwing stance. She counted under her breath, then she threw the axe.

The axe sailed through the air.

Just as the sets of the seraph's wings lined up perfectly, the axe landed between them, wedging into place and keeping the wings from spinning.

The angel dropped from the sky.

Anabelle saw her chance and charged forward, as did Terra, both of them arriving at the seraph together. They jumped into the air and brought their fists down on the seraph's black nexus.

It exploded in a bright flash of light and dust. When the dust settled, the seraph was gone.

Abby looked down at her hands. She made a fist, and her nanobots flowed over her body. "That's better." She turned to Anabelle and Terra. "Thanks for not freaking out about me."

Terra shrugged as she walked over and picked up her axe. "Why would we? The three of us have kicked every ass we've seen. We're practically gods. We knew you'd be fine."

Anabelle nodded. "It was a very good throw."

The surface of the entire lake cracked, then exploded without warning.

The DGA agents tumbled through darkness for what seemed like an eternity before hitting the ground.

Terra stood up, rubbing her neck. "You know, I'm really getting tired of that happening."

Abby got to her feet and looked around. They were in an underground cavern. Candles hung from the walls, casting flickering shadows. "This must be the end. It looks spooky enough."

"Who dares to enter my sanctuary?" a voice called from the darkness.

Abby looked in the direction of the voice. A throne could barely be seen in the darkness, with a figure sitting on it. "Answer me!" the voice thundered.

Terra rested her hand on her axes and then got a giddy look on her face. She reached over her shoulder and unsheathed her broad sword. "It's the Dark Gate Angels, fuckface."

"You've got to be kidding me."

The figure stepped down off the throne and out of the shadows.

Grok stood before the DGA agents. "What are you three doing down here?"

Abby looked from Terra to Anabelle. "We could be asking the same thing."

CHAPTER NINETEEN

Anabelle stared at Grok from across the throne room. Even though an entire year had passed since she'd seen the orc, Anabelle still wanted to rip her face off.

She could probably do it now; her strength had continued to grow. But that wasn't why the Dark Gate Angels were down here, and feeding her personal vendetta wasn't going to help anyone. "Don't tell me you're the boss of hell now?"

Terra, who had her axe out, chimed in. "Yeah, what happened to the Devil? Isn't he supposed to be the one in charge down here?"

Grok approached the DGA agents and waved her hands. The lights on the wall grew brighter, but it wasn't all that happened. The walls blurred and then stretched outward until the room increased tenfold in size.

Terra jumped back in surprise when she saw the reality manipulation. "Whoa. You could not do that last time."

Grok did not look happy to see any of them, but she also didn't look like she was spoiling for a fight. "Only here. Comes with the territory of ruling the inner circles of hell. Unfortunately, it doesn't extend outward."

Anabelle pointed an accusatory finger at Grok. "Were you the one who sent those demons after us?"

Grok shook her head. She looked worn out. She had dark bags under her eyes, and the fierceness and intensity that had terrified Anabelle were gone. "No, those were demons or angels I had forgotten about. Hell has been going through a shift in management over the last year. Namely, our management."

Abby sighed as she looked around the cavernous room. "Don't tell us—"

The ceiling exploded, sending rock and magma flying, only to freeze in the air and separate from each other.

Rasputina floated through the hole.

The lich wore a gray cloak that stretched out and clung to the rocks and ceiling around her as if it had a mind of its own. Her skin was lively for a lich's although still as pale as death, but the rotting bits and exposed muscle had healed.

Her feet softly touched the floor as the ceiling reformed above them. "Hmm. We weren't expecting company. Did Myrddin make the ill-informed decision to send you after us?"

Grok rested a hand on Rasputina's shoulder. There was a familiarity between the two that Anabelle had never seen before. From their body language, you would assume they liked each other. "I don't think they came here for us. They were as surprised as I was."

Rasputina cast a quick glance at the DGA before turning around, her cloak sweeping behind her. "I did not want to deal with this today."

Grok followed Rasputina, leaving the DGA standing there as if they were intruding.

Terra followed their former-enemies-turned-tentative-allies. "You two the ones sending all the Dark Melody and weapons to humans?"

Grok looked over her shoulder. "Stop being stupid."

Terra halted in her tracks. She raised an eyebrow as she looked at Anabelle. "What the fuck is going on?"

Anabelle shrugged, still uncertain what to make of all this. "Might as well find out."

The DGA agents followed Rasputina and Grok farther into the room as it broke apart and reset itself, forming into a dimly lit living room, complete with furniture and bookcases.

Rasputina collapsed into a chair and pulled back her hood as she kneaded the bridge of her nose. Grok took a seat in the chair next to her.

Chairs appeared behind the DGA agents, and they sat down. Anabelle noticed they were much more comfortable than the chairs in Myrddin's study. "If you're not sending the Dark Melody, what are you doing here?"

Rasputina opened one eye, looked at Anabelle, and closed her eye again, then turned over on her side so she didn't have to look at anyone.

Grok leaned forward. "We've been hunting the Dark One."

Anabelle's heart stopped. "He's still alive?"

"Barely. He's alive in a way that he wasn't before. Rasputina could still feel him in the Netherverse. We hunted him down and confronted him when we finally found him. He was weak, weaker than I thought anything could be and still be breathing." She sighed heavily. "He was still too strong for us. Very strong, but not strong enough to kill us. That was when Rasputina found hell."

Rasputina was curled up in a ball, whimpering softly.

Grok rubbed the lich's back. "She fractured the bit of her soul that was left to break hell open. We've been slowly enlisting souls and demons into our army. It's been draining for her."

Abby looked concerned. "What's wrong with her?"

Grok didn't look up, still staring at Rasputina. "She broke her soul again. There's an even smaller fraction than before, and she's trying to hold onto it in this place. Staying sane in hell is hard. She's spending a lot of energy down here."

Anabelle sneered. "You almost sound like you care about her."

Grok helped Rasputina lean over and cradled the lich's head in her lap. "I do. She's going to go insane down here, but she won't leave."

"Why? Too much power to gain?"

Rasputina's eyes were vacant. "Because if I leave, I might become a monster again."

The lich's face went rigid and then softened quickly. She dried her tears and sat up, rubbing her face vigorously before clearing her throat. "There are moments when I'm lost. I don't want to be what I used to be. I'd rather be down here. Once we rid the universe of the Dark One, I'll be able to rest down here."

Grok nodded. "I'm going to stay with her. To keep her safe."

"By ruling hell?"

Grok shrugged, the glint of her teeth harkening back to her vicious nature. "I make no excuses for the person I am. I want hell to be ordered and safe for Rasputina. It's a win-win situation. I will keep Rasputina safe, and Myrddin won't have to worry about an uprising in hell."

Anabelle rested her forehead in her palm. "Honestly, I don't believe this."

Terra was leaning back in her chair, smiling. "I don't know, I think it's kind of sweet. You evil assholes are all reformed and everything. It's because of us, isn't it? You can admit it."

Grok tensed and looked away. "Shut up. You three are here on business, correct?"

"Yeah, Myrddin thought the Dark One might have been behind the influx of evil shit that's been leaking onto Earth since we opened it up to all the realms. Guess he was right. How have you guys been trying to fight the Dark One?"

Rasputina sat up straighter. She and Grok looked as if they were running on fumes. "There are other demon generals in hell. A good chunk of them serve the Dark One and have migrated to the Nether-verse. We've been doing what we can to sway them to our side. If they choose to stay with the Dark One, we kill them. We've been trying to thin the herd, but the Dark One is also trying to grow his ranks. We've caught wind of what he's attempting to do."

Abby spoke for the first time. "He's got a plan? He's not just trying to regain power?"

Grok shook her head. "He's angry. Before, the conquest was an ideological one. He doesn't care about that anymore. There's only one thing on his mind, revenge. From what we've gathered from former generals, he's planning on wiping the Nine Realms out of existence."

Anabelle scoffed. "There's no way he has that much power. To completely destroy all Nine Realms?"

Rasputina reached out, and a book flew over to her from the bookcase. "There are two ancient prophesies in hell, and they work in tandem with each other. One tells of a Dark One with a pale child who will unseat hell and drag the Nine Realms into it. It's obviously the Dark One."

Anabelle's curiosity was piqued. "And the second one?"

Rasputina looked up from the book. "It speaks of angels from the Nine Realms. They 'close all the doors and seal all the windows. The candles will be snuffed by drowning in air.' I think it's talking about you three."

Anabelle tossed her arms up as she stood. "What does that even mean? It doesn't make sense. More air would just feed a fire. Is it saying that we're going to help the Dark One?"

Abby raised her hand, cutting Anabelle off. "That's not true. A fire needs oxygen, yes, but if you overload it, like when you blow at a candle, it goes out. Maybe it means we need to give the Dark One too much of what he wants, or at least what he thinks he wants."

Terra sank down into her chair. "None of this makes any sense to me."

Abby stood and walked over to Rasputina. "Are there more prophecies? Maybe we could make sense out of it if we had more sources."

Rasputina nodded slowly. "There are, but it's a lot to read."

"I'll help. We need to figure this out soon. We've already sent what you said to Creon and Cire. Hopefully, they can help make sense out of this."

Rasputina stood, her legs shaking as she moved. "Let me show you."

Anabelle watched Abby and Rasputina go. She couldn't believe how ready Abby was to work with Grok and Rasputina again.

Terra's eyes flittered from Grok to Anabelle. "I'm assuming you two have some talking to do. I'll excuse myself." She got up. "You got an armory around here?"

Grok pointed at the hall on the left. "Knock yourself out."

Anabelle and Grok sat there, staring at each other. Finally, Anabelle spoke. "So, you suddenly have a heart now?"

"I've always had a heart. Its concerns simply aren't anyone's but mine."

"And you're going to spend eternity down here. With her?"

Grok looked at Rasputina, who was showing Abby her arcane tomes. "She gave a lot to keep me safe in the Netherverse. It is the least I can do to repay my debt. You would do the same for either of them."

Anabelle couldn't disagree.

Anabelle and Terra killed time while Abby went over the tomes with Rasputina. The elf was surprised she didn't seem to have a problem working closely with someone who had nearly removed her intestines. Apparently, Abby's professionalism far exceeded hers.

Her professionalism was being tested by being with Grok. The elf was determined to figure out how long she could sit across from her nemesis and not say a word.

Naturally, it was Terra who broke first. "So, what about these generals you've been gathering?"

Grok stopped picking her nails and looked up. "Interested in starting an army?"

"Well, I kinda have one already, but you could say I'm still interested."

"So, you and the shaman have managed to keep the twelve tribes together? That's more than I would have expected. That in itself is a victory."

Terra tried not to look too proud of herself. "I mean, we do have to put down a small insurrection every couple of weeks, but they've been slowing down recently."

Grok laughed as she leaned forward. "Only makes sense. What's the fun of being an orc if you can't start a rebellion every so often?"

It wasn't long before Grok and Terra were talking heatedly, comparing the strength of each other's armor. After an hour or two, Anabelle would have assumed they were friends.

Guess time heals all wounds, Anabelle thought.

Her comm pinged. It was Creon. "What's up?"

"We've got a problem. A really big problem."

CHAPTER TWENTY

Creon and Cire watched a holoscreen with an image of what looked like the sun projected on it. Their eyes were glued to the holo when Roy and Myrddin walked into the room.

Roy glanced at the screen, obviously unimpressed. "This is what you called us in here for?"

Cire nodded, not taking his eyes off the holoscreen. "When I saw it, I also did not think it was anything of merit. Your sun is hardly even hot, not compared to the orcs' sun, but this is abnormal."

Myrddin walked to the holoscreen to take a better look at it. "What exactly are we looking at, Creon?"

Creon swiped down on the screen, but nothing changed. He typed in a couple of commands. Still nothing. "This isn't the sun, but some other star, I think. Truth is, I don't know what it is," Creon said. "It appeared on the screen, and I have not been able to remove it, analyze it, or view anything else on this or any other terminal."

Roy leaned closer. "What's it doing?"

"So far, nothing. It's just been sitting here like it wants us to watch it."

Myrddin stroked his beard. "Hm. That is interesting."

"I think it's trying to communicate."

Roy let out an exasperated sigh as he found a chair to sit in. "You're saying this sun is trying to talk to us? That's rich."

Creon spun around in his chair. "We've both seen weirder things. A celestial body taking over my computer is one of the lower things on the list."

Myrddin stood behind Creon, watching the holoscreen. "There are always strange things to behold. Let's hope this is one that brings good tidings."

<hr>

Abby and Rasputina sat on the floor together, poring over books. She wasn't sure how long she'd been reading, but it didn't matter. She felt like a kid. That was the last time she could remember being this over-whelmed with things to read.

Rasputina did not disappoint with content either. The lich gave Abby book after book. At first, she seemed wary of what Abby could understand, but she was warming up to sharing the information.

Luckily, Martin was boosting Abby's cognitive abilities. Because of that, she was able to read at an insane rate and retain all of it. There was a specific folder in her mind for arcane knowledge now, as if it were a computer.

She felt a pang of insecurity, then remembered her fight with her doppelganger. She wasn't her nanobots or Martin. She was the person who created those two things to augment herself. She was a genius. It was a big difference.

Abby looked up from her book to watch the lich, who was lying on the ground, staring at the ceiling and muttering to herself.

Whatever losing part of her soul had entailed, the lich seemed much different from the last time Abby had seen her a year ago. Even if the lich's sanity hadn't improved—and it seemed like it had gotten worse—she didn't radiate malice or violence anymore.

Abby wouldn't have said it to Terra or Anabelle, but she thought Rasputina was pleasant to be around, if slightly unsettling. She'd almost forgotten that the lich had tried to disembowel her. Now that Abby had thought of it, she was determined not to dwell on it.

Rasputina looked at Abby. "When did you become interested in magic?"

Abby closed her book. She wasn't finding anything useful for the current situation, and she knew she could go on reading indefinitely. "Right before we got here. Cire was teaching us sigil magic. We hadn't really thought about it before. All anyone ever told us was that humans couldn't use magic."

Rasputina nodded slowly as she returned her attention to the ceiling. "Yes, that is the unfortunate state of humanity. But the shaman was right. There are ways around it, especially when there are so few of you left."

"What are you talking about?"

"How many Abbys did you watch die?"

The girl's heart wrenched. She hadn't thought about that in forever and had done everything in her power to keep from letting her mind drift to it.

During the battle with the Dark One, Abby had traveled between different alternate realities. She'd gone to absorb her counterparts' power, which had involved watching nearly all of them die in battles with Tesla.

A tear ran down the lich's face. "I did the same thing. Not as humanely as you. As variations of yourself dwindle, it increases your likelihood of everything. I wouldn't be surprised if you were much more magical than you give yourself credit for."

Abby bit her lip, not knowing what to say.

Rasputina sat up. Her eyes were softer than Abby had ever seen them before. "For what it's worth, I'm sorry. No one should ever watch themselves die. Not even once."

The lich summoned a book from the wall. "You should stick with the sigil work, and once you're comfortable with it, you should teach Terra as well. You'd both do well at it."

Abby took the book and opened it. "Thank you."

"Are you two done over there?" Anabelle shouted. "Being this bored is hell."

Abby grabbed a few books and walked over to Annabelle, Grok, and Terra. She dumped the books on the table in the middle of the three. "We've got a few ideas. As far as we can deduce, the Dark One needs to be drawing power from something if he's in as weak a state as Grok and Rasputina think he is. There's a reason he's stayed in the Netherverse instead of trying to flee."

Terra picked her nails with her axe blade. "That's easy. The Netherverse is the nexus for all nine of the realms. It's the easiest way to travel between them, so it probably gives him direct access to the places he's planning on going."

Anabelle and Abby stared at Terra, dumbstruck.

Terra shrugged. "What? Do you guys think I don't pay attention to what's going on?"

Abby laughed and shook her head. "You never seem like you care."

"Just because I don't coat all of my observations in five degrees of nerd, it doesn't mean I don't care. Besides, I look cool when I look like I don't care. But I'm assuming you have another reason you think the Dark One is still hiding out in the Netherverse."

Abby nodded as she opened one of her books. "It says here necromancers are capable of restoring their power through the use of souls. Some consume said souls, and others use them as batteries. Either way, that's how they get their energy. I wouldn't put it past the Dark One to have some kind of necromantic power."

Rasputina absentmindedly scratched the hole in her thigh. "He does. I know that for a fact. If there's a way he's keeping himself going, it's necromancy."

Anabelle looked at the book Abby was holding. "And? What options does that give us?"

Abby leaned over the table, her lips hovering close to the flame of the candle in front of her. "Like the prophecy says, we blow it out. Hell is full of souls. Not only souls but demons and fallen angels. We let them loose in the Netherverse and overload him."

"Or just turbocharge him."

Rasputina's glinted green. "Grok and I can control them. Many are our soldiers, and I am well enough versed in necromancy to keep their energies in check."

Anabelle jumped to her feet. "Great! Now, all we need to do is flood the Netherverse with souls and go end this once and for all."

All of the DGAs' comms pinged. "Ugh, this better be important."

Creon was on the line. "You know that problem I told you I'd get back to you about?"

"Yeah," Anabelle answered.

"It just got worse."

Creon, Cire, Myrddin, and Roy watched the holoscreen of the sun as solar flares ripped from its surface, stretching out through the blackness of space.

Blood tickled from their nostrils as the walls of the room vibrated, a low hum ringing in their skulls.

"Yeah," Creon said into his comm, "it's definitely worse."

A voice rumbled through the minds of everyone in the room.

"I will speak to the Dark One," it roared.

The solar flares on the holoscreen grew even wilder, stretching farther out as if they were hands grasping in the darkness.

Creon touched his finger to the blood trickling from his nose. "It's gotten so much worse."

PART II

The gates of hell shook, rocking Grok's throne room and cracking the walls down to the ground.

Anabelle, who was looking at her holoscreen, had to fight to keep from falling over. "What was that?"

Grok walked to the wall and ran her hand over it as if searching for whatever meaning could be found within its construct. From the expression on her face, she found no answers.

Creon's voice interrupted the surprised silence in the chamber. "Myrddin wants you guys back now. Something's happening. All hands on deck."

Terra checked her comm as well. "Sounds serious. Do you think it has anything to do with what we just felt?"

Abby nodded. "It must. I mean, a quake just shook hell. That hasn't happened in thousands of years."

Anabelle gave Abby a suspicious glance. "How do you know that?"

"Some of those books that Rasputina has are history books. Turns out hell's history has been meticulously recorded."

Anabelle stared at the ceiling of the throne room. "Is there an easy way to get out of here?"

Abby pulled a piece of chalk from her pouch and crouched, then started drawing elaborate sigils in the shape of a circle. When she was done, the sigils flashed bright red and a portal opened in the middle of the throne room. "This'll take you back to the restricted area and the portal we first took to get down here. We're going to stay with Grok and Rasputina. We have a feeling we're going to have to keep researching. Whatever is going on up there, it gives us a bad feeling."

Anabelle nodded as Terra came around the portal. "All right. Keep in contact. We'll let you know what we find out up there." She turned to Grok and Rasputina. "Guess we'll be in contact with you too."

The elf and the human walked through the portal that Abby had opened, vanishing instantly.

The transportation felt as if Anabelle had been hooked by her belly button. The ground rushed out from her, making her queasy enough to vomit before the feeling was suddenly gone and she was standing in the restricted area of the library with Terra. "Ugh. That's even worse than the Hadron Collider."

Terra, who was clutching her stomach, nodded somberly. "Travel between realms really needs to get more enjoyable. Otherwise, the tourism industry to hell will never pick up."

Anabelle chuckled. "Let's go figure out what's going on. Creon will probably be in his lab."

Anabelle and Terra left the library behind and made their way through the labyrinthine HQ, eventually descending into the science department. They walked through the glass hallways until they found Creon's lab.

Cire, Roy, and Myrddin were crowded around the gnome's holoscreen. They all seemed to be in a particularly bad mood.

Myrddin looked up as Terra and Anabelle walked into the room. "That hardly took any time. Glad to see you made it out of hell in one piece."

Anabelle walked up to the holoscreen to get a better look at what everyone was looking at. "What did you need us here for?"

Myrddin pointed at the image on the holoscreen. It looked like a sun, solar flares flashing hot off of its sides. "Initially, we called you concerning what is on the screen, but the situation has grown exponentially worse. Something similar to what we're looking at has appeared over New York. I need you, Terra, and Roy to investigate it."

The image on the screen made Anabelle's skin crawl, but she didn't know why. "Anything to do with this?"

"I have my suspicions. Report back on what you find out."

The New York skyline was blood-red, the clouds black and crackling with lightning.

The scene reminded Anabelle of the Netherverse. She'd never seen anything like this on Earth before.

Tumultuous winds buffeted the helicopter as they approached the city.

Roy, who was strapped into the back with Anabelle and Terra, was busy checking his comm. "We should be coming up on the anomaly in a few minutes."

Anabelle looked out the window, still concerned by the sky she saw. "You ever see anything like this, Terra?"

The Hand didn't seem to be bothered by the blood-red skyline. "I think I saw something like this in *Ghostbusters*."

"I meant in real life."

Terra laughed as she popped a piece of bubblegum into her mouth. "Nope, never. Looks kinda exciting, right? You think it has to do with the weapons that have been cropping up in New York?"

Roy undid his seatbelt and headed toward the back of the helicopter. "Doubt it. That was some small-time stuff, and most likely tied to the Dark One. Whatever we heard in the lab wanted to speak to him."

Anabelle's stomach swirled, and she felt pressure in the back of her head. A headache was coming on, and from the way her body felt, it would be a whopper.

She also felt something wet, warm, and sticky trickling down onto her lips—a nose bleed. She gingerly dabbed at the blood. When she looked at Terra, she saw that her nose was bleeding as well. "What's this all about?"

Terra wiped the blood off of her face. "Ugh. Gross."

Roy lowered the back door as the chopper rounded the last row of towering skyscrapers. "Jesus Christ. You two are going to want to see this."

Anabelle undid her belt and went over to check out what Roy was talking about.

A brightly burning sphere was hanging above the skyscrapers, blocking out the sun. The sphere was blood-red, and massive flares burst from its surface, the raw energy unleashing unbearable heat.

As Anabelle stared at the false sun, she felt an overwhelming dread crawling up from her stomach. Her nose started bleeding again, as did Terra's and Roy's.

Terra wiped her face. "That's straight-up anime shit."

A voice thundered in Anabelle's head, overpowering her thoughts. It vibrated loud enough to make her fall to her knees and grab her skull in pain.

"We will speak to the Dark One."

The voice disappeared and Anabelle looked around, noticing that Roy and Terra had fallen to their knees as well.

Anabelle grabbed the door handle of the copter, unsteadily making it back to her feet. "That thing can talk?"

Roy pulled up his comm. "It's exactly what showed up on Creon's holoscreen. Hold on, I need to get in touch with Myrddin."

As Roy walked to the front of the chopper, Anabelle and Terra stood together, watching the flaming ball in front of them.

It wasn't the Dark One.

It was something worse.

The whole world was watching the flaming ball that hung over the New York skyline. It seemed that all the inhabitants of New York had heard the sphere's incessant demand, and their heads vibrated with the sound as blood trickled from their noses.

"We will speak to the Dark One."

This event wasn't just in the human world. Similar reports were coming out of all Nine Realms.

Anabelle and Roy were in the war room with Myrddin, listening to him speak to the United Nations. Anabelle could hear the frustration in his voice as he encouraged the United States' representative not to panic.

The balding representative's frightened face took up the majority of the holoscreen. "How are we supposed to know these things won't start appearing all over the country? The people of New York are already having extreme reactions to whatever the hell that is. When we agreed to open up our world to all of this magic nonsense, you assured us we would be protected."

Myrddin rubbed the bridge of his nose as he sank into his seat. "And you will be. We are in the process of putting together a coalition to handle the recent—"

Anabelle stepped in front of the wizard. "This is why we need you to keep your shit together and keep giving us the information we need to keep you safe. All of us are trying to figure this out, and you are no exception. The more you work with us, the better we'll be able to do our job."

The representative looked taken aback by Anabelle's words. He cleared his throat and looked around as if the rest of the representatives in the room were watching him. "Uh, fine, we'll do what we can to cooperate."

"Good. Now, we have agents getting in touch with their offices. If you have any questions, speak to them. We have to figure out what to do about this thing. Goodbye."

Anabelle swiped the holoscreen away, and Myrddin nodded at her gratefully. "I'm getting far too old for this," he muttered. "Goddamn bureaucrats."

Roy stood beside Anabelle, brushing his hand against hers. "We're still waiting for reports from Terra and Cire. So far, we haven't been able to establish communication with the sphere. We can hear it, but it doesn't seem to be able to hear us. You thinking it might be alien? Or interdimensional? Maybe like that thing Boundless came across?"

Myrddin shook his head as he watched the holoscreen showing the sphere over New York. "Perhaps, but that doesn't explain why there are so many of them. None of this makes any sense yet, and it's only a matter of time until people start to panic. We have to find something to tell the public."

Anabelle didn't think they needed to be wasting time coddling the public about what was going on. That was valuable time they could spend trying to figure this thing out. "We don't even know if it's hostile. It could want to talk to the Dark One for the same reason we do—to destroy him."

Myrddin shrugged as he swiped up on his holoscreen. "That won't matter if we can't find a way to communicate with it."

Terra appeared on the holoscreen. She and Cire had been dispatched to the orc homeworld to manage the situation there.

"How is everything?" Myrddin asked.

Terra smiled and jerked her thumb over her shoulder at Cire. "Great. The orcs don't care much. They're kinda stoked to have another sun. Some of them are curious about whether or not we can kill it, but you know, nothing out of the ordinary."

Anabelle sighed; she wished humans would comport themselves as well. She realized that she was embarrassed by them the same way she would have been for a friend who had spilled wine on themselves. It was an interesting feeling.

Myrddin sat up, his ancient face sagging slightly and his blue magic-infused veins shining beneath his thin skin. "I'm glad to hear you don't have to do too much damage control. That's good. We've waited long enough. It's time to see if we can communicate with this thing again. Mobilize your forces. Prepare for engagement if it's necessary, but first and foremost, this is an attempt at conversation. No trigger-happy hero antics."

Terra flashed Myrddin a thumbs-up. "Gotcha. We'll keep in touch."

Myrddin closed the holoscreen and turned back to Roy and Anabelle. "Same thing goes for you two. Oh, and one more thing… Team Boundless will accompany you. We're going to use Alex's psychic abilities to try to make contact."

CHAPTER TWENTY-TWO

The orcs' flying squadron was mobilized at dawn.

Terra stood on the balcony of her room, overlooking the arena where she had battled Grok and suffered through the trials necessary to learn the Path of the Lost. She looked up at the flaming sphere that hung over the arena like a massive eye full of malice and hatred.

Even if the sphere wasn't evil, it sure as hell looked like it.

Hell, she thought as she remembered the battle in the Circle of Lust. Things here were a bit too similar to that dream for her liking.

She didn't want to think about how excited she had been to see her troops. It felt wrong. Lustful. She'd beaten the vision in hell, but it had revealed what she really desired in the core of her being.

Power.

Terra thought back to the first few days when she'd fought in the arena after she'd been abducted by the Dark One's orcs. It had been the first time she felt strong. In control.

Unbeatable.

Was it so wrong to love that feeling?

Cire walked out onto the balcony. He was dressed in his shabby fur cloak. "They're waiting for us."

Terra looked at the sphere. "What do you think it is?"

Cire craned his neck to follow Terra's gaze. "Honestly?"

"Honestly."

"Something dangerous."

The orcs were lined up throughout the arena, standing in front of their steeds, which were phoenixes. The giant birds looked like the most beautiful cranes Terra had ever seen, the smallest of them easily nine feet tall. Each possessed pale white wings that rested on the ground as if they were the train of a regal gown, but that was not what made them beautiful.

No, their true beauty sprang from the bright red plumage that looked like crowns made out of flames.

One of the orc generals approached Terra and Cire as they walked toward the giant birds. "We're prepared for the ride, and your orders have been stressed to the Fireflies. Nothing close to an attack until you call it."

Terra raised an eyebrow. "Fireflies?"

As soon as the word left her lips, the platoon of riders stamped their feet. Fireflies was the battalion's name.

Cire nodded. "We should check them over."

Terra led the way to the assembly of orcs. They looked more official than any other troops from the twelve tribes. They all wore a patch on their shoulder.

The Crest of the Phoenix.

A few of the Fireflies petted their steeds, running their hands through their elegant, sleek feathers.

Two phoenixes were saddled but had no orcs next to them.

Terra smiled widely when she saw the creatures, one of them clawing the dirt beneath its feet and craning its neck backward as it picked at its feathers. "Don't tell me that these are for us?"

The general of the Fireflies nodded. "Two of our best. You do know how to ride, don't you?"

Terra didn't answer. Instead, she walked over to the taller phoenix and scampered up its side, quickly fitting her feet into the stirrups. She retrieved the reins around the phoenix's neck and snapped them to urge the bird forward. Without hesitation, the phoenix spread its wings, flapping them. Within an instant, they lifted into the air as its wings burst into flames.

Hovering a few feet above the ground, Terra laughed loudly. "Seems easy enough to me."

Cire climbed onto his phoenix and coaxed it over to Terra. "Obviously, you are a natural. Are you ready?"

Terra stared at the fiery sphere. "Yeah, let's go see if we can get a couple of words with it."

She turned her phoenix around so she was facing the Fireflies. "Come on, boys, let's see those conversational skills at work!"

With that, they took off, the Fireflies whooping and hollering as they followed their chieftain to whatever hung in the sky.

Terra couldn't help but smile as she raced through the clouds. Even with the flaming sphere in front of her, she felt an ever-flowing amount of joy. These were her people. They'd accepted her. There wasn't anything wrong with that.

Closer now, Terra could see how large the sphere was.

It was hot, too.

Beads of sweat rolled down her body, yet somehow the heat was inviting, almost as if it were calling Terra to it. As if the fire itself was reaching out to her, inviting her to join it.

Then its voice rang in her head with such force it nearly knocked her off her phoenix. "We will speak with the Dark One."

Anabelle was on top of Roy's mech, flying over the skyline of New York, breathing in as much of the rushing air as she could. She'd never been on a run with Roy before—not like this at least. The only thing keeping her from being tossed into a free-fall was her mana, which was anchoring her to the steel of the mech.

The two of them were flanked by Alex Bound and her squad of dragonriders. Anabelle hadn't seen the group since the wedding. They looked battle-scarred, and Anabelle realized that it wasn't just the DGA tasked with policing the Nine Realms.

Roy's voice came through on Anabelle's ear comm. "How you doing out there?"

Anabelle let out an ecstatic "Woo-hoo" as she pumped her fist in the air. "I think I'm going to have to learn how to ride a dragon after this."

"Might not be a bad idea. You could always get one of these bad boys. Just as fast with twice the firepower and half the upkeep. You don't want to see what those dragonriders have to do to take care of their dragons."

Alex's voice came over the comm next. "It's not that much. Besides, you actually have a relationship. Can't have much of one with a flying bucket of bolts."

"Obviously, you've never owned a car," Roy countered.

The group headed toward the sphere, talking about the info that they had just received from the orc homeworld. At HQ, Creon was doing everything he could do to relay intel to them in real-time. Terra and her group had just gotten to their sphere. So far, the conversation was not going well.

Anabelle's head throbbed as her eyes fell on the burning sphere in the distance. She recognized the feeling as being similar to when the Dark One had spoken to her—a blunt-force attack on the inside of her skull. Whatever this thing was, she didn't like it.

Boundless moved to the front of the convoy, swooping close to the burning sphere. They spread out, ready for whatever was going to happen.

Roy came in after them, flying above the group. "Time to do your thing, Anabelle."

The elf cleared her throat and tried to train her eyes on the bright sphere of unearthly fire. In any other situation, she would have felt stupid trying to talk to a celestial body, but there was something about this one that made Anabelle feel like it was listening intently. "We want to talk. We heard you say you wanted to speak with the Dark One, but before that, we need to know what you want. Why are you here?"

The voice thundered through Anabelle's head, and it felt like it was stripping her brain down to the nerves. "We will speak with the Dark One."

"I know you want to speak with the Dark One, but first you have to answer a few questions."

"We will speak with the Dark One."

Anabelle hung her head, massaging her temples. The voice was giving her more than a headache. She was feeling sick to her stomach and light-headed. She hit her comm and connected to Creon. "Doesn't seem like the thing can understand me. Either that or it doesn't give a shit what I'm saying."

Creon replied, "Sounds like the same thing Terra is experiencing. Does it seem hostile to you?"

"I can't tell if it's hostility that's radiating from this thing or if that's just how it communicates."

Alex flew up to where Anabelle and Roy were. "Let me give it a shot. Maybe Chine and I can reach it telepathically."

Anabelle nodded.

Alex's eyes narrowed at the flaming sphere, then blood spurted from her nose in a torrent of red. She swayed to the side, as did Chine, his wings going limp as he crumpled and dropped out of the sky. Alex's dragon anchor disengaged, and her feet separated from her dragon as she fell.

Anabelle released the mana from her feet and jumped off Roy's mech, pulling her arms in tight to increase how aerodynamic she was. She zoomed toward Alex and wrapped her arms around the girl, holding her close.

The rest of Boundless swooped after Chine, and the dragons caught him.

Roy hit his thrusters and rocketed downward, flying under Anabelle. The elf exerted her mana to cushion her fall onto Roy's mech.

Anabelle laid Alex down as the mech stabilized.

Alex's eyes fluttered open. They were bloodshot and wild with fear. "What the..."

"You blacked out," Anabelle said. "As soon as you tried to speak to it. Did you see anything? Hear anything?"

Alex shook her head. "There was something, but it was confusing. It was...I don't know, like getting hit in the head with a baseball bat. Even talking to the Dark One didn't feel anything like that."

A flare tore loose from the sphere. As it exuded heat, it increased in size, pulsing as it radiated.

Anabelle watched as the sphere's body grew more liquid, looking to have been composed of liquid flame. "What is that thing?"

Abby's voice crackled through Anabelle's comm. "You won't believe what just showed up in hell."

Anabelle sighed as she helped Alex to her feet. "You know, I'm pretty sure I only need one guess."

CHAPTER TWENTY-THREE

The shape of hell had changed. Abby didn't know how to describe it to Anabelle in their brief exchange, but once she stepped outside of Grok's modest throne room, she could tell that its very fabric had been contorted to something more bizarre than it already was.

Grok had left Abby and Rasputina to carry out the first part of their plan, cutting the Netherverse off from souls to create a backlog that they would eventually use to flood it. She'd been gone for some time, leaving Abby and Rasputina to marvel at the deconstruction of hell.

In some ways, it was similar to the Netherverse, chunks of rock and platforms floating around as if they had never been introduced to the law of gravity, the difference being that the circles of hell were also loosed. They spun around each other like a gyroscope, the final circle of hell which Abby and Rasputina were on being the nexus.

The scientist watched as the circles slowly moved past overhead in alternating patterns. It reminded her of the seraph that she and the other DGA agents had fought.

Hell looked like a giant angel.

Above that infernal machine of an angel was the flaming sphere. "You ever see anything like that before?"

Rasputina had donned her cloak and pulled it tightly to her body. "Yes. A few times, but only in dreams. In between places when I was exploring multiverses, never in person. Never right in front of me."

"What are we supposed to do? Can we speak to it?"

Rasputina hobbled toward the sphere. Even though her body was younger than when Abby had first met her, the lich still occasionally moved like a broken creature. Perhaps she always would. "Who knows?" Rasputina wheezed. "No doubt they've already tried to speak with it on the surface. Or attack it."

Abby shook her head as she thought about what humans might do with an omen such as this. It didn't seem too far of a stretch for them to panic.

Panic led to mistakes.

Abby tapped her comm, patching herself through to Terra. "What's going on with your fireball?"

A holoscreen projected of Terra. "Nothing," she replied. "We've been here for a minute, and it just keeps repeating the same thing. Not much of a conversationalist."

Anabelle popped up on the holoscreen. "Same here. We've tried a couple different methods too. Obviously, talking. Signing. Even a couple of ancient magical forms of communication. We're getting nothing as well."

Abby returned her focus to the sphere. She heard a dull voice in the back of her head. It was quiet, as if she were hearing it from far away, but she could still make out the words. "We will speak to the Dark One."

The psychic communication must have been filtered through all the tech in her head. "You hear that?" she asked.

Rasputina nodded, her eyes never leaving the sphere. "Yes. Not as loudly as I believe I am supposed to, though. Being the ruler of hell gives me certain privileges."

Abby raised an eyebrow at the lich. "Ruler? I thought we were in Grok's throne room."

"Grok and I have different forms of rulership. There are things I am trying to build here. You may see them eventually."

One of the rings passed overhead and Abby could see demons scuttling across its surface, craning their necks to get a look at the fiery sphere floating in the nexus of the spinning circles.

Suddenly, the sphere surged, growing nearly twice as large as sunspots grew over its surface and energy flashed from its sides, slashing at the sky as if it were a whip. "What was that about?" Abby wondered aloud.

Anabelle appeared on the holoscreen again. "We sort of have a situation here!"

Anabelle watched in horror as a squadron of fighter jets sped toward her and the dragonriders. She hadn't received information that any of the human armed forces had been given clearance to interact with the sphere. She also couldn't make out any insignia or markings on the planes.

Roy pulled his dragon mech around to get a better look at the approaching aircraft. "Who the fuck approved this?"

"Wait, you didn't know about this either?"

"No. Myrddin made it very clear that we were going to be handling this. Probably the States. Figures that they wouldn't be able to just sit back and let us take care of it. Guess someone wants to attempt to play the hero. I'm going to try and call them off."

Anabelle could hear Roy patching into the planes' communication. "This is Roy from the Integration Initiative. You are to stand down. Do not engage with the bogey. Stand down."

A voice came over the comm. "No can do. We have our orders, you have yours. It's about time for humans to start taking care of themselves instead of relying on all you magical people. That's probably what got us into this mess."

The comm went dead, and the planes flew past the dragonriders.

"Fucking idiots," Alex muttered over the comm. "We're not going to be able to save their asses."

Anabelle looked after the planes heading toward the sphere. "Maybe we won't have to save them. They might have a better chance than we do."

As the planes closed in, the sphere grew larger again. Energy flares lashed out from the surface of the sphere as they neared. One of the flashes tore straight through the closest plane, shearing it in half, and the rest vaporized.

Roy cried out as he and the dragonriders backed up. "That's not going to look good for any of us. Fucking idiots."

Alex flew over to Roy's side. "What'd I tell you?"

Anabelle was annoyed with Alex's tone of voice. "You don't have to sound so smug about it. Those people just died serving—"

"They died listening to stupid orders."

Anabelle could hear the pain in Alex's voice. Obviously, whatever had happened to have turned the dragonriders and Myrddin against her still weighed on her. "You're right, it was a stupid order."

They were quiet, the unspoken tension between Roy and Alex returning. Luckily, Abby started talking. "Did something happen on your end?"

Anabelle tapped her comm to bring Abby's face up. "Yeah, that thing just wiped out six fighter jets. And nearly doubled in size, too."

"Did it attack them with flares?"

"Yeah, how did you know?"

"Terra, what happened to your sphere?"

Terra popped up on the holoscreen. "Ours grew too. Just about double. And it let out a bunch of solar flares as well."

Abby furrowed her brow. "We're not looking at different things, we're all looking at the same one."

Anabelle scoffed loudly, although she was aware that it might not make sense to doubt Abby, even if what she was proposing sounded insane. Still, it was difficult to wrap her head around it. "What do you mean, the same one? We can't all be seeing the same thing."

Abby nodded as she crossed her arms. "It's the same. Everyone is reporting the same phenomena at the same time. Sounds unlikely, but I think that's why we can't talk to it."

Terra rubbed her shaven head. "Not following here."

Abby turned away from her screen for a second. "Okay, give us some time to figure this out, and don't get too close to that thing. If anything changes, get in touch with us ASAP, all right?"

Anabelle and Terra agreed, and Terra and Abby disappeared from the holoscreen.

"Guess we're on guard duty," Anabelle muttered.

Abby sat in front of the sphere, her legs crossed as she tried to think of a solution. Her theory still seemed too far out there, even for her.

How could the same object appear over multiple planets at the same time?

It stretched her understanding of the planes of reality. Each realm being interlaced over each other was one thing. If the sphere had appeared over the different geographic locations that lined up with the alternate realm versions of New York, that would have been one thing.

But the sphere had appeared in wildly different places that only seemed to have superficial things in common, the primary one being that they were heavily populated.

Not counting hell.

Hell was different. There, the sphere appeared above the throne room.

Abby looked at Rasputina, who was also watching the sphere. "You said you've seen something like this before. What was it?"

Rasputina scratched her face, tearing a little bit of flesh off. "Never could say. Out there, nothing really makes sense. I thought it was an angel or something. Maybe a planet caught in a time loop. But you've been in between the realms. You know how nonsensical it is."

Abby knew exactly what Rasputina was talking about. When she had slipped between the realms and space-time, she'd seen some weird stuff. She still didn't know what to make of all of it. "Maybe we're only getting a slice of it. You know, like fourth-dimensional interaction limited because we're three dimensional. That could be why..."

An idea flashed in Abby's mind, and she pulled Martin up on her comm. "Hey, those drone pods ever get installed in the other realms?"

When the integration process first started, Abby had thought it would be a good idea to work on a central communication hub. She'd built a handful of drones infused with her nanobots, those grown within her body, to use as communication ports between the realms, rather than routing communications through the older systems.

It had been a novel concept, but Creon had already been working on a system with the elvish and gnomish governments. Abby's project was a lower priority. As far as she knew, the drones were going to be installed as a backup plan in case anything happened to the main communication network.

Creon slid over to his computer and started looking. "Yep, they were installed a couple of months ago. They're running in sleep mode."

"Can you do me a favor? Broadcast my signal to all the drones."

Creon gave her a puzzled look. "Wait, you mean *all* of them? That's all nine realms, Abby."

"Yeah. We need to make a construct first, though. Give us...twenty minutes or so?"

"All right. Message me when you're ready."

Rasputina watched Abby as the young woman closed her eyes.

Abby concentrated on increasing her nanobot count as quickly as possible. She could feel them multiplying in her veins and the nanobot consciousness growing stronger. It felt almost like another person was in her skull, watching her actions. She hated the feeling, even though she knew the consciousness had nothing but her best interests in mind. It still felt eerie.

Martin appeared in Abby's peripherals. "Finally got something cooking?"

"Yeah. Could you reduce our bodily functions to sleep mode? Only cognitive after we finish constructing."

"Will do."

Abby knew when she'd reached her threshold. Her body could deal with more nanobots than a year before, but she still had her limits. She pressed her hands to the ground and nanobots flowed out of her pores, stacking on top of each other to build a satellite that pointed in the fiery sphere's direction. Then she sat down and leaned against the satellite.

A cord snaked out of the satellite and wrapped around her neck. She pulled her hair up in a bun, exposing a hole in the back of her neck. She grabbed the plug and jacked herself into the satellite.

Abby's body disappeared, or at least she lost feeling in it. Everything was dark. Nine lights shone in the darkness: her drones. She reached out to them with her mind.

The signal passed through the realms, boosted by Creon at HQ.

Suddenly Abby could see again. At first it was difficult to make sense of, but she started to get the hang of it. She was seeing through the eyes of all nine drones simultaneously.

Martin whistled. "Okay, that's pretty impressive."

Abby pinpointed the location of the spheres on all the planets, then she focused with everything she had and teleported the drones directly under their planet's sphere.

The voice from the sphere rumbled, Abby's drones picked it up and digitized it back to her.

"We will speak to the Dark One."

Abby's signal was broadcast by all the drones at the same time. "Hello. We are Abby. We want to talk."

There was silence, then the voice thundered.

"Abby. We will speak to the Dark One, but first, we will speak to you."

CHAPTER TWENTY-FOUR

The voice spoke, and Abby heard. It spoke not only in words but in visions, images that felt like they were stitched together from eternities that had come into existence and been snuffed out within moments. The visions reverberated through Abby's mind as she grappled with them, trying to make sense of what was before her.

It was like drowning. Every statement from the sphere hit Abby like a crushing wave. She wanted to pull away, to end all communication, but she knew that if she just held on a little longer, maybe, just maybe, it would all start to make sense.

Just a little longer...

"We will speak with the Dark One, Abby."

The inside of Abby's skull was vibrating. No, that couldn't be right. She couldn't feel the rest of her body. She was somewhere in cyberspace, a frequency free of physical form, yet there was throbbing pain somewhere, and she knew it was inside her.

Abby suddenly felt very grounded in her body. She opened her eyes. She'd been disconnected from the satellite. When she tried to stand, she found that she couldn't move her legs.

Rasputina was beside her. "Are you okay?"

Abby rubbed her face, and her hand was smeared with blood. "What happened?"

"You were talking to yourself, rambling as if you were having a conversation. Then you started convulsing and screaming. That was when I unplugged you."

Abby looked at the sphere. Or the Omniverse. She wasn't sure how she knew that was what it was called, but she did. "We need to see Myrddin."

Rasputina held out her hand and the reality around Abby split open, forming a portal.

Abby looked at Rasputina, confused. As far as Abby knew, getting in and out of hell was extremely complicated. "How are you doing that?"

Rasputina picked Abby up. "I've had a long time to be in hell. More than enough time to learn the necessary things."

The lich stepped into the portal, instantly stepping out on the other side.

The two of them were at HQ in the medical department. They were standing in front of an elvish nurse whose jaw dropped the moment he saw Abby and Rasputina.

Rasputina placed Abby on a bed and headed back toward the portal. "Wouldn't be good for me to stay here any longer. Keep in touch." She stepped through the portal and disappeared.

Abby sighed and rested her head on the soft pillow. "Could you find Myrddin and the rest of the DGA? We need to talk to them."

The nurse rushed out of the room as Abby tried to recall what had happened between her and the Omniverse.

Martin appeared before Abby. "Hey, how you holding up?"

"Terrible. Head is all fuzzy. What happened?"

Martin's paperclip body straightened out and then curled into a slinky. "Still trying to figure that out too. What I do know is that you interfaced with that thing. Nearly shorted out your whole system. It was some kind of direct link. I recorded what you were saying when it made sense, but for a lot of the time, you were dreaming. A lot of REM. I also recorded an imprint of what you were seeing."

"You can record our dreams?"

Martin shrugged. "Don't worry, I don't make a habit of it."

"Go ahead and play it back to me."

Martin disappeared. "You might want to grab some popcorn for this one. It's a doozy."

Abby closed her eyes and watched her dream while she listened to the recording of her mutterings. "Oh," she murmured, "this isn't good."

Roy, Anabelle, Terra, and Myrddin gathered in Abby's room in the med-bay.

Abby was already sitting up, surrounded by a host of holoscreens.

Terra took a seat on the bed. "When did you get back from hell?"

Abby looked up at the clock. "An hour or two ago. Rasputina brought me back."

Myrddin's eyes narrowed. "She was here? How?"

"She opened a portal and brought me back after I spoke with the Omniverse."

Anabelle moved over near Terra so she could get a better look at the holoscreens. "Hmmph. You leave a lich alone in the Netherverse, and she'll figure out how to become stronger. At least she seems like she doesn't want to start any problems with us. And what's this about an Omniverse?"

"That's what is hanging in the skies. It's called the Omniverse."

Abby activated the holoscreens. Her dreams were displayed on them while her voiceover played. There was a thundering noise in the background of the audio. "Have you heard about this, Myrddin?"

The wizard shook his head slowly.

In Abby's dream, she was standing before the Omniverse. The world was shifting around her. She could see the Netherverse. Suddenly, it flipped upside down, and there was another plane beneath it.

"You know that question we had about where good souls go? Apparently, they go to the Omniverse. We don't know the criteria for what a good soul is, not that we knew about the bad ones, but we do know they're sent to the Omniverse. By now, it should be apparent that the Omniverse wants to speak to the Dark One, but I guess we did something to upset it at some point. Sending Grok to turn off the valve to mess with the way that souls are housed apparently rubbed the Omniverse the wrong way."

Abby posted the audio so everyone could hear her voice.

"The disruption of souls must be stopped," Abby's recorded voice said in a trancelike tone. "Restore the nature of the Netherverse. The souls will flood until this has been fixed. I will speak with the Dark One. The time for judgment is near. The dead will walk the land of the living. Restore the valve."

The holoscreens went dead.

Anabelle looked from Abby to Terra. "How did Grok say she was going to turn the valve off?"

Abby shrugged. "She didn't say, but she didn't leave until after the Omniverse arrived. This thing not only has something close to omnipresence but also omniscience. It knew what Grok was going to do before it was done."

"We're going to have to talk to it again. Figure out what it wants with the Dark One and what it's talking about with the whole valve thing. Probably should get in touch with Grok too."

Everyone in the room's comms went off at the same time. Creon's frantic voice came through. "Guys, we have a problem."

Terra chuckled. "Let me guess. Little sun meteors with axe-wielding polar bears are attacking the Nine Realms?"

Creon didn't laugh; his face was deadly serious. "The dead. They're…they're rising. Everywhere. All over the world. And they're attacking people."

Intel was gathered as quickly as possible. The DGA waited in the war room as reports flooded in. Creon and Abby were trying to get as many video recordings as possible. It wasn't hard. From the looks of it, Earth was experiencing a full-on zombie apocalypse.

The first reports indicated that the undead were digging their way out of their graves in cemeteries throughout the city, their rotten bodies hardly holding together as they shambled after citizens. These zombies weren't the fast kind from *28 Days Later*. They were more the slow, ineffective ones from the *Walking Dead*.

People could outrun them and hide in their homes, but that was a temporary solution at best. Soon enough, people would run out of food and supplies.

Roy came into the war room, talking into his comm. He hung up. "We're mobilizing all of our forces now. Looks like the only big problem spots we have are in large urban cities. We're hitting New York, LA, Chicago, and DC in the States first. Myrddin has our overseas departments gearing up to handle their shit."

Roy's comm went off again, and he looked down at it. "Shit, it's not just Earth."

Abby had assumed that, but she hadn't heard anything from the other realms. She figured that wherever the Omniverse was, there were going to be zombies.

Terra was leaning back in her chair. "So, what are we doing? A zombie apocalypse should be pretty easy to deal with, right?"

Roy pointed at the holoscreen in the middle of the room as it projected a map of New York. "This is where we're getting hit the hardest. From what we can gather, the zombies are heading toward the Omniverse, tearing up anything in their way. We're going to need you to fight your way through that and get back in touch with the Omniverse."

Anabelle regarded the map. "Can't you just drop us off at the Omniverse? You know, since you have a flying mechanical dragon and all?"

Roy shook his head grimly. "I'm afraid not. There's some kind of disturbance coming from it. Can't get anything mechanical close to it. My guess is that it's more responsible for this zombie bullshit than any of you were with what you were doing in hell. Either way, you're going to have to haul ass to it while we try to clean this up. If we can."

Abby unplugged from cyberspace and gave her full attention to what was going on in the room. "What do you mean, if?"

"There are millions of corpses coming out of the ground all over the world, and we have no idea when it's going to stop. We're already spread thin, and we haven't even started yet. Now we're getting reports that we're going to have to organize efforts in the other realms as well? This is a shit show that just got tossed at us."

Terra chuckled as she stood up. "Myrddin didn't have a zombie contingency plan?"

Roy headed out the room, motioning for the DGA to follow him. "No, we had a plan. It just wasn't meant for all nine realms at the same time. We didn't have you three as part of it either."

They headed toward the hangar where Alex Bound and the rest of Boundless were waiting.

Alex saluted the DGA when she saw them. "We'll be getting you as close to the Omniverse as possible." She pointed to a table that had three dragon anchors on it. "You'll have to use those. They're makeshift versions of what we have. They won't do much but keep you from falling off."

Abby walked over to Alex and gave her a quick hug. "We haven't seen you in forever. How have you been?"

An unsteady smile crossed Alex's face. "Keeping out of trouble. And you?"

"Just saving the world again."

Alex laughed, and it sounded genuine. "Yeah, never gets old, right?" She turned to face Roy. "Anything else we need to know?"

Roy shook his head, looking grim and uncertain. "Nope. Get in and out fast. Stay off the ground. Make sure to keep your eyes peeled for anything else. Good luck."

CHAPTER TWENTY-FIVE

The orc capital had been erected in the year since the Dark One was expelled from the Nine Realms. It was sprawling and beautiful, a city that was both a testament to the orcs' nomadic way of life and their vision for a united future. In that single city, one could see practicality and artistry woven together in a simple execution, built the way only orcs could.

The capital was considered a jewel in the Nine Realms, proof that the orcs were a species capable of great growth and wisdom.

Now that city was on fire, homes smoking, the air filled with ash and the screams and cries of children.

The dead had arrived.

In less than ten hours, the capital had been overrun. A child had noticed the shuffling zombies first. He had called his mother out in excitement. There were strangers at the gates.

The excitement turned to terror as the orc zombies rushed the capital, moving faster than their decaying limbs should have allowed, leaping through the air, tearing into the soft flesh of the living. Seemed orc zombies behaved differently than human ones.

The orcs retreated, not knowing what else to do. They holed

themselves up in their homes and boarded up the windows. That did not stop the zombies.

Cire had sent a small squadron of soldiers into the town but had heard nothing back from them. It was nightfall now—no more waiting.

He stood before the squad of Fireflies, who were flanked by the council's private army. There was no time for speeches. Cire climbed onto his phoenix and took off into the night, the Fireflies rising into the air after him as the ground troops marched.

When Cire arrived at the town, he noticed that it was silent. He could see the dead in the streets, frozen as if they had been turned to stone.

Cire brought his phoenix around toward the front entrance of the town and leaped off, landing softly on the ground. He raised his staff as the zombies near him raised their heads, sniffing their air and curling their lips.

The shaman wasted no time. He rushed the first zombie and slammed his staff into its head, cracking its skull, then called forth vines and roots from the ground to swallow the remaining zombies near him.

The rest of the squad swooped through the streets. Their phoenixes blasted bolts of fire from their wings that burned through the zombies, who screamed in rage before they were reduced to ashes. The ground forces swarmed into the town, and the three groups made their way toward the center.

Cire stopped once they got to the town square and looked on in horror.

The streets were filled with fresh corpses. Zombies were hunched over them, cracking chests open, drawing out intestines and lungs, gorging themselves on the bodies of the townspeople.

Cire let out a scream of rage as he drew his sword and ran into the fray. The zombies' ears perked up, and they left the entrails they were slavering over and raced toward Cire and the orc squad behind him.

On the outskirts of the town, hundreds of hands burst out of the ground, rotting and grasping for lives to snuff out.

Sarah and Kravis were riding across the Black Plains on hoverbikes, heading toward a gnomish settlement on the outskirts. They'd been overwhelmed with reports of dead gnomes rising from their graves and marching into villages.

They only seemed to have one desire: to dine on the flesh of the living.

A comm message pinged for Sarah. It was Blackwell. "We've put up a perimeter around the area, but they're still coming for us. There are too many of them. We're going to be overrun soon."

Sarah could see the settlement in the distance. "We're going to be there in a moment."

"Are you bringing reinforcements?"

"There are some following us, but not many."

Blackwell looked over his shoulder and fired. "That's better than none."

Sarah gauged the distance. She was close enough. She turned to Kravis, who was riding beside her. "There's a horde up ahead. I'm going to try and break through. Meet you at the front?"

Kravis pulled his helmet up. "Be safe."

"May the stars always guide you home."

"May they always guide you as well."

Sarah put her hoverbike on autopilot and punched in the coordinates of the resistance up ahead. Then she leaped off of her bike and opened her chakra gates one heavenly portal after the other until she came to the ninth. She took a deep breath and took the plunge.

A burst of energy flew from her and her body vibrated with power, her eyes burning bright white. She leaned forward, concentrating on where she needed to go. Then she shot toward that location at nearly the speed of sound.

Sarah slammed into the wall of zombies who were stacking on top of each other to climb over the wall that protected the settlement.

The sounds of cracking bones were accompanied by an explosion of zombie body parts.

Sarah spun through the air, roundhouse-kicking the zombies in front of her to carve out space for herself. Then she punched the air in front of her, sending out a concussive blast that tore through the zombies who hadn't given her their attention yet.

She leaped up, her lungs filling with fire, and let loose a bolt that scorched through the remainder of the zombies trying to climb the gate.

Her body returned to normal as she walked past the mayhem she'd created and climbed the gate.

Kravis came around the other side as a general handed Sarah a plasma rifle. "Glad to see you made it," the general said.

After Sarah situated herself on top of the gate, she and Kravis looked out at the plains. They could see thousands of eyes watching them from the dark.

Sarah aimed down the sights of her rifle and fired, taking off one of the zombies' heads. "This is going to be a long night."

Boundless and Roy were starting their descent into New York.

Terra wished she could have enjoyed her ride on the back of a dragon, but she was too tense. Cire was fighting on the orc world without her. Even though she knew the right place for her was with the DGA, she couldn't help but worry about him.

Not that he couldn't take care of himself. He was one hell of a warrior.

Below, the streets were pulsing with zombies. Many of them were still moving toward the Omniverse sphere. The rest were hunched over dead bodies. Terra didn't want to think about what they were doing, but she'd seen enough zombie movies to know.

Alex's voice crackled over the comm. "We're going to make a quick dive and free you up some space with our breath weapons. You guys ready?"

Terra flashed a thumbs-up.

The dragons shot toward the ground, launching fire, ice, and ether fire attacks at the streets. They burned away a solid chunk of zombies before Anabelle, Terra, and Abby leaped off of the dragons' backs.

As Abby landed, she launched a thin, precise laser, spun in a circle, and cleared the area even more.

The zombies slowly took notice.

Anabelle pointed at the Omniverse about four blocks away. "Okay, we move hard, and we move fast. The army is right behind us, so if you see anyone still alive, get them out of the way for the boys in green to pick 'em up. And you keep moving forward."

Terra glanced at the pavement beneath her feet, which was slick with blood and intestines. She doubted they were going to find anyone still alive.

Anabelle let out at a scream as her body filled with energy and she slipped into the Path of the Lost. Terra did the same and drew her axes.

Abby stood behind them. They were going to move in front of Abby to let her conserve her energy until they got to the Omniverse.

Terra slashed at the zombies in front of her, cutting them down like paper dolls as Anabelle broke to the left diagonally, burning through the zombies with her fire.

A zombie came rushing in, moving faster than Terra had anticipated. It hit her in the side, tackling her as more zombies flanked her, threatening to overrun her.

Terra hadn't been expecting them to be this strong. She rolled back onto her feet and slashed outward with her axe, taking off the zombie's head before throwing her axe into the next one. Then she leaped onto the small group in front of her and took care of the rest of them with her hands.

Anabelle fell back a little and threw up a wall of fire. She kicked it and sent it cascading over the zombies.

There was more space now, and the DGA agents moved forward.

As they continued to cut their way through the zombies, Abby put up two plasma walls, one on each side of them, to keep zombies from coming in from the sides.

It was messy, gruesome business and slow going, slicing through the wall of meat that had been built up as the zombies headed toward the Omniverse.

Terra wondered what it was about the Omniverse that attracted them. What was the point of bringing the dead back to life like this, just to have them gather under the sphere? It didn't seem like much of a plan.

The DGA was getting closer to the Omniverse, close enough to feel the effect it was having on the world it was watching. Terra's head was swimming, and it was getting difficult to focus on what was in front of her. Luckily it was just a horde of mostly mindless zombies. All she had to keep doing was punching, cutting, and slashing.

She fought in a daze as she tried to ignore the blood gushing down the front of her face.

Finally, they were close enough to stop. Anabelle and Terra cleared a perimeter as Abby got set up beneath the Omniverse, constructing a satellite while she linked up with the rest of her drones across the other realms.

Anabelle cast a protective shield around them so they wouldn't have to worry about zombies during the conversation.

Terra watched Abby work. "Kinda gnarly that she can do that, huh?"

Anabelle nodded. "Yeah. Good thing she's not evil or anything. Goddess, I hate to think about what she'd be capable of doing if she turned on us."

Abby looked over and smiled. "Don't even worry about it. Wouldn't ever happen. Who wants to come with me?"

Anabelle jerked her thumb at Terra. "I'll watch the barrier. You two go for it."

Terra walked over to Abby, who held out her hand. There was a headphone bud in it. Terra took it and popped it in.

All of a sudden, Terra was floating in front of the Omniverse. "The Dark One. Where is he?"

Abby's voice thundered nearly as loud as the Omniverse's. "We don't talk until you stop this nonsense. You need us, and you're not getting our help until we know our people are going to be safe."

The Omniverse trembled and flexed. "Souls are in disproportion. Netherverse corrupted. Hell corrupted. Omniverse will stabilize. Understand?"

Abby held out her hand, and it looked as if she were trying to keep something back. "What do you need from us?"

"Stabilize souls. The reckoning is halted. You have twelve moons. On the thirteenth moon, the reckoning will recommence. Disproportions will be rectified. Balance will be restored."

Then Terra was back on the ground, gasping for breath as Anabelle stood over her and Abby, trying to help them both to their feet.

Anabelle took down her mana shield. "I don't know what you guys did, but it worked. Check 'em out."

Terra glanced at the zombies. They were as stiff as statues. She turned to Abby. "You make much sense of that?"

Abby was rubbing her temples. "Some of it. We got the gist of it, and at least now we know we have a time limit."

CHAPTER TWENTY-SIX

The cleanup crew in New York was massive. Most of the city had been shut down, and those in the ten or so blocks near the Omniverse were moved to temporary housing that Myrddin set up. In true Myrddin fashion, it was something to behold…lavish apartment buildings floating in the sky.

The apartments wouldn't last forever, but they were good enough for now.

After the city was closed off, the practical work began. Quarantine zones were set up around the largest concentrations of zombies. Abby wanted to study them, but only after a two-hour argument with Myrddin did she get permission to go down to the ground.

Terra accompanied her after she verified that Cire was okay and didn't need any help.

The zombies in the other realms had frozen as well. The large-scale attack had been put on hold, but nobody was sure for how long. All the DGA had to go off of was the cryptic message Abby had received from the Omniverse.

Martin was in the process of decoding the dream imagery that had been downloaded into Abby's brain. Until that was done, she and Terra were momentarily left to their own devices.

The two of them wandered through Queens, which had the fewest zombies.

The streets were devoid of life. The air smelled of rancid flesh, the decomposing bodies of those who hadn't been lucky enough to make it to a shelter. The smell of the zombies was nearly unbearable. Terra had to wear a filtration mask that Abby rigged up for her.

It was eerie, standing in a city that had bustled with life, but was now full of frozen flesh-eating corpses whose expressionless eyes stared into the distance.

Every now and then, one of them blinked or moved ever so slightly. That was the worst part, in Terra's opinion. The zombies weren't completely frozen, just inactive.

Abby led the way, occasionally stopping to scan one of the zombies.

Terra shivered. "What are you looking for?"

Abby put away her scanner and walked around one of the zombies, watching it closely. "I want to know how they were resurrected. The ghouls the Dark One and Tesla brought back were a combination of tech and the Dark Melody, and we know necromancy leaves a magical aura around whatever is resurrected or composed."

Terra kicked a rock at one of the zombies, and it blasted through its abdomen, not that it seemed to notice. "What difference does it make how they were brought back?"

"Back-up plan in case they come back before we're ready to deal with it. After we did enough studies on the Dark Melody, Creon was able to synthesize a compound to break down the ghouls if anyone tried to do something like that again. It would be better to have the science department work on a solution while we try to figure out what the Omniverse was talking about. Cover all our bases."

Terra nodded approvingly. "You know, you've gotten pretty good at this."

Abby smiled appreciatively. "Thank you. You have, as well. Helping run an entire government on another world? That's kind of big."

Terra waved away the compliment. "Nah. Cire does most of the boring stuff. I just punch people when I need to. Got any better understanding of what the Omniverse was trying to tell us?"

Abby shook her head before turning her scanner back on. "No, still waiting to hear from Martin." She sighed as she walked past the ripped-open corpse of an old woman. "You know, we thought stuff like this was over. We beat the Dark One. Even with that, so many innocent people died yesterday."

Terra rested her hand on Abby's shoulder. "You know this isn't our fault, right?"

"Yes, we know. Doesn't make us feel any better.."

A large shadow fell over Abby and Terra. An ether dragon was flying above them.

Alex, on Chine, swooped down and landed in front of Terra and Abby. "Find anything interesting?"

Abby and Terra informed Alex of just how little they'd found. The rider crossed her arms and clicked her tongue. "That's unfortunate. Everyone's hoping that big brain will be able to figure this out. Well, I have to get back to the edge of the quarantine zone. The dragonriders are helping transport the zombies to a holding pen. See you guys later."

Terra raised her eyebrow at Abby. "Anything I should know about there?"

Abby chuckled as she went back to scanning. "Hardly. We're friends. Kept in touch with each other after we first met and while she was on the run. One of the only people I could talk to about what was going on who was my age, and we could swap tech notes."

Martin projected from Abby's and Terra's comms. "You guys able to wrap up what you're doing? Anabelle wants to get together and figure out where you're going from here."

Abby checked her scanner. "Looks like we've got enough. Thank God this isn't like a zombie video game. Scanning for a dozen variants would be such a hassle. Let's head back to HQ."

Abby and Terra knocked on Anabelle's door and waited for it to open.

The elf slid the door open. She was dressed in sweatpants and had three beers in her hands. She passed one to Terra and another to Abby. "Come on in."

Abby looked around the studio. The carpets on the floor were insanely detailed, reminding her of Eastern Orthodox iconography. "Why aren't we meeting in the War Room?"

Anabelle flopped onto her couch. "Myrddin and Roy are busy, so I don't see the point being cooped up in that uncomfortable room. This room is a little easier to relax in, don't you think? "

Terra and Abby exchanged glances. "Anabelle? Relaxed?" Terra asked. "Did someone kidnap our Anabelle and replace her with a good clone?"

Anabelle tossed a pillow at Terra. "Fuck off. I figured...I don't know, this is our first big real mission in a while, and it's starting to feel like it's going to all be on us. There's way too much going on to wait around for Myrddin and Roy to plan this."

Abby cracked her beer open and sat on the floor, folding one leg over the other. "What are you thinking?"

Anabelle smiled. "Resources are spread extremely thin as it is. The whole integration thing has been a double-edged sword. One hand, everyone's in contact with each other. On the other, there are so many channels to go through and people you need to get authorization from. Besides, we know what's going on better than anyone since we're on the ground level. So, what do we have, Abby?"

The girl tapped the side of her head. "We just received the information on my chat with the Omniverse from Martin a few minutes ago. Working on processing it right now."

Terra raised her arms and said in a robotic voice, "Computing possible situations for viable combat. Analysis complete. Anabelle is freaking everyone out by not being uptight."

Abby laughed while the elf scowled from the couch. "I bring you to this beautiful room and give you the finest cheap beer I could hunt down, and you insult me? On my couch?" Anabelle mock-gasped.

Terra chugged her beer. "What can I say? I'm a savage. You have any more?"

Anabelle pointed to the fridge. "You have to get it yourself. So, while we wait, what was hell like after Terra and I left?"

Abby scrunched her face as she thought. "It was weird, to be honest. Rasputina...she seems so different. Not like the person we knew a year ago."

Anabelle bit her lip as she nodded. "Yeah, I didn't want to admit it, but I thought the same thing. Both of them. Nothing like when we left them in the Netherverse."

"Maybe people can change, even if they were as bad as those two. Anyway, there's no reason for us to think they're involved with this."

Terra came back with her beer and jumped on the couch. "Besides the fact that Grok was doing something with the gates to hell, you mean?"

Anabelle nodded. "Yeah, but they're trying to help, and from what I gathered, they weren't far enough along to warrant...that!" She pointed out the window at the Omniverse.

Terra shrugged. "Whatever. I don't trust them." She turned to Abby. "You done with that processing?"

Abby made a cartoony ping sound. "Is that what you were waiting for?"

"It would have been cooler if it came through the speakers."

Abby smirked.

"Computation complete," Abby's voice said through the speakers in Anabelle's room.

She projected a holoscreen from her wrist. "This is everything the Omniverse was trying to say and some things we picked up from running deductive analysis with Martin."

Terra hung her head. "Jesus, when you're not joking, you sound much freakier."

Abby didn't listen and continued speaking. "The Omniverse is composed of a material similar to the Dark Melody. Not quite the same, but they are built of similar compounds. That means this might be an actual manifestation of the Omniverse, not an avatar or something."

Anabelle studied the holoscreen. "What does it want?"

"It repeated multiple times that it wanted some kind of balance to the souls between it and the Netherverse, but Martin compiled a bunch of information based on what was being said by the Omniverse that I couldn't understand because of how we were communicating. This'll work for now, but we're going to have to figure out how to actually talk to the thing."

The screen changed to what looked like a series of mathematical equations.

Anabelle turned to Abby. "You're going to have to explain those."

Abby swiped through the holoscreen. "Those are a list of demands. For the most part, they're pretty much the same, only slightly different. Apparently, it all boils down to the Omniverse wants us to bring it the Dark One. It knows the Dark One is still in the Netherverse, and it's holding our realms for ransom until it gets him."

Terra stretched out on the couch, throwing her legs on top of Anabelle's. "What does it want with the Dark One?"

Abby shook her head as she closed down the holoscreen. "Didn't say, and we can't deduce why, other than it has something to do with the Netherverse and a balance of souls."

Terra drained the last of her beer and sighed. "And how are we going to do that?"

Anabelle leaned forward, cupping her hands together and staring into the distance. "Grok and Rasputina. They've been raising an army to find the Dark One. The two of them have to know where he's hiding, or at least have an idea of where we can start looking. I guess we gotta get back into hell."

CHAPTER TWENTY-SEVEN

HQ was buzzing with bodies. No one stayed in the same space for longer than five minutes. The sheer amount of effort that HQ was having to put in to plan around nine different realms was astounding.

Creon had been glued to his holoscreen for what felt like three or four days straight. He still wasn't sure if it had even been a day.

He was on his seventh cup of coffee, and all of the information on the screen looked like nonsense. "Gods be damned," he muttered as he reached over to the conjuring pad next to his pad and summoned another cup of coffee.

Cire walked into the lab, carrying two plates of food. "How's it going?"

"Dismally. But I'm happy to have the company."

Creon was being honest. He'd grown used to having Abby in the lab with him. Someone to bounce ideas off of was always appreciated, and Abby had the added benefit of being able to improve on them. Martin was nice to work with, but the AI's smart-aleck attitude made conversations difficult at times. Cire was proving to be a solid stand-in. Even if the orc didn't understand everything Creon said, he had enough curiosity to probe each idea.

Creon pointed at the holoscreen. "I've been trying to break down the composition of the Omniverse based on the information Abby provided, but I'm not getting anywhere. As far as I can tell, it is composed of something entirely different from anything we have in the nine realms. Which doesn't help me at all."

"What about the zombies?"

Creon looked away from the holoscreen and pushed up his glasses. "That is supposed to be your department, isn't it?"

Cire took a seat across from Creon. "Still, I'd like to see if you found anything out."

The gnome shook his head as he sighed. "No, nothing. I can't seem to find a link between the Omniverse and its ability to raise the dead."

"It could be a combination of things we don't know," a voice said from the hallway.

Sarah walked into the lab, holding a cup of coffee. She looked as ragged as Creon did, hours of sleep deprivation hanging heavily under her eyes.

Creon jumped when he saw her. "They brought you in too, huh?" He looked at Cire. "Guess they want all the heavy-hitters in one place to solve this."

Sarah walked past Creon and took a seat behind Cire. "It's all over my head at the moment. Zombies are being stored, which I'm assuming they are across all of the realms. There isn't anything to do. I figured I could maybe do something useful over here, but I showed up, and the DGA is already gone. I guess I'm just looking for someone to bother."

Cire grinned sheepishly at Sarah. "To be honest, I don't think I'm doing much other than that at the moment as well."

"Shouldn't you be with the orcs?"

Cire laughed. "Unlike the rest of the nine realms, the orcs are handling things quite differently. We haven't penned up any of the zombies. We've gone through and taken care of the problem. Dead bodies burn easily enough."

Creon gasped and looked at Cire with an open mouth. "Are you saying—"

"We do not believe in desecrating the dead. If you didn't leave a mangled corpse, you weren't living, so there is no way to desecrate our dead."

Creon tried not to look horrified as Sarah laughed. "All of our lives would be much easier if we were taking the same route," she said. "Also, concerning this whole Omniverse, have you thought that it might be magical?"

Creon nodded as he leaned back in his chair. "Crossed my mind. Or maybe a combination of tech and magic. But the more I look at it, the harder it is to figure this all out. It's proving difficult to pinpoint how it resurrected the dead."

"You know, this isn't really my thing, but..." Sarah's voice trailed off.

Creon turned around in his chair, obviously exasperated. "Whatever you have, I'm more than happy to hear it."

"During my training, I heard many stories of balance, stories that were taken very seriously by the monks who taught me but aren't widely known throughout the nine realms. Mostly because they were human ideas, but there are philosophies that speak about the innate balance in existence. There is a dark side and a light side, a yin and a yang. They are linked together, and to create an unbalance on one side would naturally tip the other. Hence the state of chaos we're experiencing now."

Cire stared at Sarah, his eyes cold and stony. "Are you talking about *Star Wars*?"

Sarah burst out laughing. "How do you even know about that?"

"Terra has been acquainting me with human cinema. She says it is a quality I lack as 'boyfriend material.' It has been entertaining."

Sarah shook her head. "I'm not talking about *Star Wars*, but the movies were definitely lifted from a tradition passed down in human stories. Maybe the Omniverse is trying to restore a universal balance, and when you look at the scope of things, if it's for the sake of the universe, it doesn't really matter how it gets us to listen to that message."

Creon snapped his fingers. "You know, I've never even thought of this before, but...maybe the humans do have a grasp on this. Martin, are you available?"

Martin popped up on the holoscreen. "What do you want?"

"Cross-reference everything we know about the Omniverse with all of our databases on celestial bodies and communication. Learning how to talk to this thing should be our first priority."

Martin yawned. "Why didn't you ask that before? Here you go."

Martin's findings came up on the screen.

Creon rubbed his hands together. "Great. This might be exactly what we've been looking for."

Anabelle, Terra, and Abby stepped through the portal Abby opened into Grok's throne room. "Do you think it's going to be hard to find her?" Terra whispered.

The dark halls were instantly illuminated by hundreds of candles.

Grok sat on her throne, staring at the DGA agents as if they were roaches. "I was wondering how long it would take for you three to come back here."

Anabelle didn't want to waste time with pleasantries. "I'm assuming you've had a problem with zombies over the last few hours."

Grok stood, and her throne vanished as the hallway contorted and stretched farther back. "Not zombies, but yes. Hell has its own version of the undead. And as for having a problem..." She shook her head. "I would have considered it a problem if we'd handled it the same way you did up top."

Terra leaned over to Abby. "Probably did the same thing we did," she said as she mimed slicing her head off.

Anabelle approached Grok. "The Nine Realms have a problem. You and Rasputina might be the solution. That thing hanging in the sky wants the Dark One, and it's prepared to wreck all nine of the realms to get him."

Grok crossed her arms and sneered. "How is this my problem?

This is the land of the damned. A couple thousand zombies aren't something we're worried about. What do you have to offer us?"

Anabelle wracked her mind for an answer. "You know what, we don't have anything. Absolutely nothing. All I can do is ask you for help because we need it, and I think you might be able to provide it."

It was hard to read Grok's face. There was no emotion on it. Finally, she answered. "We both want the same thing—the end of the Dark One. If that's all the Omniverse wants, I'd be more than happy to help. But we're going to need Rasputina for this."

Abby scanned the throne room. "She isn't here?"

Grok headed past her throne. "The new order in hell isn't as simple as it may have seemed when you first got here. I take care of the circles and the lesser demons. Rasputina has been working on something much more complicated."

The DGA agents followed Grok as she walked down the length of the hall, the walls eventually opening up to a balcony that looked out over a sprawling vista of rocky canyons and bare valleys. In the distance was a beam of light, shooting up to an infinite sky.

Grok pointed at the beam of light. "That's where Rasputina is. She's been building a city for our new order. Curbing the demons under her heel. It's a never-ending struggle, but we're building down here."

Anabelle stared at Grok, uncertain of what to believe. It was difficult to imagine Grok and Rasputina doing anything other than trying to create an army for their own selfish purposes. But it seemed as if Grok was more than willing to share their resources.

The orc straddled the rail of the balcony, preparing to jump down into the darkness below. "Rasputina is meeting with the various old generals of hell, the lords of death, right now, trying to rally our final assault on the Dark One. If you want to add your strength to our forces, I'd be honored."

Terra and Abby looked at Anabelle, who took a deep breath before answering, "We'd be honored to fight by your side."

CHAPTER TWENTY-EIGHT

G rok jumped, but instead of falling, she floated to the ground beneath.

Anabelle followed, using her magic to slow her descent. On the ground, she turned to Grok and said, "When did you get magical powers?"

Grok didn't turn to face Anabelle. Instead, she stared grimly ahead. "A perk of being friends with Rasputina. Unfortunately, it only works in the circles of hell. Once we leave my domain, we will be on equal ground. I'd like to take this time to remind you to pull your own weight while we are out there."

Ahead, a sliver of light could be seen.

Terra scoffed good-naturedly. "What do you mean, 'pull our own weight?' All of us can walk the Path of the Lost, and Abby is built out of pure intensity."

Grok shook her head as she raised the flashlight she'd brought higher. "Just as I thought. Did you think the Path of the Lost was as strong as you could get?"

Anabelle didn't answer, but that was exactly what she'd thought. She still couldn't imagine anyone being stronger than Grok had been when they had fought. It was still hard for her to wrap her mind around how strong she and Terra had gotten.

Terra spoke in the absence of anyone else. "Dude, we wreck everyone we come across. We haven't fought anyone we couldn't take once we take the Path."

"Why don't you use it during every fight?"

Anabelle knew the answer, but she wasn't sure if Terra had put it together yet, or if she'd even noticed. The Path of the Lost was exhausting. Anabelle hadn't noticed it when she'd been pushing her body a year ago. She wasn't sure if it was the adrenaline of the fights or something else, but once she had reached the Path, her usual strength had been amplified. That was the other reason she only traveled the Path when it was necessary.

Terra's answer was quite different. "Because if I do that every time, I'll never have a good fight."

Grok laughed as they came to the end of the hall, which was on a cliff that looked out over a vast red valley covered in scraggly dead trees. "Spoken like a true orc warrior. Well, let me explain this to you since Anabelle hasn't. You're naturally stronger once you access the Path of the Lost for the first time, but that isn't the limit. Just like any of the other Paths, you can continue to get stronger, but it's up to you. You have to push yourself. Fight stronger enemies. Search out tests. Otherwise, you're just coasting."

Grok leaped off of the cliff's lip, and the DGA followed.

Terra hit the ground hard and turned to face Grok. "Are you saying you could take us now?"

Grok chuckled, smiling slightly. "Down here, even the weaker demons might give you trouble."

Terra was already stretching her arms. "Fuck that. You and me, right now, baby. Let's see if your fists can keep up with your mouth."

Anabelle sighed, but she couldn't deny she was interested to see if Grok was talking out her ass or really believed she was stronger than Terra and her, particularly Terra. Anabelle didn't like to admit it, but Terra was unstoppable if she was really pushed. The fight in the circle of hell had been a reminder of that.

Abby walked over to Anabelle and crossed her arms. "Do you really think this is the best use of our time?"

Anabelle watched Grok, wishing she could sense her energy. *What if she is right? If Grok is that much stronger than we are, it could prove to be a problem later.*

"Assuming Grok doesn't betray us," the elf answered.

Abby shook her head. "If Grok and Rasputina have been building an army, they could have attacked already. HQ isn't exactly weak, but our efforts have spread us thin. That would have been the time to strike."

"Or when three of HQ's best are down in hell."

Abby nodded as she scratched her head. "Good point. Might as well watch."

Terra and Grok were circling each other. "Ready to show me what you got?" Terra asked.

Grok nodded. "Come at me with everything you have."

Terra flexed, her eyes burning white. She launched herself forward with her arm pulled back, ready to strike.

Grok lifted her hand as Terra's fist came down, catching it in her palm.

Terra's eyes widened as Grok slapped away her attack.

Grok hopped on one foot, hanging in the air for a moment before kicking Terra in the face.

The Hand went flying.

Grok turned to look at Anabelle and grinned. Then she was gone, moving faster than the elf could see—just like the first time they'd fought.

Grok appeared in front of Terra and cracked her across the face again, driving her to the ground.

Terra's head bounced after it connected.

Grok's eyes flashed white and the air pulsed around her. She slammed her fist into the ground, and the earth exploded.

Once the dust settled, Terra rolled over and opened her eyes.

The ground was split next to her head as if it had been hit by an earthquake.

Terra sat up, rubbing her jaw. "What the fuck? How did you do that? I gave that everything I had."

Grok leaned over and helped Terra up. "I know. I could feel it."

"And you...you didn't even take the Path. I could tell."

Anabelle could as well. She and Abby approached Grok and Terra. "You could take us both, couldn't you?"

Grok shrugged as she looked toward the horizon. "Probably all three, which means you all need to be training more instead of coasting on your past victories. Today is going to be the first step in that."

Anabelle nodded as she followed Grok. Even if she didn't want to admit it, the orc had a point. She had achieved a level of strength that Anabelle now knew was possible.

Abby had caught up with Grok. "What are we expecting?"

She pointed into the distance. "There is a wildland of demons out there. Nothing like you experienced in the circle, so like I said, try to keep up."

They descended into the wilds of hell, a place vastly different from the defined circles above. This was the true hell. Anabelle knew the difference as soon as she started walking. Her body was heavy, as were her lungs. The heat was beyond the physical. She felt it in her bones, searing into her mind.

Abby wiped sweat off her forehead as the four of them climbed up a canyon's wall. "What's the deal with this place? Why is it so different from the circles?"

It figured that Abby would be the one to ask about the technicalities of this section of hell. Anabelle knew it was different, and that was all she needed to know.

Grok hoisted herself over the lip of the wall. "We tried to figure it out for a while, but Rasputina just came back with more questions than answers. Hell has a similar makeup to the Netherverse. It isn't a physical realm, more like a place made up of psychic energy that has found a way to imitate a physical realm. Rasputina couldn't understand why it would want to do that, but it *can* be manipulated. It takes a large amount of energy, though."

Anabelle looked ahead at a forest that was not unlike the one they had seen in the circle of violence but much denser. "Are you implying that someone created the circles?"

Grok nodded, her eyes grimly following Anabelle's line of sight. "That's exactly what I'm saying. I created the throne room where you found me. It...lacks the imagination and structure of what Rasputina is capable of, but it was a creation. When I leave, it barely exists."

They stood at the foot of the forest. Anabelle could hear screams coming from within. "What's this place?"

Grok shrugged as Terra and Abby caught up to her and Anabelle. "Depends on the time of day. Nothing here is constant unless someone is forcing it to be. This might be a forest full of demons right now, and in an hour, it could be an ocean full of demons."

"How do you know there are demons?"

Grok reached out and snapped one of the branches. Blood dripped from the tree. "That's what causes the terrain to change—the combined egos of the demons. It's not a conscious effort. Many of the demons here are no more sentient than an animal after living in the chaos for too long. The same thing that happens if you're in the Netherverse for extended periods of time. But you'll see for yourself. Remember, fight with everything you have. These things aren't people. They won't show you any mercy."

The forest was dark, any light blocked by the trees' thick branches. Anabelle was surprised she didn't feel the same measure of dread that she had in the circles of hell. She started to wonder if those negative feelings were a creation like the rest of the circles.

A loud, mournful wail soared through the air. It was echoed by others.

Abby winced at the sound. "Ugh, it sounds like they're in pain."

Grok stopped walking for a second, listening to the screams. "Everything is in pain in this part of hell."

Soon they came to the source of the wailing. The forest floor was littered with the naked bodies of humans. Their chests had been split open and their entrails flung about. Dozens of six-eyed birds pecked at the gore covering the ground.

Terra covered her mouth as she tried to avoid vomiting. Anabelle almost had to do the same, the smell was so overpowering. "What the hell did this?"

Grok pointed at the tree branches.

A hairy creature the size of a large man was crouched in the shadows of the branches. It had a dozen visible eyes crammed into its face, and the hair across its body looked to be covered with mud.

The creature leaped down into the scarce light. As soon as it was in front of them, its back split open, forcing a mound of sickly, pulsing, fleshy material up from the wound. Its head slanted to the side as the bottom of its face began to run like wet paint.

The creature let out a pained moan as it scuttered forward, its fingers splitting down the middle to show razor blades.

Grok took a fighting stance. "A lesser demon. Manageable. Stay on your toes, and let's end this fast before it gets worse."

The demon bounded toward Abby.

Grok leaped in front of it and grabbed it, the razorblades cutting into her hands. She managed to twist the demon midair, using its momentum to slam it into the ground.

Terra pulled out an axe and lobbed it at the demon, but the monster was shockingly fast. It got to its feet in time to catch the axe in its mouth and crush it between its jaws. Terra's eyes narrowed as she gritted her teeth. "I liked that axe. A lot."

She ran at the demon, shoulders lowered, ready to tackle it. The demon's legs cracked, the joints popping, shooting it up a few feet as if it were on stilts. Its jaws stretched open to reveal a tongue that reached the floor. The demon's tongue snapped toward Terra, wrapping around her waist and then slamming her into a tree.

As she crumpled to the ground, Abby swooped in and peppered the demon with plasma blasts. They didn't seem to affect it since it whirled and slashed her with its tongue.

Flames covered Anabelle's body a second before its tongue hit her, then she dissolved into smoke and reformed behind the demon. She grabbed its back legs and pulled hard, causing the creature to fall onto its face.

Once it was down, Terra slugged it, putting everything she had into the punch and cracking its face.

Abby flew overhead, charged her body with kinetic energy, and slammed into it.

Before the demon could get back to its feet, Anabelle's blazing fist slashed through the demon's neck, severing its head.

Anabelle and Terra were both breathing heavily. Abby was covered in a thin sheen of sweat. Grok, on the other hand, was leaning against a tree, looking as if she was thoroughly enjoying the show.

Terra hunched over, catching her breath. "What gives? We killed a dozen demons up top and didn't have a problem with them. Well, not like this."

Grok clicked her tongue as she walked forward. "The demons from the circles aren't nearly as powerful as those down here. That's why they use illusions and temptations. They're like spiders trying to catch you in their webs. The demons down here are tigers."

Terra looked at Anabelle, exasperated. "I know I was talking about wanting a challenge earlier, but this is ridiculous."

Anabelle turned to Grok and swallowed her pride. "Okay, seriously. No bullshit. Do you think we can make it through here without ending up dead?"

Grok gave that devious grin. "I think it's possible, but that depends on you three. We can take the quickest path to Rasputina, but it's going to be the hardest. If you survive, you'll feel the results instantly. But it will be very difficult."

The DGA agents looked at one another. Anabelle wasn't sure what the rest of them were thinking, but she knew her answer. "Well," she started, "we were looking for something—"

Simultaneously, the other two agents interrupted, "Harder."

Grok's smile softened a little. It almost looked pleasant. "Good. That's what I was hoping you'd say."

CHAPTER TWENTY-NINE

The middle of the day was Sarah's favorite time to meditate. It had always bothered her teachers. She'd stay up all night working on her practical skills, then sleep in far past scheduled morning meditations and chores, only to wake up around noon and meditate for three or four hours. Her teachers had tried to break Sarah of the habit, but her will was too strong. Eventually, they let her be.

The heat from the Omniverse was powerful, and she dripped thick beads of sweat as she sat underneath it. She was on Middang3ard, having left Kravis on the gnomish homeworld to deal with the technicalities of caging the zombies that had risen all over the planet. At first, like all the other realms, the gnomes had assumed that the outbreak was small, but as the days passed, they'd found that the dead walked throughout the whole world. All of the burial mounds and cemeteries were empty.

As far as Sarah was concerned, that was a problem the gnomes needed to deal with themselves. Same for the humans or any other race. The care of the dead was a cultural thing, not to be taken lightly or trifled with. She knew watching over the dead of her own planet was not going to be easy, or a task she would have taken lightly. That was for others to worry about. She was going to try to figure out what she could about the Omniverse.

Sarah had been there for three hours already. She could feel the weight of the Omniverse on her shoulders, as if it was trickling down her body like molten lead.

There was a presence in there that she knew she could reach; all she had to do was push. Clear herself of everything. Cease to exist. It would take time, but it was possible.

Another hour passed, and blood dripped from Sarah's nose in a rhythmic pattern that counted down the seconds.

Then, without warning, she felt something open within her. It was as if her throat had been slit, an outpouring of her very life. She gasped but did not know why. It wasn't a physical sensation.

She knew the words for it before she realized what it was.

The Path of Pain.

Sarah looked at the Omniverse above her, wondering where those words had come from. She hadn't thought them. They seemed to have come from something outside of her.

When she stood, the world swayed, and she nearly toppled over.

Whatever this new Path was, she had to inform Cire and Creon instantly. It was the key to reaching the Omniverse. She hoped they could help her understand.

"I don't understand why you think these guys are such a big deal."

Terra was speaking about the demons that lay before them in the flatlands of hell. There were thousands of them, but the demons ahead didn't look any more terrifying than the last. In fact, they looked relatively harmless. Simple humanoids, nearly transparent and completely black, as if they were shadows separated from their bodies.

Grok, Terra, and Anabelle were also watching the shades shuffle and amble through the flatlands. They did not look to be trying to go anywhere. There wasn't anything of interest. Only red emptiness and dust swirling about with no discernable wind to command its movements.

Anabelle knelt and picked up a handful of red dirt. "Terra's right. Other than the numbers, they are nothing, and Terra and I have blown through this number of soldiers before."

Terra cleared her throat. "Abby has too."

Anabelle smiled apologetically. "I know. I didn't mean Abby couldn't, but her power isn't in question. She beat the shit out of both of us."

Abby, who was still staring at the shades, shrugged. "Still, we could probably stand to get stronger."

Grok chuckled softly. "Good to hear that you have a warrior's spirit as well. And trust me, these shades are some of the most pathetic hell has to offer. They don't even try to cloak themselves in false identities. They're beyond that. They've suffered here forever and live only to enact violence. The only reason that they don't attack each other is that they've grown bored with that specific kind of torture. They want something fresh, namely us."

Terra pulled out her remaining axe. "Uh, Abby, could you help me out?"

Abby held out her hand and constructed an axe from nanobots. She handed it to Terra.

Terra flipped the axe up and smiled. "Perfect balance. Thanks. So, now what? We just keep carving our way to Rasputina? Sounds easy enough."

Grok smiled as she nodded. "I think you might want to take a better look at their numbers."

Terra strained her eyes. She didn't know why but she hadn't noticed the clouds hanging low, nearly touching the ground, ahead of the shades. The closer she looked, the more it became obvious that they weren't clouds. "Wait, are those shades too?"

Grok tightened her belt. "They'll come in waves. The weaker demons stay on the outside. The red shades are stronger. Once we move past those, we're stepping into the elementals, the most powerful of these kinds of demons. They've abandoned the shackles of natural form. They don't try to be perceived by the eye; they simply exist, constantly changing and adapting. What we will face down there in the last wave of shades will be difficult to anticipate."

Terra turned her attention back to the waves of shades. "What do you mean?"

Grok was silent for a moment. "Don't let up, not until we're on the other side of that valley, no matter what you see. Don't let anyone out of your sight. That's all I can say. The Valley of Demons is different every time. Are you ready?"

No one answered, and Terra was ashamed of what she was feeling.

Excitement. Pure, unadulterated excitement.

Before Terra could say anything, Anabelle spoke up. "Yeah. I am."

"Me too," Abby said.

Terra reached down to touch her toes, stretching her muscles. "Yeah. Let's do this."

Grok flexed and her eyes flashed, energy pouring from her body. She dashed into the valley.

The Dark Gate Angels sped after her.

Grok threw her body through the air and landed in the thick of the shades. She unsheathed a sword from her back and slashed through one as another's arms exploded open, thousands of hands reaching out for her. She stepped to the side, slashing through shade's arm as she leaned in and punched it. Its head cracked open, and dust flew into the air.

Anabelle's eyes widened with surprise as she pushed herself to keep up with Grok. She could still hardly keep track of the orc's movements. All she could make out were the dozens of shades tossed into the air as Grok made her way through the horde.

"She makes our run look like amateur hour," Abby remarked.

Anabelle looked at the girl. "Didn't think you were one for competition."

Abby shrugged. "She's pretty impressive."

Anabelle was coming to the edge of the horde. She took a deep breath and slipped into the Path of the Lost, then filled her arm with mana and punched a shade. As a follow-up, she sent a blast of pure mana through the horde.

It was the most mana she'd ever put into a punch. The exertion almost made her dizzy, which was troubling since the horde was already regrouping and Grok was still a good way ahead.

Terra cleaved the heads off three shades and then stomped, causing a shockwave that knocked a few more off their feet. Then she bounded forward and landed on a shade, crushing it.

Abby's body charged with kinetic energy and she blasted forward with her thrusters, connecting with a shade and sending out a ripple effect. She grabbed one of the shades that had been thrown into the air, swung around, and tossed it, clearing a narrow path.

Anabelle could see that both Abby and Terra were giving it everything that they had. She wondered if they would be able to make it through the horde before they burned out. They would have to watch each other's backs because Grok didn't seem interested in that, regardless of what she'd said.

The elf let out a blast of fire to make space and leaped forward to catch up with Terra and Abby.

A shade grabbed Anabelle by the hair and pulled back, yanking her off her feet and slamming her into the ground.

Terra turned around, threw her axe into the shade's chest, and then jumped back to grab Anabelle's wrist and toss her into the air.

Electricity crackled from the elf's body as she dive-bombed the horde, sending dozens of bodies flying.

Like before, Anabelle had tried to force every ounce of mana from her body. She could feel her skin burning from her energy, but she wasn't going to stop.

As soon as she got to her feet, she sprang forward as fast as she could, straining against the limitations of her body. She hit a shade and tore straight through it as three more dog-piled her.

Plasma blasts cut through the shades as Abby caught up with Anabelle.

Five shades behind Abby melted into one and then swirled around as if they were made of liquid, forming a tidal wave filled with screaming faces and outstretched hands, that crashed on Abby, sweeping her away.

Terra, who was next to Anabelle, clasped the elf's hand and spun in a circle, slinging her around. She built momentum before releasing her, sending the elf straight into the tidal wave.

Anabelle grabbed Abby as she came out the other side and the two of them skidded across the ground, ripping through any shades in their way. Anabelle tried hard not to lose her footing.

There was no time or room for strategy. All Anabelle had was brute force, so she was going to have to make it work. In the distance, she could still see Grok's warpath.

Anabelle let out another discharge of mana to give herself space, then took a step forward and fell to one knee, coughing blood.

The physical exertion was starting to take its toll.

A shade stomped Anabelle in the face as another climbed onto her back.

Instinctively, Anabelle let fire cover her skin, reducing the shades to ashes. She continued on.

The three Dark Gate Angels battled their way through the horde, pushing themselves to the limits, their bodies screaming in agony as they struggled to catch up with Grok.

Anabelle couldn't even imagine what the next wave was going to be like. This was already shaping up to be the hardest fight of her life. "We're not losing her!" Anabelle shouted.

Terra slammed her skull into a shade's. "Speak for yourself. I don't know if I can keep this up."

Abby blasted her plasma cannon, the energy output significantly lower than before. "We're fading."

Anabelle reached down deep, farther than she'd ever had to before. "We're doing this!"

A wave of mana shot out of her, shredding hundreds of shades and leaving a smoking hole that the DGA agents stood in.

Anabelle grabbed Terra by the collar and pointed at Grok. "We're not fading. We're strong enough to get through this."

Terra nodded and bounded after Grok.

Anabelle turned to look at Abby, who was hunched over, breathing heavily. She rested her hand on the girl's shoulder. "Come on. We need to keep moving."

CHAPTER THIRTY

Sarah stormed into Creon's laboratory.

The gnome was passed out in front of his computer, the Omniverse sphere projected on his holoscreen. Cire was sitting next to Creon, reading an ancient-looking book. He looked up as Sarah walked into the room. "You seem excited about something."

Sarah smiled widely. Her eyes were half-mad, and there was dried blood smeared across her face. She looked as if she had just gorged herself on a living creature. "We can talk to it without any of the bullshit Abby had to do just to get that thing to listen to her."

Cire closed his book and leaned back in his chair as he watched Sarah intently. "How do you know that?"

Sarah pointed to her bloody nose. "Because I spoke to it. Sort of. Mostly, I guess I just heard it speaking to me, but it wasn't repeating that nonsense about the Dark One. I heard something completely different."

"What was it?"

Sarah told Cire what the Omniverse had said to her about the Path of Pain. "Have you heard of anything like that?"

Cire shook his head. "Since becoming an orc lich, I have gained access to the orcs' sacred archives, but most of the books about the

Paths of the Travelers are housed in the elven archives. Even with all the strides we've made to improve interracial relationships, I still find it hard to believe the elves would allow us access to their libraries. Based on your expression, I'm assuming you haven't heard of it before this."

Sarah shook her head as she took a seat. Her mind was still racing. The Omniverse's voice continued to echo in her skull. "No, but I never received the proper training as a Traveler. Also, the way I access the Path of the Lost is completely different than Terra and Anabelle. I doubt Anabelle knows about this. She was surprised when she found out Grok could walk the Path of the Lost. I think there's a lot she doesn't know...or maybe wasn't taught."

Cire stood and placed his book on Creon's desk. "Hm..."

A random thought crossed Sarah's mind. "Wait, why did you refer to yourself as a lich? I thought you were the orcs' shaman?"

Cire smiled, his face looking somewhat tired. "Slip of the tongue. I am the orcs' shaman, but I am also a lich. When I consider it, I think of myself as a lich. 'Shaman' is simply a title. I'd prefer not to allow myself to forget what I'm capable of becoming."

Sarah nodded. She could see the validity in that.

Cire softly tapped Creon on the shoulder. The gnome jumped out of his chair and pulled a dagger from his side. He hissed something in Gnomish before realizing where he was.

Creon cleared his throat awkwardly as he pulled his greasy hair back. "Sorry about that. Bad dream."

Sarah smiled approvingly at him. She was glad to see he still was armed, even if he spent his entire day in a magically protected lab. "I'm coming with you," Sarah said as she turned to Cire.

The orc headed toward the door. "I assumed so." He looked at Creon. "Would you please send a request to start the Hadron Collider? The destination is the orc homeworld."

Creon, whose eyes were still half-closed, nodded as he fumbled with the conjuration pad, which put a cup of coffee in his hand. "Will do," he muttered.

Abby was having a hard time keeping up with Terra, Grok, and Anabelle. She'd been trying to produce more nanobots as fast as she was burning them, but it was too hard. Martin had already informed her that if she increased production too much, she would overheat, throwing her body into shock.

She was slightly bitter that she couldn't just push through the pain like Terra and Anabelle could. Their resilience was noticeable. The two of them were in the lead, and even though they were both tired, it was obvious that they weren't going to give up.

Abby wasn't as strong as they were, but she did share their determination. She would give it everything she had, choosing death over giving up.

The first wave of shades was nearly behind them. Grok was somewhere ahead, lost in the red fog that blanketed the valley. Grok knew where Rasputina was, which implied that she'd made this journey before.

There was a clear path behind Anabelle and Terra, so Abby slightly diverted her course, blasting her thrusters to catch up with the other two agents as they relished the brief respite from the onslaught of attacks.

Terra suddenly stopped running. "I need a break. I feel like I'm going to snap in half." Her eyes returned to normal, and the white aura of energy around her disappeared.

Anabelle did the same, and her fiery red aura vanished. "There's no way Grok is still alive."

Abby looked around, trying to see through the red fog. "It's getting worse. The fog. The farther in we go, the thicker it gets."

Terra clapped Abby on the back. "How you holding up, kid? Must be nice not to have all those pesky muscles to hold you back."

Abby smiled weakly. "Yeah. It's pretty great."

A shadowy figure approached from the fog. "I'm definitely still alive," Grok said as she stepped into view. "Glad to see you three are as well."

Anabelle's eyes flashed white for a second as she walked up to the orc. "Where do you get off leaving us behind like that? We could have—"

"Been killed? Yeah, that's the point. If you can't survive this, you're not going to be ready for anything ahead. But you guys aren't doing too bad. It took me and Rasputina ten attempts to break through the first wave. Just keep at it. You're already getting stronger."

Terra looked at Abby uneasily before leaning over to whisper, "Still not sure what I think about Grok trying to win Coach of the Year."

Grok pointed into the fog. "It's coming. I advise you to get ready to fight." With that, she ran into the fog.

Abby pulled out her scanner and took readings in the direction Grok had pointed. "What is she talking about? We're not getting anything."

The fog suddenly sucked itself in as if there were a giant vacuum before the DGA agents. Then it shot outward, forming into a variety of shapes before breaking apart and coming back again, this time taking the shape of a giant dragon.

Terra snorted as she crossed her arms. "So, what, we're fighting clouds now?"

Abby raised her hand and charged her plasma cannon. "Technically, it's fog."

The fog solidified, turning to flesh and blood, and collapsed on the ground, its red flesh moving back and forth in a rhythmic manner. The dragon's eyes were attached by stalks that swayed like those of an insect. Five wings were attached to the dragon's back, the odd wing stretching down the spine like a mohawk.

The dragon opened its mouth, and dozens of red shades were vomited out. They were greasy and oily creatures with malformed bodies, limbs hardly set in their bodies, their heads lopsided and caved in, and mouths ajar, rows of teeth lining their insides.

The shades moved as fast as Grok had as the dragon breathed fire into the sky behind them.

Abby launched her thrusters, flying backward to pick off the shades, but they were too fast. One leaped onto her and drove her into the ground. It roared and opened its mouth, its jaw stretching wide enough to fit her entire head inside.

An axe hit the shade in the neck and severed its head. Terra's foot came next, hitting the shade in the waist and sending it into the fog.

Terra helped Abby to her feet. "Think you can take the dragon?"

Abby looked up at the dragon and tried to swallow her fear, but it stayed in her throat, a massive knot. She didn't think there was any way she could take down that dragon. "We...we're not as strong as you two."

Anabelle was fighting four ghouls at once, her movements as fluid as water as flames and electricity crackled from her body. She was holding her own.

Abby could see that Grok hadn't been lying. Fighting down here was enough to increase Anabelle's and Terra's strength.

Terra spun and caught one of the shades flying at her. She lifted it and brought its back down on her knee as Abby watched.

That was all Abby could do, stand there and watch. She was frozen with fear. Everything was moving too fast.

Terra looked over her shoulder at the girl. "Come on, kid! We don't have time for an existential crisis. You can do this. You always figure something out."

The dragon vomited out another pack of red shades just as grotesque as the last. They wriggled their way out of the dragon's sludge, screeching.

Abby tried to clear her head. She took off toward the dragon. As she leaped into the air, one of the slithering shades shot off the ground and wrapped its body around her. It dragged her down, and the other shades quickly piled on top of her.

There were too many of them, their bodies too slippery, and they were far too strong. Abby struggled to get out from under them, but she couldn't find the strength.

Panic set in.

Abby had forgotten what it felt like to panic. Now she was watching her life flash before her eyes.

Terra's words echoed in her head. She could figure this out. She always did. There had to be a way for her to get strong enough to handle this. After all, she'd figured out how to handle the trial of fraud without her tech. All she had needed was her mind. This wasn't any different.

Actually, it was. She still had her tech.

A pair of sharp fangs sank into Abby's leg, and she screamed in pain as she tried to fly away.

She couldn't. The shades had her pinned.

Another set of fangs bit Abby's arm. The shades were going to eat her alive.

A memory passed before her eyes—sitting with her father at his computer. He had been having a hard time playing video games on it since the graphics card wasn't up to date and the processer wasn't running fast enough for the game. He was disappointed since he'd been looking forward to locking himself in the barn to play all night.

Now Abby was a little girl, standing next to her dad, watching him pout as if he were a child. "There's got to be some way to get more juice out of this thing," he muttered to himself.

Suddenly, it clicked.

Abby stopped trying to struggle. She felt another set of jaws sink into her skin. "Martin, open all my operating procedures."

Martin popped up in the blackness of Abby's mind. "You sure this is the best time to be running a diagnostic?"

"First off, cut all my pain receptors. I need to concentrate."

"You're the boss."

A bright web of icons showed up in front of Abby. She knew exactly what she needed to do and rearranged a few of them, turning off certain functions. "That's it. Initialize, Martin."

The paperclip showed up again and looked at the changes. "Shit, I would never have thought of that. You sure you want to do this?"

"Do it. And turn my pain receptors back on."

Abby's body woke up with pain, but that wasn't all. Newfound power surged through her like a live wire. It was almost too much to contain, so she didn't try. Instead, she let it out.

Anabelle looked over her shoulder to check on Abby as an explosion went off near the dragon. It looked like a giant dome of light.

Abby leaped out of the explosion, leaving the charred remains of the shades beneath her.

She raised her hand and aimed her palm at the dragon. "We found the juice."

A plasma blast the size of a small house shot from Abby's palm and hit the dragon square on the face, burning through it and instantly vaporizing it.

Abby floated back to the ground as Terra walked over to her. Anabelle was still dealing with the last of the shades.

Terra whistled loudly. "Now, that is some serious power. I dig the new look too."

Abby's hair had a techno-organic covering, as did the rest of her skin. Her armor had lost its bulk, and there was barely a distinction between her skin and the nanobots.

Anabelle approached the two. "How'd you do that?"

Abby smiled bashfully. "We figured we should try something like you two. Instead of trying to operate at the same level all the time, we'd make a different combat profile, one that conserved certain energy so we could use it for other things. Also, we overhauled the entire system. Why limit nanobots to our bloodstream? Now they're infused with our skin cells, nerves, and brain. A more precise arrangement."

The fog began to clear, revealing Grok, who had been watching them. "If I had to pick one of you that I didn't think was going to make it, would have been you, Abby. Didn't think she could do this without going back to HQ and adding something to her current rig. Guess I was wrong."

Abby tapped her head. "The weapons don't make the fighter."

Grok smiled. "That's what I like to hear." She turned and walked into the fading fog. "Follow me. We're almost there. You're going to want to see this."

CHAPTER THIRTY-ONE

Sarah paced. She was in the orc archives with Cire and was starting to get bored. It felt like she'd been waiting for him to find the answer for a long time.

The shaman had encouraged her to search with him, but she was hampered by her inability to read Orcish. For a while, she had busied herself looking through the different armories of orc weapons that had been passed down through the generations, but there were only so many swords and axes to look at. That being said, there were a lot.

Sarah flopped on one of the large ottomans near Cire and groaned loudly. "I didn't think you were going to have to read every book here."

Cire looked up from a book and smiled politely. "Most of the archive hasn't been updated yet, and hardly any of it has been transferred to HQ. We're going to have to do this the old-fashioned way."

Sarah picked up one of the books on the ottoman and languidly flipped through its pages. When she got tired of looking at what could have easily been a picture book, she stood up and went to the window.

Outside, orcs were walking back and forth, transporting building materials as large container ships flew behind them. "Do you know how the containment's going?" Sarah asked.

Cire made a few arcane gestures in the air, causing his book to disappear and be replaced with another one. "Wouldn't be much of a shaman unless I did. It's been difficult is the answer. Initially, we thought that only a few of the larger cities had been invaded by the dead. We were very wrong. They are all throughout the planet. Anywhere the dead fell in this world's history, the dead rose."

Sarah looked over her shoulder at Cire. "Fuck. Part of me was hoping Earth was the only one that got hit that hard, but it makes sense. How are you going to contain them all?"

Cire stood and stretched, groaning slightly as he touched his toes. "As best we can. Holding pens for the larger infestations. The entire army is working on the cleanup. How about you humans?"

"Pretty much the same thing, except our governments have been ridiculous about it. Myrddin won't step in because he says it's treading on too many people's toes—which he never seems to have a problem with."

Cire joined Sarah by the window. "He's been pulling the strings of humanity for years, prepping them for war with the Dark One. I wouldn't be surprised if he was simply tired. Nor will it be good for humans if they're babied throughout the integration. Your government will have to quickly figure out how to deal with the many crises of the realms."

Sarah chuckled. "Yeah, it does seem like there are a lot of them. I'll catch you later, Cire. I'm going to see if I can find someone to spar with."

Cire nodded and headed back to his books, tripping over one that had fallen off of a pile. He reached down and picked it up. "Hold on. You might want to take a look at this."

Sarah, who was already at the door, looked over her shoulder. "Cire, I told you, I can't read orc."

"Humor me."

Sarah joined Cire in the middle of the archives. "Why would you want me here for this?"

Cire handed Sarah the book.

The book's cover was an etching of a black orb in the sky. A white orb was at the bottom of the cover. Six humanoid figures stood in between the two orbs. Each of the figures was in a different martial arts stance. "Any of those look familiar?"

Sarah recognized three of the stances instantly as being those of the three Paths of the Traveler. She'd never seen the other three, though. "Worth taking a look at."

"I'll translate. Let's get to work."

The red fog was fading and a structure was visible in the distance, reaching up like a finger pointing to God.

The irony of something like that being in hell was not lost on Abby.

The fog continued to clear, showing that there was a walled city lying beneath the spire.

There was now a road beneath Abby's feet. Behind her, scores of demons still battled among themselves. The red fog was still there, but Abby and the rest of them had passed through it. The gnashing of teeth and screams were still loud enough to hear, though.

The road began as dirt, but as Abby followed it, she could see that there were stones, shaved and ground down to be as smooth as possible. The farther down the road she walked, the more ornate the stones became. There were geodes and jewels sprinkled throughout the surface, making it look as if she were walking on stars.

It was far too beautiful a thing to be in hell, but so was the spire. Now that the fog was completely gone, Abby could see more details.

The spire had been built from what looked like ivory. Its sides were smooth, painstakingly ground down so that it looked like a weather-worn bone. Grooves had been cut into it that followed its rounded body, creating an illusion of clouds frozen in time.

Terra whistled loudly. "Are you saying that this is where Rasputina lives? When did they start building cities in hell?"

Grok laughed as she quickened her pace. "They started building cities in hell when Rasputina started building them. Before this, there were only circles meant for torturing and the wild thought energy of hell. Now there's a city, made with her own hands."

The walls extended much farther than Abby had initially thought. They stretched far to the right and left, eventually becoming invisible under the tumultuous red sands and fog. There were also more buildings than just the spire. A row of skyscrapers built in a similar design was visible.

The DGA and Grok walked up to the front gate, where two guards stood. They were both demons but were wearing armor that almost distracted from the fact that they did not have heads. Fire and smoke fumed from the empty wounds in their necks. They gripped battle-axes. "Halt. Who wishes to enter New Sodom?"

Grok raised her hand to the guards. A sigil appeared on her palm. "These are my guests."

Both guards bowed slightly, and the one on the right apologizing profusely. They stepped aside, and the gates opened.

The streets of New Sodom were bustling, packed with demons wearing loose-fitting, cloth garb that looked like it had been pulled out of a medieval fantasy. The more humanoid demons could have easily been mistaken for undiscovered races if it were not for the utter lack of uniformity.

The other demons were things to behold. Some were made completely of smoke, occasionally taking human form before contorting into something else and then shifting back into a cloud.

There were bipedal demons, bizarre mixes of animals that one would have never thought of combining. Yet, somehow, they were nothing like the broken demons the DGA had come across in the circles of hell. These demons didn't look wrong. They looked like they had been lovingly put together.

Shops and homes lined the streets of New Sodom, and the shopkeepers leaned out, encouraging the mass of bustling demons to stop and take a gander at their wares. Tonics, memories, lost things, glimpses into the lives of mortals, and profane texts.

One of the vendors, an imp with two horns instead of eyes, shambled up to Abby. "Care for a taste?" he croaked as he produced a shimmering apple of glazed crystal that looked sickly-sweet. "Should sit as well in a mortal belly as any other."

Abby cast a glance at Anabelle, her eyes wide with surprise and bewilderment, before looking at Grok. Anabelle shrugged and said, "When in Rome..."

Grok grabbed the apple from the imp and then showed the imp her palm. It yelped excitedly before opening its back and pulling out another apple. "Thank you, m'lady," it said before scrambling away.

The orc stepped out in front of the DGA, leading them down the street. "The markets are always hectic. You should get a better idea of this place once we get to the square."

Abby continued to watch the street vendors and demons interacting with each other. Even with the business of the market, it was obvious that all the demons were civil to each other. Nothing like outside the walls. "Rasputina really built all this?"

The crowds thinned out. The town square was much less busy but interesting all the same. There were demons sitting on benches in a park with black grass and trees with what looked like small fairies flying in and out of branches covered with blood-red leaves.

Terra pointed at three statues towering over the square. "Well, fuck me twice while standing."

Abby gasped when she saw what had caught Terra's attention, then wondered why she hadn't seen it as soon as she had walked into the square.

Statues of Annabelle, Terra, and Abby were the centerpieces of the square. They were made of some kind of living stone, giving them the illusion of breathing. The craftsmanship was superb. Whoever had created these had perfectly captured the fiery haughtiness in Anabelle's gaze and the glint of joyful violence in Terra's eyes. Looking at her own statue made Abby feel as if she were looking in a mirror that knew more about her than she did.

Abby looked at Grok, confused. "Why are these here?"

Grok shrugged as she headed closer to the statues. "Rasputina thought it was appropriate. I think the statues speak for themselves."

She sat on one of the benches near them. It was a bizarre sight, and a lot to take in.

"How did she do it?" Anabelle asked.

Grok looked at the statues and smiled. "When we got here, we were lost. We'd fought through the Netherverse and found our way into this section of hell without realizing it. We were exhausted and stupid, and Rasputina got away from me. She had a break with reality and fled into the unformed part of hell we just came from. I could still sense her, so I went after her. When I found her, she was surrounded by thousands of dead demons, and she was making this place out of their bodies. She kept building after her materials were gone, trapped in some kind of haze. From there, we started our work, gathering demons who were tired of lives they had to live out in the violence and bringing anyone who didn't want that life under our heels."

Abby watched a one-eyed imp chase a four-footed chicken demon with the head of a bull. "Do you think that's right? Forcing demons under your rule?"

Grok shrugged. "Someone always rules hell. Why not Rasputina? She might be crazy, but at least she's trying to make it a better place. And I think it's worth trying to do. Besides, no one is forcing anyone to stay here. The demons can come and go as they like. They prefer to be inside the walls."

Abby didn't have anything to say. Judging by the silence of the rest of the DGA, neither did they.

Grok stood up and looked at the tallest of the spires. "Come on. We've already wasted enough time with the tour. Let's see if Rasputina can help us."

The DGA agents followed the orc.

Abby continued to marvel at the city Rasputina had built. She was interested in the mechanics of how she had done it, but the why was as interesting as the how. She had more than a bit of interest in the lich and her motivations, mostly because Abby had never seen this kind of change in someone.

Granted, the lich had been insane. Now she seemed just as insane, but much less evil.

Grok was different too. It was more than the simple fact that Grok and Rasputina didn't want to kill the DGA anymore. The change was much deeper.

The two villains seemed like they truly wanted to help people, and in that way, they weren't much different from the DGA. Well, there was one major difference…they were more concerned with demons than mortals.

Abby wished she could talk to Anabelle and get her perspective. Of the three of them, the elf was the least likely to trust Grok or Rasputina, but even Anabelle seemed taken in by the town they walked through.

They made their way through the square into a residential section that reminded Abby of an old English hamlet. The smell of fresh baked goods and cooked meats filled the air. From there, they found their way to the largest spire.

A dozen guards stood before it, their empty necks flaming just like the guards who watched the gate. These recognized Grok and saluted her as she approached.

Grok returned the salute. "I'm here to see Rasputina."

One of the guards stepped forward. "She is currently meeting the Lords of Death within the citadel."

Grok sighed and shook her head. "Perfect. Just what we need." She turned to the DGA agents. "I thought she'd be done by now."

The guards stepped away, and the surface of the spire melted into a door. Grok opened it and stepped through.

Abby and the rest of the DGA followed her.

CHAPTER THIRTY-TWO

Persephone held a one, a three, a five, and a ten in her hand. Her foot was bouncing nervously. Naota and Blackwell were staring her down. She could sense murder in Naota's eyes. He held the deck beneath his hand and made something like a smile with his lips, but Persephone knew the truth. He was ready to end this all in a second.

Roy had left the game, much to Persephone's irritation. He had been helping her for the last hour, and she'd been winning. Blackwell didn't seem to mind. There might not be a competitive bone in his body. But Naota...that was another story. Persephone thought that even Rasputina might have folded under the intense pressure of his gaze.

Naota tapped his hand on the table. "So, what's it going to be? Hit? Or stay?"

Persephone looked back down at her cards as she tried to remember the rules of the game. She was only a few points away from having twenty-one. Roy had cautioned her to play it safe once she got that high up, and she was already in the lead, having taken most of the pot already.

But there were Naota's eyes to still deal with—those cold, brown, dead eyes peering at her from underneath those bushy eyebrows.

Persephone leaned forward. "You want me to hit, don't you?"

Naota folded his fingers over each other like a collapsing piece of origami. "Honey, I don't want anything. I'm just a dealer, slinging cards. I ain't got no stake in the game. I'm neutral."

"Don't call me 'honey,' and stop trying to psych me out."

Naota grabbed the cigarette hanging from Blackwell's lips and took a puff. He exhaled a cloud of smoke that obscured his face. "Trying? I ain't ever tried anything my entire life."

Blackwell snickered as he snatched his cigarette back. "You know that doesn't make any sense, right?"

Naota pretended to continue smoking. "Sense? I don't even know how to spell the word."

Persephone glanced at her cards one last time. She knocked on the table.

Naota pulled a card from the top of the deck and placed it face-down in front of her. "How about we make this extra spicy? If you get twenty-one on this card, you take the whole pot, plus my gold teeth. If you lose, I take the pot and…your shoes."

Blackwell burst out laughing. "Are you serious? You know those things aren't comparable, right?"

Naota grinned. "Remember what we were saying about making sense?"

Persephone narrowed her eyes as she ran her finger over the card. "Fine. I'll take it."

She flipped her card over.

An ace of diamonds stared up at her.

Persephone picked up the card to survey it. "Uh, what's an ace again?"

Naota tossed his cards on the table. "An ace is 1 or 11, Percy. That means you win the game."

Blackwell hooted as he slapped his knees. "Goddamn, Naota. I didn't think your luck could get any shittier."

Persephone passed her cards to Naota before pulling the pile of cash, magical artifacts, and trivial items such as buttons and bus tickets toward her. "Naota, you don't have to worry about it. I don't want your gold teeth. Honestly, that's pretty gross."

Naota hooked his fingers into his mouth and spread his lips wide as he let his jaw drop. "I don't have gold teeth. That right there was a golden-mouthed bluff."

Blackwell yawned as he took the cards from Naota and began shuffling. "That was not a bluff, that was lying, you idiot. If you pull that shit in a real game, someone's liable to break your legs."

Naota reached into his pocket and pulled out two gold coins. "That should be about the same amount." He turned to Persephone and gave his usual, good-natured, goofy smile. "Not bad for beginners' luck. If you want to play again, just let me and Thomas know."

Persephone was surprised to hear Blackwell's first name. Naota was the only person who used it.

Blackwell put out his cigarette and stood. "All right, who's making rounds with me?"

There wasn't anything else to do this late at night, and Persephone didn't think she was going to be getting any sleep. She raised her hand and followed Blackwell as he walked into the camp.

The camp was a makeshift construction, a containment center for the zombie outbreak. Myrddin had been organizing them across the world through a combination of funding and magical tech. Each country supplied military forces to take care of the dirty work, putting everything together and moving the zombies. Myrddin's forces were overseeing the process and helping out wherever they could.

The work had been a pleasant change for Persephone. Integration workshops and jumping between worlds every couple of days had been draining. She was glad to be in one place long enough to feel like a person again.

Persephone and Blackwell walked down the rows of zombie pens.

On the surface, they were little more than giant steel cages, but that was only on the first look. If you had any knowledge of sigil work, which Persephone knew a small amount of, you could see that all the cages were rigged with the same sigils, linked together. If anything set off one, they would go off at the same time, incinerating anything inside.

It seemed like a disrespectful end for the dead. The drow would have never done anything like this. But then again, having your body reanimated by a giant floating sphere in the sky also seemed fairly disrespectful.

Blackwell stopped at one of the cages and peered inside. "Kinda disturbing, isn't it? Never been a fan of prisons, and here I am, playing guard and everything."

The zombie within the cage was frozen, its dead eyes looking at nothing.

Persephone was sad for the thing. "Not quite a prison. They aren't alive."

"We don't know that yet," Blackwell corrected. "HQ is still trying to figure out what the hell is going on with these guys. They're not undead. Not like we've seen before, at least. Whatever they are, they're a problem. Still, I'd rather be the one watching shit down here than waiting for something to go wrong."

Persephone agreed with Blackwell, but she wasn't sure what to say. Instead of speaking, she watched the zombies inside the cage. That was when she noticed one of them blinking. "Dark Goddess, did you see that?"

Blackwell shook his head as he leaned in to get a better look.

Persephone pointed at the zombie that had blinked. "Watch."

The two of them stared at the zombie, holding their breath.

Blackwell left out a sigh. "It was probably nothing."

The zombie blinked.

Blackwell stuck a cigarette in his mouth and lit it. "Fuck. That's not good."

What Anabelle saw in front of her was difficult to fathom. Even if she'd had it explained, it still would have been hard to wrap her mind around. Yet here it was before her.

She had stepped through the door of the spire into a large chamber. In its center sat what looked like a snow globe. That, in and of itself, wasn't impressive. What was inside was, though.

There were at least a dozen continents, each of them built from the ground up. The trees, plants, mountains, each piece of nature had been handcrafted, and the detail was immaculate. Some of the continents had buildings, replicas of places Rasputina must have seen over the course of her life. Anabelle could have sworn she saw New York.

That is to say, Anabelle noticed for a brief moment before her perception was altered again. If she'd been looking into a snow globe, what happened next was akin to the snow globe's glass dome cracking open and the contents being tossed on the floor, the miniatures sinking roots into the ground and swelling in size until you were in the scene.

Anabelle whirled, trying to understand where she was. As she searched, she could see Abby and Terra trying to figure it out as well.

Abby looked the most confused. "Wait, are you saying Rasputina did all this? This is an entire planet!"

Grok pressed her hand to the floor, her sigil burning into the stone. "No, this is one planet out of at least twenty. It's her sanctuary. She keeps building. I think it's part of her process to deal with everything. She can't create life, but she can make constructs." The orc lowered her eyes, sadness painting their edges. "She can make worlds where nothing grows. It just exists."

"That doesn't make it any less beautiful."

Grok stepped back from the glowing sigil. "True. It is beautiful, but it's a pain in the ass to navigate when I need to find her."

Anabelle stared at the stars above her. It was both night and day, the sun shimmering in and out of clouds that shifted into the shape of the moon as stars breathed themselves into visibility before exhaling and vanishing. "This is the most beautiful thing I've ever seen!"

Grok knelt and scratched more lines into the sigil. "It is. Being here has been good for her."

The ground slipped away, and space swallowed them all before sucking inward and belching out a new planet covered in blue grass that rose to the knee. Long-legged creatures walked in the distance, their tube-like necks reaching down for the grass in unison.

A small human sat on a rock, watching the creatures. Bennington. His skin looked to have been whipped for a lifetime and left to heal. He looked over his shoulder, and they saw that his face was growing new skin, soft and powdery. The look in his eyes was hard to place. It might have been sadness. "What do you want, thief?" he spat at Grok.

She narrowed her eyes at Bennington. "Where did she put the council chambers?"

"What do you care? Are you back to take her away from me again? Why don't you let her be what she is?"

Grok's eyes flashed, and she took a step toward Bennington. "Do not play with me, human. I will tear you open, and Rasputina will have to put you back together again."

Bennington sneered as he turned around and stood. His body was hardly more than bones with flesh stitched over him. "Threaten me all you want. You can't hurt me, not like my mistress would. You lack her creativity, her conviction. And you took that from her! You were jealous."

Grok rushed Bennington and held him up by his throat. "Tell me where she is. I don't have the time to scour each of these worlds."

Bennington shook his head. "You took my mistress from me. If you can't find her in time, you don't deserve her."

"You know she's meeting with the Lords of Death, don't you?"

Bennington smiled, his beady eyes flickering beneath his rotten brow. "Mistress is doing what she does best. She's tearing flesh, breaking bone, and spilling blood. BLOOD! You can try to make her into whatever you want because she's weak, but I remember what Mistress is. I won't ever forget." He spat in Grok's face.

The orc's eyes flashed as she screamed in rage and slammed Bennington on the ground headfirst, cracking his skull open.

His brains oozed into the grass, and flowers sprouted around his emptying skull.

"Jesus," Anabelle muttered as Grok walked back.

She waved away Anabelle's concern. "His head will heal in an hour or so, and then he'll be whining again. Goddamn it!"

Abby stepped forward, holding the sigil book Cire had given her. "Wait, I think I might have something to help. You're looking for something you lost, right?"

Grok sighed. "Yeah, something like that."

Abby's finger converted into a laser and she carved a sigil into the ground, looking at the book for reference.

Once the sigil was etched, it glowed brightly. A faint echo of another sigil appeared beside it. Grok knelt and carved it into the ground.

The world lurched, and this planet was gone.

A regal throne room stood before them. Thousands of statues lined the sides, their faces mournful, twisted in fear, many of them crying.

Twelve cloaked figures sat around the throne, which was empty.

Grok took a step toward the figures when something flew out of the sky and smashed into her, then landed on the floor.

A four-armed demon fell from the sky, beating its bare chest as it roared, its mouth filled with sharpened teeth. Scars covered its body, and it wielded a sword in each of its hands.

The demon stepped forward and kicked the orc out of the way. Rasputina lay beneath her. The demon picked the lich up by her hair.

A plasma blast hit the demon in the face.

Anabelle, Abby, and Terra stepped forward.

"You're going to want to put her down," Anabelle growled.

CHAPTER THIRTY-THREE

The four-armed demon straightened, showing how tall he actually was. He towered over the three DGA agents. He laughed caustically as he raised one of his swords. "Ah, so the would-be queen of hell allows any mortal into her domain as she wishes? Is hell to be overrun by the foul scent of the living, much like she has turned our rugged wild into a sterile imitation of the realm of the living?"

Rasputina's eyes creaked open as she groaned softly.

The demon slammed her into the ground. "Today you face Skah-haj, avatar of the Blessed Lord Shiva, his finest warrior, scourge of the underworld, the Blade That Never Dulls."

The DGA agents exchanged glances. Terra cleared her throat. "Uh, do you guys have any titles?"

Abby and Anabelle shook their heads. "Sorry, no one's ever asked," Abby said.

Terra sighed as she unsheathed her axe. "All right, we can forgo the titles. I don't want to look like I'm bragging or anything. Let's just kick this guy's ass."

She lunged toward the demon and drop-kicked him.

He stumbled back, dropped one of his swords, clutched his chest, and coughed loudly as he tried to catch his breath.

Abby appeared in front of him, her hand charging a plasma blast. She fired, and the blast was large enough to cover the demon's body.

He was thrown back.

Anabelle ran and flipped over the demon, moving nearly as fast as she'd seen Grok moving in the wildlands.

The demon opened his eyes to see Anabelle's fist colliding with his face. He hit the ground hard and did not get up.

Terra ran over to Rasputina and helped her to her feet.

The lich looked around, confused as to what had gone on after she was knocked out. "What happened?"

Terra smiled proudly. "We took care of that asshole for you."

Rasputina's eyes flashed bright with green fire. "You did what?"

"Uh, we helped you out?"

Rasputina grabbed her hair and pulled at it as she stomped off. "You fools! You have no idea what you've done."

The world shifted, and Rasputina and the DGA were standing before the twelve lords of hell.

The lords of hell removed their hoods. They had been the gods of death and the afterlife throughout humanity's existence.

Anubis' jackal head stared at the DGA. Freya sat by his side, her armor covered with shards of ice. On one end of the council stood the Orisha Eshu, his eyes white, a flame in one hand and staff in the other, his hood swooping toward his back. A tall, slender man in a black suit with a blank face sat at his side.

Anubis took a step forward, snarling. "It would seem that we have interlopers destroying the sanctity of the challenge. Is this the sort of rule you propose, Rasputina? Insulting our traditions in the name of disrespect?"

Rasputina cast an annoyed glance at the DGA. "Hardly. I've fought beside these three before. They found their way here through a friend of mine. None of them were aware that I was fighting to rule."

The Slender Man stepped forward, his arms stretching as he moved, nearly touching the ground. "Humans can be...impetuous, to say the least. That does not change the fact that you violated our rules."

Rasputina's face tensed as she spoke slowly, enunciating each word. "Quiet, fool. I destroyed worlds before your name was even on the lips of children. Let your elders speak of matters you wouldn't understand."

The Slender Man hissed loudly but stepped back, giving the floor to another.

Hades, a pale-skinned god who smelled of wine and decay, stood. "Everyone quiet, quiet. It was a reasonable if unfortunate mistake. There must be something we can do to rectify this grave injustice."

Eshu met Abby's eyes. "Hm, one of my children. As it stands, I would be interested in seeing how this new situation plays out. If Lord Shiva is allowed to send a proxy, why should we not allow Rasputina to fight with hers?"

The Slender Man curled around his chair, his body moving like a snake's. "Because they were not part of the bargain. Some of you may be keen to lose our hold on hell, but that cannot be said of us all. That is not even taking into account the potential battle with the Dark One."

Anubis and Eshu laughed. "Child, none of us is losing anything other than you and Hades. We weren't stupid enough to put all our stock in the Christian idea of the afterlife. We all have our own domains," Anubis said. "This is nothing more than a condo to rent out for us, though one I am quite partial to. And concerning the Dark One, not all of us are afraid of a god's death."

The Slender Man turned to Hades. "What about you? You're in the same situation as me."

Hades shrugged as he ran his hand over his bald head. "What do you think, Freya?"

The goddess picked at one of the shards of ice on her shoulder. "Hades and I are looking to start a new death cult together. We could go either way."

The Slender Man's body shrank slightly and then expanded vertically. "You all may have forgotten your roots, your pride, but I have not. If Rasputina wishes to take the throne and be helped by her friends, who have already disrespected and violated our sacred ways, then they should be held to a trial worthy of the kingdoms of hell."

Anubis snickered. "Why would we care about the 'sacred' things? This is hell."

A chorus of laughter erupted through the lords until silence eventually overtook. Anubis spoke again. "But you have a point. Who are we taking bets on? I think the bald human will be the first to die."

Freya jumped up from her seat. "We haven't even chosen our champion. Who wants to pick?"

The lords were silent, each of them thinking of an apt demon, monster, or hero for the occasion. Finally, Hade said, "Why not have the stickler for the rules make the choice?"

The Slender Man slithered forward. "Very well. You will face one of my offshoots, a lesser demon than my great glory but one of intense power nonetheless. Today you face the Scungilli Man!"

Terra cracked up, holding her sides as she stepped back. "Wait? Are you serious? Scungilli Man? Like the pasta dish?"

The Slender Man's body pulsed and vibrated. "Do you accept?"

Anabelle looked at Rasputina, who solemnly nodded. "Please. Bring him on."

The Slender Man floated into the air, raising his tentacled hands. "Scungilli Man." He repeated it three more times.

Terra, still laughing, rested her hand on Anabelle and leaned against her. "Oh, my God, are you really doing a Bloody Mary thing? This is unbelievable. Are we at a high school sleepover?"

Abby was also having a hard time not laughing.

The Slender Man repeated the name three more times.

The sky began to darken. In the distance, waves could be heard crashing. The air was suddenly filled with the salt scent of the ocean.

The name was spoken again.

Lightning crackled in the pitch-black sky, and the ground beneath the DGA agents' feet began to roll as if it were rocked by the sea.

Abby leaped into the air, firing her thrusters. "This is a little more than I was expecting."

The smell of the ocean turned rancid, like rotting carp and shark skin reduced to decay and death.

A conch sounded in the distance. A chorus of whales answered, their voices rising, long and mournful, the dirge of death come from the sea itself.

The Slender Man let loose a foul cackle. "Scungilli Man!"

Blackness settled over all. The only light came from the sliver of a moon on the ground beneath the Dark Gate Angels' feet, which rolled and rocked.

A terrible screech tore through the air, a high-pitched violent noise full of anguish and melancholy, accompanied by the Slender Man's cackling laughter.

Tentacles reached up from the ground, grasping the legs of the DGA agents and Rasputina, wrapping tightly around them.

Another long, mournful blast of the conch and the agents were pulled beneath the rolling ground.

Terra wasn't sure how long she'd been in the sunken black place. She knew she'd been awake most of the time, but that only made the time seem to have passed even slower.

She tried to move, but her range was limited. When she looked up, she could see the Lords of Death looking at her through a small box.

Across from her, Anabelle and Abby floated lifelessly.

Terra tried to run to them but could not move. Realizing the situation she was in, she flopped onto her stomach and kicked her feet like she was swimming. She easily glided toward her fallen comrades.

She shook Abby as hard as she could.

The girl's eyes slowly opened. "What happened?" she asked, air bubbles escaping her mouth.

Terra shrugged before swimming over to Anabelle and waking her up.

The three of them glanced up at the Lords of Death standing over them.

Terra didn't care about them. They weren't the problem at the moment. The Scungilli Man was the issue, whatever he was. "Can either of you see Rasputina?"

Abby popped one of the air bubbles that had come from Terra. "This doesn't make any sense. How are we talking underwater?"

Terra grabbed Abby by the shoulders. "We're fighting something called a Scungilli Man that was summoned by an internet meme in a kingdom in hell built by a lich who tried to kill us a year ago. Are you really going to try to look at this logically?"

Abby nodded, defeated. "You have a point. Where is this guy, anyway?"

Something dark bolted past Terra, knocking her to the side. "What the fuck was that?"

Another black bolt blew past Abby, shoving her as well. "Don't know. Don't really want to find out."

A black bolt came racing toward Anabelle, who braced herself, the water around her bubbling from the mana she was shooting out.

The black bolt rammed into Anabelle, who caught it in her hand. It was a snout. The snout was attached to a shark's head, which was attached to a muscular human body with fins.

The mershark snapped at Anabelle, trying to chomp through her hands.

The elf punched the mershark in the face before kicking it, which sent her floating backward.

The mershark swam away, only to return within seconds with a team of ten other sharks.

The sharks rushed the DGA agents, and the water boiled with blood and energy.

Abby tried to fire a plasma blast at the sharks, but the water dampened the attack, resulting in nothing happening. A shark rammed into her side, clamping down on her leg with its two rows of teeth.

She tried to swim away, but the shark held on tightly.

Anabelle was in a similar situation, trying different attacks that were nullified by the water.

Terra wasn't affected at all. She pulled her axe from her back and slipped down the Path of the Lost, her eyes flashing brightly. She sliced through two of the mersharks before slamming her feet into another and kicking off it, heading toward Abby.

She cut through the shark that was holding onto Abby, slicing its head from its neck. Then she swam over to Anabelle and swung around in a slow-moving circle, cutting up any of the beasts who were close enough for her to reach.

Another school of mersharks was rapidly approaching.

Terra grabbed Abby and Anabelle, pulling them close. As long as they stayed together, they would be able to handle this.

Suddenly, the mersharks were sucked downward as if someone had pulled the plug.

Terra looked down and saw Rasputina, her arms outstretched. Thin strings of energy stretched from her fingers, attaching to the corners of what looked to be reality.

The lich let out a scream and swung her arms down.

Water drained from above, and Terra, along with Abby and Anabelle, got caught in its pull, swirling down with the mersharks toward Rasputina.

Terra hit the floor and coughed up water as she struggled to her feet. As she straightened, she saw Anabelle and Abby standing as well.

The mersharks lay at Rasputina's feet, their gills flapping as they gasped for breath.

Rasputina sighed as she swayed to the side. "Scungilli Man! Face us!"

A conch sounded, and the room shook.

The Scungilli Man was coming.

CHAPTER THIRTY-FOUR

Thick fog spread through the chambers as rain poured from a nonexistent sky. A low, pitiful moan echoed throughout the dim room as lightning crashed and shadows danced across the floor.

Rasputina joined Terra and the rest of the DGA. "Have you heard of this...thing? I'm not familiar with it."

Terra shrugged. "I think it's like an online meme. How long has the Slender Man been a god of death? I remember seeing him in a video game or something."

Rasputina looked at the Slender Man, who was rubbing his long fingers together greedily. "A few years. Compared to the other gods, a couple of hours. No doubt why he feels he has something to prove. He's extremely irritating."

Her words were cut off by another loud moan. A massive, hulking figure came out of the shadows, his head nearly touching the clouds above. Red eyes peered out of the darkness as the monster's barnacle-covered body heaved into the light. Its arms were covered with thick, corded muscles, but there were no hands. Instead, its wrists trailed off, splitting into hundreds of blood-stained spaghetti-like tentacles.

Beneath the creature's cracked legs rowed dozens of gondolas, each with a lantern sitting in it, casting light upon the Scungilli Man, who now stood at his full height, nearly that of a ten-story building.

The Scungilli Man let out a pained roar, his red, beady eyes peering out from behind a swooping conch that stretched to his chest, a gondolier's hat resting atop it. Squids, octopi, and jellyfish fell from the opening in the shell as the profane creature lumbered toward the Dark Gate Angels.

Abby raised her hand cannon and fired.

The plasma blast eviscerated a few of the gondolas on the path to the hulking creature.

The Scungilli Man raised his hand, creating a wave of water to shoot up and block the plasma attack.

Terra glanced at Abby and grinned. "Looks like we're going to have to get close and personal with this one."

Abby sighed. "Yeah."

Anabelle's eyes flashed white. Terra flexed and slipped onto the Path as Abby's armor reconfigured, shrinking down to its bare minimum, her body pulsating with invisible energy.

Rasputina joined the DGA agents. "Let's end this quickly." She slashed the air in front of her, tore open a portal, and stepped through.

Abby teleported out of sight.

Terra groaned as she tilted her head back. "So, we're the ones who have to do the anime run now?"

Anabelle grabbed Terra and sprinted forward. The floor came up in massive chunks from the force of their feet.

Abby appeared behind the Scungilli Man and fired her cannon.

The barnacles on his back detached and flew at Abby. Some of them opened into flowering jellyfish that absorbed the bulk of the blast, while the others latched onto Abby's body, sprouting tentacles that wrapped around her, causing her to lose flight.

The lich stepped out of her portal onto the shoulder of the Scungilli Man, flicked her wrist, and caught the bone spear that shot out of her palm. She raised the spear and drove it into the Scungilli Man's shoulder. As Rasputina gripped the abomination of the sea's shoulder, Abby fell out of the sky only a few feet away.

Rasputina leaped off of Scungilli Man and grabbed Abby, then slashed in front of her and opened another portal, which brought her out on his other side.

Small laser canons formed across Abby's body and sliced through the barnacles' tentacles.

Terra plowed into the behemoth's leg, driving her axe as far into its putrid flesh as she could. Once it was anchored, she crouched, still holding the handle, and leaped, dragging the blade of her other axe up the length of the sea creature's leg.

Scungilli Man roared as he leaned down to swipe at Terra.

As he attacked, Anabelle went after the other leg. She pulled whatever liquid was on the ground up and flash-froze it around his foot, causing the creature to fall forward.

Terra landed on the ground and ran toward Anabelle, who knelt and positioned her hand to boost Terra up. When her foot hit Anabelle's palm, the elf launched Terra up into the air.

The human rose at the speed of a bullet, and Abby flew around her and then upward, catching Terra's hand and flinging her higher still.

Tears eased out of Terra's eyes as she tried to see. Stars twinkled above, billions of them. Then gravity came for her. She positioned her body for the descent, trying to make out which part of the Scungilli Man's body she was going to slice open.

The conch seemed like the appropriate spot. She'd crack the thing open and see what was on the inside.

As Terra descended, Abby flew past her once more, taking Terra's hand and swinging her to increase her momentum.

By this point Terra couldn't see anything, but she knew whatever she hit was going to have a hard time getting up.

Below, Anabelle and Rasputina were trying to pin the Scungilli Man to the ground. Annabelle had frozen the floor, making it impossible to walk on. She was skating in a circle, using her mana to keep her feet moving on the surface of the ice as Rasputina floated around, pulling bones out of the ground to cage the Scungilli Man.

The lich shot several bone spears into his thick, soft neck, then anchored them to the set of bones protruding from his torso, trapping the sea beast.

Terra let out a riotous scream as she descended, axe held out in front of her, and crashed into the conch, splitting it down the middle. When she landed, a shockwave shook the ground, and dirt and debris were kicked up by the impact.

Abby landed as well and scanned the area for Terra's vital signs. When she found them, she teleported to the Hand, grabbed her, and teleported back to her previous position. Shock absorbers formed on her heels, digging her into the ground as she pressed her wrists together, aiming her palms at the tip of the exposed conch. "Let's shuck this fucker and see what's inside."

Terra, who was safely out of the way, looked at Anabelle. "She's good at the trash talk. You might want to take lessons."

The elf's eyes narrowed. "Shut up, Terra."

Abby screamed as she fired her plasma blast. The force of the attack had burned through her fingers as the plasma left her hands.

The plasma blast hit the conch, and there was an explosion that sent debris and shell particles everywhere.

Once the smoke settled, the contents were visible.

Terra flipped her axe. "Now let me show you guys how to shuck... Oh, wait, goddamn it, Abby already got that one. Uh-oh! I'm gonna kick this one right in the pearls!"

Anabelle crossed her arms and sneered as she walked with Terra toward the conch. "Conchs don't have pearls. Oysters do."

Terra pointed her axe at Anabelle. "Keep it up, and we're going to have a rematch," she said with a laugh.

Scungilli Man's wheezing moan was getting louder. Terra slammed her axe's blade into the shell's crack and pulled it to the side, trying to pry it open. "Give me a hand!"

Anabelle charged her hand with pure mana and punched the crack, deepening it enough for Terra to split the conch down the middle.

A torrent of saltwater poured from the shell, washing both Terra and Anabelle away.

Thousands of crabs scuttled out of the conch as thick, green slime poured from what had to be a wound. The gondolas floated eerily around the still body of the Scungilli Man.

Abby looked at Terra and Anabelle and the lich. "It's dead, right?"

Rasputina stared long and hard at the beached corpse in front of them. "Doubtful. Even if the Slender Man is new to the council, there's no doubt he earned it. That means this will prove to be more than a minor inconvenience."

The body of the Scungilli Man pulsated, its arms growing large and bulbous as its torso swelled. The scents of onions and rotten fish wafted from the corpse.

Terra and the rest of the DGA grabbed their noses or covered their mouths, trying to keep from vomiting. Rasputina didn't seem to mind the smell.

More sea life spewed from the shell halves, predominately crabs and other bizarre crustaceans.

Then the spine of the corpse bulged upward. The skin burst open, and a humanoid figure stood. It wore the hat of a gondolier, which cast a shadow on his face. His skin was a sickly green, covered in barnacles, and his hands were long, spindly things with no structure. His face was the head of a squid, its tentacles stretching to his chest like an oceanic beard. The tentacles lifted to show a mouth devoid of lips or jawbone, only rows and rows of jagged teeth. A whale song escaped from the gaping maw.

Terra kicked away a crab scuttling near her. "At least he isn't as big this time around."

The corpse dissolved, and his body reformed in front of Terra. The limp, stringy hands twisted and became large crab claws.

"Goddamn it," Terra muttered when he punched her. She was barely able to throw her hands up in time to block the attack.

Anabelle rushed him, her arms crackling with lightning. She swiped at the demon but he stepped back, easily blocking the attacks. His foot melded with the water and he swung it back, then brought it forward with a tidal wave attached to his heel. The wave connected with Anabelle's face.

Rasputina lunged at the Scungilli Man, thrusting her spear at him. His body split in half to avoid her attack. As he reformed, his hand came down on the bone spear, breaking it in half.

He grabbed Rasputina and bit her throat.

The lich screamed, pressed her hand to the Scungilli Man's gelatinous head, and shot a bone spear through it.

He tore away half of Rasputina's throat and shoulder and dropped her to the floor, where she lay clutching her wound, blood pouring out at an alarming rate.

Abby teleported behind the Scungilli Man, seeking to strike the back of his neck, but before her hand could connect, he sank into the water and reformed behind her. Abby teleported away from his grasp, firing her plasma cannon. She was too close. He couldn't dodge her attack.

The blast connected and threw him backward. He skidded across the floor, caught himself with his claw, and dove into the floor with a splash.

Abby took off into the air, but she was too slow. Watery tendrils snaked up and wrapped around her legs, pulling her down into the water.

Terra slid across the floor and slashed through the tendrils, freeing Abby.

The Scungilli Man leaped out of the water, bringing both of his claws down on Terra's head as Anabelle burst into smoke and reformed behind him. She got him in a chokehold, attempting to pull him back. His skin hardened into a shell and he fell backward, sandwiching Anabelle between him and the watery surface.

Anabelle's back hit the floor, and the water didn't release her. It began dragging her slowly below the surface.

Terra reached for Anabelle, and the Scungilli Man's claw caught her across the face.

Abby flew over and he dodged her attack by stepping to the side, grasping Abby's arm with his claw. A gurgling sound like a laugh wheezed from his mouth hole. He closed the claw, cutting straight through Abby's forearm.

Abby screamed as she hit the ground, holding her stump as Terra leaped over her, axe raised high, only to be caught by the Scungilli Man's claw.

As Terra hit the ground, the creature's legs split apart into crab legs and he scuttled to Terra, his squid head bobbing comically as he cackled before slamming his claws down on her and vomiting rotten fish bones onto her.

Tendrils from the water reached up and grasped Terra, holding her arms, legs, and neck as he continued to vomit decayed sea detritus into her face.

Terra choked, trying to get air and not swallow the filth being dumped onto her face.

Water tendrils clung to Abby as well, pulling her down into the water.

Anabelle was gone.

The Scungilli Man's body grew more bulbous and gelatinous, and it jiggled. He coughed and wheezed, still spewing into Terra's face.

"Enough!" a voice shouted.

Rasputina stumbled to her feet, still grasping her wound. She cupped blood in her hand and tossed it onto the ground before shooting a bone dagger out of her other hand. She drove the dagger into the ground and cut it open.

Dark sludge bubbled out of the ground as the Scungilli Man tilted his head, staring at her.

The lich plunged one hand into the hole and raised the other. Thin, barely visible threads were connected to her fingertips.

Rasputina pulled her hand out of the hole, holding onto what looked to be a black vein. She yanked it upward, and the ground beneath her shifted. Then her other hand moved downward, the threads gleaming brightly as she tied them together.

The Scungilli Man dropped Terra and scuttled toward Rasputina, screaming his whale song.

Before he could get any closer, Rasputina leaped into the air, holding onto the black vein as she flipped over the sea monster. She yanked on the vein, trapping him.

The demon looked up at Rasputina, eyes filled with fear as the lich summoned a bolt of black lightning. The unnatural electrical charge squirmed and moved like the Dark Melody. She rammed it into his soft head.

The lightning bolt impaled him to the ground as his body convulsed and trembled, the blackness traveling through it, burning him alive.

Rasputina stood and picked up the bolt as his hat fell off. She tossed it up and spread her arms, sending the Dark Melody to the farthest corners of the chamber.

With the monster vanquished, Rasputina fell forward.

The Lords of Death had returned as well and were standing at the back of the room. The Slender Man crossed his arms as he returned to his seat. "Fine. Rasputina has the victory."

CHAPTER THIRTY-FIVE

Creon sat before an array of holoscreens stretching from one side of the room to the other. They displayed the zombies locked up around the nine realms, the images shifting every few seconds as they cycled through the entire system. It was too much for regular eyes to keep up with, so Martin was helping him watch. The strain was even a bit much for Martin to deal with, stretching his computing abilities to their limits, but the two of them were managing to stay on top of the workload.

They were looking for the slightest movement, the faintest hint of life.

Other lab technicians were doing the same in their own rooms, Martin was watching all of their screens as well. There were thousands of zombie pens across the nine realms.

Blackwell had been the only person to see a zombie blink, and he had waited for an hour to see if it happened again. It did not. This didn't change or sway his and Persephone's opinions. They knew what they had seen. The zombie had blinked, and that meant the other ones might as well.

Actively surveying the zombie pens had been Creon's idea. He understood the ramifications of what Blackwell and Persephone had seen. If even a quarter of the zombies woke up on any one planet, it could be disastrous. The number of the dead far outweighed the living.

Creon wondered if the Dark One was behind this as well. If the Omniverse was just a pleasant distraction or a double agent or any number of other things that he was glad Roy and the DGA took care of so that he didn't have to think about it.

The door to Creon's lab opened, and Cire walked into the room. "You seem busier than I expected."

Creon didn't look away from the screen. "There's been a development in the zombie issue. We haven't come up with a solution to this yet, so I can talk, but I'm afraid I can't look away from the screens in case a zombie moves."

Cire raised an eyebrow as he stroked his chin. "That does seem like a problem. You need watchers?"

"Diligent watchers."

"Give me a few minutes. I require your undivided attention. Sarah and I have need of you. I'll be back."

Cire left the room and headed toward his and Terra's room. Or at least it was when he could manage to get time away from the orc homeworld.

Their room was in one of the lower sections of HQ, where the orcs had originally been housed when they'd arrived from the Arena a few years ago. Cire could still remember the way most of the races in HQ had looked at them, and how they'd been caged away from everyone else.

Things had changed. Now there were orcs working in HQ in all departments, and that was just here. Across the nine realms, orcs had easily integrated into the different societies without any issue. Still, it always made Cire happy to return to the lower levels, away from all the noise of HQ, to spend time with his lover.

Cire stepped into Terra's room to look for one of his books, an ancient tome on constructions. He found it buried under a pile of her dirty underwear. He wondered why his books always ended up in places like that. He flipped through the book, which was full of arcane knowledge, the likes of which most had never seen.

If an alchemist wannabe ever got hold of this book, they'd be successful in any search they made for the philosopher's stone. But that wasn't what Cire was after. For one, it didn't interest him. Since his soul had been removed from his body, he'd found there were few things he desired, and gold was low on that list. What Cire needed at the moment was infinitely more valuable than gold.

He made his way from the bottom of HQ to the gardens that were overlooked by Myrddin's office. As he walked the paths, looking for a bit of untouched dirt, he saw Myrddin poke his head out of his office's windows.

Myrddin waved, a friendly gesture from a man who looked very tired. "Fancy seeing you down here, Cire. What brings you to the garden?"

Cire pointed at a mound of dirt. "Simple alchemy. I require a member of your staff, but he is tied up with mindless work at the moment. Creon."

Myrddin nodded as he stepped out of his window, waving his wand to create stairs beneath his feet. "Yes, I believe he is running surveillance on the zombie pens. A rudimentary solution, but effective for the time being. What are you thinking?"

"Anything with eyes that can watch. A false beholder, perhaps."

Myrddin smiled faintly. "Your magical skills have grown quite impressively. It was a surprise to see the next lich be such a gentle orc."

Cire frowned. "Did you not know of the orc shaman's tradition?"

Myrddin knelt and sighed as he regarded the pile of dirt Cire stood before. "No, I did not. Contrary to what people think, there are a large number of things I do not know about the nine realms."

"You don't try to eliminate that view."

Myrddin didn't look up but continued to stare at the pile of dirt. "No, no, I do not."

Cire knelt beside Myrddin and began scratching sigils in a circle around the pile of earth. "While we're on the topic of things you do or do not know, have you ever heard of any additional Paths of the Travelers? Paths other than the three?"

Myrddin shook his head as he stepped away from Cire's work. "No, I'm afraid not. My knowledge of the various elvish martial arts is unfortunately lacking, as is my knowledge of most elvish magic."

Cire raised his eyebrow in surprise. "You? I'd assume you'd be the human who knew the most."

"Hardly. That knowledge is heavily protected by the elves. Only an initiated few are privy to that kind of information. You should have seen the faces of the elvish delegates when they found out that two humans now walk one of the Traveler's Paths. Why do you ask?"

Cire touched his hand to his sigil. The pile of dirt that he had carved the sigils around shook as it shot upward, the dry earth turning soft and muddy and forming the body of a broad-shouldered man. Multiple dull eyes opened on the body of the golem.

The orc walked around the creation, admiring his work. "Sarah received some words from the Omniverse sphere that we think might be used for communicating. The Path of Pain."

Myrddin was silent while he thought. "No, I'm afraid that doesn't bring anything to mind, but I will keep an eye out for anything that pertains to it." The wizard raised his wand and conjured stairs that led up to his office's window. "By the way, your magic is coming along quite well. I'm glad to see that you've managed to hold on to your sanity."

Cire looked at the golem standing before him. "I am too."

The golem was placed in Creon's laboratory and given the simple task of alerting Martin if it saw any movement from the zombies. Creon, being uncertain about leaving the task to a golem, ran visual tests to see if it was up to the task. Once he was satisfied, he left with Cire.

Sarah was waiting for them in the training room.

Creon looked around, bemused by all the weapons hanging from the walls. "Out of curiosity, why have you brought me here? What does this have to do with speaking to the Omniverse?"

Sarah approached Creon, eyeing Cire. "You didn't tell him why we needed him?"

Cire shook his head, the briefest shadow of shame passing over his face. "I believed it would be easier if we both were present."

Sarah locked eyes with Creon. "I think I've found a way to talk to the Omniverse, but it isn't going to be easy. I need your help to keep me alive."

Creon frowned as he tried to figure out what Sarah was talking about. "How are you going to need my help?"

"There's a new Path, one I don't think I can reach on my own. The Path of Pain."

Sarah walked away from Creon and Cire toward the wall. She removed her shirt and placed her hands on the surface, revealing a heavily scarred back.

Cire took a deep breath as he turned to face Creon. "We believe pain is the door to open this path. Sarah already has a high pain tolerance. We will need someone who can revive her quickly if she passes into death. Someone who can do that fast and often in a short period of time. Do you think you can do that?"

Creon sighed and shook his head. "How many times has she—"

"Twice so far. Reviving her was...difficult, but she believes she is getting closer. Will you help?"

Creon pulled up a holoscreen on his comm unit and displayed Sarah's vital signs. "You both will listen to me and not question my judgment. And yes, I should be able to help you."

Sarah looked over her shoulder and shouted impatiently, "Come on, Cire, let's get this over with."

Cire raised his hand, muttered under his breath, and pointed it at Sarah.

Six long, deep slashes tore open across Sarah's back.

Creon gasped as Sarah's screams filled the room.

She fell to one knee as she took a deep breath and bit down hard on her lip.

Cire looked at the open door of the training room. "I think it might be a good idea to close that door."

The Lords of Death were talking quietly among themselves. Rasputina and the DGA agents waited for them to finish their discussion.

Abby was curious and wanted to start her own conversation. "What did you do, Rasputina? Earlier, with those black veins?"

Rasputina looked at Grok hesitantly but answered before the orc could say anything. "That's how Grok and I have been building. Hell is made up of energy similar to that of the Netherverse, a type of the Dark Melody. I don't know where it comes from or why it's different from what's in the Netherverse, but it can be bent if your will is strong enough."

Terra's eyes widened as she whistled. "Are you saying you can control the Dark Melody?"

Rasputina shook her head. "I'm not sure I can control all of it, but whatever is in hell is easy enough for me to manipulate. I can bend it to my will and create my own reality here."

Anabelle hadn't taken her eyes off the Lords of Death. "What about the statues of us. You decided to make those...why?"

Rasputina avoided the eyes of the Dark Gate Angels. "That's not important."

Anabelle laughed quietly. "There are huge statues of us in the middle of your little world. Why wouldn't that be important?"

Rasputina's eyes looked wild for a moment before they filled with tears. She looked away from the Dark Gate Angels. "Because you're heroes, more so than anyone I've ever met. And..."

The lich turned to face the DGA, her face reverting from its youth back to the hollow skeletal visage she used to show the world and then quickly filling out with bright, living skin. "You gave me another chance—a chance to become something more than a lich. I am remaking hell into a better place for souls like me. That is something I can do."

Anubis cleared his throat and waved Rasputina and the DGA over. "Your victory is substantial, and we formally grant you the right to rule hell. But there are some conditions to this rule."

"What are they?" Rasputina asked.

"For starters, do not make a habit of allowing mortals to enter. These three, understandable. They've proven themselves worthy of standing on hellish ground. And the orc, of course."

Grok smiled and politely nodded her head.

Anubis continued, "Second, we will be allowed in the realm for whatever business we need as long as it does not interfere with your rule. Third, the Slender Man would like to resurrect his Scungilli Man to do with as he pleases."

Rasputina agreed to the conditions.

"And fourth," Anubis said, "the material of hell's creation must remain in hell, not mined by or for mortals. Understood?"

Rasputina extended her hand to Anubis, who took and shook it.

He and the other lords bowed slightly. "Very well, Lord Rasputina. Enjoy your rule."

The lords disappeared in puffs of smoke, and behind the Dark Gate Angels, the Scungilli Man's corpse dissolved into water and disappeared.

Rasputina turned to face the DGA. "Now, I assume there was something that brought you here.

CHAPTER THIRTY-SIX

Abby watched as the council chamber disappeared, the ground sliding out from underneath her feet as the ceiling stretched away, revealing stars. What was behind the stars caught her attention. Blackness swirled about, waves crashing over each other like a dark sea.

It was calming, and she felt like she could watch it forever.

Rasputina floated up toward the swirling blackness, turning for a moment and motioning for Abby and the rest to follow her.

Once they had all passed the stars, reality started to shift into focus again. Columns stretched up out of the nonexistent floor, which quickly covered itself in intricate black and blue tiles that spread from the floor to the walls, then changed the ceiling's color and coalesced to form multiple golden chandeliers.

Rasputina sat down on a throne in the middle of the room. "Thank you for the help. I don't think I could have killed that beast if you hadn't provided me with a distraction."

Terra kicked her feet up on the ottoman between the four of them and leaned back in her chair. "No problem. It was horrifying, but at least... *HOLY SHIT, ABBY, I COMPLETELY FORGOT ABOUT YOUR ARM!*"

Abby's right arm was no longer bleeding, but it was a messy stub cradled next to her chest. She hadn't noticed that she wasn't reeling in pain anymore. Martin must have killed her pain receptors, and the disorienting, mind-bending transition in Rasputina's Citadel had been distracting enough.

But the distraction was over now, and looking down at her stump, she stammered, "Oh, shit, we…uh…hm… Hold on, we need to take care of this."

Abby knew what she had to do. The thought crossed her mind whenever she thought of worst-case scenarios. Even though she had already entertained the idea, she still felt somewhat melancholic.

Martin popped up. "So, you're finally taking the plunge?"

"Don't really have a choice," Abby answered. "Right now is as good a time as any."

"All right, kid. Hope you like the new arm."

Abby's attention returned to the conversation around her. Nanobots crawled out of her wound, which they had cauterized earlier, and began building, adding protein chains to nanobot chains to craft an entirely new arm.

Terra was trying not to look like she was staring, and Abby ignored her friend's eyes.

After a few minutes, Abby had rebuilt her arm. Anabelle, Terra, and Rasputina watched with amazement.

"Damn, girl," Terra muttered.

Rasputina nodded. "Impressive."

"Thank you," Abby said. "But please, you were saying about hell…" She gestured for the lich to speak.

"Very well. It's simple enough. The Lords of Death refused to share any of their information with me until I was officially one of them. At first I thought they cared about hell, but apparently, this place hasn't had a ruler for centuries. Each of them has their own underworld to rule, and it's assumed that one must have their *own* underworld to rule."

Anabelle leaned forward, her eyes hungry for information. "And they know what the Omniverse is?"

Rasputina nodded as she rubbed her temples. Her face looked tired and strained. Even when she relaxed into her chair, she looked tense and uncomfortable. "I do not know everything. The Lords are still wary about giving away all their information. As far as they're concerned, I am a child, barely older than that idiotic Slender Man. But they did tell me what the Omniverse is. Its true name is the Light One."

Terra bust out laughing and slapped her kneecap. "You've got to be fucking with me? The Light One? I thought the only reason we called the Dark One by that name was that Myrddin lacked imagination. Those things actually call each other by those titles?"

Rasputina rested her head on her hand. "No, they do not. Those are simply the names they give to us. Names hold an extremely large amount of power, and it would be foolish to assume that any being of that much strength would reveal its real name."

Abby remembered something that she had read in one of the dossiers on the Dark One. "Wait, two different groups found the Dark One's name—the Mundanes, and Team Boundless, the dragonriders. They said it was Jodin or something like that."

Rasputina looked up, her eyes interested. "The Dark One is a master of magical names. Some would consider his name to be the same as the Norse God of War, the One-Eyed Prophet. But even that is a name he allows mortals to know. We might not find out what his true name is until we kill him. But the Light One is...something different than the Dark One. It is perhaps the strongest thing in existence."

Terra cracked her knuckles. "I'm pretty sure that's what everything says until it meets us."

Rasputina shook her head slowly. "No, it might be. According to the Lords, the Light One is the very embodiment of life and death. It is...sort of a piece of the multiverse... No, that's not right. It's more like...the Omniverse and the Netherverse are two sides of the same coin. They are inseparable. A balance must be maintained between them at all times. The Light One is the caretaker of the balance."

"So, are you saying I can't kill it?"

Abby ignored Terra's question. "That would make the Light One a good guy, right? If it cares about the balance, it would help us destroy the Dark One."

Rasputina reached out for a glass of wine that had magically appeared on the table. "Balance and morality are two very different things. The Light One doesn't care about anything other than balance. It will destroy whatever it needs to in search of maintaining that balance. There is no emotion in it. No empathy. If wiping out the nine realms would restore the balance between the Omniverse and the Netherverse, it would do it in a heartbeat."

Terra snagged one of the cups of wine on the table. "It sounds like a huge bag of shit."

"The Dark One, it would seem, is something of an avatar of the Netherverse. The lords don't know if he's one of the elder gods or he predates them, or if he *was* the Netherverse at some point. But now, for whatever reason, he is trying to do something other than he initially was intended to. Conquering realms, destroying life at a whim on a massive scale. The Dark One has gone rogue, and the Light One is here to fix the damage that has been done. I don't know why the Light One has decided now is the time to fix this, but for whatever reason, we need to make sure the Dark One does not provoke the Light One into any more action."

Anabelle sighed as she shook her head. "The Light One gave us a time limit. Twelve moons or some shit like that. What exactly are we supposed to fix?"

Rasputina stood and wrapped herself in a cloak she pulled from nowhere. "The lords of death have agreed to fight the Dark One. They've also shared some of their observations. Anubis believes that since the Dark One is weakened and can no longer be in control of the Netherverse, he's opting to flat-out destroy everything."

Abby snapped her fingers as she jumped up excitedly. "That's what we thought he was going to do! But we couldn't figure out what kind of weapon he could use that could destroy all of the realms. It would have to be—"

"He doesn't need a weapon," Rasputina said. "The imbalance *is* the weapon, and he's been working on it for some time. His massive culling of souls, finding ways to send them to the Netherverse regardless of where they belong. Tricking Grok and me into closing the valve was just a drop in the bucket of what he's been trying to accomplish. By creating an extreme imbalance, he's hoping to trick the Light One into destroying everything."

Abby was trying to track what the lich was saying. She understood the metaphysics of what Rasputina had explained, but she still wasn't certain about the motives...or the technicalities of how it was to happen. Truthfully, that didn't matter. She understood the Dark One had found a way to destroy the nine realms, regardless of his defeat. "We don't need to understand how or why he's doing this. If we kill him, the problem goes away."

Rasputina's true age shone on her face for a moment. "True. Regardless of his reasoning, he's a vicious animal backed into a corner, and he's lashing out. All we need to do is put him down."

A high-pitched giggle came from the far side of the room.

Rasputina jumped to her feet, waved her hands, and pulled up a wall of bones between her and the DGA and the source of the laughter. She pulled her arms close, which yanked Abby and the others near her. "Who dares enter my sanctum?"

A small child wearing a deer skull mask, his skin as pale as snow, stepped into the light. His hands were covered in deep red blood, as was his chest. Thick black hair was clutched in his hand, and a decapitated green head swung from his fist.

The Pale One threw the head, and it hit the ground with a smack as it rolled toward the bone gate.

Rasputina screamed, her voice hollow and pained as Grok's face looked up at her.

The Pale One giggled, his voice echoing in the heads of all in the room. "You never fail to impress, Rasputina. You've learned and gained so much...in so little time...even without a soul. Look at you, caring about mortals. Obviously not enough, or this one wouldn't be dead."

Rasputina sank to the floor, clutching her heart as she screamed, "You killed her, you killed her!"

The Pale One waved his hand, shattering the bone cage separating him from Rasputina and the DGA. "There is still much you do not know."

Rasputina grabbed Grok's head and pulled it close to her chest, weeping as she prayed inaudible words over her friend, rocking back and forth and trembling.

The Pale One's wooden mask's mouth turned up in a grin, the wood groaning as it stretched. "Still so much to learn."

***

Sarah could hardly stand. Her back was carved up, and she didn't want to think about how much blood she'd lost, but she knew her skin was too slick to dress again. She felt weightless, but that was because Creon and Cire were holding her up, dragging her to the Omniverse.

She had commanded them to bring her to the Omniverse. It had reached out and spoken to her. It knew she could hear it, and it knew she could speak to it.

The night was freezing, and Sarah held her arms close to her chest to try to warm herself while Creon and Cire placed her before the sphere.

Sarah closed her eyes, focusing and trying to hear the voice she'd heard before.

There was a shred of her still here; she could sense it. That was what had to leave her body. She looked over her shoulder, her back erupting in pain. "Cire, I need to go over. You'll know when."

Cire's face was blank of emotion, but he nodded nonetheless.

Sarah pulled into herself, opening each of her gates one by one, each gate flooding her body with energy that made her skin feel as if it were unraveling down to the bone. She needed to get to the last one, to make it to the Path of the Lost.

The last gate opened, and Sarah's eyes flashed with fire as she threw her arms outward as if she were trying to embrace someone.

Cire muttered under his breath, and Sarah's back exploded with fresh wounds.

Her mouth clenched as her mind went white. Her body fell forward, but she didn't feel the ground against her skin. Instead, there was a warm caress across her cheeks.

The sphere burst into flames as her limp body floated into the air.

Sarah could hear the Light One speaking quietly into her bones, setting everything within her on fire.

She could speak with the Light One, languages she'd never heard before pouring out of her mouth.

The Omniverse vanished.

Sarah's feet touched the ground, her wounds healed, and Cire ran to her, wrapping her body in her cloak. "Did it work?" he asked.

Sarah looked up at Cire, her eyes burning with the same light that had been cast from the Omniverse. "I will speak to the Dark One. This one is my vessel now, and there will be balance."

CHAPTER THIRTY-SEVEN

Abby stared down at Grok's lifeless eyes as she backed away from Rasputina's shrieks. Before she realized what she was doing, she was flying toward the Dark One's child avatar, screaming with rage, her blood creating and pumping nanobots.

A wall of bone ripped up out of the ground, separating Abby from the Dark One, slowly coating itself in hell's variation of the Dark Melody.

Abby hit the bone wall with a heavy thud and scrambled to her feet, looking for her teammates. They were behind her, and rather than attacking again, she decided to join them to do what they did best: fight as a team.

Rasputina clutched Grok's head to her chest. "Stop! Don't you see what he's trying to do?"

Anabelle stepped forward, her face stony and her lips trembling. "He killed her. That's what he did."

Rasputina shook her head. "Not here. Not in my domain. He doesn't have that kind of power here. This will still be hard, and I will need your help. Please?"

The angels came over to Rasputina's side and knelt next to the lich, whose face twitched as if someone were pulling on her skin, trying to tug it away and show what was buried deep within.

"What do you need?" Terra asked.

Rasputina circled her hand above them, her eyes rolling back in her head. "Your energy. Relax your bodies, your spirits. I need extra strength to bring her back. She can't be too far. And then I will have to rebuild. But I will need you to do it quickly. Usually in a few minutes. Please, focus."

Abby realized the lich was no longer talking to them, but she knew to listen. She closed her eyes and focused, letting her body give up whatever energy Rasputina needed.

Her energy was sucked out of her in an instant. It felt like having the wind knocked out of her. She fell over on her side, gasping for breath. Anabelle and Terra hit the ground beside her. When Abby tried to move, she found she had no strength. The most she could do was twitch as she watched Rasputina.

Rasputina reached up as if she were trying to grasp something, her hands wrapped around an invisible shape. The ceiling above her split down the middle, revealing a cyclone of flames above—millions of souls caught in a sort of limbo. A lash of flame wrapped around Rasputina's arm and she wrapped it again quickly, winding it up her forearm and pulling as hard as she could. The skin of her arm burst into flames, searing down to the bone.

Rasputina did not stop pulling. Bones stretched up from the ground and latched onto her feet and knees, anchoring her to the ground as the flaming spirit above tried to escape. Arcane words spewed from her mouth, a dark incantation that yanked the soul from the sky and slammed it on the ground.

The lich dove forward and grabbed the soul, rolling it in her hand until it was like dough and shoving it into her mouth. She pressed her lips to Grok's as her hands grabbed at the little bit of bone exposed in the orc's severed neck. The lich's fingers worked as if they were a spider's hind legs, knitting new bone from her own fingers.

A scream escaped the lich as she leaned forward, her hands gone, only the nubs of her bones left. She closed her eyes, rocking back and forth as her hands rapidly grew back. Then she went to work again, bone arms ripping from her back, continuing the work along with her other hands, building Grok's skeleton.

Once the bones were all in place, Rasputina pressed her hands to the orc's sternum and let out a whimper as all of her skin and muscle unraveled and attached to the bones, building new muscle and skin.

Rasputina's bones crumpled to the ground as a small spark floated from her open jaws and settled on Grok's lips.

Grok's eyes snapped open and she jerked up. "The Dark One, he's here. The Dark One!" She looked around, trying to piece together what had happened. Her eyes fell on Rasputina's bones. "No!" she shouted as she fell next to Rasputina's head.

Rasputina's green eyes burned brightly in the hollow of her skull as the jaw fell open. "I will not let him take you away. Not here."

The ground beneath Rasputina erupted and covered the bones in the Dark Melody, which formed into a new skin.

Rasputina slowly got to her feet, setting her jaw as the last bit of skin grew over the bones.

Abby felt her strength come back to her. She sat up as the bone wall between the Dark One's avatar and the DGA agents disappeared.

Rasputina ran her hand over her naked body, creating a black cloak that draped over her head. "Who dares disturb my domain?"

The child with the deer mask let out a cynical laugh. "*Your* domain? The recently crowned queen of hell?"

The child floated into the air, his body as limp as a doll's as he swayed. "This monument to your hubris, your broken mortality...this is your domain?" He fell back to the ground, digging his hands into the fabric of the place and pulling at it as he stood. "It barely holds together."

Rasputina's eyes flashed. "State your name and purpose or be banished. Your true name."

"Can you not tell? I'm the Dark One."

Once the words were out of the child's mouth, the skin of his back tore open, caught in a heavy gust that threatened to tear him away from this plane of existence.

The wind disappeared, and the child fell forward. He slowly got to his feet.

Rasputina smiled. "This is my domain, and you will be held to my rules here. Now, your name. Your true name. And your purpose."

The child lifted his mask, and a sound came from underneath, an obscene jumble of low notes that seemed to come from hell, burning and boiling within Abby's mind. It was a cacophony of malice and violence with no limits; the sound of his name made her want to run screaming into the whiteness of the Citadel.

Abby looked off to her side and saw that Anabelle and Terra were affected the same way.

The child returned his mask to his face. "Grimnir, for you mortals. And my purpose is to make a deal. It seems we have come across the same enemy, the Light One. I believe we might be able to help each other if we put aside our past differences."

Anabelle laughed loudly. "You're fucking kidding, right? Your idea of beginning negotiations is killing our friend?"

Grok looked at Anabelle, who blushed before clearing her throat and returning her gaze to Grimnir, the Dark One's avatar.

His mask turned up in a caustic parody of a smile. "It was necessary to get your attention. And to let you know I am quite serious."

Abby wracked her mind, trying to see what didn't add up. She could have sworn she'd heard about this small avatar of the Dark One before, but he'd had a different name.

And he hadn't been aggressive.

Suddenly, Abby remembered. She'd heard about the Dark One's masked avatar from reading Boundless' reports, the dragonriders. Alex had encountered the avatar within the meteorite that had almost destroyed Middang3ard.

But this avatar was nothing like that one. He had helped Alex.

Even if Grimnir looked like whatever Alex had seen, there was a good chance this was simply another trick.

Terra took a step forward. "Obviously, your shit must have gotten more fucked up than we realized if you think we'd want to make a deal with you."

Grimnir's masked smile faded. "Hardly. By now, you must have found out what the Light One is. It does not care about your noble battle to destroy me and bring peace to your realm. Balance is all the Light One cares about, and if you are on the wrong side of that balance, you will end up dead, along with anything else it deems worthy of that fate."

The DGA agents looked at Rasputina, who still hadn't taken her eyes off Grimnir. "What do you propose?" the lich asked.

The mask's smile returned as he casually paced, his toes barely touching the ground. "You swear loyalty to me—"

Terra snorted derisively. "Oh, you've got to be kidding me. That line again?"

The boy waved his hand, and Terra went flying.

Anabelle and Abby prepared to rush forward, but Rasputina held out her hand. "You know the rules of my court. Another slip-up, and you will be banished."

Grimnir's mask sneered. "You can risk me being taken out of here, along with my offer?"

Rasputina didn't reply.

Terra picked herself up off the ground and wiped the blood from her nose as she returned to the group, grumbling under her breath

Grimnir continued, "The valve in hell was never your problem. The one in the Netherverse, of which I have complete control, is all that will save you now. My armies guard it, so any attempt to take control will be met with overwhelming force. If I were to have your loyalty, I would reopen the valve in the Netherverse. I would also allow the souls of the dead into my domain. That, and only that, will satisfy the Light One's desire for balance, and by extension, save your lives and the lives of those who reside in your precious Nine Realms."

Anabelle crossed her arms. "What's in it for us?"

Abby couldn't believe what she'd just heard come out of Anabelle's mouth. Was the elf thinking about trusting the Dark One?

The mask's smile widened. "Aren't the lives of everyone in the Nine Realms enough?"

Anabelle shook her head. "Not if it means being in your service."

Grimnir couldn't hide his frustration. "Very well, then, I leave this universe and never come back. All of the Nine Realms and anything else that happens to exist in this universe will be safe from me. As for your loyalty to me, let us say that I am not a very demanding master."

Anabelle shook her head. "But you would be free to do whatever you want in the other universes? And with us loyal to you, the Nine Realms will be under your control by proxy? Is that the game?"

"Your loyalty is merely a convenience, so the other lords of the Netherverse do not think they have a chance against me. I tire of killing them. I would much rather have their subservience, which is why I need a public show of your loyalty. That, and nothing more. Once I have it, you and yours will never hear from me again."

Anabelle crossed her arms. "Funny how I don't feel comfortable just taking your word for it."

Grimnir placed his feet back on the ground. Then, putting his hand up as if he were a Boy Scout swearing an oath, he said, "I vow on my existence that I will not betray my word. I do believe Rasputina's realm is particularly partial to vows of this sort, correct?"

The lich shot a furtive look at Anabelle. "True. Vows hold power over life and death here. If he were to break it, even after leaving hell, it would kill him."

Grimnir's head shook. "Believe me, there is a reason the Light One came to you, searching for me. Even the light is afraid to come for me. You may have defeated me once, but you will not do so again. The light knows how strong I am. That is why it hides, waiting for you to do its bidding. I offer you a way out, do I not?"

No one answered.

The boy snickered. "Perhaps you would like time to speak among yourselves. See how much you value your precious universe when compared to the fates of others."

He turned, and the air in front of him folded in on itself before splitting down the middle and swallowing Grimnir.

Rasputina slumped and ran her hands through her hair. "No, no, no."

Grok knelt beside her. "Rasputina, I need you to stay here with me. We have to figure this out."

Terra raised an eyebrow as she smirked. "Wait, you guys are actually thinking about this? That's fucking crazy. There's no way we can trust him, and even if we did—"

Abby cut Terra off. "We'd be releasing him on every other universe and reality to do as he pleases. We can't do that, right?"

Anabelle wouldn't meet Abby's eyes. "I don't know what we can do."

The words hung heavy in Abby's heart. She could hear the truth in the elf's voice.

CHAPTER THIRTY-EIGHT

A magical projection of the Nine Realms appeared in front of the DGA. They were stacked on top of each other, floating in the middle of the table before them.

Terra took a seat and grumbled, "Do you think we really need this visual representation?"

Rasputina ignored Terra as she scanned the display of the Nine Realms. "He can't lie to me here. My magic would alert me. Surprisingly, of all the things you can't do in hell, lying and breaking vows are highest among them."

Terra gave Rasputina a doubtful look.

The lich rubbed her face, looking tired and frustrated. "The only reason the lords of death agreed to help me was because of an old vow between them and the Dark One. He made a deal with many of the older lords that they would stand by his side as long as he remained undefeated. Because of you, that vow was broken."

Anabelle shook her head in disgust. "So, what? He suffers one defeat, and everything they swore is null and void? "

Rasputina nodded. "But there's more to it. The lords are responsible for things incomprehensible to mortals. Things that are essential for balance."

"Blah, blah, blah, balance. Who can I hit? That's all I want to know," Terra said.

Rasputina's voice was hard as she ignored the human gladiator. "Things necessary for all of existence. Mortal Death and the places where their souls go is chief among them. As cold and heartless as it sounds, all things—animals, plants, people, worlds, even—must all die. Nothing can go on living forever. If it does, it becomes corrupted. Evil. Like me. Or worse, like the Dark One. And the lords are an essential part of the natural order of things, of the balance."

"Makes sense," Anabelle said. "Live as best you can. Prepare yourself for what comes next. The Path of the Traveler teaches that."

The elf reached out and touched the realm projection. "So, what do we do? Decide to preserve our own lives, thus damning the other universes, or let the Light One wipe us out? Wait, why are we assuming that's what the Light One is going to do? All it said before was it wanted to speak to the Dark One. It didn't say anything about wiping us out of existence. Granted, it did unleash zombies across all the realms."

Rasputina frowned and nodded. "The Dark One is first and foremost a creature of manipulation and lies. Grimnir is no different. The mask hides what he thinks, what he feels. That's probably why he was the avatar the Dark One sent to speak with us. He could be bluffing, trying to con us into making a decision before we understand everything that is going on."

Terra ran her hand over her shaved head. "Ugh. I am so not down for mind games. Why can't we just beat the snot out of the little shit? He was hardly bigger than—"

Grok interrupted Terra. "He ripped my head off without so much as a thought."

Terra crossed her arms and nodded. "Righto, mate. Guess you got a pretty good point there. Strong and moderately smart. I'm still not going to buy into this whole 'the Dark One is trying to pull the wool over our eyes.' His plans haven't been the smartest. They all basically boil down to 'throw as many troops at something as possible.' He's probably scrambling as much as we are. Maybe even hoping we make a mistake and fuck ourselves by assuming he's got a James Bond villain level of cunning."

Grok grunted in response. "That holds. But it's always a mistake to underestimate your enemy. It could easily end with our deaths. On the off-chance he is smarter than he looks, we end up dead."

Anabelle turned to Abby, who seemed to be deep in thought. "Can you still communicate with the Light One? Maybe we can get some perspective on what the game is."

Abby shook her head. "We can barely keep in contact with Creon and HQ at the moment, and even that's a barebones connection. We haven't received anything from them for a while." She sighed. "This feels wrong. It feels like we shouldn't even be talking about it. If we agree, he'll be on top again. He'll be free to keep on killing and conquering. Everything we've been fighting for means absolutely nothing."

Anabelle shook her head as she stared down at her hands. "No, we've been fighting for our realms. We can't conceptualize other universes. Before this was brought to our attention, we weren't thinking of them."

Abby's eyes watered as she slammed her hand on the table. "*We've* seen them! We watched thousands of versions of ourselves die in battle against the Dark One. We saw all of you dead across thousands of timelines. Even if it's not this specific universe or this specific time-line, he is going to kill."

Anabelle nodded, thinking about what the girl had said. "I under-stand this is hard for you, Abby. You've experienced something we could never understand. But we have to be practical. Throughout all those alternate universes, did you find anywhere the Dark One didn't win?"

Abby shook her head.

"Exactly," Anabelle continued. "We have a chance to save at least one."

"That's not true," Abby countered. "If we die, so does the Dark One, and every other universe stays safe. They'll never experience what we have."

Silence fell over the table as they all weighed the option.

Terra groaned. "Fuck, when you put it like that, it does seem pretty selfish. I don't know if I'm ready for that, though. I've had a pretty good run, but I'm not ready to throw in the towel yet. There's got to be another way."

The lich cleared her throat, catching everyone's attention. "There is another option. We lie."

Terra threw her arms up. "Oh, my fucking God, you said we couldn't break any vows made in hell! That's the reason the Dark One wouldn't be able to attack us."

Rasputina nodded. "True, but don't forget this is my domain. My rules. If the vow was broken, it would be of no consequence. Grimnir is hoping we are tired of the war against the Dark One and will prioritize our own existence... "The lich absentmindedly tugged her skin. "That we believe our battle against him is pointless. That it will go on forever. He believes we're ready to quit."

Terra pulled a dagger from a side sheath and slammed it into the table. "I cannot express how much I am not done fighting this asshole."

Abby nodded. "Same. We would give our life if it meant destroying the Dark One and keeping others safe."

Anabelle took a long time to answer. "Shit, don't look at me like that. Of course I'd fight the Dark One to the bitter end. I'd prefer to still have some semblance of a normal life after all of this but...oh, who am I kidding? I had a normal life. A glamorous life. And it wasn't enough. I wanted in on this fight. It's all I wanted."

Abby nodded as she relaxed into her chair, looking at the nanobots covering her hand in sleek black armor. "We started this looking for revenge. Everything was simpler back then, but we quickly saw what was at stake. Besides, we missed the whole graduating high school thing. There's no way we're going to go back for a GED and do the college route. This right here is what we are here for."

Terra picked at her teeth with her knife. "Oh, is it my turn to say something inspirational? Uh, yeah, fuck the Dark One, orcs are the shit, blah blah blah, let's fuck this asshole over."

Anabelle turned to Rasputina. "If we lie, what happens? I thought you said he'd die if he broke the contract. Why won't we?"

"Because we will use a different bartering tool than he did," Rasputina said. "When the contract is voided, he will be able to attack our universe."

"Which basically means we're back at square one, and we don't lose anything. Why stop there? If we break our loyalty from him, we could go to other universes and prep them for the battle ahead. One of the reasons the Nine Realms got so fucked was because we didn't see it coming. We could train his next targets. He'd be walking straight into a trap, and then we'd be there. If he tries to retaliate against our realms, we'll still be ready."

Grok scoffed. "This war of yours could go on for the rest of our lives. Are you prepared for that?"

Terra groaned. "Dude, did you not hear the speeches they gave?"

"What if it goes on beyond your mortal lives?" Rasputina asked. "Are you prepared to do what you must?"

Anabelle looked at Rasputina. "What do you mean?"

"There are ways to live forever. Granted, you as an elf will go on living for hundreds more years. Terra's life will be expanded because of her tie to Cire and his lichness."

Terra sat bolt upright, her eyes bright and a huge smile on her face. "Wait, what? No one told me that!" She jumped out of her seat and did a bizarre jig, jumping on one foot while holding her palm to her head. "Extra human life," she sang to herself. When she was done, she sat down with an unbelievable amount of dignity.

The lich cleared her throat, ignoring Terra's outburst, and continued, "But you may need more time. I could show you how to become liches. It is a difficult path to walk, one I believe most liches have misunderstood for a long time. But having found that orcs have a tradition of long-lived moral liches, it is a possibility. When the time draws nearer..."

The DGA agents thought it over for some time before Anabelle answered, "Like you said, death is part of existence. If I have to give the next five hundred years of my life to fighting the Dark One, so be it. We'll train a generation to fight under us, and when we die, they'll be there to carry on."

Terra pointed her dagger at Anabelle. "Yeah, what she said." Across the table, Abby nodded in agreement.

Grok smiled, her teeth glinting. "I never would have assumed any of you were warriors of this caliber when we first fought." She stood. "It would be my honor to fight alongside you against the Dark One until we breathe our final breaths."

"Ah shit, Grok's finally finished her Goku/Vegeta story arc." Terra smirked as she looked at Abby.

Rasputina conjured a paper and quill pen. "Then it is decided. Let us draft the agreement."

"And prepare for one hell of a fight," Anabelle added.

CHAPTER THIRTY-NINE

As Rasputina scribbled symbols and sigils on the paper, the Citadel around her began changing. The walls broke apart into boxes, shifting around each other as colors poured from the blank space as if the Citadel was bleeding. The space the DGA occupied turned into a glass prism.

Abby could see outside where the demons walked around living their lives, the populace unaware of what transpired in the crystal spire Rasputina had built.

The spire continued to mutate, shifting in space and rising above the rest of the Citadel, floating through the air as the lich continued to work.

The rest of the DGA stood and wandered around with Grok, watching the changes happening throughout the spire. Abby stayed and watched Rasputina work. Some of the symbols and sigils the lich used were familiar to Abby.

Rasputina looked up, noticing Abby watching her. "I see your interest in magic is more than general curiosity."

Abby pulled her seat closer to her. "May I?"

The lich pushed the paper closer to Abby to allow the human to get a better view. "Each of these symbols is tied to the world around us. It's one of the more complicated ways for me to manipulate the Dark Melody in here. But they are also tied to the contract, the language of what I'm creating. This whole place is built from my vows, my promises to the people here, to Grok, and to myself. Anytime one of them is broken, the thing I've created disappears. That makes the creation of vows complicated."

"What do you mean?"

"If I know a vow is going to be broken, there's only so much I can create. I have to make something I understand will eventually go away, that no one here will depend on or need. It only requires mindfulness. Take this one, for example..."

Rasputina waved her hand, and a statue of a golden pig rose from the table's surface. "This was my first attempt at a creation meant to be broken. Naturally, no one would miss this. But as the stakes grow higher, the language becomes more demanding, and the constructions must grow more complicated. It can be a time-consuming process, but we have a little bit of time. A full day until we meet him again."

Abby continued to watch her work. "There are a lot of rules to magic."

The lich nodded as she traced runes on the paper. "For this kind of magic, yes. There's no heart in it, not like the elemental magic Anabelle uses, only structure. You find the creativity in that."

"What if you built a trap?"

Rasputina raised her eyebrow. "What do you mean?"

"If you're building something that is going to fall apart when it's broken, what if you built something that fell apart in a way that would hurt the Dark One? The same way you're thinking about creating something unneeded, what if you created something that caused another effect by not existing?"

Rasputina smiled deviously. "You will make an excellent sigil worker. I see you have the creativity in you. Once you get the sigils down, you might be a force to be reckoned with."

Abby laughed softly. "Doubtful."

Rasputina scratched at the back of her head, insanity creeping into her eyes for a moment before receding. "No. You have a hunger for knowledge. I can see it. You're not much different than I used to be. Except for your methodology. And maybe your heart."

The sadness in Rasputina's eyes made Abby want to move away, but she stayed. "You're strong," the lich continued. "And you have strong friends. Remember them while you walk your path."

"What are you talking about?"

The lich returned to her writing. "There are many ways one may become a lich. Not all of them are intentional."

Abby nodded slowly as she took in her words. There was no malice in them. It seemed like a genuine warning. "What do you mean?"

"There is an interesting dichotomy in magic. We lose a little bit of ourselves with every use. You see it most among the spell weavers. I trust you've seen the magical veins running through Myrddin's skin."

Abby thought back to the thinness of Myrddin's skin and the electric-blue veins that shone through. "Yeah, I have."

"They grow back what magic takes. Over time, everyone does. But your mortality is necessary for growth. Once you lose that, you start taking from something you can't replenish."

Abby looked down at her robotic arm. "You think they're the same thing? Our growing lack of humanity?"

"Be careful."

Rasputina toiled long into the night, leaving the DGA agents and Grok with time to kill until the next meeting with the Dark One and the lords of death. According to Rasputina, the lords had to be present. It also would work as a show of power for the DGA and Rasputina's coalition.

So, Terra, Anabelle, and Grok walked throughout the spire while Abby stayed with Rasputina to learn.

Back in the Nine Realms, Creon watched Sarah from behind a sheet of thick glass. A handful of Abby's drones were taking readings on her.

After Sarah had communicated with the Light One, she'd come along quietly, her eyes burning with the same light as the Light One's sphere. She hadn't said much, simply repeated her desire to speak with the Dark One.

What Creon was seeing now was astonishing. Sarah's body was radiating with the Light One's unique energy. It was as if she wasn't just possessed by it.

She *was* the Light One.

Creon sighed. He wished Abby was here with him. Her razor-sharp mind would have been appreciated, even if it was just to cut down on Martin's sarcastic commentary. It also would have been nice to share such a massive discovery with someone who understood the implications.

Which were only starting to dawn upon Creon.

Sarah sat silently in the glass room. She looked as if she had been frozen in time. She rarely blinked, but when she did, all the power in the room went out for a moment.

Within her, the Light One waited.

Of that, Creon was sure.

CHAPTER FORTY

The Lords of Death arrived first, wearing sweeping gowns and robes, dressed in the finest clothes of their societies and cultures, appearing like dreams in the pearly-white confines of the spire's courtroom.

The room was a new and beautiful marvel of Rasputina's imagination. The walls seemed to have been formed from conch shells, their smooth silvery-pink glimmer catching the light from the candles in the room and casting it in new and interesting configurations.

The lords of death sat on elevated chairs that floated near a circular table. Around the table were six seats, five for the DGA, Rasputina, and Grok.

Another single chair faced the triangular double doors. That was where the Dark One would sit.

Terra and the rest of the DGA had arrived a little after Rasputina. The lich's butler Bennington had personally come to collect Terra and led her to the rooms of the rest of the DGA agents. They woke them up one at a time and brought them to the main chamber.

Bennington had seemed sullen to Terra, although he was hard to read. She was surprised the butler was back in Rasputina's service. The last time she'd seen him, he was obstinate about keeping Grok away from Rasputina. Whatever problem had existed must have been put aside for the current situation.

Once the DGA had been led to the chamber, Bennington busied himself taking care of the lords, providing them with exquisite food he pulled out of the ether.

Rasputina had leaned over to explain it was customary in hell to show respect to the lords. Even if this wasn't their domain, they were still considered a form of astral royalty there.

When Bennington was done serving the lords, he moved on to serving the DGA while Hades cracked jokes about not eating any of the food.

Terra stared uneasily at the delicious-looking plate of fresh fruit in front of her. "What's he talking about?" she asked

Rasputina waved away Terra's concerns. "An old joke among gods."

Abby picked up a grape and plopped it into her mouth. "Hades tricked his wife into getting stuck in the Underworld by giving her food. Her name was Persephone."

Rasputina took a piece of bread and spread butter on it. "Those rules do not apply here, so enjoy. This may be our last meal, after all." She chuckled.

No one else did.

The doors of the chamber opened and Grimnir stepped in, his mask devoid of any facial expression.

Bennington rushed over to him and bowed politely before guiding the small child to his chair, which lowered and then raised of its own accord to accommodate his stature.

Anubis stood and raised his hands. "Now that the Grimnir is present, we can begin."

One of the lords at Anubis' side, a cloaked figure with the rotting head of an ox, snickered. "The best the Dark One can do is to send one of his avatars? He doesn't even have the respect to show up in person?"

A smile spread across Grimnir's mask. "Are you challenging me, Nous?"

The god Nous leaned forward and grinned. "What does it sound like to you?"

"Unlike you, my form is far too powerful to be held within one vessel. It would be indecent for me to present myself as such in front of you, but if you have any doubts about my power..."

The boy casually slapped the air in front of him. Across the room, an invisible force struck Nous' head, cracking it on the table in front of him. His skull shattered, sending the insides splattering across his plate.

Nous lay dead on the table.

Rasputina sighed and shook her head. "Bennington, would you please attend to that?" Then she turned to the DGA, who were aghast at what had happened and said, "Old law of hell. If anyone issues a formal challenge of power, the challenger and the challenged have a right to settle the matter to the death. Nous was probably hoping to end this quickly and go back to whatever he had planned for the day. Now he's dead, and unless he has a strong group of followers to resurrect him, we have lost a lord today."

Anubis cast an indifferent glance at Nous' corpse while Bennington cleaned up the mess. "As we all know, we are gathered today to speak of the potential vow between the mortals and the Dark One. Have you read through the articles of the vow, Grimnir?"

Grimnir shook his head. "No, not yet."

Rasputina waved her hand and conjured the document in front of Grimnir, who leaned forward to read it.

Grimnir nodded and leaned back in his chair. "It all seems to be in order. My only issue is that I feel we haven't exhausted all of our options. I suggest we bring the Light One into this."

The lords all looked at each other. "How do you propose we summon one of the most powerful entities in existence?"

Grimnir jumped out of his seat. "Here I was, thinking you would never ask. Allow me."

Rasputina tensed in her seat. "He can't bring her here. There's no way."

Most of the arcane subtleties were lost on Terra, but she knew the

Light One hadn't been able to summon the Dark One. Was he strong enough to summon her?

Grimnir got out of his chair and took a few steps forward. He traced a circle in the air before rapidly scrawling a series of sigils, fire appearing in the lines. When he was done, he pressed his hand to the middle of the circle, and the foundations of the Citadel trembled. There was a bright flash of light.

Sarah stood before the council. Her eyes were bright and flashing with the power of the Light One, and her hair was swirling as if it were made of flames.

Anabelle jumped to her feet. "What is Sarah—"

Sarah turned to face Grimnir. "I am here to speak to the Dark One."

Anabelle slowly sat back down. "I'm not going to act like I understand what's happening."

Grimnir slightly bowed his head. "I figured since we're discussing things that concern you, we might as well have you in the room. Long time, no see. How have you been enjoying nearly infinite power?"

Sarah whirled to face Grimnir, white fire burning from her hands. "You have created a severe imbalance by cutting off the valve of the Netherverse, and do not try to blame the mortals for turning the valve in hell. That was hardly a—"

Grimnir raised his hands. "Understood. But that is not the topic currently at hand."

The fire in Sarah's eyes cooled. "Speak. Quickly."

"The ladies and I have come to an agreement. They will swear loyalty to me, and I will turn the valve back on. Then I will leave this universe for good. You'll finally get your precious balance back. How does that sound?"

"I do not care how it is done," Sarah growled, her voice growing deeper as she spoke. "Fix it."

Terra was on her feet before she realized it. Rasputina glared at her, but then her face softened. "Uh, excuse me," Terra started. "Sarah, or the Light One. What if *we* opened the valve?"

Sarah turned around as Grimnir hissed. "Speak."

"We were going to make a vow with the Dark One to save our universe, but only because we couldn't talk to you. But now you're here, and we've done the whole Netherverse thing before, and we could do it again. Our only problem is that asshole standing behind you. What if we made a vow that was something like, we turn the valve back on, fix the problem, and you vow to keep the Dark One out of our universe and any other universes he wants to conquer?"

Grimnir stepped forward to say something, but the Light One raised her hand. Surprisingly, the boy stopped in his tracks, looking up at the Light One before stepping back.

"Interesting," the Light One said. "There is a problem, though. Starting the valve requires a level of pain tolerance I do not believe many mortals are capable of, much like holding my power. This vessel is the only one I have seen thus far. Perhaps it would work if you could find mortals who are trained in the Path of Pain. They should—"

Terra's eyes widened with surprise. "Are you serious? We totally already have that down. Three of us know the Path of the Lost. Check it out." She flexed, her eyes blazing white as she slipped into the Path of the Lost. "If Sarah could learn it, we can too. Probably wouldn't take much time."

The Light One stroked her chin as she thought. "That would be a more convenient vow, and I could deal with this mischievous imp once and for all. You *are* aware of how vows in this plane work, correct? If you were to fail, I would have no choice but to rip out your universe to maintain balance."

Terra looked at Anabelle and Rasputina, who nodded. "Yeah, we got a pretty good handle on how these things work."

"And what of the Dark One?"

Anabelle cleared her throat. "You're pretty powerful. Could you keep him off of our backs until we finish the job?"

The Light One glanced at the boy. "I believe I will be able to keep the imp entertained. Stay. I will not tolerate your tricks today, Grimnir."

Grimnir crossed his arms and sat back in his seat.

The Light One approached the DGA. "Let us work out the final details."

Abby slipped Terra a high five under the table. "That was some quick thinking."

Terra winked at Abby. "Gotta try and keep up with the rest of you nerds."

Anabelle stood as the Light One approached. "Consider yourself kept up. I'm interested to know what this new Path is as well."

Before the Light One could reach the table, a high-pitched scream broke the silence. The Light One looked over her shoulder at the source.

Grimnir had fallen forward, and he was clutching his neck as blood spurted from it. The wound was glowing with a golden aura. He crawled forward, his mask clattering on the ground. Behind Grimnir stood Bennington, holding one of Rasputina's bone daggers.

The Light One whirled back around. "What is the meaning of this?"

Rasputina was on her feet as the lords of death opened a portal and fled. "That was not our doing!" the lich shouted.

As she approached Bennington, the husk of flesh threw up a magical barrier before grabbing Grimnir and jamming the blade farther into the child's body. He pulled at the flesh, separating the wound and tearing it wider. He shoved his arm down into Grimnir's body.

"*NO!*" the lich shouted.

The magical barrier exploded, throwing Rasputina backward and knocking the Light One over.

Bennington forced his whole arm into Grimnir's body, the pale child's form expanding to make room, Bennington's fingers and knuckles visible through the child's skin.

Grimnir tried to crawl forward as Bennington continued to tear into him, shoving more and more of his body into the boy's.

The avatar's face exploded, thick, black sludge rolling from his eye sockets, and a five-foot-long tongue lolled from his mouth when his jaws opened. The bones in his legs and arms cracked and extended, thin, almost fragile-looking things, as his arms grew huge claw-like paddles on their ends. The thing drew itself to its full emaciated height like a starving jackal given the power of the raging demons of hell.

Bennington stood hunched over, his ribs visible, and reached down for Grimnir's horned mask. He placed it on his face before letting loose a pained howl.

Terra drew her axe. "What the fuck is going on?"

Bennington dashed forward and scooped Rasputina up in one move, his hand around her neck. He slammed her into the wall. "How could you abandon me?" he howled. "What we had—how can you toss it away? You built a home in pain across my body. Took me to levels of experience that I have never known. I know you felt it as well. My Mistress! Now you wish to be Queen of the *Good*?"

Rasputina struggled to breathe as she tried to pry Bennington's hands off her throat. "Bennington! Stop! This isn't—"

"I will not be forgotten, Mistress, nor will I let you forget what you truly are."

Bennington raised Rasputina high and then slammed her body into the ground. He leaped on top of her and bit her throat while two more arms ripped from his side, each of them scribbling sigils around him as he tore ribbons of flesh from his mistress' screaming body.

A beam of green light shot down from the top of the spire, consuming Rasputina and Bennington. When the smoke cleared, Bennington stood, leaving Rasputina's body on the ground. He took a step toward the DGA. Grimnir's mask was fused to his face and cracked across the middle when a wolf's snout forced its way out.

The Light One turned to Terra. "What is the meaning of this?"

Terra shrugged, looking around for an explanation. "Dude, I'm trying to figure it out as well."

The light faded from Sarah's eyes. Her body went limp, and Abby grabbed her before she hit the ground. Sarah opened her eyes slowly. "What's going on?"

Anabelle tapped Terra's shoulder. "Come on, you and me. Abby?"

Abby held Sarah up. "I'll stay with her."

Grok joined Anabelle and Terra. Their eyes burned bright with the Path of the Lost, and they charged after Bennington.

Terra whirled her axe, and Anabelle's hands burned with fire. Grok's sword slashed through the air.

Bennington bounded forward, two of his hands moving too fast to see, his fingers tracing arcane symbols.

The three women froze in the air.

Bennington knocked them over as he ran past them. He touched his hands to the floor and it opened up beneath him, a tear in hell leading straight into the Netherverse. Bennington leaped down into it, and the hole resealed itself.

A voice came through on Abby's comm. It was Roy. "What's going on down there? The Light One's sphere just vanished from everywhere, and we're getting reports. The dead are waking up."

Grok rushed over to Rasputina, who lay on the ground. Her throat was torn open, and bright green sigils glowed across her body.

"Whatever's happening, you guys are going to have to clean it up quickly," Roy said. "If these fuckers all wake up, we're not just losing Earth, we're losing everything."

The DGA agents looked at each other as Rasputina gurgled on her own blood.

Things had taken a turn for the worse.

PART III

CHAPTER FORTY-ONE

The spire's walls were crumbling. Chunks fell like autumn leaves shed by a tree. Rasputina lay in the middle of the room, choking on her blood while Grok and the DGA agents knelt by her side, trying to figure out what could be done.

Anabelle calmly pulled off Grok's hand. "We will."

"No! You don't understand. If she dies, all of this comes apart. Not just the spire, everything in hell that she's built. It'll come crashing down."

Abby pulled out the book of sigils Rasputina had given her the night before. "Wait, let us see if we can help." She flipped open the book, her eyes racing back and forth as she searched for a solution. "Here, maybe this."

Abby's index finger converted to a laser and she stood, then walked in a circle, cutting sigils into the ground and muttering under her breath as she read. Then she knelt beside Rasputina, lifted the lich's head, and scrawled a sigil underneath. "Everyone, get out of the circle."

Anabelle and the rest did as they were told, moving outside the magical sphere that shot up around Abby and Rasputina.

The interior erupted in light, making Abby and Rasputina invisible. When the brightness faded, Abby was still beside the lich. She slung Rasputina's arm over her shoulder and helped her to her feet.

Rasputina rubbed her face, trying to gather herself. "What happened?"

"Bennington," Anabelle explained. "He did something to Grimnir. Forced himself into Grimnir's body, and then he attacked you. After that, he disappeared."

Rasputina felt her neck. "He planned this. He must have stolen one of my daggers, one of the few things it's hard for me to heal from. And he cut deep, it would seem. Deep enough so I could have died. But he didn't finish it."

Terra looked around the chambers. "The Lords of Death split too. Guess they figured out what was going on. So did the Light One. Just left Sarah's body here."

"We should see how she's doing."

Anabelle, Terra, Grok, and Rasputina walked over to where Sarah lay.

Abby held her wrist to Sarah's forehead. "She's stable. She'll wake up in a little bit."

Anabelle crossed her arms as she bit her lip. "We need to figure out what's going on. Is there a way you can reach out to the lords of death?"

Rasputina nodded. She bit her thumb, drawing blood, then leaned over and pressed her thumb to the ground.

A portal opened a few feet away, and a group of twenty cloaked figures stepped through. One of them walked forward. "We are the emissaries of the lords of death. They regret that they cannot appear themselves since they have judged this situation as problematic at best."

Rasputina sighed. "They understand this is out of our control, right?"

The emissary nodded. "They do, but they will not put themselves at risk for you."

Sarah opened her eyes and coughed quietly. "What's going on?"

Abby helped Sarah to her feet. "Glad to see you're okay. Do you remember anything?"

Sarah rubbed her head. "Yeah, everything. Getting your body hijacked by an interdimensional being isn't something you forget, especially since I was conscious for all of it."

"Can you still communicate with her?"

Sarah shook her head. "No, she's gone, but she left me with a message. The vow is still on the table. If we fix this shit with the valve, no repercussions for any of us. The Dark One is done for, and the Light One will fix everything that's going on with the undead."

"Okay. Then we go to the Netherverse and fix the valve problem before Bennington or the Dark One or whatever that thing is can stop us."

The ground began to shake. A violent earthquake knocked everyone off their feet, and the walls of the spire continued to crack.

Anabelle stumbled to her feet. "Okay, now what?"

The spire's floor cracked down the middle, sending jutting pieces flying. The crack widened, and the Netherverse could be seen underneath.

Bennington, wearing the emaciated, stretched-out body of Grimnir, climbed out of the chasm. Black sludge hung from his arms and legs, tethering him to the Netherverse, yet he moved unencumbered.

The head emissary threw back his cloak, showing a body made entirely of Dark Energy. He held two swords in his hand. "The lords of death do not take kindly to this violation of the laws of hell. We've been sent to put a stop to this."

The other emissaries removed their cloaks. They wielded a variety of weapons: swords, chains, and maces.

Bennington laughed as he straightened to his full height. "Do you think you will harm me? My Mistress has shown me the true Path of Pain. What will you be able to do that she has not already done?"

He rushed past the DGA and took hold of the first emissary, lifting him into the air. He shook him violently as he laughed before tearing into the being with his teeth, ripping through his throat before discarding the lifeless body.

Then he turned to the rest.

It was nothing less than slaughter, and the butchered bodies of the emissaries fell to the ground as if they had run through a blender.

Bennington turned his head toward the DGA, Rasputina, and Grok. He drew a series of sigils in the air and then slammed his hands on the floor.

Terra flipped her axe and caught it. "All right, let's fuck this asshole up."

She ran forward, Anabelle at her side, then tripped over her feet. As she stood up, she saw that Anabelle was also picking herself up. "Uh, what's going on?"

Bennington wheezed and sneered. "Strength in numbers has always been your game. Not anymore."

Grok dashed to join Anabelle and Terra but fell, skidding across the floor. She stood up and brushed off her knees. "Rasputina?"

Rasputina sighed as she scanned the sigils on the floor. "He's split us up. We can't all attack together."

Bennington hunched over, growling. "I want to feel your individual pain. Specific. Intricate."

Grok unsheathed her sword as she approached Bennington. "I have no patience for this." She flew at Bennington, slashing at him with her sword.

Bennington took a step back and fell to his knees, then sprang upward and caught Grok in the face with his fist.

The orc flew backward, landed on her feet, and rushed forward. She slid underneath Bennington, got back to her feet, and thrust her sword behind her, catching him in the back.

The monster roared in pain, then chuckled and reached behind him. His spine broke and contorted, allowing him to bend over backward, and he grabbed Grok by the head and lifted her, squeezing her skull. "What do you have to show me?"

Grok let out a scream, her eyes flashing bright as she slipped into the Path of the Lost. She kicked Bennington in the face and flipped away under him. She attacked before her feet touched the ground, discarding her sword and relying on her fists instead.

Bennington's hands deflected each of Grok's attacks even as they grew faster, the orc screaming as she threw everything into each punch.

One of Bennington's hands missed the mark, and she slipped in close and slammed her fist into the monster's jaw. She straightened, ready to continue to the attack.

Bennington leaned into her fist, taking the full brunt of the attack as two of his hands grabbed Grok's arms and the other two delivered two solid blows.

Grok froze, her eyes glazing over before she spat blood and went limp.

Bennington chopped Grok across the neck and then threw her body into the wall. He turned, his mask's face ominously blank, and stared at the DGA. "Next?"

Terra cracked her knuckles. "I'm going to fuck him up."

Anabelle raised her hand. "No. You saw how quickly he dealt with Grok. You two have similar fighting styles. Hold off a moment. I'll go. If I can't take him down, it'll give you time to figure out a different approach than Grok's."

Terra looked ready to argue but relented. "All right. How about you make sure I don't have to get my hands dirty?"

Anabelle let out a surge of mana as she went down the Path of the Lost. She approached Bennington slowly, circling him, keeping her head.

Bennington leaned forward. "Scared?"

"Hardly," Anabelle replied. She raised one of her hands and sent a pillar of stone rocketing up from under Bennington. As he twisted in the air, Anabelle jumped, dissolved into smoke, and reformed behind Bennington. She curved the stone pillar toward her, bringing Bennington with it as her hands filled with electricity.

Anabelle's fist hit Bennington square in the jaw, shooting electricity through his body, then threw her arm up and drew another stone pillar into his stomach. The pillar burst into flames and engulfed the butler in a column of fire.

Anabelle didn't let up. Once her feet touched the ground, she stretched out her fingers and pulled four stone pillars from the ceiling and two more from the ground, freezing the former butler in mid-air before converting them to water and then ice and freezing him in place. Then she lunged at him, her body bristling with electricity.

Before Anabelle's fist could connect, Bennington's chest split open, and a dozen sludge-covered hands reached and grasped Anabelle. They pulled her close to his chest and he spun to break free of the ice, dropping to the floor as his fists pounded her head.

The two hit the floor with enough force to create a crater.

Anabelle scrambled to her feet, but Bennington was ahead of her. He drew a sigil, and a piece of paper appeared in front of him. Another hand attached the paper to her head, and a third slammed into Anabelle's chest, pushing her backward. Her skull hit the ground hard, and Bennington held her there until the paper exploded.

Bennington stood as smoke wafted up behind him. "Who will show me pain?" he roared.

Abby looked at Terra. "Do you need more time?"

Terra shook her head, her face nervous. "He tore through Anabelle and Grok like it was nothing."

Abby grabbed Terra and shook her. "You need to keep it together." She turned to Rasputina and Sarah. "Can either of you fight?"

Sarah shook her head. "Not yet."

Rasputina looked from Bennington to Abby. "I don't know."

Abby stood up. "We'll whittle him down. Be ready, Terra. If anyone can end this, it'll be you."

Bennington laughed darkly from the other side of the chamber.

Abby charged her body with kinetic energy, bypassing her energy blockers as she prepared to go all out. She increased the production of nanobots in her blood and her skin. Her reflex speed increased significantly, and the world slowed around her.

She'd watched the last two fights closely, trying to see if Bennington had any weak spots. She hadn't seen any. He'd handled

Grok's physical attacks well enough, and Anabelle's elemental magic hadn't fazed him.

Abby hit her thrusters and sped in Bennington's direction. She slammed into him and discharged all of her kinetic energy, then flew backward as she tossed three sticky plasma grenades, which attached to three of Bennington's four arms.

Bennington swiped down at the grenades, trying to knock them off, but the grenades exploded.

"Finally," he murmured. "Pain!"

Abby slammed her hands together to form her hand cannon and fired, unleashing a steady stream of plasma that hit Bennington with the force of a Mack truck.

Half of Bennington's body was blown away, leaving only charred flesh as he stumbled forward.

Abby zoomed toward Bennington but pulled up at the last minute and rose above him to launch another attack.

Bennington's entrails connected with the ground, sucking up the Dark Melody the spire was built from and remaking the part of his body Abby had destroyed.

The girl deconstructed her cannon and landed in front of him instead, putting all of her energy into her fists. She unleashed a barrage of quick punches, hitting Bennington hundreds of times in the stomach as he stumbled backward. She launched her thrusters and slammed him into the wall.

As Abby pulled away, another arm burst from Bennington's chest and slapped her.

The butler thrust himself away from the wall, his hands tracing sigils.

Ten energy blades conjured around Bennington as he stepped forward, circling him as if he were the nucleus of an atom. "What else do you have, child?"

Abby shed most of her armor, dumping more energy into her power reserves. Her hands smoked from the amount of energy coming from them. She rushed at Bennington and caught him with an uppercut, then grabbed one of his arms, snapping it as one of his blades pierced her shoulder.

She ignored the pain, grabbing the man by the throat as another blade slashed her. She punched Bennington in the face, breaking his jaw before pressing her hand to his head and firing a blast that ripped straight through his skull and then the spire's walls.

Bennington grabbed Abby's hair and spun her around.

As she spun, she burned her thrusters, taking away Bennington's momentum. She raised her hand to fire.

Bennington's chest arm drew a sigil in the air in front of Abby's hand.

She fired.

A small portal opened in front of Abby's hand and caught the blast, then a portal opened behind her. The plasma blast came through and hit Abby in the back, knocking her across the room.

Bennington landed on the floor and cracked his neck before turning to face Terra. "Looks like you're the last one."

Terra swallowed and stood up, looking at the bodies of her fallen comrades. "Yeah, looks like it. I'll try to make it count." She rushed Bennington, swinging her axe over her head as she found her way to the Path of the Lost.

Bennington raised his arms to counter Terra, who threw her axe instead of using it to slash and hit the butler in the chest. As he stepped back from the force of the blow, Terra leaped, used her axe as a steppingstone, and brought her fist down on Bennington's head, slamming him into the floor.

The two hit hard, and Terra was first to her feet. She grabbed Bennington's leg, swung him around, and tossed him into the wall.

The spire's wall cracked down the middle from the impact, but he was up instantly and bounded toward Terra, his mask off-kilter, the wolf snout that extended snarling and salivating. He tackled the Hand, and the two of them skidded across the floor. Terra tried to roll out from under him.

The butler dug his feet in, stopping both of them. As Terra flew past him, he grabbed her by the back of her suit. Terra wrapped her hands around one of Bennington's fingers and pulled it back, snapping it.

Bennington screamed and hit her in the face twice as his free arms drew sigils in the air, and a magical barrier formed around the two of them. Lightning began striking Terra from inside the barrier, bolt after bolt until she collapsed.

The barrier opened, and Terra fell at Bennington's feet. He laughed harshly as he walked away. "These are the Dark Angels who gave you such a hard time?" Bennington called to Rasputina.

"Where the fuck do you think you're going, sweetheart?"

Bennington looked over his shoulder as Terra picked herself up off the ground. She cracked her neck and spat. "You ain't even knocked a tooth loose yet. Come on, puppers, let's tango."

Terra walked toward Bennington, an uncanny sense of calm radiating from her as her power grew, her eyes flashing even brighter.

Two of Bennington's hands traced sigils as he sauntered toward Terra.

Suddenly, she flashed forward and grabbed his hands, the ones he was using for sigil work. "Uh-uh. These are going, pronto." She gripped them until the bones crunched and leaned back, ripping them out of his chest.

Bennington howled in pain and stumbled backward. Terra pushed forward and cracked the butler across the face.

After he hit the ground, Terra squatted over him and brought her fists down like sledgehammers, relentlessly pounding the butler's face, cracking his mask further. "We got one big thing in common, puppers!"

Bennington's arm snaked around Terra, and he slashed her back as he drove his other hand into her stomach, puncturing her skin.

Terra slumped onto Bennington's wrist.

He grinned as he stood up, Terra impaled on his hand. "What is that, human?"

Terra's hands wrapped around Bennington's wrist. "We both dig pain." She twisted Bennington's wrist, snapping it, then threw her body to the side, knocking him off-balance. As her feet touched the ground, she twisted again, wrenching the butler into the air with sheer strength. Once he hit the ground, Terra threw one leg over his arm and pulled up, tearing his arm off, then delivered a solid blow to Bennington's skull. "Now, stay the fuck down!"

Before Terra could walk away, Bennington rose, black goo feeding into his body from the spire. He grew to twice the size he was before, towering over Terra, his wolf's head breaking through the bottom part of the mask. He fell on top of the human, his body a mass of swirling blackness and claws and teeth, and enveloped Terra completely, only to spit her out.

Terra hit the floor, covered in blood. She groaned quietly as she tried to keep from slipping into unconsciousness.

CHAPTER FORTY-TWO

The dead woke across the Nine Realms.

They had lain in wait for days, their soulless eyes staring at the living from behind walls in cities where the folk were lucky enough to have them built. But there were more out in the fields, in the jungles, in the suburbs where there were not nearly enough resources to offer protection.

Roy, Blackwell, Persephone, and Naota were in a helicopter on its way to Los Angeles. LA was an epicenter of the zombie infestation. Initially, most of the state had been swept, and the zombies had been taken to pens in LA. The idea was, if something were to happen, it would all be centralized. Halfway through the extraction, it had become obvious that if anything happened, it would be far too large to control.

As Persephone looked at the burning city, she could easily see that. "Why would zombies burn anything?" she wondered aloud.

Roy came over to her side and looked through the window. "It's not the zombies. They're the root of the problem, but anytime you throw a terrible situation at human beings, they're going to make it worse. Luckily, we're not tasked with dealing with humans, just zombies. That being said, anything that acts like a hostile is a hostile today."

Persephone looked at Roy, shocked. "Are you saying we have permission to use lethal force on people?"

Roy shook his head. "No, I'm saying that if something tries to hurt you, don't hesitate. We're on a rescue mission today, folks. That means anything even remotely dangerous to the mass population is going under. You got it?"

Blackwell and Naota nodded.

Outside the helicopter, a squad of dragonriders flew by, headed by Alex and the rest of Boundless.

Roy held his hand to his ear, turning on his comm. "You guys got that too?"

Alex's voice came through the comm. "I highly doubt anyone is going to try to stand up to a herd of dragons. We should be good."

Roy turned off his comm and muttered under his breath, "Obviously, she's never been to LA. The place is worse than New York. The fucking raccoons might eat you here."

The helicopter pilot banged on the cabin's panels as he looked over his shoulder. "All right, we're getting close to the drop zone. You ready?"

Roy looked at his crew. Persephone was standing. Blackwell was strapping himself into an improved exo-suit. Naota had already secured his.

Blackwell looked at Roy. "Sir, have we heard anything from the DGA?"

Roy shook his head. "Nothing yet, but we haven't heard from them in hours." He turned to Persephone and offered a weak smile. "That doesn't mean shit's gone south. Probably just means they're doing their job."

Persephone nodded. She was worried about Abby, but there were other things to attend to at the moment. Lives were at stake, and she knew there was a job to be done. If she didn't stay focused, people would end up dead. Abby wouldn't want that on Persephone's head, and neither did she.

Blackwell finished loading into his exo-suit and grabbed a plasma rifle hanging from the interior panels of the helicopter. "What's the plan?"

Roy pulled up his holoscreen, which depicted downtown LA. "We're swooping hard into the shit. There are four clear zones around downtown. We're going in hard and fast, clearing everything we see around us and hunting down civvies. We're the heavy hitters today. Got it?"

Naota attached his plasma blades to his exo-suit. "Ain't we always?"

Blackwell sighed and shook his head. "We're flying beside a group of dragons. A drow infused with elder god goo is in our helicopter. Terra, Anabelle, and Abby are in hell, fighting demons and shit. We are *not* the heavy hitters."

Naota shrugged as he swung his plasma blades and caught them. "Maybe you aren't, not with that attitude. I'll make sure to watch your back." He blew a kiss to Blackwell, who sighed and turned to join Persephone by the window.

The drow was still watching the zombie horde below. "You hear anything from Cire's squad?"

"A little while ago. They're making moves on the orc world. Kravis is doing the same on the gnome homeworld," Blackwell said. "Don't worry, we'll get this cleaned up. Make sure there's a world for the DGA to come back to."

Blackwell opened the back of the helicopter and leaned out. "Okay, team, it's go time."

Roy walked over to Blackwell. "You know that's my thing, right?"

Blackwell smiled. "Yeah. Always wanted to give it a try, though." Then he jumped out of the helicopter, spiraling down as he maneuvered his body so his exo-suit could take the bulk of the impact.

Roy and Naota leaped out next and headed in the same direction as Blackwell.

Persephone watched them go, forcing herself not to look at the thronging masses of undead in the streets. She didn't want to think about what they were doing to the defenseless humans down there. She swallowed her anxiety and jumped out of the helicopter.

The ground floor was worse than Persephone could have imagined. The view from the helicopter did no justice to the sheer volume of the chaos they had landed in.

Roy and Blackwell had hit the ground a second before her, and zombies were already swarming the two of them.

Persephone launched her tentacles in their direction, breaking through the zombies and clearing a path. Once they got some space, they climbed on top of a car and started lining up headshots.

When Blackwell reloaded, he scanned the area. "Have any of you seen Naota?"

"*Yeehaw!*" came a scream from down the street.

Naota swung around the corner, using his blades, which were connected to energy tethers at his wrists, to catapult himself forward. He landed in the sea of zombies and spun in a circle, taking their heads off.

Roy opened his scanner and searched for anyone living while Persephone, Blackwell, and Naota held the zombies at bay.

Hundreds of zombies were in the streets. Most of them trudged by without paying attention, but enough were interested in the Middang3ard agents to create a problem.

Roy pointed at an apartment building. "Okay, we got some! Blackwell, Naota, this one is you. Persephone, clear a path."

Persephone whipped her tentacles out, lashing the zombies lining the street to the apartment. That gave Blackwell and Naota time to break down the apartment building's door and run inside. She pulled a plasma rifle from her back and started taking shots, backing up to the car Roy was on while he took care of clearing the other side.

"Would have been nice if we knew it was this bad!" Persephone shouted.

Roy aimed down his sights and blew through a zombie's skull. "No way we could have known. This has been getting worse by the minute."

Alex and the rest of the dragonriders descended, launching fire attacks that burned through the zombies on the street.

Despite being aflame, the zombies continued on their death march, some of them falling to the ground, only to be crushed under the feet of the others.

Above, the windows of the apartment burst open, sending glass flying. Naota leaped out, holding a child, and a woman hung from his back. He was followed by Blackwell, who held two teenagers in his arms. They landed in the open space the dragonriders had cleared.

Roy pointed east at a street full of zombies shambling by, taking no interest in them. "The DZ is that way." He turned to the civilians. "Can you walk?"

All of them wearily nodded.

"Good, follow me."

Roy turned to go and heard one of the teenagers inhale sharply. He turned around to see the kid struggling to stay on his feet. Without saying a word, he walked over, slung the kid's arm over his shoulder, and turned back around, ready to face the odds. "Blackwell, Persephone, I want you on point. Naota, you're taking up the rear."

Persephone and Blackwell moved into their positions, standing side by side and waiting for Roy's order.

"All right, move it!" he shouted.

They slowly made their way up the street, watching the zombies around them, who didn't seem to notice or care. The dragonriders had cleared enough space, and they were due for another burn soon. All Persephone needed to do was keep a level head and make sure not to fire unnecessarily to avoid drawing attention to themselves.

The blood pounded in her ears. She tried to keep from looking too long at the decaying corpses crowding the street. She felt like she might open fire out of disgust.

Then there was a sharp, shrill screech of pain.

Persephone looked over her shoulder.

The woman had tripped and fallen onto a piece of broken glass, cutting her hand open. She'd already covered her mouth, silencing the brief scream.

Persephone didn't need to turn around. She could hear the growling. It was obvious what was about to come.

"We're pushing through," Roy growled. "Don't let up."

The zombies ahead turned around, and their dead eyes locked onto the mortals in the street. They started their slow yet relentless attack.

Blackwell and Persephone opened fire, mowing down the zombies in front of them. When Persephone's rifle was empty, she threw it to the side, shooting her tentacles out and lashing the zombies to clear more room.

But the zombies didn't stop. They continued to pour into the street from all sides, creeping as slowly as death itself.

In the distance, Persephone could see the DZ tower. "Can we get some fire?" she shouted to Roy.

Roy checked his HUD and shook his head. "Boundless is engaging more shit right now on the other side of town. Just called it in. This is on us."

Blackwell opened fire again, shouting in frustration. "There are too many. Goddamn it!" He threw down his rifle. "Sir, permission to do what needs to be done."

Roy looked past Blackwell at the horde of zombies. "Permission granted."

Naota broke formation and ran up to Blackwell. "Wait, hold on, you're being a little rash. You should—"

Blackwell placed his hand on Naota's shoulder. "Hey, buddy, we talked about this. Remember what we promised?"

Naota hung his head, tears forming in his eyes. "That we would never keep the other from doing their duty."

"And what else?"

"That no sacrifices would ever be made in vain."

Blackwell turned to Roy. "Tell the DZ we're coming and to get those doors ready." Then he turned to face the horde of zombies. He reached behind his neck and grabbed the power reserve on his exo-suit. "Get ready to run." Then he tanked it out.

Energy surged through Blackwell's exo-suit, and his body started to vibrate. He took a step forward, his boot cracking the pavement. He took a deep breath as he closed his eyes, then he made his move.

Blackwell sprinted forward, moving faster than his body should have allowed. He was overclocking it, pushing the suit and his body to their limits. He zoomed right and left, tearing through zombies with his bare hands as the veins in his neck throbbed, threatening to burst.

Within less than two seconds, he had cleared ten feet.

Roy shouted, "Get moving!"

Persephone picked up Blackwell's rifle and started firing. Naota was at her side, crying softly as he fired at the zombies.

Blackwell continued to rip through zombies, but there were still too many.

"He's not going to make it," Persephone whispered.

"No, but you are," Roy said. He helped the teenager he held hobble over to Naota. "Take him."

Naota shook his head. "Sir, you can't—"

Roy reached back and jerked his exo-suit's cord. "That's an order." He turned to face Persephone, his face vibrating, the blood vessels in his eyes beginning to pop from the strain. "Tell Anabelle I love her." Then he removed his pistol and rifle, handing them to the woman and the boys.

He bolted forward, joining Blackwell in the mass of zombies. The two worked in tandem to clear the path.

Persephone and Naota followed closely, picking off the zombies who escaped Roy's and Blackwell's combined wrath.

The men in the exos made their final push, bounding forward like wild animals and savagely ripping through the zombies that tried to claw their way up the DZ's gates.

Persephone and the rest ran as the guards opened fire, keeping the zombies at bay.

Roy and Blackwell slipped through the gates as they were closing, the both of them stumbling, hardly able to walk. The exo-suits had overexerted their muscles and bones. They had practically been liquified in their bodies.

Roy managed to lean against the wall while Blackwell collapsed, spewing blood as he coughed.

Naota ran to Blackwell's side. "It's going to be okay, buddy," Blackwell muttered.

Naota nodded, his lips stiff as he tried to keep from crying. "I know. It's going to be okay."

Blackwell coughed up blood as Naota helped him sit up. "This isn't going to last forever, Naota. This war. It's going to be over, and then you have to keep on living your life, you understand? This is just a moment. You have a whole life." Blackwell's head slumped to the side, his chest rising slower and slower until it finally stopped.

Naota clutched Blackwell and kissed his forehead, finally allowing himself to cry. He sobbed softly into Blackwell's hair.

Persephone couldn't comfort Naota, not now. There was nothing to be done.

"Hey, Mister!"

One of the kids was trying to talk to Roy, who was still leaning against the wall with a lit cigarette hanging from his mouth. His eyes were closed, and for the first time since Persephone had met him, he seemed at peace.

Persephone walked over to the child and guided him to his mother. "You should let me talk to him." Then she went back to Roy.

His cigarette had fallen to the ground.

He wasn't breathing.

But he still stood, a defiant smile on his face.

CHAPTER FORTY-THREE

Anabelle's eyes snapped open. There was something wrong. She felt it deep in her stomach, an overwhelming sense of terror, pain, and suffering.

Her body had lost all feeling.

The only thing she could register was a sinking feeling in her stomach.

Roy was dead; she knew it. Deep in her gut, she knew he wasn't coming home.

Part of her snapped. Whatever had been holding her together was gone. Something sleeping within her woke up. This was the first time Anabelle had ever felt hopeless, and along with that feeling came something else—a pain even Grok hadn't been able to bring out.

Anabelle's skin smoked as small flames flickered across her body. There was nothing more for her. Nothing to fight for. Nothing to love. There was only the well of pain growing within her. Still, her eyes couldn't remain open.

Across the room, Bennington was walking away from Terra, who was lying unconscious on the floor. He was heading toward Rasputina and Sarah.

Rasputina put herself between him and Sarah. "You don't care about them. Just take me, and let's be done with this."

Bennington laughed and pressed his hand to his heart in a mockery of embarrassment. "You think this is only about you, Rasputina? You thought of me as a plaything, never taking into account that I might have feelings. Have you forgotten what I was before you?"

Rasputina winced at his words. "I tried to forget."

Two arms sprouted out of Bennington's chest again as he lumbered toward Rasputina. "Why? Do you fear what *you* used to be, or are you afraid you made a mistake?"

Rasputina stood and plunged her hand into her side, pulling out a dagger-like bone wand. "I did make a mistake, and I will never again become what I once was."

"Your only mistake was not killing me. Only a fool would cow one of the most powerful sorcerers in the universe and make a plaything of him. Only an idiot would spend centuries torturing him without expecting to have some kind of vengeance taken on them."

Rasputina gripped the handle of her dagger wand tightly. "What do you assume you will get from all this? My death? Then what?"

Bennington raised his hand, his sorrowful eyes peering out from Grimnir's mask. "Power. In your foolishness and the Light One's, in your fear of the Dark One, you failed to see what I have seen. Grimnir was not the Dark One's avatar. He was the last of the Dark One's strength—the Dark One distilled down to raw power, and the very last of it. And now that power is mine!"

Rasputina stared at Bennington blankly for a few seconds. "No, no, that can't be."

Energy swirled around his hands. "Once I rip the bones from your bodies, I will use this power to do what the Dark One could not. I will kill the Light One, and I will rule *everything*."

Rasputina pointed her wand at Bennington. "You will do no such thing. This ends now. I defeated you before, and I will do it again."

The former butler leaned over, clutching his heart in feigned concern. "You defeat me? Maybe before when you had true power, but look at you now. A third of a soul, hardly able to tap into the true power of a lich. Face it, Rasputina, you've gone soft, and as long you cling to that pathetic semblance of humanity, you will never defeat me. You simply don't have the strength."

Rasputina flew at Bennington and drove her blade into his shoulder, her flashing bright green eyes mad with rage. "Do not insult my power!" she screamed.

Bennington grabbed Rasputina by the hair and tossed her away.

Rasputina spun and opened a portal behind her, passed through it, and came out on the other side behind him. She slammed her dagger wand into the floor and spikes shot up, impaling Bennington.

He screamed in pain and rage as he tried to lift his body off the spikes, nearly tearing his stomach open, then flopped back onto the floor. Black tendrils snaked again into him, healing his wounds.

Rasputina gripped the blade of her dagger and split open her palm. She smeared blood across her face and floated into the air, green balls of energy circling around her hand. Then she rushed at Bennington.

He threw up a magical barrier, and flames burst from the lich's body as she passed through. She collapsed onto the ground, her skin melted off, nothing more than bones and muscle.

The bloody mess plunged her hands into the floor, drawing out the Dark Melody and coating herself in flesh again. She drew sigils in front of her and then blew gently, and a giant ball of green flames streamed from her lips.

Bennington leaped into the air to avoid the fireball, but Rasputina appeared behind him and drove her dagger into the side of his head. The butler cackled as he turned around and grabbed Rasputina. "Yes, Mistress! Give me the pain you've so long denied me!"

The two of them hit the floor hard. Rasputina scampered away as fast as possible, then whirled, trying to find where Bennington had disappeared to. The air in front of her tore open and Bennington's arm flew through, cutting in from the Netherverse, and slashed Rasputina across the face.

As she stumbled back, Bennington stepped out of the portal and lunged after her, cutting her across the stomach. "From where I stand, it doesn't seem as if you have even half of your power as a lich."

He grabbed Rasputina and lifted her into the air. "Perhaps I should show you some of the exquisite experiences you've gifted me over time?"

He rammed two fingers into Rasputina's eyes as she screamed and writhed. He dropped her body, and as she tried to crawl away, he brought his hand down on her head.

The butler let out a triumphant roar as he stood tall, then his eyes fell on Sarah. "I believe all that is left is you."

Sarah shakily got to her feet, swaying as she tried to keep from falling over. "So be it."

Across the room, Anabelle heard Sarah's voice, and it stirred her. Her eyes opened, and she could feel the deep pain in her heart again. No, there was something else. Her friends—they were all that mattered now.

The small flames on Anabelle's skin bloomed, covering her entire body, and her hair became a mane of fire. Electricity crackled inside and across her skin as she let herself succumb to the pain within her. She crawled forward, the ground exploding beneath her touch. As she got to her feet, she let out a scream of rage.

Bennington stopped walking and turned to look for the source of the noise. "What's this?" he asked.

Anabelle glared at him, her body made of fire and electricity. She seemed to be some demonic elemental from a plane of hell not yet discovered. When she spoke, her voice echoed. "The Dark One is in there still, isn't he?" she growled as her eyes narrowed.

Bennington took a step back. "What does it matter? Just because you're made of fire now, it doesn't mean you've changed anything."

Anabelle took a step forward, melting the floor beneath her feet. "He's responsible for this. All of our pain, all of our suffering. *He's responsible.*"

An aura of flame and electricity encircled Anabelle. "I'm going to pull you out of his body and burn you both alive." She shot forward and slammed into Bennington before he was able to put up a defense.

She brought both hands down on his head and smashed it on the floor.

As he tried to crawl away, Anabelle grabbed him by the scruff of his neck. "You aren't going anywhere."

The butler laughed maniacally as he rolled over. "That's what you think." He slashed beneath him, opening a portal into the Netherverse, and slipped out of Anabelle's grasp.

The elf screamed in rage. As the portal started to close, she grasped the edges, distorting space and time, and held it open. She looked over her shoulder at Terra, who was stirring. "Help me!"

Terra rolled onto her feet and ran over to Anabelle. She didn't ask any questions, just grabbed the tear in reality and lifted with everything she had, her muscles and veins bulging as she tore the Netherverse rift even wider.

"Wider!" Anabelle screamed.

Rasputina, who was only a few feet away, was quickly healing herself with the Dark Melody, pulling it from the foundations of the spire. As her skin regrew, she came over to Anabelle and Terra, pulled out a dagger, and carved into the tear, widening it even more. "We can go after him, but he'll be even more powerful in there. He'll have even more access to the Dark Melody. His reality manipulation will be even stronger than it was here."

Terra yanked on the tear. "Can you do the same?"

Rasputina nodded. "Yes. With less affinity, but I can."

"Where's Abby?"

"Right here," was the answer. Abby was shuffling over to the Netherverse tear, her body healing itself with nanobots. "Are you guys ready to go?"

Rasputina shook her head. "Before we go, you all need to understand: this version of the Netherverse is drastically different than the last time you were there. Even before Grok and I left, it had become unstable. Dangerous. Wait, where *is* Grok?"

Grok grunted from afar and limped over with Sarah hanging on her shoulder. "She won't be able to fight, and I'm not sure how much help I'll be, but we can't leave anyone behind."

"If we do this, there is a chance that none of us will come back. But if what Bennington said was true, if this really is the last of the Dark One's power, we can end this here, now and forever. It'll finally be done."

Anabelle's body returned to normal. She was tired, not physically, but emotionally and spiritually. The idea that this could finally be over was almost too much for her. "We can't know what to expect in there. Unless the bastard redraws the sigils in the Netherverse, which I don't think he knows how to do, we won't be bound by the one-on-one combat rule like we were here. So, everyone play to your strengths. DGA, we've been doing this long enough to know what those are. Don't waste time. We go in hard, and we go in fast."

Terra chuckled. "Play to my strength. You know, I almost had him. He's strong, but I'm fairly sure I can get stronger. And whatever you did earlier—"

Sarah and Grok interrupted Terra at the same time. "The Path of Pain." They looked at each other awkwardly before Sarah continued, "I don't quite know what it is, but Cire helped me find it. It was how my body could hold all the energy of the Light One. Maybe it's even stronger than the Path of the Lost."

Terra narrowed her eyes at Sarah. "How did you get there?"

"I had to experience a lot of pain."

Terra turned to Anabelle. "And you?"

Anabelle looked down into the Netherverse. "Roy died. I felt it."

Terra nodded solemnly. "I'm sorry, Belle. I'm sorry you couldn't be there with him."

Anabelle sniffed as she wiped away tears. "Not now, Terra. We focus now. Do you think you can get there too? The Path of Pain?"

Terra nodded as she stood up. "I can try." She leaped down into the Netherverse.

Anabelle followed her, as did Rasputina and Abby. Grok went last, still supporting Sarah.

If there had been an order to the Netherverse before, it was gone now.

Bits of rock and planet jutted out from nowhere, tearing through the fabric of the realm. Dark Melody dripped from the gashes. Shimmers of other realms drifted across the sky and the ground like reflections in a lake. The elder gods were nowhere to be seen.

There were few instances of there being anything like a surface. Even when there was ground, it could easily swallow itself like a cannibalistic Venus flytrap.

It was this chaotic maelstrom of bastardized reality the DGA found themselves in, floating around as they tried to make sense of the madness the Netherverse had devolved into.

Stars were born and died within a blink of an eye, and souls bloated and withered within seconds. They transformed into giant spiders, only to break apart into birds and eventually melt into skulls that floated atop nothing like wax on water.

The DGA agents searched for each other, calling out in this blackness reeking of sulfur and honey. In the dark, they could not see each other, but they could all hear the tearing of flesh and the snarls of the gluttonous.

Bennington.

They each found their way to him, working through the mind-numbing madness of the Netherverse as they thought through their best course of action. If he was stronger here, they were going to have to be as well.

Abby was the first one to reach real consciousness and she spread it among her allies, watching Bennington hunched on a comet, ripping into the flesh of a defeated elder one.

He stood tall, his mask dripping with blood as he held the entrails of the elder one in his hands. "So, foolishness is a trait you all share?"

Anabelle landed on the rock first, her skin crackling with flames and electricity. She didn't waste any time. She surged forward like a bolt of lightning, delivering dozens of punches to Bennington's body. There was no grace, no technique, only pure and simple aggression.

Grok landed behind him and slipped into the Path of the Lost.

Arms tore out of Bennington's back, blocking Grok's attacks as another head burst from his shoulder, breathing fire as the Dark Melody latched onto his back. His front forearms grew thicker, splitting down the middle until they were as sharp as blades. He slashed back and forth, forcing Anabelle to step back.

As the elf took a second to breathe, Terra came flying in, drop-kicking one of Bennington's heads and forcing the monster off-balance.

He stumbled backward, his abdomen splitting. Dozens of hands shot out and grabbed the corpse of the elder one, pulling it closer and pulling it into the chasm he had opened, the stomach's teeth gnashing and gnawing.

A plasma blast the size of a small car hit Bennington's stomach, ripping clean through it. The butler hit the ground, still trying to pull away as he laughed. Abby flew in and used short blasts of plasma to tear through his chest arms before slamming her hands together and firing a plasma blast that tore through his chest.

He swung around, ripping apart at the waist, his lower half separating from his chest. His halves ran in different directions as the elder god's guts began to pour into him.

Rasputina ran past the bottom part, heading toward the piece that was directly linked to the elder god's entrails. She severed the connection between him and the elder one with her dagger wand.

The bottom half of Bennington ran away and leaped into the darkness of the Netherverse. Lightning cast by Anabelle struck Bennington's bottom half and destroyed it.

The rest of him howled with laughter as his guts reached out again to the elder one. They covered the comet he stood upon, giant mushrooms sprouting from his entrails as he tried again to combine with the corpse.

Anabelle slammed her hands into the comet, sending fire and lightning through it until the rock broke apart from the inside. "Everyone, hold on!"

Terra whirled, looking for something to grab. "Onto what?"

Rasputina raised her dagger wand and cast a field around the DGA, keeping them afloat as the comet exploded.

Bennington bit the black space between him and the DGA and tore it open like a rabid dog. He reached into it and dragged out another elder one's body, which he quickly started to consume.

"Why is he doing that?" Abby asked.

"He's trying to synthesize the Dark Melody into himself to gain more control and power," Rasputina answered.

"We're stopping this now," Anabelle said. "This is our final push."

CHAPTER FORTY-FOUR

Abby wracked her brain to figure out what she could do to make the situation better. From what she could see, there were only so many approaches to handle Bennington. The butler had the use of the Dark One's ability to manipulate the Netherverse. The only thing the DGA had was brute force, and that didn't seem to be enough.

She could see Bennington in the distance, warping reality around him. He was intoxicated by his power. Unsurprising. The only thing he had said he wanted other than revenge was power, and it didn't seem as if he had any plans outside of that.

He was creating worlds around himself, spiraling black orbs of slushy Dark Melody that orbited him, expanding and contracting as he grew larger, becoming something of a feral galaxy.

The girl watched in horror as he flexed his power, obviously delighted by his strength. "We're still going to need a plan. Something, at least."

Anabelle shook her head. "I don't have anything. He's got the advantage here. Rasputina isn't up to snuff, and we're cut off by ourselves. All I can say is give it everything you got. You have a better idea?"

Abby thought it over for a few seconds. "I might have something, but I'll need time to myself. I won't be able to help for a little bit."

Terra shrugged. "Well, if it goes anything like it did last time, that shouldn't be a problem. We'll try not to die until you show up."

Abby couldn't help but chuckle at Terra's bleakness. "You could try not to die at all."

Terra turned her attention back to the growing galaxy of Bennington ahead. "Yeah, but I don't want to make any promises I can't keep."

Rasputina stood. "We should get going. The longer he has to get caught in his own mind, the more bizarre everything we're going to have to face will be."

Terra looked around, confused. "Uh, just out of curiosity, how are we going to get over there? There isn't really a walking path."

Rasputina kicked off the ground and floated. "The rules of reality here aren't working as clearly as usual. The more Bennington manipulates the fabric of the Netherverse, the more we can use these things for ourselves."

Terra jumped and slowly rose. "Are you fucking kidding me? I can *finally* fly? This is one hell of a fucking climax. Let's go, let's go. Shit, if this is the way I'm going out, I will die happy."

Anabelle's flaming body floated into the air. "I want him dead!" She rocketed toward the dense galaxy forming around Bennington.

Terra flew after Anabelle, easily keeping pace with her. Grok and Rasputina stayed behind with Abby and Sarah for a moment. "What are you planning?" the orc asked.

"We need more magic," Abby answered. "We can only keep throwing punches at him for so long, and it's not doing enough. His body reacts differently and draws in the Dark Melody to make him stronger. If he can manipulate reality, we need to be able to do that as well."

Rasputina looked at Abby closely, her eyes narrowing and growing dark. "How are you planning to do that?"

Abby avoided her eyes. "We don't know yet, but we're going to figure it out."

Rasputina sighed and glanced at Bennington. "I know you want to win this, but don't forget what I told you earlier. There are reasons we hold onto our humanity. Remember that."

Abby nodded slowly as she watched Grok fly toward Bennington. "We will."

Rasputina took off after the orc, quickly closing the distance between them.

As the DGA closed in on Bennington, the monster cackled and slashed at the planets that floated above him, destroying them and sending Dark Melody flying around. His eyes doubled in size when he noticed the DGA coming for him. "Gnats? Flies? Insects to me!"

Anabelle arrived before anyone else. She stopped and watched him, the flames around her body pulsing even brighter than before. "You're not the Dark One. You might have his power, but you aren't him. Get out of his body, and we'll let you go. We want *him*."

Bennington sent a planet flying at Anabelle.

Anabelle pointed at the planet. "Fine. I'll pull you out of his body myself." A beam of fire and electrical energy shot from her palm, cleaving the planet in half. Then she turned to Rasputina. "We need to get him out of that bullshit galaxy he's creating. Any ideas?"

Rasputina nodded. "If you can keep him busy, I can undo his reality manipulation. Then you can fight him on your terms rather than whatever this is."

"I'll do what I can."

Rasputina flew over the duplicating, refracting universe Bennington was creating and raised her dagger wand, muttering arcane words under her breath. Bright green light shot out of her wand, piercing the blackness overhead.

Bennington looked up at the lich, letting out a roar as his body swelled. His mask fell off, revealing the head of a deranged six-eyed wolf, its jaw broken in multiple places. A human head had forced itself up through the wolf's mouth. "What are you doing, you dead bitch?"

Lightning cracked above, illuminating the elder ones, the giant floating gods of old hidden by the distortion of the Netherverse. Dark Melody flowed from their bodies to Rasputina, who etched sigils into the air in front of them. The fabric of the reality started to shift.

Suddenly, Bennington's universe no longer seemed to be as large as space and time. The planets were diminishing, and he grew smaller. Now he was only the size of a skyscraper.

Anabelle and Terra flew forward, the elf taking the lead. She crashed into the butler, sliding between the energy orbs knocking them out of their strange orbit.

He swiped his hand down, and a meteorite hit Anabelle. She careened away from him.

Terra hit the butler next, her boots coming down on his chest. He grabbed her ankles with a speed that shouldn't be possible for someone his size, then drew back his arm to launch her into space.

Grok came up behind him as he continued to shrink and threw her arms around his neck, then pulled as hard as she could to flip him over.

Bennington raked the black and tore it open, and a host of Dark Melody versions of him scuttled through the hole.

Across the black, Sarah stood with Abby, who was sitting quietly on their floating asteroid. "You have a plan, don't you?" Sarah asked.

Abby opened one of her eyes. "Hold on, I'm focusing."

Sarah paced, watching the climactic battle happening ahead of them. "I should be out there."

Abby stood up and shook her head. "We have something we need you to do."

Sarah smiled weakly. "Yeah, about that. You remember I can hardly walk, right?"

Abby opened her palm, revealing two obsidian balls the size of walnuts. "Take these. The smaller one is for you."

"What are these?"

"Nanobots to heal you, and the other is a nanobot infusion of the Dark Melody. They're timed for an hour max, which means you don't have to worry about becoming like me. It should give you all an extra push."

Sarah took her nanobot ball and rolled it over in her hand. The ball exploded in a faint cloud of dust, which she breathed in. She coughed for a second, then stood up straight. "Oh, shit. I feel better. A lot better. I'm ready to get in there."

Sarah floated up, her eyes glowing.

"Wait," Abby called. "There are two more things. All you have to do is throw that at Anabelle or someone. As long as it bursts, it'll work. Second, the Path of Pain. You said Cire showed you. How?"

Sarah shrugged. "He practically tortured me to death. Why?"

Abby opened her other palm, which held a red sphere. "Tell Terra to take that into consideration when she's ready for the Path of Pain."

"What about you?"

Abby took a deep breath. Millions of nanobots flew out of her mouth and streamed from her pores. Hundreds of small lasers were created across Abby's skin. "We're not finished preparing yet, but we'll be ready soon."

Sarah didn't ask any more questions. She sped off to join the fight.

Abby closed her eyes, focused her breath, and drew a sigil in her mind's eye. It was her own creation, designed by synthesizing everything she knew about the Dark Melody as taught to her by Persephone, plus all of the runes and sigils she'd memorized. She and Martin put all of their processing power into creating something new and potentially terrifying.

Sarah joined Anabelle, who was blasting Bennington with an ongoing stream of electricity and fire. The butler screeched in pain as Rasputina tried to rip him from his tethers to the Netherverse. Grok and Terra were busy hacking pieces off his legs. "Here, it's an upgrade from Abby!"

She tossed the sphere at Anabelle, and it exploded. The cloud of nanobots split up, some of them heading toward Grok and others to Anabelle. Then she flew down to Terra, who was standing atop a comet that was sprouting trees which instantly bloomed and then died. "Hey, Abby says when you're ready for the Path of Pain, take—"

Terra grabbed the red sphere out of Sarah's hand and bit into it. "Bring it on!" As soon as Terra bit into the sphere, she bent over and clutched her stomach, her eyes bulging as she coughed blood.

Sarah knelt beside her. "Holy shit, are you—"

Terra waved Sarah away. "Take care of business. I got this."

Sarah flew over to aid Grok.

Terra shook as her body convulsed. It was worse than anything she'd ever experienced. She felt like she was going to die.

But she knew it was going to pass, and once she crossed the threshold, she'd be stronger than ever.

Terra let loose a roar of anguish as wounds broke open across her body. Her eyes glowed flaming red as her muscles tensed and pulsed, growing larger and then shrinking. She straightened and noted smoke coming off her body, then looked down at her hand. A nearly psychotic calm washed over her. "So, this is the Path of Pain?"

She grabbed Bennington's leg and ripped it off, causing the monster to fall over.

He was growing again, still sucking energy from the Dark Melody, regardless of what Rasputina was able to pull away from him.

Terra let out a feral roar as she jumped onto his thigh and ripped through his skin, continuing to climb and tear and bash every part of his body as she made her way to his head.

Then everything froze.

Abby's voice was heard in everyone's head. "We will separate him from his power source. The rest is up to you."

Abby walked toward Bennington and the DGA agents. Her armor was gone. Instead, billions of nanobots floated around her like an eerie black aura as she glided toward the fight. As she moved, the tentacles of the elder ones floating above reached down to her and connected to her nanobots, which connected to her.

Rasputina looked at Abby and gasped. "Oh, gods, she's done it."

The Dark Melody and the tentacles pulled Abby toward the elder ones, and her eyes burned with black fire as she opened her mouth and shot forth ether flames. The nanobots surrounding her took on the form of an elder one, and a mass of tentacles reached toward Bennington.

The tentacles wrapped around the sections of his body that were connected to the Netherverse.

He screamed, his eyes mad and frantic as he struggled to get away. Abby's tentacles held him fast while she tore him away from the Netherverse, then plugged into what he had been drawing power from.

Terra and Anabelle observed Abby's awful power. "Dude, she would totally kick the shit out of us in another fight."

Anabelle nodded. "She almost looks like a god."

When Abby lifted her hands, the Dark Melody of the elder gods flowed into her and the world exploded in white light, blinding everyone.

When the light faded, the Netherverse was different. Rolling green hills stretched as far as the eye could see and the sky was a deep black where stars twinkled, the tentacles of the elder ones hanging overhead.

Bennington stumbled forward, back to his regular size. He let out a howl and shook his head. "I will not be defeated."

Abby landed, her nanobots circling around her as trees and flowers sprouted around her feet. Rasputina walked up behind her and placed her hand on the girl's shoulder. "I guess you *were* paying attention to what I said."

Abby smiled and nodded. "We figured if we used those sigils on Persephone's arm to control the Dark Melody within her, we could use a similar one to harness the power of the elder ones and their Dark Melody. That way we could cut off Bennington's power, and we figured this place could be spruced up as well, the same way you took care of hell."

Bennington let out a roar. "You're not done with me!"

He raced toward Abby, his chest arms reaching out.

Anabelle waved her hand and a wall of fire rose around Abby and Rasputina. "Where do you think you're going?"

Terra stepped between Bennington and Abby. "You still owe me a dance."

Anabelle stepped forward, but Abby stopped her. "You should let Terra handle this. She's the only one who is physically strong enough. Bennington might be able to warp your magic since he still has the

Dark One's power, but there's nothing he can manipulate in a full-on fistfight."

Anabelle nodded and took a step back, joining Grok.

Bennington sprinted at Terra, knocking her to the ground, then brought his fists down on her.

Terra in turn head-butted him, then pushed him off her and leapt up, bouncing from foot to foot as she spat out a tooth. "Come on, puppers. You told me Rasputina taught you all about pain. Let's see how our lessons match up."

Bennington and Terra circled each other, their eyes locked. The Hand waited for the first sign of attack, and when she saw the slightest twitch of Bennington's leg, she prepared herself.

The butler lurched forward with speed on par with Anabelle's, but Terra was ready. She turned to the side, grabbed Bennington's striking arm, and let his momentum do the work of tossing him onto his back, then snapped his arm in three places and took her time straddling him. She brought one fist down on his head.

The force of her punch smashed his head into the ground, shaking the earth around the two of them for twenty feet. The sound of Terra's fist hitting Bennington's head was like thunder. "That's for wasting so much of my goddamn time!"

Another crack of thunder. "That's for ruining our meeting with the Light One."

Yet another crack. "And that's for...oh, fuck it."

Terra punched Bennington again, and his head split and spilled black sludge on the ground. The DGA, Rasputina, and Grok came over and stood over Bennington's limp form. "Is it finished?" Sarah asked.

Rasputina shook her head. "Almost." She knelt, pulling a dagger wand from her side, and made a cut in the body, then reached into the wound and pulled out Bennington's shriveled body. She held it in her arms as the wrinkled flesh suit on the ground returned to Grimnir's form, the mask still broken, the young child bleeding from a hole in his head.

Bennington looked up at Rasputina. "I didn't think you were really going to leave me. That you were going to change."

The lich shook her head. "You could have changed with me. "

He glared at her. "You deserted me. After you took everything from me, you deserted me."

Rasputina pressed her hand to Bennington's forehead, and he burst into flames. She dropped the burning corpse.

Anabelle, Sarah, Abby, and Terra stood over Grimnir, who was muttering under his breath and coughing up blood while trying to move away.

"Please, please," he sputtered. "Not like this."

Sarah looked at Anabelle. "I can't believe this is what we've been fighting for years. He's pathetic."

Grimnir removed his mask. There was no face underneath, only a gaping mouth full of teeth far too large for the orifice.

Abby knelt beside him. "How did you think it was going to happen?"

Despite not having eyes, Grimnir looked up at Abby. "All I wanted was order. All of the universe, the multiverse, so much chaos. You've seen it. Individuality is nothing more than chaos. I thought I could fix that. Rewrite it all. A single organism to control and be spliced into everything. Then there would be order."

Anabelle sneered. "You really think that would have worked? That it justifies all the death you've caused? That you're still causing?"

Abby turned to Rasputina. "Are you sure this is him? All of him?"

Rasputina nodded, looking around the Netherverse. "There isn't a trace of him left in this place. This is all."

Abby cradled Grimnir, the Dark One. "We've all suffered because of you. I lost my father. Rasputina lost her humanity. Grok and Terra almost lost their lives. Anabelle…" Her eyes hardened. "You brought nothing but pain into the universe. You should know that. The last thing you will see as you die are those who stood against you and your insanity. You failed. You failed because you were wrong. Life is chaos. You were just too stupid to see it."

Grimnir sighed and struggled to move, choking as he writhed.

Abby pressed her hand to his cheek. Nanobots poured from her flesh, covered Grimnir's body, and slowly ate him alive.

Grimnir screamed as he thrashed about but Abby held him still, refusing to let him leave as he was devoured. Finally, the screams subsided, and there was nothing but bones.

Anabelle took the bones in her hand and they burst into flames, leaving only ash, which Terra trampled under her feet.

They all stood in silence for a while, letting the momentousness of the moment sink in. Finally, Anabelle said, "Come on. We need to find that valve."

CHAPTER FORTY-FIVE

The Netherverse stretched before the DGA agents, Grok, and Rasputina. They had to find the valves and close them as soon as possible. The Light One was waiting for them to accomplish that task, and there was no way to find out how bad things were in the other realms right now.

Anabelle turned to Rasputina. "Where should we start? You've spent more time down here than any of us."

Rasputina stared into the distance, watching the tumultuous, shifting parts of the Netherverse fade and combine into each other. "We never came across the valves, and the Netherverse is too vast for us to have traveled the whole of it. Not that it would have helped, but we should have asked Grimnir."

Abby, who held a ball of nanobots in her hand, shook her head. "It wouldn't have helped. We felt his indignation as he died. He wouldn't have told us anything."

Terra leaned over to Abby. "Hey, what exactly was that thing you did with him?"

"Ate him. Converted everything he was into something our system could process. Waste not want not."

Anabelle paced, scratching the back of her head. "Sarah, any ideas?

You had the Light One in your head for a while, right? Did you retain anything?"

Sarah nodded but looked uncertain. "She left me with a lot, but that wasn't part of it. I don't think she knew the makeup of the Netherverse any more than we do."

Anabelle threw her arms up. "Well, great. We don't know where these valves are. Do we at least know what they look like?"

Grok stepped forward to offer her opinion. "In hell, they were valves. They were built into the outer circle. Looked like living plumbing. But that was hell, a place that had been constructed."

Rasputina looked up at the elder gods, who were floating above like indifferent jellyfish. "It's a living realm, always changing, made of dead and living elder gods and the souls of those who have passed. Maybe I could use the Dark Melody to find them."

Terra sat down on a rock and sank her head into her hands. "It would be a pretty shitty climax to all of this is if we managed to kill the Dark One and still didn't save the universe because none of us got our Netherverse plumbing certification."

Rasputina knelt and pressed her hands to the ground. Black tendrils snaked up and floated in front of her, and an eyeball grew on the end of each stalk and peered into her eyes. They looked from one to the other as more tendrils pushed out of the Netherverse's soil.

Abby, who was standing next to Terra, grimaced at the bizarre garden of sprouting stalk eyes. "Every time we think we can't see anything freakier than we have, we do. Never thought bean sprouts with eyeballs would be so disturbing."

Rasputina was humming something under her breath as she swayed. The eyeball tendrils watched her, swinging in time with her movements.

Suddenly, Rasputina looked at the elder gods above them. "That's where we have to go. Up there."

Terra laughed nervously. "You're joking, right? I've read enough Lovecraft to know you don't want to go toward the big ancient things that have tentacles. That's instant death."

Rasputina stood, her eyes still locked on the elder gods. "That's what this place is telling me. Whatever controls how souls get in and out of here is up there."

Anabelle's gaze drifted to the mass of floating tentacles above the clouds. "That was what the Dark One did? Braved that shit? Even though he was an asshole, I have to admit he had guts."

Terra cracked her shoulders as she got to her feet. "So, everyone can fly now, right?"

They looked at each other. "Yeah, I guess we all can now," Anabelle finally said.

Terra's eyes flashed white as she let her energy flow through her body. "Well, doesn't make much sense to sit around and keep jabbering. Let's get ready to pump it!" She looked around, smiling at her joke.

The rest of the group didn't seem to have noticed.

Terra crossed her arms as she floated into the air. "I swear, I give you guys quality content and you don't even care. *Quality content!*"

The rest of the group drifted into the air, Abby laughing quietly at Terra's indignation. They headed toward the elder gods, who were much farther away than they looked.

Thick clouds still obscured them. They no longer looked as ominous, but the elder ones still looked vast and terrifying, even if the DGA had become somewhat used to seeing them floating overhead.

As they got closer, Abby commed Creon. She wanted to know how bad things were on Earth. "Hey, Creon, you there?"

Creon's voice came through a wall of static. "Abby? Abby, is that you? How are you guys doing down there?"

"The Dark One is gone. Finally. We're done with him."

"That's good news," Creon said, hardly sounding enthused. "Glad one problem is taken care of."

"How are things on your end?"

"Terrible. Utterly terrible. The dead are running rampant. We're trying to contain them, but...gods, it doesn't look like there's a chance. They're everywhere. Myrddin's leading an assault on a group of them in the Midwest. Whatever you guys are trying to do, please make it quick. I'm not sure how long we're all going to be able to hold out."

"Will do. I'll keep you posted."

Anabelle looked at Abby. "Full-scale apocalypse?"

Abby nodded. "Sounds like it. Creon doesn't know how long the realms will survive."

"Then let's push this!" Terra shouted, blasting past everyone else.

The air was hot, brimming with energy and life. Small creatures drifted through the tentacles of the elder ones like plankton. Past the clouds, the sky was pale pink, strokes of blue looking as if they'd been painted on.

The group floated directly below the unbelievably massive bodies of the elder ones.

Anabelle humbly watched their swaying tentacles. "What now?"

Rasputina flew past everyone else, heading straight toward the mass of tentacles. When she got closer, she let out a scream as one of the smaller tentacles touched her, shocking and flinging her back.

Grok caught her. "Doesn't look like we're flying straight through them."

Terra nodded. "Yeah, but I'll give you props for trying. Any ideas, Abs?"

Abby pulled out her scanner and took readings on the elder ones. "They're made out of the Dark Melody, and there's something in them —a network of some kind. It's hard to make out, but they're all connected to each other. Kinda like a Portuguese man-of-war."

Everyone exchanged confused looks. "What do these things have in common with someone from Portugal?" Anabelle asked.

Abby shook her head. "It's just a weird name. They're a kind of jellyfish that all hook up to each other to create a massive nervous system. That's kind of what it looks like the elder ones have done."

Suddenly, Abby snapped her fingers. "Wait, remember what the Light One said about the Path of Pain being the only way to access the valves? Maybe that's how we get through. Those tentacles are filled with energy that would probably fry any of us if we get too close. But maybe Terra, Sarah, or Anabelle can."

The two humans exchanged wary glances. "She did say that," Terra finally agreed.

Sarah clenched her body, opening the nine gates until flames ripped from her body and fire poured from her eyes.

Terra did the same, her body taking on the same hue and aura as Sarah's. She looked at the other woman. "Ready?"

Sarah nodded, and the two of them rocketed toward the tangled mass.

Lightning cracked from the elder ones' tentacles and snapped at the two humans, who made no effort to dodge. They both screamed as they pushed past the initial burst of lightning and flew straight through the tentacles into the soft underbelly of one of the elder ones.

As Terra and Sarah got closer to the elder one, something unexpected happened. The elder god rolled in the sky and pulled its tentacles up, exposing its underbelly to Terra and Sarah.

There was a clear path now. The rest of the DGA raced to them before the elder one changed its mind.

Abby got there before anyone else. "Can you touch it?" she asked, warily watching the tentacles that floated around her.

Terra reached out to touch the elder one. As her fingers got closer, the elder one's skin rolled back, creating an opening large enough for her to walk through. "Oh, that's weird. Uh, are we going in?"

Abby looked at her scanner. "That's where the network is, and we couldn't have gotten here without the Path of Pain. This might be our best chance to find the valves."

Terra nodded and floated toward the hole. "All right. Into the giant, ancient jellyfish gods I go."

She slipped into the opening. The skin remained open as she disappeared into the darkness.

After a few seconds, her head poked through, covered in Dark Melody goo. "You guys have to check this out. It's fucking wild." She vanished again.

Rasputina smiled as she stared at the hole. "Of all the things I've seen, I never would have thought this possible. Walking into the body of a living god..."

Terra's head popped out again. "Okay, are you guys coming or not?"

No one answered, but they all floated toward the open hole.

Anabelle passed through, and everything went dark for a moment. A few seconds later, thousands of lights appeared, each shining brightly. The lights multiplied from thousands to millions, then billions within seconds.

The sky was full of neon lights in the shapes of tentacles, waving as if caught in the slow ebb and flow of an ocean tide. As the tentacles touched the surface, electricity ran through them, brightening the entire world. Each flash came with another small bead of light.

Terra floated past Abby, watching the electrical flashes above. "What do you think that is?"

Abby scrunched her forehead. "Looks like a nervous system, which means that's probably information being relayed through electrical systems."

She reached out and allowed thousands of nanobots to float to the thin red and purple tentacles above.

The nanobots joined the lights, flashing along with the bright bursts of multicolored energy. Then they drifted back down into Abby's palm, glowing the color of the clouds above.

Abby closed her eyes as her body hummed slightly. "They're so much more than neurons. It's their thoughts, their whole essence. This is where the valves are."

Grok spun, obviously annoyed at not being able to track what Abby was saying. "What are you talking about? Where are they at?"

Abby held her arms up, her eyes glowing with the light from above. "All of these are the valves. Each of them is a connection point to other universes and dimensions and timelines, an infinite number of entry points from the multiverse."

Anabelle furrowed her brow as she scanned the floating lights. "And we're only supposed to find ours and open it up? How did the Dark One manage to pull this off?"

Abby shrugged. "We don't know, but we better figure it out."

CHAPTER FORTY-SIX

Abby marveled at the infinite number of valves before her. She wasn't sure where to look or even how to start, but she was excited. The brief connection she'd shared with the elder ones had shown her a snippet of their thoughts, their existence. It was still difficult to understand, but she knew it was the key to figuring this all out.

Terra floated forward a little, spinning in the gravity-free place. "So, are we just going to kick each one of these or something?"

Anabelle shook her head, deep in thought. "If these are part of the elder ones, it would be stupid as hell to go around kicking shit. Who knows what they could do? If I had to guess, probably not anything good. I say we split up and investigate whatever is directly in front of us. Maybe if we figure out how to interact with them, we can figure out how to turn ours on when we find it."

The women split up and drifted over to a node near them.

Abby reached out to a node, and its shining light condensed into a hand-sized orb. Her skin warmed as she got close to the orb. Suddenly, she was filled with an intense fear of what would happen if she touched it. She wished she could have done some experiments ahead of time and gotten a better idea of what to expect, but it wasn't a possibility right now. The only way to find anything out was direct experience.

With that in mind, Abby touched the orb. It was smooth and cold despite the warmth coming from its surface. She wrapped her hand around it; it wasn't connected to anything. She could have walked away with it.

Feelings flashed through Abby. It was like having a camera flash go off multiple times in front of her eyes. She felt like her brain had been blinded, and she searched for words to call to the rest of her group, but nothing came to her.

Abby saw all of the orbs around her connecting to a grid she hadn't seen before. There was something in the middle of them, a nexus of sorts. That was what it felt like, at least. Abby didn't have the words to describe what she was seeing.

It was gone as quickly as it had appeared.

When Abby's awareness returned, she spun to watch what everyone else was doing.

Terra had picked up two of the orbs and was weighing them in her hands. Anabelle was poking another one tentatively. Rasputina and Grok floated next to an orb as the lich held her dagger wand at it, muttering under her breath.

Abby floated over to Terra. "Did you see anything?"

Terra rolled the orbs in her hand and shrugged. "Nope. Didn't see anything strange. Well, stranger than this."

Abby turned to Anabelle. "How about you?"

Anabelle shook her head as she continued to poke the orb. "Were we supposed to?"

"We saw something like a vision when we touched the orb. Confusing but kind of direct. If these are the elder ones' thoughts, we think we might have interacted with them directly. These lead some-place. We have to follow them. That's probably the proper valve, or at least a control point."

Anabelle called Sarah, Rasputina, and Grok over. She quickly explained what Abby had told her. "So, we're following Abby and hoping things don't get any weirder." Then she turned to Abby. "Lead the way."

Abby touched another orb and closed her eyes, trying to prepare herself for the onslaught of information. The same vision flashed in front of her. Since she was prepared this time, she memorized the grid and direction it showed her. Before the vision faded, she saw something else. It was a quick, condensed history of the universe she was holding in her hand.

Abby backed away from the orb and looked at her hand in shock. "Whoa. These are more than thoughts. These are entire universes. Complete."

Rasputina picked up the orb Abby had let go of it. "Beautiful. I've always wondered what the purpose of the elder ones was. And the Dark Melody. Who would have thought all of reality was held in them? Floating in the Netherverse, full of all our lives."

Terra scrunched her forehead. "Wait, are you saying *our* universe is in here? Like, it's floating inside a bunch of giant jellyfish?"

Abby smiled as she looked around. "That's exactly what we said."

Terra shook her head as she sighed. "How can we be in here and out there is actually in here? That doesn't make any sense."

Terra was right, Abby thought. That was what made this all the more beautiful.

"You know, we would never have thought we'd experience anything like this," Abby said. "Never. Not in our entire lives. This is beyond anything I have ever dreamed of."

She pointed in the direction the vision had shown her. "This way. All we have to do is keep going this way. I'll keep checking and see if we're on the right path."

Abby floated ahead almost lazily, brushing her hand against an orb here and there to make sure she was still going the right way. That was only part of the reason, though. Every time she touched an orb, she caught a glimpse of another universe or dimension. Some of them were drastically different from her own.

It would have been easy to spend an entire lifetime here, Abby thought. Peeking into every universe that would and could ever exist. It would never get old.

Even though no one else was able to see what Abby did, it didn't diminish the wonder in their eyes.

Reality was in flux in the bosom of the elder ones, much like the Netherverse had been, the difference being that there wasn't any violence or chaos. As reality shifted around them, it was hardly noticeable. It was difficult to put your finger on since the changes were so microscopic, but they could be felt.

Abby could feel something creeping into her, almost like a voice, a whisper. On a basic level, she understood it was the Dark Melody, the fabric of the elder ones, making itself known. She didn't know how much the elder ones were aware of.

Persephone had told her the Dark Melody that existed within her was self-aware. It had desires and needs which were much different than those of a mortal. For a while, it had caused Persephone a large amount of discomfort. Abby assumed this place was similar.

She wasn't sure if the Dark Melody was what the elder ones were made of or if it *was* the elder ones. Either way, whatever the DGA was floating through was aware of what was happening.

The DGA continued to follow Abby as she floated along the grid imprinted in her mind.

Terra wasn't far behind Abby. She was floating on her back, leisurely backstroking through the ethereal plane. "You know, this is much more relaxing than I thought it was going to be. Usually, there's the whole hanging sense of dread thing, you know?"

Anabelle floated closer to her. "It's a pleasant change. I feel like we deserved a break, even if it's only going to last until something else tries to kill us."

Terra casually picked up one of the universe orbs and tossed it at Anabelle. "So, Grimnir or the Dark One or whatever the fuck that thing was is finally gone. What are you going to do with all of this new freedom we're going to have?"

Anabelle's jaw tightened. "Bury Roy."

Terra's smile disappeared as she rolled around and righted herself. "Fuck, Belle, I didn't—"

Anabelle shook her head as she stared grimly ahead. "It's not your fault. You don't have to apologize, and now isn't the time to think about all of that. We'll do it when we get home."

Silence descended over the group as they made their way through the infinite universes surrounding them. Finally, Anabelle spoke, her voice tight, as if she were trying to keep something in. "You know, I didn't think it could ever happen. I've known him for decades. Seen him pull through everything. I guess I didn't really believe he could die."

Abby nodded, uncertain of what to say. Maybe it was better to let Anabelle talk. There probably wasn't anything *to* be said.

Anabelle wistfully brushed one of the universe orbs. "You know he was worried about me being embarrassed about us dating? He used to talk about it all the time. Worried that I'd be embarrassed to date a human. Funny, right?"

Terra shrugged as she floated ahead of Anabelle. "I don't know, you did seem like you had a pretty big problem with humans when we first met. I kinda thought it was an elf thing."

Anabelle shook her head, her eyes sad and her lips tight with grief. "No, I was stupid, that's all. Roy and you two did a lot to change that." She clenched her jaws as she blinked back tears. "Sorry," she muttered. "We should pay attention to the mission. The Nine Realms are still depending on us."

Abby wished she could think of something to say. She knew Anabelle would have had a comforting word for her if anything had happened to Persephone, but there was nothing she could think of that would ease her friend's pain. Not now, not here.

Terra, who was staring ahead at the path Abby was leading them all down, cleared her throat. "You know he loved you a lot, and he went out like a hero. There's no way he didn't."

A few tears made their way out of Anabelle's eyes as she bit her lip and nodded quickly. "Yeah, I know. He probably took a lot of assholes with him."

The orbs were beginning to appear with more frequency, and they bunched together as if they were being generated too rapidly to expand further.

Abby touched another of the orbs and saw the grid in front of her. Their destination was getting closer. "Wherever we're heading toward, we're almost there."

Rasputina drifted closer to Abby. "Do you feel that?"

Abby looked at Rasputina quizzically. "What do you mean?"

"The heart of it all. You were right when you said this was like a man-of-war jellyfish. There's a central point. Not a heart. Not a brain. Something else entirely. I can feel it. I know you can too."

Abby let herself listen to her nanobots, which were linked with the elder ones through the sigils she'd carved.

The nanobots were singing. Abby hadn't noticed it since she was used to ignoring the nanobot consciousness in her, but now she could hear it. They were singing a choral arrangement unlike anything she had ever heard. "That's the center, isn't it?" she asked.

"Whatever we're heading is bigger than a valve to let souls in and out, just like this place. There's no telling what we're going to come across."

Abby looked at the lich. "You sound excited."

Rasputina smiled shyly. "It has been a long time since I've seen anything new, and you Dark Gate Angels keep surprising me." She hung her head and avoided Abby's eyes. "Thank you for believing in us and for giving us another chance."

Abby stared ahead. A bright light was floating in the distance. "Who would have thought this was how things would end up?"

Terra floated over to her and Rasputina. "You two having a heart to heart?"

Rasputina looked away quickly.

Terra lightly punched the lich in the arm. "Cut that shit out. You guys are honorary Dark Gate Angels, the both of you. What do you think, Anabelle?"

Anabelle glanced at the lich and the orc. "They're here trying to save the Nine Realms with us, so I'd say full-on members. As long as you don't try to kill us again."

Grok laughed. It sounded like she was choking. "Easily, if not for the simple fact that we might not live past the next few hours."

Terra sighed as she stopped to admire the gleaming light ahead. "You know, you could have said, 'Sure, no problem. We won't do evil shit anymore.'"

Grok came to a halt beside Terra and rested her hand on her shoulder. "We'd be honored."

Anabelle walked between Terra and Grok. "Cut out the cute shit." She turned to Abby. "What now?"

Abby reached toward the light. "Now we see if we can make contact."

C H A P T E R   F O R T Y - S E V E N

L A was burning. The sky was dark with smoke, and an eerie red cloud hung over the skyline.

Most of downtown had been cleared of civilians, who'd escaped to Myrddin's floating buildings.

The few souls who were not able to escape were thought to be doomed. Since Roy had passed, there was not an immediate chain of command to follow. It probably would have fallen to Blackwell, but he was gone as well.

Persephone watched zombies ambling out from behind a gated structure. She'd been picked up with Naota and the civilians they'd rescued and taken to another DZ. Across from the table she sat at were recordings of soldiers stranded in the field, hunkered down during their search for civilians who were left behind.

There were still people out there, and these pitiful soldiers were too afraid to go get them.

Persephone shook her head. She wasn't any different, though. There were people suffering outside the walls, and she was holed up in safety.

Naota sat at the table with her. He was slouched over it, his head resting on his arms. He hadn't said anything since Blackwell died.

Persephone wondered where Abby and the rest of the DGA were. Roy had sounded so certain that they were going to be able to fix what was going on, but the longer the day wore on, the less likely that seemed. There hadn't been any word from Myrddin, and communication from the other realms was sparse at best. The orc homeworld had gone silent.

Naota suddenly looked up. He watched the soldiers walking back and forth, staring at the zombies with frightened expressions. Many of them ignored the snarling corpses outside the wall, trying to pretend nothing was happening. "Fucking pathetic," he muttered. "When are we getting out of here?"

"What do you mean?"

"We're rested enough to get back out there. What the hell are we still doing sitting here?"

Persephone laughed softly to herself. "You want to go back out there? You know that's a death wish, right?"

Naota met Persephone's eyes. His stare was broken and cold, but not without hope. "You want to stay in here and let people die?"

Out loud, it sounded ridiculous. "Of course not, but we don't have any orders."

Naota stood and wrapped his energy chains around his wrists. "What do we need orders for? We know what needs to be done. We have the equipment. Might as well get back to work."

Persephone nodded as she stared down at her hands, the sigils on her possessed hand glowing brightly. "You know it might mean a court-martial for you, right? We were told to stay here. Those might as well be orders."

"I didn't sign up with the Initiative to sit on my ass while people get hurt. Did you?"

"No, but I wanted to make sure you knew what was at stake."

Naota grabbed a rifle from the arms rack near their table. He slung it over his shoulder as he put more ammo into his pack.

Persephone pulled up her comm and pinged Creon. "Hey, I need a favor."

The gnome appeared on her holoscreen. He looked beyond frantic.

His hair was frazzled, and his glasses kept sliding down his nose. "What can I do for you?"

"We need you to patch into the army's intel. There are people who need our help throughout the city. We need to know where they are."

Creon leaned out of screen range and shouted something, then came back and said, "That seems like something Martin can help you with. Let me connect him."

Creon was replaced by Martin's sarcastic paperclip face. "So, you two ready to play hero? Well, just give me a second and voila! Instant access. Looks like you have your job cut out for you. If you need anything else, just ask. You shouldn't be bothering Creon; he's got enough on his plate. If you think Earth is bad, you should see the gnome world. Actually, you probably shouldn't."

Persephone and Naota headed toward the main gate. Two soldiers guarded the gate, both of them armed to the teeth.

One of the guards raised his gun. "Halt. You aren't authorized to leave."

Both guards' guns flew out of their hands.

Alex walked up behind Persephone and Naota. "Didn't know you two were here. If I had, I would have tried to get out of this shithole sooner. What's the plan?"

The two guards left, no doubt to find their commanding officer.

Alex raised her hand and teleported the two rifles to her. "You believe the nerve of those guys? Fucking grounded me. Who's even in charge here?"

Naota shrugged. "I'm surprised you let them."

Alex checked her rifles. "Too much going on. Best to be a team player. I figured I'd be a better team player in the air."

"Probably, but like you said, there's a lot going on. The brass is using our limited resources as best they can. Right now, we're working with human forces who have never faced off against zombies. Not like any of us have."

She threw one of the rifles to Persephone. "Unfortunate. At least Team Boundless is still up there, even if they're ferrying civilians to the floating cities. Speaking of which," Alex connected with Chine, who was encumbered with numerous civilians, including two kids who sat in Alex's seat. He was doing well but wished he was with Alex. That made two of them.

Alex shook her head. "Well, we're hoofing it until I can get back in touch with the rest of my squad. Let's get going before anyone puts forth a decent effort to keep us in."

She rose into the air and pulled Naota and Persephone up with her. The three of them went over the top of the wall and hovered there for a second, taking in the severity of what they were up against.

Persephone pulled up her map. Martin had dropped pins where there were civilians and wounded soldiers holed up for protection. "I'm sending the details to both of you. Let's hit the closest one."

Alex dropped Persephone and Naota into the pit of undead as she pulled her scythe from the ether. She dive-bombed the horde of zombies, and Naota swung his chained blades at her side.

Persephone aimed her arm, and tentacles burst out and lashed through the pile of bodies.

Alex surged forward, swinging her scythe. She cut a path for them to move forward as Naota sheathed his daggers and fired, clearing away the zombies who were starting to take notice of them.

The going was slow and methodical, the three of them carving a narrow path for them to get away from the DZ. Once they could catch their breath, they headed into a building, figuring it would be easier to move through the city on rooftops rather than contesting the streets with the swarm of undead below them.

Naota glassed the building across from them from atop the roof. He pointed to the room the civvies were in while Persephone coordinated with Martin for a dropship to come to their position in an hour.

Alex and Persephone leaped from the roof. The dragonrider telepathically guided herself and Naota through the window while Persephone used her tentacles to latch onto the sill and pull herself over.

An older man was curled up in the corner of the apartment, holding a young girl in his arms. He hardly looked up when Persephone approached him.

She reached out to the man, who flinched toward the corner. "Sir, we've come to get you out of here."

The old man looked at Persephone, dazed. "Can you help my daughter?" He held the young girl's body up. The girl's head slumped lifelessly.

Persephone swallowed the gasp that threatened to escape. "Come on," she said as she helped the man to his feet. "Let's go."

They made their way back to the window as Alex and Naota headed out of the apartment to sweep the rest of the rooms for survivors.

On the rooftop, Persephone placed the old man on the ground. He continued to stare at his dead daughter as if he were puzzled and said nothing.

After a few minutes, Alex and Naota returned. Alex watched the man from afar. "Give me a minute." She walked over to him and held her hand over his forehead.

The old man closed his eyes and rocked back slightly. When he opened his eyes, they were full of tears. Alex whispered something to him, and he handed the dead child to her. She walked over to the corner of the roof, laid the child down, took off her jacket, and covered the child, then returned to Naota and Persephone. "We have more to find."

"What did you do to him?" Persephone asked.

"Pulled him out of shock telepathically. Tried to ease the pain. He'll be okay for a few hours. After that, I'm not sure."

They continued their mission, leaping from rooftop to rooftop and breaking into the apartments that were flagged, bringing whoever they could find back to the rooftop pick-up point. After a half-hour, they ran across a group that was stranded at ground level.

The small, squat house was surrounded by zombies who clawed the walls, their eyes dumb and glazed, their mouths gaping with frightening hunger.

Alex pointed at the door. "I'll hit the door and provide a distraction. You two can slip in through the back and get them out fast. Sound good?"

Persephone and Naota nodded.

Alex leaped off of the roof, spinning her scythe. Before she hit the ground, she telekinetically pushed all of the zombies out of the way. She backed up against the door and pulled out her pistol, quickly getting six headshots on the zombies around her before slashing with her scythe to maintain a perimeter.

Persephone led Naota through the back door of the house. She took point, clearing each corner as she stepped into the room, her pistol raised in case of an attack.

The two of them reached the living room, where they found a group of wounded soldiers huddled together. One of them drew his gun, prepared to fire. When he saw it was Persephone and not zombies, he sighed and relaxed. "What are you doing out here?"

Naota leaned next to one of the soldiers and helped him to his feet. "Doing what needs to be done."

The soldier nodded as he wiped blood off the side of his face. "We didn't think anyone was coming. We lost contact with the rest of the squad. Been stuck here for hours without…fuck, I thought I was going to die in here."

Alex's scream came from the front of the house.

Persephone turned to Naota. "Get them to the back. I got Alex." She took off toward the front door.

The door exploded in as Persephone's tentacles tore it apart.

Alex was cutting through anything that got close to her. A zombie's head was attached to her ankle, separated from its body.

Two zombies flung themselves onto the dragonrider and knocked her down. The larger one sank its teeth into her neck, and blood spurted as she screamed and dropped her scythe. She clenched her fist and fire bloomed on her skin, incinerating the two zombies. She struggled to her feet as more zombies massed behind her.

Persephone ran to Alex, and they made their way back to the house. Alex held her neck tightly, trying to stem the loss of blood.

Once they made it through the house and past the back door, Persephone scooped Alex into one arm and used her tentacles to pull herself up to the rooftops again. She took them back to the pick-up roof.

Alex leaned against the parapet, breathing heavily. She was losing a lot of blood, and Persephone was worried.

Alex waved away the drow's concern with her bionic arm. "Cut it out. I'm okay." She pulled a patch from her dragon anchor and slapped it on the wound, where it instantly cauterized the skin. "Looks like we were just in time." She pointed at a helicopter heading toward the roof. "I'm not sure how long this can keep going."

Persephone looked down at the zombies clawing the side of the building. "Neither am I."

Naota watched the helicopter. "As long as it takes us to get everyone out of here."

Persephone nodded. "Yeah. I guess it's going to have to."

The door to the helicopter opened. Cire smiled down at Persephone before leaping onto the rooftop. Behind him were more helicopters, all with the insignia of the shaman's tribe.

Persephone approached him. "What are you doing here?"

Cire walked to the edge of the rooftop and pointed at the streets as orcs leaped from the helicopters into the thick of the zombie horde. "Us orcs have handled the issues on our planet. I thought it would be helpful to provide our services to the other realms. Our platoons should be able to handle some of the worst areas."

Persephone smiled as she breathed a sigh of relief. "So, I guess the horde is finally back."

Cire nodded, smiling slightly. "Yes, and the realms will see the extent of orc strength. I think they might have a different opinion of the horde once this is over."

Persephone threw her arms around the shaman. "Thank you so much."

Cire patted the top of her head before breaking their embrace. "This is a huge moment for us, and one the Nine Realms will remember."

CHAPTER FORTY-EIGHT

Abby reached out to the light, letting her nanobots stretch out from her so she could communicate with it.

The nanobots passed into the light.

Abby received a surge of information. This was it, the heart of the elder gods, but it was more than that. The hearts of all of the universes met right here.

Each universe was before her, waiting for her to grasp it. Abby concentrated on her own and felt it rushing toward her.

She reached out to touch it, to flip the switch and reopen the valve.

An unearthly screech tore through Abby's head. It sounded like a thousand voices asking different questions at the same time. She recoiled as her nanobots returned to her. A lingering thought remained in her head, the last bit of information communicated to her through her connection with the nexus of the elder ones.

Danger.

Abby returned to regular consciousness and backed away from the nexus valve. "Something's coming. I think it's a defense system. It's preparing to defend itself from us."

Terra looked around wildly. "Why is it trying to defend itself from us? We're not trying to hurt it? Wait, we *aren't* trying to hurt it, right?"

Abby was still trying to find the source of the impending danger. "This place is like the neural network of the elder ones. It probably sees us as something like a virus, and that means it's going to try and flush us out."

The nexus valve split down the middle, pumping Dark Melody out on the ground. The liquid spread quickly, reaching up to the DGA's ankles.

Abby took to the air as an intensely primal fear filled her heart. The rest of the DGA was doing the same.

The Dark Melody stopped pouring now that the ground was sufficiently covered. Shapes started to form in the Melody, large humanoid figures that rose slowly.

Terra reached out to Abby. "Hey, can you help out with a sharp thing?"

Abby quickly constructed two axes and tossed them to her.

One of the humanoid figures took on the form of a balrog. Slowly, the other shapes did the same.

Terra backed away. "I know that balrog. It's the one from the arena."

Another shape formed from the Dark Melody, a face slowly coming into existence as electricity crackled around the body. It was Tesla.

Abby shook her head, trying to understand what was happening. "No, it's impossible."

The Dark Melody swirled up and Grok stepped out of the darkness, her eyes glowing the same color as the sky above.

Grok and Anabelle looked at each other, confused. "Uh, what's going on?"

Terra landed back down on the ground, swinging an axe in both hands as she stared at the balrog. "Guess we're doing a Greatest Hits."

Abby charged her hand cannon as Tesla rose into the air, his eyes locking with hers. "The nexus must be reading our minds and creating memories from our pasts. Our biggest challenges."

Thousands of figures popped out of the goo and coalesced into elves, wearing the uniform of an old mage college. Their dusty robes and hoods covered their faces, and their wands glowed with other-worldly energy.

Rasputina gasped and shook her head. "No, not here. I can't face this here."

Anabelle's eyes widened as she looked at the elves. "The College of Shogarethak? You were responsible for that massacre?"

Rasputina was trembling as she backed away from the rest of the DGA, muttering to herself, her eyes frantic and half-crazed. "Not again," she kept repeating.

Anabelle grabbed Rasputina. "What you did in the past was the past. These are just memories."

Rasputina pushed the elf's hands away. "I don't want to do this again. That's not me."

Anabelle looked over her shoulder at the replica of Grok. "We're all doing this again. You understand?"

She glanced at Grok. "How come you don't have anything?"

Grok smirked quietly. "Because I have no regrets or fears. Doesn't seem as if Sarah does either."

"Less talking, more fighting!" Terra shouted as she ran toward the balrogs. She leaped into the air, bringing her axe down on the balrog in the middle as the other two circled her, preparing to pounce.

Grok sprinted in Terra's direction. She rammed into one of the balrogs, knocking it off-balance as it pulled out a fiery whip.

Tesla charged Abby, unleashing a torrent of electricity as he hit her that sent her flying backward.

Sarah walked over to Anabelle, who was sizing up Dark Grok. The three of them took their fighting stances.

The army of elf wizards faced off against Rasputina, who tore open her sides and pulled out two bone daggers. She growled, her eyes bright green and feral as she hunched over, her skin rotting away to its former lichness. She was as pale as a skeleton and nearly as emaciated.

She dashed toward the elves as they raised their wands. A fireball headed toward her and she dodged to the side, throwing a dagger that hit an elf in the head.

The fireball exploded near Sarah and Anabelle as Dark Grok attacked, moving faster than Anabelle or Sarah had ever seen.

Dark Grok spin-kicked Anabelle, who threw up a mana barrier at the last second.

The elf dropped to her knees and pressed her hand to the ground, sending a column of stone up at Dark Grok, who dodged it. She kicked the pillar, causing it to separate and fly at the doppelganger. The orc chopped at the stone, breaking through it as Sarah came up behind her and tossed a handful of ninja stars at the memory. They hit Dark Grok in the chest and exploded.

Sarah came through the smoke from the stars and uppercut Dark Grok, who wrapped her legs around Sarah's neck as she fell backward and flipped her into Anabelle.

As the elf rolled to her feet, a whip wrapped around her ankle and flung her toward the balrogs.

Abby flew past and fired a plasma blast that severed the whip around Anabelle's ankle. Tesla chased after her, launching small EMP bombs as he cackled,

Anabelle hit the ground and swung her leg out, unleashing a torrent of water at the balrogs Grok and Terra were fighting.

Terra was on the back of one of the balrogs, hacking at it with her axes and shrieking curses when a whip wrapped around her waist and slammed her into the ground. The balrogs were multiplying near the nexus.

Grok screamed as she slipped into the Path of the Lost. She flew at one of the balrogs and slammed her fist into its flaming head, breaking the creature's jaw. She leaped up and brought both of her feet down on its skull, which split open and leaked lava and flames.

As Grok turned to the next balrog, a blast went off near her feet and propelled her into the air.

Anabelle caught Grok in mid-air and flung her toward Dark Grok.

The orc tackled her dark doppelganger.

Dark Grok let out a blast of energy as she went down the Path of the Lost.

Grok circled her doppelganger. "Looks like this will be good."

She charged her, ramming her shoulder into the other Grok's face. The other Grok took a step back, dropped to the ground, and swept Grok's feet out from under her.

Grok hit the ground and her doppelganger flipped through the air, bringing her feet down on the orc, who threw up both arms and absorbed the attack.

Abby flew by and grabbed Dark Grok by the hair, then flung her across the battlefield.

Dark Grok landed in the mass of elf mages Rasputina was tearing through with the ferocity of an animal, her blade shearing flesh as she dashed and rolled through the elves. She wasted no time between movements, not even bothering with magic, instead relying on pure animalistic destruction.

Rasputina was nothing more than bones and blades. Still, the masses of elves began working their magic, dozens of them raising their wands and sending projectiles through the air that bombarded the area.

Terra released the balrog she was wrestling to move out of the way of one of the projectiles, which hit the balrog and eviscerated it. "Hey, you want to do something about that?" she shouted. "Someone's going to lose an eye."

Abby burned her thrusters, heading over to the elves. "On it!"

She flew over them as she constructed a small turret in her hands. She dropped the turret into the thick of the elves, and it began firing plasma bolts.

Tesla's hands wrapped around Abby's leg, stopping her in her tracks.

Abby turned around, fists raised. Tesla jabbed at her and she teleported behind him, her hand full of plasma. She slapped it across Tesla's face, where it burned through his skin.

Tesla fell as he unleashed an electric shockwave that knocked Abby out of the sky, temporarily disabling her system.

Dark Grok burst from the cover of the elves and tackled her. As the two hit the ground, Dark Grok punched her in the face, delivering a blow that shook Abby and shattered her jaw.

Anabelle screamed in rage as her body went down the Path of Flames, then rocketed toward Dark Grok and caught the orc memory by the throat. She slammed Dark Grok on the ground and followed her attack with a flaming stomp.

Abby slowly got to her feet as her nanobots healed her jaw. Her hands glowed with a plasma blast, and she unleashed it as Anabelle launched a fire attack. Both attacks consumed Dark Grok, reducing her to ashes.

Anabelle looked at Rasputina, who was still waging war with the elves. "I'm going to give her a hand."

Across the way, a fiery explosion rocked the plane.

Terra was hunched over a balrog, her eyes glowing red with blood lust. She gripped a balrog's jaw and was splitting it down the middle. The balrog was spewing a column of fire from its mouth.

Anabelle rocketed toward the mass of elves, flinging fireballs that crackled with lightning at the mages.

A few of the mages raised their wands, deflecting the attack.

Anabelle slid in between them and spun in a circle, shining the light everything around her as Rasputina leaped toward her, blades cutting down the elves.

A balrog landed amidst the army of elves. Sarah flew after it and dropped on its shoulders, holding the balrog's whip. She wrapped the lash around its neck and pulled back.

The balrog's head popped off.

Sarah threw the decapitated head to an elf who raised his wand too slowly.

The balrog head hit him and exploded.

Anabelle reached out and wrangled the flames, manipulating and growing them into a flaming dragon that soared into the sky.

The DGA made room as Anabelle brought the fire dragon down on the mass of elves, torching them all.

Anabelle returned to normal.

The ground was littered with the enemies of the DGA. Tesla's body was among them, Terra standing over his smoking corpse.

"Now we close the valve," Anabelle said as she walked toward the Nexus.

The nexus started glowing brightly again.

Terra sighed as she wiped balrog blood off. "Are you serious? How many times are we going to have to do this until it realizes we don't want to hurt it? To be fair, it probably looks like we want to."

A hand reached out of the nexus, followed by a foot, and then a head that congealed into a shape, then a face. Abby's face.

A Dark Melody version of Abby stood before the DGA.

Abby laughed as she looked at the other DGA members. "Okay, real funny. Which of you is afraid of us?"

The rest of the DGA didn't seem to think it was funny.

Terra took a step back. "Dude, this isn't a joke."

Anabelle took a fighting stance. "Was it everybody?"

Rasputina drew two more daggers. "I didn't think I was the only one who could see Abby's potential."

Abby couldn't believe what she was hearing. There was no way her friends feared her this much. "Guys, you can't be serious. It's just me."

The Dark Melody Abby raised her hand as she smiled. Nanobots flowed from her fingertips as she raised her other hand and fired at Abby.

The plasma blast knocked Abby off her feet. "Holy shit, *that's* what it feels like?"

Dark Melody Abby's hands began tracing sigils as the cloud of nanobots grew behind her.

Anabelle helped Abby to her feet. "We're not afraid of you, only of what you can do. And I guess we're about to find out."

CHAPTER FORTY-NINE

The Dark Melody version of Abby stepped forward with a treacherously sweet smile on her lips. She raised her hand, and the swarm of nanobots behind her rushed the DGA.

Anabelle cast a magic barrier, diverting the majority of the nanobots, which flew into the air and constructed a dozen drones while Dark Abby drew a sigil into the ground.

Dark Abby stomped on the sigil, sending a wall of fire at Anabelle's magical barrier.

The drones flew down from above, firing lasers at the DGA.

Everyone scattered. Grok hid under Rasputina, who threw up a magic shield. Terra and Sarah bunched under Abby's and Anabelle's shields.

Terra nudged her in the side. "Any idea of how to kill yourself?"

Abby grimaced at Terra. "We would rather not think of it like that."

"You know what I mean. You had to have had a backup plan for when you went evil."

Abby looked incredulously at Terra. "Did everyone believe we were *going* to go evil or something?"

Terra shrugged. "More like daydreamed about it. Come on, you gotta admit, evil you is pretty sick."

Above, the nanobots were circling Abby as she constructed a plasma cannon on her shoulder. She signed another sigil, opening a portal.

A smaller portal appeared directly in front of Anabelle, on the other side of her shield. "Gods be damned!" Anabelle sighed as she dodged to the side.

Dark Abby fired her cannon into the portal.

The blast came out on the other side, hit the ground, and exploded.

Dark Abby teleported behind Anabelle and cracked her across the head.

Terra tossed her axe at the impostor, who raised her hand, causing her nanobots to fly in front of her and harden. The nanobots swarmed over the axe and broke it down into nothing.

Dark Abby burst through the nanobots and landed in front of Terra.

Before she could attack, Grok came in from the side and slammed the palm of her hand into the side of Dark Abby's head.

Dark Abby went skidding across the ground, launching her thrusters and righting herself, preparing to take to the air.

Black tendrils shot up from the ground and wrapped around Dark Abby, pulling her to the ground.

Rasputina leaped on top of Dark Abby and drove her dagger into the construct's chest.

Dark Abby opened her mouth and fired a plasma blast that tore through the side of Rasputina's face.

The lich fell back, reached into the Dark Melody, and drew some up to heal her face.

Dark Abby traced another sigil, and the Dark Melody Rasputina was pulling from froze as if it were water.

Abby flew past her doppelganger and fired a plasma blast as Sarah and Anabelle rushed her counterpart.

Sarah slipped into the Path of Pain, as did Anabelle.

Dark Abby squared off against them and her armor thickened, blocking her assailants' attacks. She managed to keep pace with them.

Terra joined the assault on Abby, and the three of them attempted to overwhelm her.

As Dark Abby stepped back, her drones flew overhead and dropped plasma grenades. One of the grenades hit Terra and exploded, throwing all three women through the air.

Dark Abby teleported above Anabelle and brought her fist down on the elf's chest.

Anabelle crashed to the ground, then struggled to her feet, coughing blood.

Dark Abby teleported in front of her and converted her hand into a blade.

Abby appeared behind Dark Abby and grabbed her counterpart's shoulder. She pulled her off Anabelle.

Dark Abby turned around and sliced through Abby's nanobot arm.

Abby stumbled back, trying to stay on her feet as she became the focus of her dark counterpart's attention.

Three daggers hit Dark Abby in the back, but she didn't bother turning around. Instead, her drones flew back, each targeting one of the DGA members and engaging them.

Abby struggled to keep up with her opponent's moves while repairing her arm, and she eventually tripped.

Dark Abby leaned forward, her hand glowing with plasma, and rammed it into Abby's head.

Abby converted the nanobots on her head to absorb the energy blast, funneled them back through her system, constructed a cannon on her chest, and fired.

The blast tossed Dark Abby into the air. One of her drones flew by and she grabbed it, the drone converting to an oversized cannon which she fired at Abby.

Terra tackled the girl out of the way as Sarah, Anabelle, and Grok flew after her opponent. Dark Abby launched her thrusters and took off, her drones flying in between her and the DGA members to make space for her.

The drones fired lasers, creating a grid that Sarah, Anabelle, and Grok couldn't get past.

Tentacles rose from the ground and wrapped around Dark Abby's legs.

Terra came from the back and rammed into her back, pushing her into the laser grid in front of her.

Dark Abby teleported behind Terra and kicked her in the back, sending Terra toward the lasers instead.

Abby rocketed toward Terra and knocked her out of the way of the laser grid, then released her nanobots to become a huge cannon on her shoulders. She fired at Dark Abby, who traced a sigil that caused the plasma blast to slow to a snail's crawl.

Dark Abby teleported again, this time out of sight.

Rasputina used the Dark Melody tentacles to rip the last of the drones out of the air as everyone scanned the area for Dark Abby.

"There!" Anabelle shouted.

Dark Abby had teleported beside Tesla's corpse. She had unleashed her nanobots on Tesla's body and was absorbing his tech into her own.

Terra threw her axe at Dark Abby. "No power-stealing on my watch!"

The axe hit Dark Abby in the head, and she stepped back.

Abby teleported behind the Dark Melody version of herself, wrapped her forearm around her neck, and put her in a full nelson. "Finish it, Terra!"

Terra ran toward the two of them, grabbing Grok's sword off her shoulder. "Just borrowing it!"

When she was in front of Dark Abby, Terra slashed her neck while Abby held her still, cleaving through half of it.

Dark Abby screamed in pain, and Terra hesitated.

Nanobots started to rebuild the wound in her neck.

Abby struggled to hold onto her doppelganger. "Don't stop! You have to finish it."

Terra nodded, face grim, and hacked at Dark Abby's neck again, cutting through the part that was trying to repair itself.

Nanobots continued to flood the wound as Dark Abby squirmed

and sputtered blood. "Please, Terra! I'm your friend. Don't do this to me," she screamed frantically.

"Do it," Abby shouted.

Terra closed her eyes and let out a horrified scream as she swung around, gaining momentum and slashed through Dark Abby's neck, severing her head.

Abby dropped the body as it broke apart into nanobots and called them to her. The nanobots hesitated for a moment before flowing up Abby's arms.

The main nexus began to hum and glow again.

Anabelle sighed. "There's got to be a way around this. That thing is going to keep summoning crap for us to fight."

Abby shook her head. "No, not if we go about this the right way. Part of the elder one was in there. We heard some of its thoughts. There's a distinction between out here and in there."

Terra gave Abby an exasperated look. "How are we supposed to get in there?"

"It requires a sacrifice."

At those words, the nexus stopped humming and glowing.

Abby walked over to the nexus. "The only way to get in there is to sacrifice ourselves. Then we'll have access to the valve."

Anabelle's face dropped. "How many of us?"

Abby shook her head. "We don't know. We doubt all of us. If the Dark One was able to make it in, we should be able to as well."

The DGA approached the nexus.

Abby watched the light. She hadn't thought it was going to come down to this, but she was ready. Even if she hadn't thought it through beforehand, she was ready to give whatever was needed to save the Nine Realms. She was a Dark Gate Angel, and this was her duty.

Grok cleared her throat. "So, who's it going to be?"

Terra laughed loudly. "The DGA, obviously. We can't leave this up to someone else to mess up. If it works, you can sacrifice yourself along with us. Sound good?"

The orc smiled somberly. "Are you sure?"

Rasputina stepped forward. "Grok and I have hands stained with innocent blood. If there's anyone who isn't worthy of living, it is us. We should do this."

Anabelle shook her head. "That's not how this works. We were given a mission, and we're going to complete it."

Sarah rested her hand on Anabelle's shoulder. "It's not every day you get to say goodbye. It's been a pleasure serving with you three. I'll never forget you."

Grok held her fist over her heart in the traditional orc salute. "Neither will I. I will continue your legacy in hell. Your sacrifices will never be forgotten."

Rasputina nodded solemnly, avoiding the eyes of the DGA. "There's nothing I can say except thank you for everything you've done."

Terra turned back to face the nexus. "All right, it's time to do this."

Abby held her breath. She wasn't sure what was going to happen. All she knew was once she touched the nexus, it was all going to be over. "I love you guys," Abby murmured. "Couldn't imagine my life without you. I'm glad we're going out together."

She looked at Anabelle and Terra as she fought back her tears. "You two really are the best friends anyone could have."

Anabelle nodded solemnly. "I love you too, Abby. You're one of the smartest, kindest, strongest people I've ever met. There probably won't ever be another Abby. No one could stack up to you."

Terra cleared her throat. When she spoke, her voice was choked with tears. "Belle's right. We can't even begin to tell you how proud we are of you. That's why you're not coming with us."

Abby turned to face Terra and Anabelle. "Wait? What are you talking about?"

"Sarah," Anabelle said.

Sarah pulled a small EMP pistol from her side and fired at Abby.

Abby's joints seized up and she toppled, unable to move. "No! What are you doing?"

Anabelle stepped toward the nexus. "You think Terra and I only talk about who could kick each other's asses, but we talked about this a long time ago. If anything like this ever happened, we weren't letting you go through with it. You have too much potential. Both of us have lived our lives. We're not letting you throw yours away."

Abby struggled against the EMP, trying her hardest to get up as tears rolled down her face. "No! You can't leave me. You can't do this to me! I'm a Dark Gate Angel. We have to do this together."

Terra chuckled, her face tired. "We ride together, we die together. Dark Angels for life."

Anabelle groaned. "Seriously? Those are your last words?"

Terra wiped the tears from her face. "You're going to do great things, kid. Keep it up."

Anabelle and Terra reached toward the nexus.

As Anabelle's fingers neared it, they became translucent. Her bones and veins were visible beneath her skin. The same happened to Terra.

Abby kept screaming. She begged Anabelle and Terra to stop, to let her join them, not to make her watch them both die. "You can't do this to us! Please, don't do this without me!"

The elf and the Hand met each other's eyes.

"Ready?" Anabelle asked.

Terra took a deep breath and sighed.

The two of them grasped the nexus, and power flooded into their bodies as their skin burned away in a blue burst of ash. Still, their glowing bones forced their way into the nexus.

Somehow there was still life in them.

A shockwave threw Abby and the rest through the air as Anabelle and Terra pushed farther inside.

The universe nodes began to float into the air as strings of blue light connected them. They expanded as they floated outwards.

Another shockwave erupted as the bodies of the elder ones began to vibrate.

Suddenly, Abby was outside the elder ones. She floated through the air of the Netherverse, which she could now bend to her desires. She gently touched down, and Rasputina, Grok, and Sarah landed beside her.

Two pale-blue skeletons as large as the elder ones stood before them. The skeletons held one of the elder ones between them, cradling it as if it were a baby. Then they cracked it open as the rest of the elder ones separated and floated away from each other, spreading to the far corners of the sky.

A beam of light shot from the sky between the two skeletons, making it seem as if a giant spear of light had pierced the Netherverse.

The skeletons grabbed the light and pushed in the same direction, slowly twisting the beam.

The light exploded and shot upward, and the sky burned bright. The planet nodes could be seen floating in the distance.

Abby finally managed to get to her feet. The EMP had worn off.

The two skeletons turned away from Abby and the rest of them and walked off into the sunset, flecks of blue ash floating from them.

Abby ran toward Anabelle and Terra. "Wait! Take us with you!" she shouted.

The skeletons stopped walking and turned to face Abby. They knelt, looking at the girl, and gently reached out.

Abby grabbed one of the skeleton's fingers and clutched it as tightly as she could. She wasn't going to let go, no matter what. They were going to take her with them.

The skeleton Abby wasn't holding reached out and held up Abby's chin as she cried. "I need you guys. Please," Abby cried.

"No, you don't," Anabelle's voice murmured.

Flakes of blue ash continued to come off the two skeletons as they began to fade.

Abby didn't let go. She held on with every muscle in her body, every fiber of her being.

The skeletons collapsed, shattering into blue crystals as they hit the floor.

Abby cried as she held onto the skeleton's fading finger, flecks of blue crystal surrounding her like a cloud. The skeleton's finger shattered as well.

Another hand reached down for her, one covered in flesh. Sarah. "You're gonna be okay, kid," she said. "I promise. You're going to be okay."

CHAPTER FIFTY

The main hall of HQ was filled with flowers from all over the Nine Realms. They hung from the ceiling and the walls in delicate and intricate patterns. Many of them were white.

Pews had been brought in, and hundreds of people were sitting in them. They spoke to each other quietly in somber tones, their whispers filling the Great Hall.

Drones floated through the room, offering refreshments to the guests who were seated.

Myrddin wandered around the room, talking to foreign dignitaries. He wore a beautiful pure-white suit from the elvish realm. He didn't look nearly as tired as normal, but his face held no joy.

There were a handful of drones in the back of the room, recording the proceedings. The funeral was being broadcast all over the Nine Realms. Creon was sitting in the back, watching the ceremony through a multitude of monitors.

At the front of the hall were two white caskets. One was decorated in traditional orc fashion. A pile of bones sat beneath the casket, and Terra's ceremonial axe, the Shaman's Hand, rested on the top. Cire stood next to it, singing the Orcish burial rites softly under his breath while pouring mead over the shining white box.

Anabelle's casket was beside Terra's. The flowers decorating it made those that decorated the Great Hall look paltry in comparison. They ranged from dramatic blues to pastel oranges. The flowers grew from the floor of the Great Hall, their vines wrapping around the casket like a warm, embracing blanket.

Abby walked into the Great Hall. Her nanobots had formed a black military uniform with the new Dark Gate Angels insignia on the chest.

Persephone was at Abby's side, her hand intertwined with the girl's. Her flowing magenta gown, composed of individual pieces of mithril, swept across the floor as the two made their way to Creon.

As the newest member of the DGA, he wore the same insignia.

Abby rested her hand on the gnome's shoulder, smiling slightly. It barely penetrated the sadness on her face. "Hey, how's everything running over here?"

Creon patted Abby's hand before he spun around in his chair. "Beautifully. The feed to the Nine Realms is working perfectly. Everyone will be able to pay their respects. How are you holding up?"

"Six months is a long time to grieve. We're sure the both of them would have loved this."

Creon nodded as he absentmindedly typed without looking at the screen. "Avoid Myrddin if you can. He's giving small speeches. Not that they're bad, but you know he's going to give another one once this is all over. Might as well brace yourself for that one."

Abby and Persephone chuckled. "Do you want to take a seat?" Abby asked.

Persephone craned her head to take a look at the rest of the Hall before looking at her comm watch. "Might as well. Everything should be starting soon."

Abby and Persephone approached the front of the hall where the caskets were.

Cire had moved away from Terra's casket and was standing a few feet away, his back facing the crowd. Persephone and Abby came up to him, and the orc smiled at the two of them. He looked sad but not defeated, and his eyes still radiated warmth. "I'm glad to see you two. How have you been?"

Abby shrugged as she looked at Terra's and Anabelle's casket. "You know, the usual. Work, trying to save the universe. How about you?"

Cire nodded as he returned his gaze to Terra's casket. "Rasputina and I are still working to solve the complications of Terra passing into the Netherverse with my soul, but other than that, business as usual."

"He's being modest. The research is going well, and his people are thriving," a voice said.

Rasputina approached from the side, along with Grok. The lich wore a long, sweeping cloak that seemed to be covered in dust. Grok, on the other hand, wore nothing but her leather armor. They stopped on the other side of Cire.

Abby saluted the two using the traditional orc gesture. "Glad you two decided to come. They would have wanted you here."

Rasputina pulled back her hood. "It's the least we could do."

"Sure your kingdoms aren't going to fall apart while you're gone?"

Abby looked over her shoulder to see Sarah walking down the aisle. Kravis was at her side but took a seat as she approached the hall's stage.

Sarah wore a similar uniform to Abby's, although it was woven of nanofiber mesh instead of produced by nanobots. "Who's going to keep demons from trying to take over while you're gone?"

Rasputina smiled pleasantly. "There are no uprisings. They all know better than to challenge our rule."

Abby couldn't help but laugh to herself. Some things never changed.

Myrddin appeared at the front of the Great Hall and cleared his throat. "We are gathered here to honor the sacrifices of two of the bravest warriors the Nine Realms have ever seen, Terra and Anabelle of the Dark Gate Angels. They sacrificed their lives so the Nine Realms could continue existing, but I can only tell you snippets of what I learned from the two of them. Instead, we will honor them today by listening to their closest friends, those who fought side by side with these amazing women."

The wizard motioned for Abby to come to the podium.

The scientist took a deep breath. She had so many emotions and stories running through her mind, she didn't know where to start. The speech she'd written didn't seem to do justice to what she felt, or how much Terra and Anabelle had meant to her.

Myrddin walked off the stage and took a seat as Abby ascended the podium. She cleared her throat as tears began welling up. She rested her hand on the podium and took another deep breath.

"Belle and Terra were, first and foremost, my best friends. They were two of the strongest people I've ever met. Constantly growing, pushing themselves to be better. Without them, we..."

Abby tried to keep from sobbing, but she couldn't help it. She turned away from the audience for a moment while she wiped away the tears and tried to compose herself.

Two drones flew over the podium.

"Hey, dude, we said to make it sad but not like, crying-for-a-week sad," came a familiar voice.

A holograph of Terra's face projected from one of the drones. "This is too sad. I thought you were going to talk about how much I kicked ass or something. Maybe my haircut. Oh, or about that time I totally owned you in that ramen-eating contest?"

The other drone projected an image of Anabelle, who had her arms crossed and was glaring disapprovingly at Terra. "She might have gotten to that if you hadn't interrupted her speech."

Abby hiccupped as she laughed, her heart swelling the moment she saw Anabelle's and Terra's faces. "If you two don't mind, can I finish my eulogy? This is streaming live."

Terra turned around to see the crowd. "Oh, crap. I didn't think so many people were going to come to my funeral. And they're crying! Sick." She turned back to Abby. "Yeah, go on. Just remember, we're dead. Not gone."

The two drones flew off and landed near Persephone and Cire.

Abby cleared her throat. "As I was saying before I was interrupted. Terra and Anabelle were the two best friends I could ask for, and the love and loyalty they shared with me was what they gave the Nine Realms. I'll never be able to thank them enough."

Terra's hologram started clapping. "Hell, yeah! We were awesome!"

The rest of the audience broke into applause as the Anabelle hologram hung her head and shook it, laughing quietly.

When the wake was over. Myrddin magicked the pews out of the Great Hall, replacing them with circular tables and spindly, ornate chairs. The tables were filled with appetizers, and Abby's drones attended to a buffet table.

The heroes of the War for the Nine Realms were all seated together. Naota bickered with Creon and Cire while Persephone and Sarah chatted with each other. Sarah continued to drop hints about marriage to Persephone, who awkwardly tried to come up with excuses.

Abby sat closest to Anabelle and Terra. The three were engrossed in each other's conversation. It had been months since Abby had been able to speak to the two.

The month after Anabelle and Terra had sacrificed themselves had been difficult for Abby. She'd spent days in bed and had been inconsolable. But one day, she heard Terra's and Anabelle's voices. She hadn't believed it, but she told Creon anyway.

Reopening the valves had caused the Netherverse to shut down between the realms, but what Abby was hearing could have only come from there.

Creon had told her he had no idea what was going on.

But Abby could still hear her friends. Deep in her bones, she heard them every day, and their voices grew louder and stronger.

Abby realized she was still connected to the Dark Melody of the Netherverse through her nanobots.

From there, it was as simple as figuring out how to open a portal.

Myrddin walked over and took a seat next to Abby. Terra waved emphatically at the wizard. "Hey, how is it going, my dude? I have to admit, your speech was pretty good. Not nearly as good as Abby's or Cire's, but a close third."

Myrddin smiled as he conjured himself a glass of wine. "I'll take it. How are my two favorite Netherverse agents doing?"

Anabelle pointed her finger at Myrddin. "I'll be doing a lot better once you figure out how to get the Netherverse access to heaven. Roy won't stop going on about not being able to visit Blackwell."

Myrddin sighed. "As I told you before, Anabelle, it's not that simple. Having all Nine Realms be able to access the Netherverse, hell, heaven, and every other potential universe is complicated enough. He does realize that Blackwell can easily travel from heaven to the Netherverse, doesn't he?"

Anabelle nodded. "Yeah. It's weird how Blackwell can visit Roy in hell but not vice versa."

"Not that weird. I mean, would you leave heaven once you got in? Especially when hell is your alternative." Myrddin's cheeks went red, remembering who he was speaking to and, more importantly, where she was.

Anabelle laughed. "It's OK, I like it here. We all do. But like I was saying regarding Roy, he's complaining that he can't go visit Blackwell. I think he's jealous he got stuck in the Netherverse because he wasn't good enough for heaven."

Terra shrugged. "All this shit is mostly connected now anyway. Who cares?"

"Obviously, Blackwell hasn't let Roy hear the last of it."

Myrddin waved his wand. "This will have to do for the time being."

There was a flash of light, and Anabelle and Terra were sitting beside Abby.

Abby squealed and knocked the two of them over as she jumped on them to give them hugs.

Across the table, a gruff voice cleared its throat. Roy was standing wrapped in a bath towel, smoking a cigar. "Uh. Next time, you want to give me some warning?"

Terra pushed Abby off her. "I thought it was impossible for us to travel out of the Netherverse?"

Myrddin stood and smiled proudly. "It is. This spell will last for a few hours, and I probably won't be able to do magic for a week."

Terra ruffled Abby's hair and stood up. "I'm stoked to see you, kid, but I'm going to be honest—"

Abby waved Terra away. "Yeah, yeah, something gross about you and Cire."

Terra grabbed Cire and pulled him away from the table. She'd already ripped Cire's top two buttons off his shirt.

Anabelle and Abby sat together. "Missed you a lot, kid. The video chats aren't quite enough."

Abby nodded as she swiped away a tear. "Yeah, not really."

The elf grabbed a glass of wine and leaned back in her chair. "Good thing you're going to be the one stuck coming down to the Netherverse for all of our problems. Can't wait for our first catastrophe."

Abby looked up at the sky. "There's still the Light One. We have no idea where she went. That could always be the next big one. And who knows how us turning the Netherverse into a nexus could affect the balance of—"

Sarah leaned over the table and waved her hands in front of Abby's face. "Hey! How about we don't talk about work right now? We only got these two for an hour."

Music blared from the speakers in the Great Hall. Abby looked over her shoulder and saw Terra kissing Cire.

Abby stood up as some of the tables were cleared for a dance floor. "How about we party instead?"

Anabelle downed her glass of wine as she and Sarah stood. She looked at Grok and Rasputina. "That means you too."

Grok crossed her arms. "I don't dance."

Rasputina cast off her cloak and stood, then grabbed Grok's hand and pulled her out of her chair. "Come on. We're with friends."

The music pumped louder as Abby stepped onto the dance floor, the lights streaming overhead.

This party wasn't going to last forever, and that didn't matter to Abby.

Not one little bit.

The End

AUTHOR NOTES RAMY VANCE
OCTOBER 2, 2020

Most people don't know this about me (truth be told, most people don't believe me), but I didn't touch alcohol from the age of 21 to 34.

Not a drop.

There wasn't any real reason for it, except I found that when I was such a lightweight that a night of moderate drinking usually ended with me praying to the porcelain bowl.

Drinking just wasn't worth it.

Besides, I never needed alcohol to lower my inhibitions. That bar was set pretty low from the get-go.

Then the Egyptian Revolution happened and everything changed.

You see, I'm half-Egyptian, and lived most of my life in the Middle East. So when the famed 18 Day Revolution began, everyone and their mother called the one Arab they knew – aka: me – and asked what I thought would happen.

I made predictions carefully crafted from my studies of Middle Eastern History, my decades of immersing myself in Arab culture and my keen, finely-honed senses.

And every prediction I made was wrong.

Not just wrong, mind you. It was as if the divine powers that be listened in on everything I thought would happen, and did the exact opposite.

I didn't get a single thing right.

Not one.

But there was one prediction that I was confident in. President Mubarak, the dictator that resided over Egypt for the better part of 4 decades, would never step down.

Never.

I was so confident of this particular prediction that I proudly proclaimed that should Mubarak fall, I will start drinking again.

I still remember the day it happened.

I was penning a manuscript that still hasn't seen the light of day (Samurai vs. Vampire – ahem, Michael!). CNN was on mute in the background. I looked down at my manuscript, writing the very last sentence to a particularly violent fight scene, and when I looked up, the headline read: Mubarak Stepped Down.

Needless to say, I had made a promise. To my friends, my family... the universe.

A Vance always pays his debts. Standing from my desk, I searched my apartment for alcohol. Sadly, the only thing I found was two bottles of warm cider in the back of a cupboard.

Resolved to my fate, downed those two bottles and laughed my ass off as, later that afternoon, prostrated myself before the porcelain bowl and offered tribute.

13 years of abscondence ruined by hubris and the human spirit to fight for something better. Such was my fate. Such is my joy.

Thank you for not only reading this story but our *Author Notes* in the back as well!

I really don't have much to say about drinking, neither stopping and starting again nor hoary tales of stupidity during college days.

I have a cool story of a friend who was so drunk (and hungry) that when he wanted food as the party went into the wee hours of the morning, he got a fish from the aquarium and downed it.

While he admits he doesn't remember doing that, there was a missing fish the next day.

Speaking of drinking stories, I remember one—during college, we played a game of quarters. Basically, take a quarter and bounce it off the table. If it goes in, you tag someone to drink. If it fails, you take a drink.

I only drank Coke at the time, so they didn't pick me often to drink. I think they hoped I would get stupid and decide to drink due to peer pressure. My secret defense is my taste buds.

I wouldn't try to eat food I didn't like to impress a date, so I sure as hell wasn't going to drink alcohol to impress three buddies who are already having problems sitting down.

One of them was so blitzed, I remember him taking an old cheese grater (the kind with four sides for four different types of grating) and eyeing it. This is during the time of acid-washed and ripped jeans (back in the 1980s, not the present incarnation), and he looked at that grater and then down at his leg.

I was confused. I was not accustomed to being around blitzed young people and their antics, so it came as a total shock when he RUBBED IT ACROSS HIS FOREHEAD.

I'm staring, open-mouthed at him. He's staring at the table... pause...wait for it...

OWWWWW!!!

He reaches up and grabs his forehead, wincing in pain. I'm shocked his forehead doesn't look like hamburger. It was just red, no blood.

Thank God.

That game supported my decision to not forsake taste to drink a lot and do stupid things.

So, if you drink, make sure your Kindle is nearby, so when you wake up, the worst thing you might have done is purchase ALL the books in your To Be Read list.

Eventually, you will read yourself out of that mistake!

Peace!

Ad Aeternitatem,

Michael Anderle

OTHER BOOKS BY RAMY VANCE

Mortality Bites Series
Keep Evolving Series
Fatebound Series
Welcome to the Dragon Show Series

Other books in the Middang3ard Universe
Middang3ard Series
Dragon Approved Series